Reign of a Billionaire

Billionaire King Series

Eva Winners

Copyright © 2024 by Winners Publishing LLC and Eva Winners
Cover Image Designer: Eve Graphic Design LLC
Model: Kaio Q.
Photographer: Wander Aguiar
Formatting by: The Nutty Formatter

All rights reserved.

No part of this book may be reproduced in any form or by any electronic or mechanical means, including information storage and retrieval systems, without written permission from the author, except for the use of brief quotations in a book review.

Resemblance to actual persons and things living or dead, locations, or events is entirely coincidental.

Visit www.evawinners.com and subscribe to my newsletter.

FB group: https://bit.ly/3gHEe0e
FB page: https://bit.ly/3oDzP8Q
Insta: http://Instagram.com/evawinners
BookBub: https://www.bookbub.com/authors/eva-winners
Amazon: http://amazon.com/author/evawinners
Goodreads: http://goodreads.com/evawinners
TikTok: https://vm.tiktok.com/ZMeETK7pq/

Leave your feminism at the door for Kingston Ashford. Just kidding. 😉 *This FMC will make you proud.*

Reign of a Billionaire Playlist

https://spoti.fi/4acIqAe

Billionaire King Collection

The series covers each Ashford brother separately. While each book in the series can be read as a standalone, events and references to the other books are present in each one of these. So, for best enjoyment, consider giving each Ashford brother a chance. 😃

Enjoy!

Eva Winners

Blurb

Kingston Ashford.
An enigma.
The Ghost.

His skills are unparalleled. His motives clear. His lethality unquestionable. His only purpose is to obliterate the kingdom that had stolen more than his innocence from him.

Until he crosses paths with a ghost from his past and he's drawn into the woman's web.

Liana Volkov.
An ice princess with murderous plans.
The unstable killer with the face of an angel.

Something big is happening in the belly of the underworld. Realities are shattered. A deadly game is played, tearing apart the kingdom from within the beast. But that's just the tip of the iceberg.

The line between enemies and allies is blurred. Mysteries unravel. Histories clash. Desires consume. Nothing is as it seems.

A new reign is born.

Note

Timeline for Kingston's book isn't in line with Winston's book. In fact, it occurs months later and it catches up to the last book in the Stolen Empire trilogy.

Prologue
Kingston

Eight Years Ago

We moved through the moonless night like two spirits in the shadows.

I knew by heart every corner patrolled by the guards on the outskirts of the property. Our boots crunched the fresh snow, and I regretted there wasn't another storm coming to erase our tracks. Goddamned Siberia.

"Mother has security extra tight." The tremor in Louisa's voice mirrored the trembling of her cold, slim fingers in the palm of my hand. "Ivan is making a deal with the Tijuana cartel, so she's extra paranoid."

I nodded, wrapping my arms around her waist and steadying her before she could step into the spotlight circling the grounds.

"They won't get to you," I promised naively. "You're eighteen. Nobody has the right to hold you back."

"And you're twenty-four, Kingston. She's holding you captive," she pointed out. I didn't tell her that once I turned eighteen, she was the only thing keeping me here. I would have run, willing to die trying, but not without her. Not by leaving her behind and vulnerable to Sofia and Ivan's men.

The December air howled with bitterness, pulling us into its frigid embrace. It whipped at Lou's soft cheeks until they were raw, but she hadn't complained once. She was just as determined as I was.

I just wasn't as sure about her twin. She was nowhere to be found, and we were out of time. The alarms that surrounded the property would be down for precisely fifty seconds. If we weren't off the property by then, we'd miss our window.

I whispered, "Get down," and Lou crouched, making herself smaller—if that were even possible. We slinked into the shadow of the guardhouse just as two men turned and headed in our direction. We knew it was empty; every guard was out patrolling the grounds.

"Where's Lia?" she whispered, more to herself than me. "It's unlike her to be late."

"Maybe she changed her mind." Her breathing stilled, the fog around her mouth evaporating.

"No." There wasn't an ounce of doubt in her voice. "No, no, *no*."

Liana—or Lia, as her twin called her—was identical to Lou in looks, but the two couldn't be more different in personality. Louisa was a peacemaker; her twin was a fighter. Lou wanted world peace; Lia wanted to stir it into chaos. One hated the cold; the other thrived in it. In fact, if I had to guess, I'd say she got caught up in covering her tracks, unbothered by how deadly the conditions could turn.

"No, she wouldn't," she repeated again, her voice barely above a whisper. Time was running out, and we both knew it. We were moments away from getting the chance to bolt out of here and never look back. "Kingston," she breathed, gazing up at me through terrified hazel eyes. "What if they got to her?"

Her distress always stirred emotions in my chest. We needed to leave, but I kept the impatience out of my tone.

"If they did, we'll come back for her," I promised. Hesitation flickered in her eyes. "Do you trust me?" She nodded without delay, and my chest warmed. "Then trust me when I say this: they'll wish

Reign of a Billionaire

they never took her if we have to show up armed to the nines to get her back."

The first flicker of dawn peeked, smiling upward at the dark heavens and throwing shades of blue, purple, and red across the horizon. Lou nodded once, and then we took off in a run.

Right into the trap.

A metallic smell filled the dungeon.

Lou's screams pierced the dark space. The dreary gray walls and high ceiling supported by stone pillars gave this dungeon an ominous glow.

My wrists burned from the acid being poured onto my flesh, but the pain was forgotten the minute I saw her tied to the chair, folded over with her back exposed.

What was left of it had been flayed from her bones, raw and blistery. Sofia's men held her down while one poured more acid on her. Her screams shredded my heart to pieces.

I jerked against my binds, fury suffocating me. "You're all dead," I bellowed. "All of you."

Nobody even glanced my way.

"Where's your sister, Louisa?" Sofia's voice was colder than the Siberian temperatures as she watched her daughter with icy features.

"I... don't..." Lou's voice was weak. Broken. "I don't know, Mother."

"Sofia, let her go," I rasped, the lead settling in my gut. "Liana wasn't with us."

"Liar," Sofia bellowed, her manic expression alarming. I couldn't put my finger on it, but something was off.

"It's true," I gritted, the bullet that'd pierced clean through my shoulder burning like a motherfucker.

Sofia's wild eyes snapped to me, full of hate. "Because they have her," she screamed, her usually perfect silver chignon disheveled and her eyes wild. "The Tijuana cartel ended her, and it's your fault, Ghost." Lou whimpered, tears running down her cheeks, and shook her head in disbelief. "You're their bodyguard, why didn't you protect her?"

Lou's breathing escalated, her eyes darting wildly around to her mother's guards. "Mother... I... made him... run... with me. Lia didn't... c-come."

"More acid," Sofia ordered, and Lou's wounded whimper slashed through me. She trembled but fisted her hands, trying to be brave.

I roared with fury, fighting against the chains. Unsuccessfully. Instead, I was forced to watch while enduring my own torture.

I'd been holed up in the windowless room for what seemed like days as I drifted in and out.

Sanity refused to leave me. Somehow it had endured the cruelty inflicted on my body.

My limbs were frozen, my belly empty. My right shoulder was dislocated, and my entire body screamed in pain. I was filthy and naked. I couldn't hold my head up without getting dizzy. Every breath was agony.

It wasn't my first beating. The years had been hard. Time had no meaning here. Only torture did. Until I met the girl with the golden-hazel eyes.

The girl who'd grown up with me. My savior.

A cry tore through the haze in my brain, causing me to peel my swollen eyelids open.

"Don't worry, Lou. I'm okay," I grunted. All the fucking years of torture and I'd never cracked—until today, when she was forced to partake.

I was hanging by a cord that was cutting through my wrists. Lou had to watch my latest bout of torture. It was either that or have Sofia's men hurt her too.

And she had done plenty of refusing—her scars were proof.

"I'm so sorry," she croaked, her cries ripping at my heart. Her face was blotchy and pink, her split lips trembling. Sofia wanted to harden my Lou, make her indifferent to human suffering. But deep in her core, that wasn't who Louisa was.

"It's okay. You're not hurting me," I assured her while she shook like a leaf. Seeing her pain was gut-wrenching. Blood gushed out of my cuts, but still I cared more for her well-being. She hadn't actually laid a hand on me, but her presence during the sessions was enough to shatter her.

"I'm okay," I repeated, barely managing to reassure her with a smile. Before I could say anything else, another punch across my face connected.

"Please stop hitting him," she begged her mother's men.

Another punched me in the stomach, stealing my breath. I spit blood, my vision turning blurry.

Louisa's screams turned haunted, her voice hoarse. I locked on to her blotchy face, her expression full of terror. I refused to pass out. I had to hang on for her. She started fighting against the men who held her, giving her an inch only to pull her back.

"Stop! Please stop," she begged, her eyes red-rimmed. Fresh tears streamed down her bruised cheeks. "It was my fault."

"No, it wasn't."

I couldn't let them hurt her.

I lost consciousness several times. The next time I peeled my eyelids open, it was to an eerie silence. I was no longer tied up.

It'd been days, possibly weeks. I had no idea how long I'd been imprisoned. Time was an abstract concept as I drifted in and out of consciousness. Every breath was agony, and my entire body screamed in pain from the bones I was sure were fractured.

But I didn't give up.

I held on for Lou, my eyes locked on her, drawing strength from God knew where and offering it back. Except she wasn't moving, and whatever morsel of hope I had left extinguished as I watched her lifeless body sprawled on the filthy ground, her long golden locks stained with my blood.

"Wake up, sunshine," I said. *Please don't leave me.* She didn't move, lying still like a broken angel. "Please wake up. We have to get somewhere warm. P-please wake up, baby."

My voice cracked, mirroring my heart. I'd never begged for anything. Not when I was tortured and abused within an inch of my life, not when I wished death on those responsible. But now, I begged and pleaded, calling on whatever deity or divine being to spare her life.

The answer was my own whisper in the cell, my battered body too weak to move. But I willed myself to. I'd die with my hand on her beating pulse, on her chest as it rose and fell.

Crawling on all fours, my muscles shuddered, protested, and became weaker with each inch of space I covered. I felt my energy—what little life I had left—being drained as I fought to get to her.

I reached out, my hand brushing against her ice-cold skin. My breath caught as I draped myself over her unmoving body. She looked as though she were sleeping peacefully, despite her bruised body.

"Wake up, sunshine." No response. I didn't care if they continued to beat me until I was no longer recognizable, as long as she *lived*. "Don't... leave... me..." I pleaded.

Her left wrist, mangled from where they'd broken it, was cradled against her chest, her body curled up. Unmoving. But my sanity refused to accept that she was dead. There had to be a way to bring her back. I'd do anything. I'd give anything.

The small tattoo on her nape—the one matching mine—played peekaboo and I pushed her hair over it, hiding it as she always did.

"I love you." I whispered the words her romantic heart lived for.

She didn't move. Surely if she was alive, she'd open those golden eyes, a mixture of brown and hazel, and smile at me. There was only silence and my shuddering breaths. The blonde hair sprawled all over the bloodstained floor. My blood. It soaked through her golden strands, her body battered and broken. My stomach revolted, but I kept myself from retching.

The bracelet I'd given her lay on the ground by her side, ripped from her wrist and crusted with blood. I sucked in a breath and reached for it, fisting it in my palm, the silver digging into my flesh while the emptiness in my chest grew, the gaping hole expanding until I became darkness.

I couldn't live without her.

My every inhale was raw, shredding me to pieces. I gasped and clawed at my wounded chest.

I looked up when I heard a scoff and found Sofia Volkov staring down on me with wrathful eyes, surrounded by armed men.

My lip curled back from my teeth, hatred poisoning every ounce of humanity I had left.

I steeled myself and roared, "Bring her *back*."

My body collapsed on top of hers, and for the first time in years, my world went still and silent.

Then the darkness descended.

Chapter 1
Kingston

Eight Years Later

When Ivan Petrov and Sofia Volkov made a ghost out of me, they never thought I'd be back to destroy them like a vengeful king. I reigned over my empire while lingering in the shadows and used what I'd learned to go after them—those who stole my innocence and the girl who was my guiding light.

But they'd underestimated how far my hatred could go.

I'd become a shadow, almost erased from this world. I'd stalked and planned for years, revenge the only oxygen I breathed and killing the only nourishment I needed. A bleak reality of life without Louisa.

But then I'd seen her—Liana Volkov, alive and breathing, working alongside her mother, strutting along as Sofia's sidekick as though nothing was amiss. The twin sister we waited for the night we were all supposed to escape the clutches of Sofia Volkov. Years went by without a word about Liana, and I assumed she died too.

I'd been fooled. Louisa was buried six feet under in an unmarked grave while Liana walked this earth. An invisible knife speared my chest, blaming Liana for her twin's death. She was the reason we waited too long before running. She was the reason we got caught. Maybe I should let the underworld catch up to her, because it didn't take long for the Thorns of Omertà to learn Sofia Volkov had a living, breathing daughter.

The invisible wound opened right up at the sight of the woman who wore Louisa's face, leaving me gaping and bleeding. Shrill ringing filled my brain as I glared at the familiar face, every single muscle in my body immobile. Same face; wrong face. Same smile; wrong smile. Same hands; wrong hands.

The voices in my head insisted on revenge. *End her. Rip out all the teeth in her mouth. Make her pay.*

Except, there was a promise made. *Fuck!*

I'd been watching her for weeks, unable to wrap my head around the fact that Liana Catalano Volkov was alive. Living and fucking breathing, while her sister died in agony in fucking *Siberia*.

Pressure like heat in a kettle built behind my eyes as memories invaded, whipping through my skull with knife-like precision. The sound of her voice. The comfort of her touch. The softness of her heart.

A crater grew inside my chest and my mind, memories pouring out.

"I want you to marry me, Kingston," she murmured, her voice soft and reserved only for me.

Louisa. My Lou.

"You're not yet eighteen," I said, pulling her closer to me. She rolled her eyes but immediately fell into my arms, unable to keep a smile off her face. Even when shit was hard, she found things to smile about, offering her sunshine.

"I might not live long enough." She lifted on her tiptoes and brushed her nose against mine. "So why wait?"

I grasped her jaw in my hand. "You... We'll live until we've earned our wrinkles and grays. Until we've seen our grandchildren and great-grandchildren walk this earth, as living proof of our love."

I ran my fingers down the length of her silky blonde curls. Her golden eyes, speckled with hazel, met mine, and fuck, the urge to claim her drove me wild. But it was the heartbreak in them that kept me at bay.

"What's the matter?" I demanded. She smiled again, but not as brightly. "Don't tell me it's nothing or there'll be hell to pay."

Her smile vanished, anguish in her eyes wrapping around my heart like a vise.

"Don't hate me..." she whispered.

"I could never hate you."

She looked over her shoulder, her fingers fidgeting with the buttons of my shirt, before she returned to watch me.

"Ivan—"

"Has he hurt you?" I growled, a red mist creeping in. It didn't escape me that the sick prick had been eyeing the twins. Lou more than her sister. The fucker was like a bloodhound, sensing that Louisa was the softer of the two. With Liana, he risked having his balls cut off if he even contemplated touching her.

She shook her head. "No, but he..." She swallowed, her delicate throat bobbing. "He wants to marry me off to forge an alliance with the Tijuana cartel. Mother said no, but—"

We both knew it was only a matter of time though. "Sunshine, we should wait for the right time."

"I want you to be my first, Kingston." My grip on her chin tightened, and she came up on her toes, her lips brushing against my mouth. "You were my first kiss. The only man to mark me." Her full lips pursed, a soft smile curving them, and there was a pink hue that covered her cheeks. Our secret. A matching tattoo. "I just can't bear—"

Her voice cracked, as did my heart.

"Don't you see, Lou?" I rasped into her mouth. "I want to be your first, your last, your only."

"Me too," she whispered, her cheeks staining red with her admission. "But whatever happens tomorrow, we've had today. We'll have this. So why wait?"

There was so much pain in this household. Loneliness and fear. It wasn't where I wanted our first time to be. Then there was the issue of her age, with her being just shy of her eighteenth birthday, I didn't want her rushing into this. We should take our time—for her sake.

Her arms wrapped around my shoulders and she trailed her mouth down my chin, my neck, before burying her face into my throat.

"Maybe it's time we run away," she whispered. "You're a ghost. Make us disappear before they end us once and for all." She pulled away and met my eyes, her lip trembling. "She's destroying you, and I can't bear it anymore."

The fury festered in my chest, even after all these years. It made me a monster, full of hatred and thirst for revenge. I'd take the whole Volkov empire down. And no one would be able to stop me. Not even death.

I closed my eyes, washing away the memories of the only good thing in my life and focusing on this woman in front of me who had a hand in taking her away. I hated that Liana survived while my Louisa died. She was my other half. My light in the darkness. She was my everything. It was time for Liana to pay for it. Every breath she'd taken since Lou's death had earned her a punishment.

It had given me purpose for the first time since Alexei Nikolaev saved my battered body from that dungeon eight years ago.

While my appearance remained calm and collected, my insides were aflame.

There was a fine line between hatred and love. Even finer between sanity and insanity. I could no longer see that line. Not since I'd witnessed Lou die in front of my eyes.

I reached for a drink in my dark corner of the restaurant while I observed. Stalked. Planned.

The ember's orange glow of my cigarette in the ashtray was the only sign indicating my presence in the restaurant. I looked over at the table where my target sat, my eyes tracking the movements of the young woman.

This dark hole in my chest was slowly swallowing me whole.

I'd cultivated this festering hole, nourishing it with bitterness and hatred. It was red, angry and raw. I welcomed the feeling. Embraced it even. It was better than the numbness I'd felt for so long.

I would not rest until I got my revenge. Until I made her death count.

They killed her, and I would kill every last one of them for the pain it'd caused.

My fist clenched, shredding the cigarette to ashes as my enemy dined across the room. How could Liana sit there like the world was still turning when Lou was gone?

Shutting down my nightmare before it could stir to life, I focused on the present, downing the whiskey and relishing the burn in my throat.

I had a purpose, a goal that drove me forward. Revenge was within reach. No mistakes. No rash decisions. Day after day, week after week, year after year—each metaphorical step brought me closer to *her*.

Sofia Catalano Volkov.

The bitterness and hatred seeped into my cells and mixed with the ashes of those years spent in captivity. With the loss I felt when *she* was taken from me. The innocent young woman who watched me with golden eyes, promising warmth and happiness.

I rubbed my thigh absently, stroking the phantom pain that haunted me. It was always present, the result of cold, dark nights spent in that basement full of horror. Full of nightmares.

A flash of movement brought my attention back to the young woman with hair the color of warm wheat. It was identical to my Lou, but I knew it wasn't her. Lia was a fraud, the faded version of Lou.

Yet I found myself unable to tear my gaze away. It fed my broken mind. My body healed after Alexei Nikolaev saved me, but my mind didn't. Nobody came out of that shit sane. Fucking nobody.

I watched my enemy as she focused on her daughter, unaware of the ghost lurking in the shadows. If Sofia turned around, she'd spot me easily, but she was distracted by her greed. With plans of her own. Or maybe she was too confident.

They'd never see me coming.

I watched as she handed a piece of paper to her daughter, and disappointment washed over me. Liana was knee-deep in this shit now.

Lou had insisted on trying to get her twin out, sensing it'd be Liana's downfall. She was right, except my and Lou's downfall came first. Could I blame her twin? Fuck yes. She knew right from wrong, and she—along with her mother—signed their own death warrants.

Sofia Volkov apparently hadn't learned anything, keeping her daughter in that world. She'd lost two daughters—her firstborn, Winter Volkov, who was kidnapped by the Irish and then later died in childbirth, and Louisa. She was about to lose the third one.

There was no forgiveness for the pain Lou had suffered. What they did to her in her final hours.

Her punishment for trying to run with me and loving me was death.

Giving my head a subtle shake, I decided not to follow that train of thought. Lou's screams tattooed themselves onto my brain, haunting my dreams and plaguing my waking hours.

My lips curled in disgust as I studied Liana's profile, her eyes scanning over the document before she handed it back to her mother. A terse nod and her mother extended her hand to Perez Cortes's men for a handshake.

My eyes drifted to the piece of jewelry around my wrist—made of teeth dipped in silver and gold. It was Lou's, once upon a time. Now it served as a reminder to finish the job—eliminate the people who'd hurt her.

Ivan Petrov and Sofia Volkov made me their ghost. Lou was mine.

It became my signature. I craved death, wanting to follow the shadow of my dead woman, but it wasn't time yet. First, I'd make the world pay. Over the years, I'd wondered about the distinction between justice and vengeance, where one ended and the other began, but ultimately, I knew it was up to me to bring it all to an end.

My gaze flicked back to my bracelet, and memories of rare smiles and friendship dug a hole in my chest.

It was time to add more teeth to my collection.

Chapter 2
Liana

T he Godfather was the most expensive and elitist restaurant in Washington, D.C., located smack-dab in the heart of the city. You'd think the restaurant name would make it clear who ran it, but people flocked to it eagerly, ignorant to the fact that it was run by the mob families.

I hated this place.

Every single thing about it—the atmosphere, the criminals who frequented it, the corruption. That this restaurant was one of Perez Cortes's favorites made me hate it even more. The fucker wasn't here, but his presence was felt at the table.

Sinister. Deadly. Fateful.

He and his men were scum of the earth. It sickened me that my mother made deals with him. Even more, it sickened me that I sat at this table without slicing all their throats.

The ache in my wrist throbbed. Both hands on my lap under the table, I wrapped my fingers around it and massaged the tender skin while listening to my mother's plan, clenching my jaw. They held a conversation in various codes related to their latest shipment that had just arrived into the city, full of young women destined to be forced into serving sick men.

Speaking freely in front of me, unaware I broke their codes years ago, I listened and memorized. I understood that "The Raven" meant the Canton Docks in Baltimore. "The Monument" was a prostitution ring led by the Tijuana cartel using the Port of Washington yacht club. Just like Cortes, the Tijuana cartel loved to use young girls as entertainment for their soldiers. Fucking sickos. And then there were the Marabella Mobster arrangements that negotiated for high-prized girls. The negotiation took place in Brazil, and its code name was "The Dock." If only I could get coordinates for it so I could blow it all to pieces.

Locations were shared. Specifics like dates and times weren't. Much to my dismay.

"The women are of the highest quality," Mother stated coldly.

Bile rose in my throat, but I forced it down. One would think I'd be used to it by now. Instead, every fiber of my being fought against it. I sat there, listening to the men and my mother talk, and kept my expression blank while staring out the window. Happy people strolled by, unaware of the evil happening inside. Unaware of how empty I felt inside.

Ever since the day I lost something priceless.

My mother handed me a piece of paper. I took it with a steady hand, my eyes skimming over it. It was a bullshit agreement between Perez Cortes and my mother for the transport of drugs, alcohol, and *other* products. *Translation: humans.*

I used to hope Mother would get us out of the underworld, but that girl died a long time ago, right alongside my twin. My other half.

My chest twisted, the pain notched up in full. I'd been left with an aching heart and bitter truths. Guilt became the only constant in my life; grief, my penance. This was my misery—dark and poisonous—crawling under my flesh like a snake.

I fisted my hands in my lap, my nails cutting through my skin. The physical pain was better than the one in my heart. It was distracting. It was necessary. It coaxed me into someone I had to be.

"Liana." My mother's voice pulled me away from my self-pity and spiraling thoughts, only to find five sets of eyes on me.

"You look beautiful." One of Perez's men complimented me, bringing my attention to him and leading me to believe he'd repeated those words one too many times. His ogling agitated me, the urge to dig out his eyeballs consuming my every instinct. He viewed me like I was a piece of meat. I guess in a way I was. In this world, women were just that. Used to show off and abuse.

I refused to be either.

I shot to my feet, giving everyone at the table a full view of my outfit. I wore a sleeveless blue dress with straps that hugged my body above my torso like a second skin and fell to my knees in waves. My favorite pair of nude pumps gave me an extra three inches.

My mother wore a Valentino dress similar to mine underneath her signature fur coat. She refused to take that off even while seated at the restaurant because of what hid beneath it.

I barely held back a sneer at men who were too blind to see her arsenal.

Silence fell upon the table, until I broke it with my words. "Excuse me, I have to use the restroom."

My mother gave me a terse nod, the carved line between her brows the only indication that she wasn't happy. She was never happy. Not with me. Not with my twin. Not with her lovers. This life had stained her soul and destroyed her innocence. Assuming she ever had any to begin with.

Taking a deep breath, I turned around and headed toward the bathrooms, my heels clicking against the polished marble floor. The knots in my stomach seemed forever present.

I hated how my mother remained unaffected by it all—trafficking humans, being far too comfortable with the level of collateral damage her dealings accumulated.

And most of all, I hated how she seemed so unbothered by the death of my twin. It had been years, yet the wound inside my chest refused to heal.

She was my other half. The day I saw the video of Lou's death was my last straw. I died right along with her.

Unfortunately, my body and my mind continued living. Remembering some things and forgetting others.

So, since destiny refused to be kind and kill me off, I had to make a difference. Make my sister's death count. So I played my part. I stayed silent and betrayed no emotion. They would never see me coming.

Disgust thick in my veins, I held my clutch as I stalked toward the washroom. My nape prickled. My steps slowed. I could feel eyes on me. I turned around, but everyone at the table was deep in their dirty business. I skimmed over the restaurant, but nothing seemed amiss. Yet, I could feel it. It made every single hair on my body rise.

My hand reached up, twisting the single diamond stud earring—once, twice—before I gave my head a subtle shake and my hand fell to my side. Another throb in my wrist and I gripped it tightly as I rounded the corner.

Once I entered the restroom, I finally released a heavy breath and started to pace. The energy brimming beneath my skin was restless—I needed to get a handle on it, if not to preserve my cover.

I stopped in front of the sink and met my reflection, my hands on either side of the fancy marble counter steadying me. I looked like me, but I didn't *feel* like me. *Who am I?* I wondered. *What am I doing?*

No matter what I did, it didn't seem to make a difference. More women were found. More flesh was traded. I couldn't save them all.

I leaned my forehead on the cool glass and closed my eyes, remembering the first time I'd found them. The innocent, broken girls made to move like cattle.

No, it was worse.

The stench was the first thing that registered when I opened the door to the container. The terrified whimpers were what followed.

Reign of a Billionaire

My eyes adjusted to the darkness and my heart stopped. It fucking stopped beating, seeing girls and women with bruised faces huddled around each other, bodies angled to shelter themselves from what lay on the other side of the door. From me.

Some were lying in a fetal position, wearing nothing but filthy oversized shirts. Others sat with knees raised to their chest, their eyes glossed over and vacant.

It was then I saw their collars—the thick metal gripping their throats.

My nostrils flared, fury surging through me. "I'm going to help you."

And I'd make them pay.

Someone banging on the bathroom door pulled me out of my trance, my heartbeat racing at the onslaught of bitter memories. Disgust and disappointment swirled like a category-five hurricane inside of me. Unstoppable and destructive.

I'd saved some, but I'd failed more. Including my sister.

My hazel eyes, misty at the reminder of my failures, stared back at me.

With hate. With resignation. With sorrow.

Chapter 3
Kingston

I watched her golden locks bounce with each step she took, her skin glowing. She looked fragile, maybe even broken, reminding me of Lou.

My breath stuttered. My chest twisted. The resemblance was remarkable. She looked like *her*. Walked like her. Moved like her.

Don't be fooled, Kingston. The warning rang in my ears. This woman didn't hold a candle to Lou.

And just like that, it felt like losing her all over again, and the familiar fury bubbled like lava. Sofia took away my chance at redemption and left me in hell. I was no longer under her and Ivan's thumbs, but I might as well have been. What existed was a different level of hell, where I couldn't escape my failure to save Lou.

Alexei had been too late.

"I'm here to save you." *Unfamiliar voice, strange words. Nobody was saved here.* I cracked open my swollen eyes and inhaled a sharp breath. "I'm Alexei."

Pale blue eyes stared at me through the darkness.

"Save... her..." I could barely recognize the sound of my own voice as I motioned next to me, only to find the spot empty.

His eyes followed my gaze, waiting for me to explain. Frustration and despair welled in my chest when more words filtered through, this time in a more pressing tone.

"Alexei, we have to get out of here." I didn't turn my head, my eyes glued to the spot where I'd last seen Louisa. Her body was no longer there.

"The bomb's about to detonate." A third voice.

Alexei shifted my body, setting off an explosion of pain, and I clenched my teeth to stop a groan from slipping through my lips.

He raced us out of there, every one of his steps sending a shot of pain through me. My limbs were too heavy, my body too broken to fight him off—whoever he was. He raced through the castle, but I kept my eyes glued on the stairwell we just emerged from. My mind needed another glimpse of her, even as a ghost.

But destiny wasn't kind enough to give me that.

A beat later, the air filled with an ear-shattering explosion. Alexei picked up his speed, but it wasn't long before another boom sounded from the castle.

My savior stumbled and we went down hard. My head connected with something solid, and I was dragged into unconsciousness.

Alexei Nikolaev saved me to atone for his mistakes. But he only saved my body. He came too late to save my spirit. Too late to save *her*.

The years since Alexei rescued me had been hell. I couldn't sleep. Could barely eat. I had to be sedated to get rest or risk my body shutting down. I wanted to kill anyone who crossed me. Anyone who resembled the woman with golden eyes who never failed to cause heaviness in my chest.

The woman who died for me.

For weeks after I was saved, I was under Alexei's protection, but I was on edge all day and night, only a breath away from launching myself over. I couldn't forget Lou's cries, her screams, her pain.

Liana strolled in the direction of the restroom, capturing my attention. Her steps slowed as she scanned the diners. Almost as if she could sense my eyes on her. My gaze roved over her face and down her body.

She was older, curvier, but she wasn't my Louisa. No matter the striking resemblance.

She reached for her ear and tugged on the diamond. I sucked in a breath through my teeth. The world tilted on its axis and time slowed. For the first time in a very long time, I felt a flicker of something in my chest. My throat closed.

But then reason slowly filtered in.

She used her right hand to tug on her earring. Lou had been left-handed.

But then she wrapped her fingers around her left wrist and her eyes locked to where I hid in the shadows. My breath hitched. The ache intensified.

This woman's eyes were all wrong, lacking softness and passion that warmed me from the inside. Lou's eyes were the mirror to her heart and soul. Every moment of pain and torment were reflected in the depths of them. Liana's eyes were flat, the lack of fire serving as a reminder of what I'd lost.

It was fucking torture.

I shook my head.

Liana owed her life to Lou, the least she could have done was atone for it. Made her sister proud instead of joining her mother's ranks.

My mind flickered back to the young woman who'd once traced my scars and kissed my blood-drenched hands after especially brutal ring-fights. I missed the woman who used to look at me like I was a god.

Some days I wanted nothing more than to forget it all.

Instead, the rage grew darker. It tore through my chest and made it impossible to differentiate between what was real and what I was reliving. Pulling me back to that fateful night all those years ago, feeling like I was losing her all over again.

The soft din of the restaurant went silent, pulling me out of my mind.

Exhaling slowly, I let the dark memory roll off me. That was the day she broke. That was the day my woman died.

That day, Sofia Volkov signed her death warrant—not for torturing me, but for crushing her daughter's very essence.

Chapter 4
Liana

I was making my way back to the room bustling with busy waiters and chattering patrons when I felt eyes on me again. I straightened suddenly and my stride faltered.

My heart stopped. My breath hitched.

A man walked—no, sauntered—toward me like he owned every inch of this restaurant and the people in it. The hints of silver in his stubble beard were at odds with his young-looking face. Yet it matched his expression. His dark eyes locked on me, lethal power emanating from him in waves, and all the way, I stood frozen, unable to move. He was tall. Dangerous. With eyes that seemed to see too much.

His gaze drifted over my body with a dark scowl, like he knew me. But that was impossible. I wouldn't—could never—forget a face like that. His jawline spoke of determination, of grief and pain. The kind that I sometimes felt in my own heart.

Dressed in a black three-piece suit, sans tie, his muscular frame was enveloped in fine material, but it did nothing to hide the predator underneath. The color of his hair matched his suit. But it was his dark, almost-black eyes that captured me completely.

I couldn't look away.

Another step and he was close enough I could feel his warmth. The spiced vanilla scent and a cologne I didn't recognize invaded my lungs. It was more intoxicating than any alcohol could be.

A shudder rolled down my spine. Blood drummed in my ears. He was the only thing I was aware of, capturing every ounce of my attention. I could feel the chill and... something else in his gaze.

Hatred, maybe? Or was it curiosity?

I knew I should start walking, but I couldn't force my body to move an inch. I stared at the stranger's broad figure striding agilely past me.

It wasn't until I heard the ding of the door opening that I finally jolted from my stupor. He was gone. Like a ghost in the dead of night, except in this case, it was the middle of the day.

The overwhelming sense of loss weakened my knees, the confusion at my reaction profound.

Shaking it off, I resumed my path back to our table, the nape of my neck prickling and all my senses on alert. I needed to figure out what the hell was wrong with me before my mother picked up on it. I couldn't handle another one of her *treatments*.

"Ah, there you are." I turned to find my mother standing with the rest of the party, ready to depart. Her gaze bore into me, studying me. "You seem frazzled."

I shook my head, acutely aware of her suspicious eyes.

"I'm not," I said, my voice even, betraying none of my inner turmoil. Tension coiled in my belly like a beast, leaving me utterly confused but hungry for answers.

Mother nodded, accepting my answer, when one of our dinner companions extended his hand. "It was a pleasure meeting you."

I let his hand hang in the air, not interested in letting this creep touch any part of me. Locking eyes with his bland ones, I gave him a terse nod, then faced my mother. "Ready?"

"You're driving back to the hotel with me," she declared.

I gritted my teeth but didn't argue. At twenty-six, I was more than capable of making my own decisions, but my independence was something the great Sofia Volkov hated. She had guards who watched me and reported everything I did to her.

After years of practice, I'd become an expert at ditching them. Of course, they never knew that they'd been left in the lurch. Most of the time, they believed me asleep in bed.

I walked toward the exit, caught off guard by my reflection in the window. My hand on the doorknob, I stared at myself. There was an unfamiliar glint to my eyes. An odd flush in my cheeks.

Before my mother could comment on my odd behavior, I exited the restaurant and made my way to the waiting car. My mother followed, shutting the door. As I slid along the plush seats, my gaze darted back toward the restaurant while my mind reeled with questions. And then I saw *him*.

The familiar stranger lurked in the alley's shadow, his eyes firmly locked on mine. I barely contained a fresh shiver, my body throbbing as his gaze lingered.

"What are you staring at, Liana?"

My mother's voice pulled my attention to her only to find her eyes following my gaze, and as I glanced back into the alley, he was nowhere to be found.

"Nothing, Mother."

I sat poised and collected, my back straight and my gaze locked on the fleeting scenery of the city. The remainder of the short drive was spent in silence. Once we arrived at the hotel, I got out of the vehicle and started walking toward the five-star hotel.

My hand on the handle, my mother's voice boomed from behind me. "Liana, stop."

I froze just as the hotel door opened, the handle slipping out of my palm. A man in his thirties stood opposite of me, holding it open for us. He stood to the side, waiting patiently.

"After you, miss."

"Thanks," I murmured.

My mother and her bodyguards appeared beside me in a flash,

their eyes locked on the man.

"What are you doing here?" Mother spat, her Italian accent making a rare appearance.

"It's a free country last time I checked, Sofia," the stranger responded with a hint of sarcasm. I watched the exchange in amazement.

My eyes locked on him, his muscled body wrapped in an expensive suit. His striking green eyes were hard to ignore, but what captured my attention was the tattoo on his left hand. A weird symbol in the mouth of a skull. I'd never seen anything like it before.

My mother nodded once, in that polite warning that was reserved for those she held in contempt. Naturally, my interest was piqued, and this time, I memorized every line of his face.

He watched my mother with a cold expression, his lips curled in a sneer.

"He expects the delivery on time, Sofia," he said in a gravelly voice. "No mistakes."

They had to be discussing the timing of a new delivery of girls. Why couldn't anyone announce the date and time?

"It will be," Mother said with a finality that sent twin shivers down my spine.

"Ladies," he said as he nodded back, his eyes shifting in my direction, and my mother had me ushered away quickly, the two of us sandwiched between our bodyguards.

The man moved, his muscles flexing, and then he chuckled. He fucking chuckled; although, when I glanced over my shoulder, there was no amusement on his face or in his strikingly green eyes.

"See to it that it's without hiccups. Too many of your shipments have had... mishaps." And then he disappeared, leaving me confused.

"Who's that?" I asked my mother curiously.

"Nobody."

"Where do you know him from?"

"Nowhere."

It would seem two could play a game of vague answers.

Chapter 5
Liana

Loud music drummed through the floor of our shitty motel as I navigated the hallway with red walls, red carpets, and even red doors. The only thing that wasn't red was the ceiling.

With one last deep breath, I focused on the task at hand. I had to get to my target—the weak link in Perez Cortes and my mother's plan. My plan was simple: knock on the door, pretend to be lost, isolate him, then inject him with a syringe full of poison.

Simple.

"I'm keeping my promise," I whispered to the empty hallway, my throat tightening.

Blinking away tears that stung the backs of my eyes, I hinged my jaw. I proceeded down the musky, worn-out carpet, my five-inch heels silent in my stalking. A door suddenly opened and a six-foot-five giant stepped out, leaving the door ajar.

Target in sight.

The muffled thump of the bass coming from the bedroom matched the manic beating of my heart. His gaze swept down my body, lingering on my bare legs. Pervert. This was exactly the reason this man was the easiest target of those who were present at the restaurant. He couldn't resist his urges and had a reputation among the Brazilian cartel for sampling women.

So tonight, I wore a white minidress, my pink bra and panties clearly showing underneath. Of course, my clutch matched my outfit, but it served to contain everything I needed to finish this job. I looked like an underage slut, going for the jugular. Just for him. He'd sing a tune, tell me everything, and then I'd kill him.

For every woman he'd ever hurt. For my sister.

"Are you lost, baby?" Men were such pigs. I forced a smile, despite the goosebumps breaking across my arms.

"Maybe." I fluttered my eyelashes.

"You didn't seem so friendly at the restaurant." A medal for his observation skills.

"My mother's very protective," was all I said.

He smiled lazily. Predatorily. "She's not here now, baby."

If he called me baby one more time, I'd have to promptly stab him, to hell with my plan. Inhaling a deep breath, I forced myself not to lose my shit. The lives of innocent women depended on it.

"She isn't." I just needed to find out the day and time when the women would be shipped so that I could intercept them. "Is this your room?" I asked, batting my lashes and smiling flirtatiously while swallowing the bile rising in my throat.

"It is," he purred, opening the door wider. "Want to come in and check it out?"

I glanced around him as if dying to see farther into his shitty room. The dim yellow light bathed the room in a sickly glow as I made eye contact with him.

"What's your name?" I knew every organization in the underworld, every name running within them, but I never bothered learning soldiers' names. They expired too frequently.

His eyes narrowed with suspicion. "Why do you want to know?"

"My mama always tells me not to talk to strangers," I said sweetly. "But if you tell me your name, you won't be a stranger anymore."

Reign of a Billionaire

My voice was steady and unwavering, but my hands trembled. I'd done this plenty of times by now; I really shouldn't be so nervous. Maybe it was adding one more tally to my list of sins. Or maybe it was the fear of something going wrong.

"I'm Pedro, baby," he answered, visibly relaxing. "But tonight you can call me Papi."

My lips tightened, barely tamping down my cringe. Sicko. I couldn't wait to kill this asshole.

If my mother learned of my extracurricular activities, she'd kill me without batting an eyelash. But I couldn't stand by and allow those poor women to have their lives destroyed. If I did nothing, then wasn't I just as guilty?

This way, I could at least hope for a quick death once Sofia Volkov learned what her daughter did. What she *had* been doing for years now.

As I took a step into the room, I swiftly extracted the syringe that was safely tucked in my bra. I removed the cap while observing the space. The room was dark, and the stench of urine was so strong it had a physical presence. The door to the yellow tiled bathroom was wide open, revealing a bathtub.

Bingo.

The door shut with a thud, followed by the click of the lock. My stomach roiled, but I kept myself in check as I scoped out every inch of the room.

"Shitty room," I said in a bored tone. "Your boss must not value your services too much to put you in a cockroach motel." Or was it a roach motel? American slang wasn't my forte. Russian was my first language, Gaelic a close second. My formal English was perfect, but that was about where it ended.

His tall frame was in my personal space in the next breath, and I anticipated it.

He loomed over me, and sucking in a sharp breath, I twisted the syringe around in my fingers and stabbed its pointed end into his neck, pressing the plunger.

"Bitch—"

He reared back with a roar, raised his fist, and slammed it into my face.

Pain exploded in my cheek, but I persisted. The price for any errors made tonight was too steep. He pulled his fist back again, but this time I caught it and twisted it behind him. I heaved my foot on his ass, my heel digging into it with force, then pushed him forward. Losing his balance, he collapsed face-first into the filthy carpet.

He flopped like a fish, gasping for air and clawing at his throat.

"Don't bother expending your energy, *suka blyat*," I drawled lazily, cursing him in Russian. Son of a bitch. "You'll only die faster." He stilled, and suddenly I had his attention. I dug my heel into his back. "You've been poisoned. And only I have the antidote for it." I didn't, but he didn't need to know that. "Tell me where and when the next shipment will happen, and I'll administer it."

He tried to speak but the words that came out were garbled. *Suka blyat*, did I give him too high a dose? The dude was a mountain, so I'd added an extra ounce just to be sure.

I spotted a gun holster on the armchair and casually made my way to it. "Not that I'm rushing you, but the poison will kill you in exactly"—I glanced at the clock, red digits blinking angrily—"ten minutes."

I picked up the gun and turned around, finding my latest victim's eyes on me. Seconds passed, and I watched him with a cold expression until he finally broke.

"Tomorrow," he gurgled. "Ten p.m."

I flashed him a smile—more like a grimace. "Thank you."

"Anti—" His every syllable was labored. "An... An—"

"Antidote?" I finished for him, and he struggled to nod. More like an eye twitch. I smiled with menace. "Didn't I tell you, *baby*?" I accentuated the word while sneering. "I don't have it on me."

Moving around him, I reached for my clutch and pulled out a knife.

Reign of a Billionaire

"Did you know a lady never leaves the house without a clutch?" I said quietly, eerily. "And a paintbrush."

His eyes grew wide and he paled as I ran my finger along the blade.

"No, no," he cried. "Don't—"

I leaned over him. "Don't what?" I asked, raising one eyebrow in mock-interest. "Hurt you? Tell me something, Pedro. How many women have you spared when they begged not to be hurt?"

His pupils dilated, understanding sinking in that there was no escaping this. I sliced his gut, and he opened his mouth to scream. The only thing that came out was a small whimper. The drug was working.

I reveled in his helplessness. *Let them have a taste of their own medicine,* I thought bitterly.

My hand still holding the knife buried in his gut, I twisted it as I reached for the paintbrush in my clutch.

Then I dipped it in his blood, soaking in his pained moans, his terrified eyes on me as I started my process. I preferred to sketch, but blood was sure to get my point across.

Five minutes to draw a sketch of a faceless man all over the wall in my victim's blood. Admittedly, it was a creepy thing to do, but it was about the only thing that made me feel alive anymore. In the darkest recesses of my mind lived the notion that my sister was here with me when I committed these atrocities. She might be disgusted, but she'd be proud.

So I sketched with their blood for me, my sister, and every woman who'd been wronged by men like this one.

I stood over my victim like an avenging angel, watching him struggle until the life drained out of his eyes.

"Another one bites the dust," I muttered under my breath. "Bath-time, asshole."

Dragging his dead weight into the bathroom, I grunted and cursed as I pushed his body, limb by limb, into the filthy, ancient tub.

Once in there, I used the fire escape to fetch my supplies.

It took me exactly five hours to dispose of the body. A sodium hydroxide mixture with boiling water made Pedro disappear down the rusted drain. The stench—pungent, sharp, and acrid—was welcomed. I'd take it over being touched any day.

My heart thrashed with memories of my own sister. They always seemed to reach me at the worst times. I pulled out my phone and retrieved my secret folder, then pressed Play. I'd seen the recording a million times—could recite every detail of it word for word, move for move. That didn't stop my chest from fracturing with the same intensity.

The gloved and masked men tortured her. She fought them tooth and nail, yanking the chain off one's neck. I wished there was a way to zero in on the necklace. I needed clues, anything to hunt those responsible down.

In the next moment, they dunked her head into a tub filled with a clear solution, and I watched my twin's body dissolve into nothing. Pain surged across my chest, the way it did every time I thought of her.

The cartel—specifically the Tijuana cartel, who had close ties to the Cortes cartel—took something valuable from me. In return, I would take it *all* from them. When I was done with them, there'd be nothing left but ash.

Even if it included my own mother and me.

Chapter 6
Kingston

R ush hour in the city was in full swing when I entered the building that Byron called "meet in the middle" restaurant.

The place was crowded, but my family had a reserved table. A privilege of being wealthy. Our mother left her inheritance to her children, and each one of us had built our empire from the ground up. My brothers became some of the top real estate tycoons, and I became one of the top killers and trackers in the underworld.

I made my way over to the table where Kristoff Baldwin and my brother Byron already sat with drinks in their hands. Bourbon for Byron, scotch for Kristoff. They were way too predictable.

Kristoff pushed his hand through his hair, flagging the waiter over.

"Kingston," he greeted me, handing me an envelope. It was a deed to another property I acquired.

I took my spot, nodding my thanks.

"Byron, I thought you were still in France?" I remarked. "Are your wife and kids here too?"

"We're here just for a week."

The waitress was back with a refill for Kristoff, who downed it before she disappeared.

"What's wrong with you?" I questioned.

"His oldest is rebelling," Byron remarked. "He's worried because he hasn't heard from her in a few days."

"I'm sure you can track her via phone," I pointed out.

"She has it turned off," he gritted.

"Is that what I have to look forward to with my children?" Byron mused. "Sleepless nights and rebellion?"

"For your sake, I hope not," Kristoff retorted dryly. "You might be left without any hair."

My brother served a few deployments with Kristoff, the latter saving his life on his last tour. Byron was lucky to come out of it with only burns on his back.

I twisted my face as the two of them marveled at the joys and stress of parenthood and marriage. It wasn't jealousy, I told myself. It had nothing to do with the fact that I couldn't relate. Or maybe it had everything to do with it.

My thoughts drifted to Liana Volkov and a sardonic breath left me at her show of confidence back at the restaurant. Admittedly, it also left me puzzled. It intrigued me—troubled me even—that there was no recognition in her eyes. She couldn't remember me.

I shook my head, chasing the thoughts of her away. I spent more time than I liked with that woman on my mind. That had to stop.

"Is everything okay?" Byron asked, studying me.

"Yes."

Kristoff leaned back into his seat. "I recognize that look."

I gave him a puzzled look. So did my brother. "What look?" I questioned.

Kristoff smiled, amusement flashing in his gaze. "Someone important, a woman, must be occupying your mind."

He was only partially right. Liana was a woman, but she wasn't important to me. I pushed my fingers through my hair, the motion something I'd done more than I'd like to admit in the recent days.

Reign of a Billionaire

It was at that moment that a familiar figure caught my attention. Giovanni Agosti was seated at the table opposite from us.

"Excuse me," I said, getting to my feet and making my way to his table. His expression was solemn as he looked up to find me sliding into the chair opposite him.

"By all means, I wasn't waiting for a date," he muttered dryly.

Giovanni was part of the Thorns of Omertà, although for the most part kept to himself. "What are you doing in the city?"

He raised a brow. "Are you writing a book about me that I don't know about?"

Odd. He usually wasn't the dodging type. I cast a look at our surroundings. "I am."

He rolled his eyes.

"Please leave out this chapter." My lips twitched. I would swear he was about to roll his eyes but stopped himself. "I have to attend my uncle's... event."

I raised a brow. "Event?" He nodded. "Isn't your uncle in Boston?"

His jaw clenched before he answered, "This is my other uncle."

"*Other* uncle?" I repeated slowly.

"Yes." He narrowed his eyes on me, his tone matching mine. "And I want to talk about this as much as you want to talk about your kidnapping by Ivan Petrov and your time under Sofia's imprisonment."

The temperature dropped, both of us emanating resentment and eyes blazing.

"Brave of you to bring that up. Have a death wish?" The threat escaped me, so calm and deadly it stilled the air.

Giovanni watched my face, then nodded. "Then don't ask about my shit."

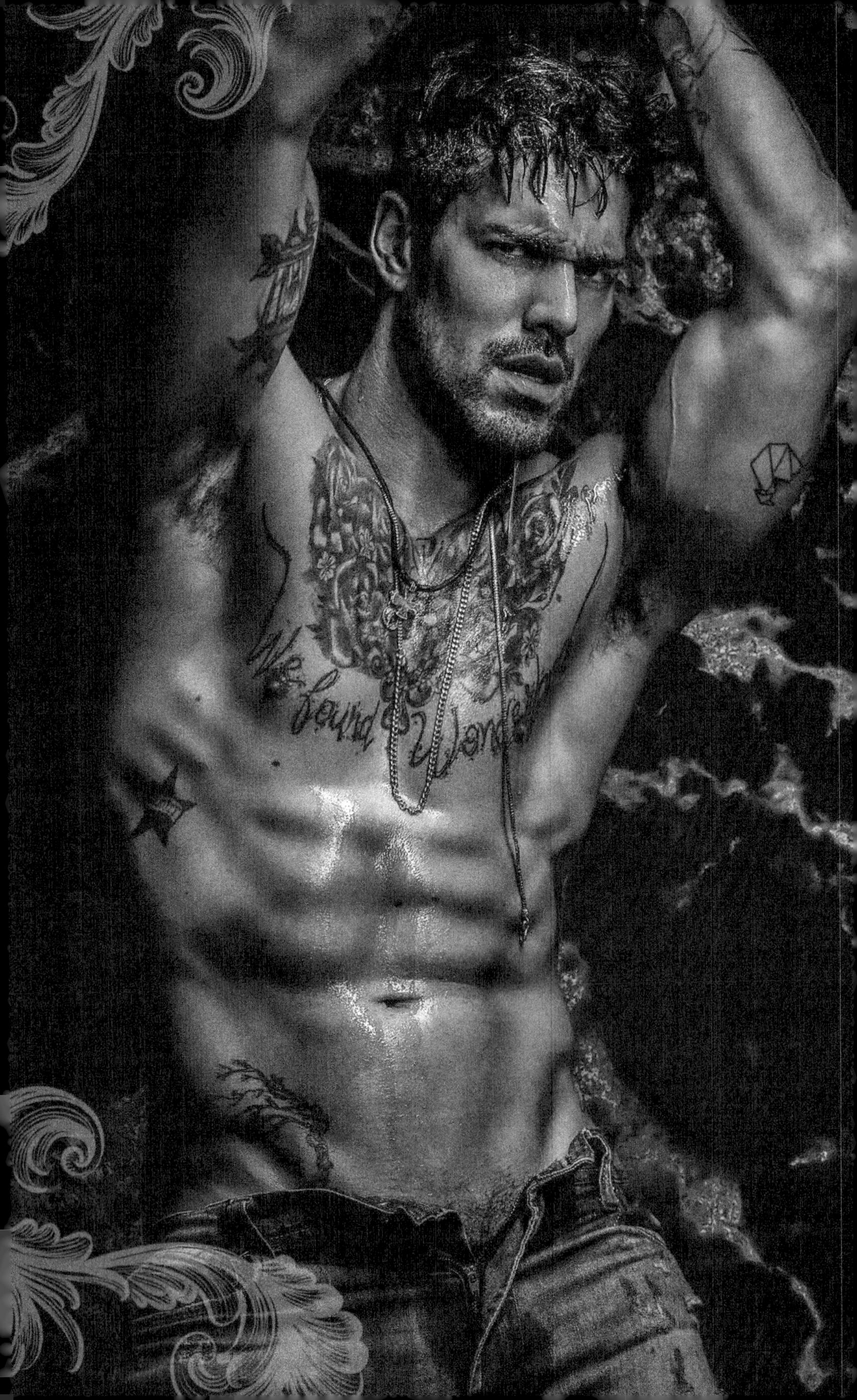

Chapter 7
Kingston, 10 Years Old

Our nanny chased my little sister Aurora through the yard as I let out an exasperated breath.

"Don't even start," Royce grumbled while Winston watched us with a bored expression, taking a puff of his cigarette. If Father found him smoking, he'd have all our ears boxed. "It's your turn to take her to the zoo."

"It's true," Winston agreed. "But if you're not up for it, I'll do it."

Rora's dark curls bounced as she skipped across the manicured lawn, brimming with energy. Despite her fancy red coat with black bows for buttons and her shiny leather loafers, she was wild. But she was happy, and I wouldn't—couldn't—be the one to ruin it today.

I waved my brothers off and rolled my eyes. "Fine, I'll do it. You guys suck."

Royce glanced around before flipping me off. Winston just shrugged and returned to his vice, pulling in a puff of nicotine-laced air. The all-boys school we attended demanded a certain level of decorum from us, but that didn't necessarily apply to our behavior in private.

"Nanny's going with you, so you won't really do much," Royce pointed out.

I called my sister over and took her hand securely into mine while the nanny trailed behind us. She hummed the whole way to the zoo—which was thankfully only a few blocks away—chatting my ear off about the Christmas presents she wanted to shop for. She'd been crazy about hippos since watching a documentary on them, and no amount of explanation could convince my stubborn little sister that we couldn't keep one in our yard, *even* if it was at the top of her list.

"Stay with me, Rora," I reprimanded in a soft voice.

"Always."

She lifted her face, watching me with so much trust it made my chest pound with pride. I tugged her pigtail fondly, and a giggle bubbled on her lips.

We'd visited the zoo probably a hundred times this year, but Rora behaved as if it were her first time every time. The moment we were past the gates, she tugged her little hand out of my hold and ran circles around me and the nanny.

"Lion," she squealed, smiling widely. "Here, come here. Bears!"

Her enthusiasm was contagious. There wasn't anyone who could resist her innocent charm. Another loud giggle sounded from her, and I couldn't help but smile along.

"Oh my gosh." She beamed, her cheeks rosy from the walk. Her dark hair was a wild mess by now, but her eyes shone like obsidian, her delight palpable.

"Rora, stay close!" I warned when she strayed too far. We made our way deeper into the zoo and finally stopped at the elephants. I watched one lift his trunk high up in the air and reach for the tree branch, then shake it with all its might.

My worries sailed away as I stared in awe at the elephants. I'd have to tell the boys at school about this tomorrow. Of course, I'd have to play it cool and not tell them that I was with my five-year-old sister. They'd laugh at that. No ten-year-old boy wanted to spend time with their little sister—at least, they didn't want to admit as much.

Reign of a Billionaire

I didn't mind it myself, but it wasn't something I bragged about.

"See, Rora. A hippopotamus can't do—" My eyes widened at the empty space by my side and I turned around, my gaze darting left and right. Pushing through the crowd, I searched for my sister's smiling face. My stomach twisted with each passing second until a thought occurred to me.

She was stubborn. Maybe she'd taken herself to the hippo enclosure.

I rushed across the path and made my way to where they were housed. I spotted her red coat, her little hand wrapped in a stranger's, and trepidation shot through me.

"Rora." My voice traveled over the air, drawing my sister's attention in my direction.

I stood on the other side of the pool pathway, but before I could run to her, I was yanked off the ground by my hair. A painful gasp tore from me, tears stinging my eyes, and I blinked them away furiously. I was being held captive by a man with an evil smile. I instantly regretted not dragging our nanny with us.

My sister ran toward me, but I shouted, "No, Rora." Her steps faltered and she came to a stop, her dark eyes widening in terror. She breathed heavily, her little coat rising and falling from the exertion. "Run, Aurora. Run and don't look back!"

Her little body trembled where she stood next to a man covered head to toe in tattoos. My eyes darted to him, praying for him to save my sister.

"I don't want to go alone," she whimpered.

"Don't worry, little girl." The man holding me grinned menacingly. *No.* I had to protect my sister. My brothers and I had made a pact. I jerked against his hold, his grip tightening on me as he leered at my baby sister. I didn't like it. "Sharing is caring. I came for you, but we can take your brother too... that could be fun, *da?*"

"Leave her alone," I snarled, pushing against the men who surrounded me. "Run, Rora!" I screamed at the top of my lungs.

She bolted while I started after her, but before I had a chance to send whispered prayers to Ma in heaven, I was knocked unconscious.

The hum of men's voices pulled me back to awareness.

"Should we tie him up?"

I stiffened at the sound of someone laughing. "Why? There's nowhere for him to go."

My nostrils filled with a mixture of blood, metal, and sewage as I lay on my side, unmoving. I cracked an eye open just in time to see a steel-toed boot swinging in my direction, hitting me in the torso.

I grunted, spitting out blood.

"Look at that, the pampered prince is awake." One of them chuckled. I pushed myself up, my limbs screaming in protest, and glared at them. My eyes darted to each one of them, memorizing their features, so when I was rescued, I could describe them to my brothers.

We'd find them and end them all.

"Someone looks pissed off." Another kick. My nostrils flared, but before another could land on me, I jumped to my feet and struck him in the shin.

A painful howl bounced off the walls of the dark room. Someone pushed my face roughly, my head hitting the wall, but this time it didn't hurt as much.

Instead, I focused on the group of men surrounding me. Ignoring their taunting glares and smiles, I searched for their faces, their positions. My brothers always said to locate the weakest link among bullies.

Except, none of them looked weak.

Before I could devise a plan, a pair of hands wrapped around my throat and my back slammed against the rocky wall. My sight flickered, and when I opened my eyes, I blinked to refocus and get myself out of danger.

"Wanna fuck with me?" I dangled in the air, pressed against the corner. The scent of stale alcohol was heavy on his breath. Nausea gripped my throat, but I refused to go down without a fight. I swung my arms and legs, unable to reach him. When I couldn't land a punch, I twisted my head and sunk my teeth into his wrist.

He dropped me, and I landed on my feet.

"I'm glad we have a fighter here." The sound of the metal door opening drew everyone's eyes away from me and landed on the man who just entered the room.

Expressionless face. Bottomless eyes. Menacing smile. I knew no saving would come from him.

His eyes zeroed in on me, taunting and cruel. Dread settled in my stomach, and somehow I knew running away from this situation wouldn't be easy.

The door behind him remained open, and I took my chance, my heart soaring with hope. Bolting through the group of men like I was in the Olympics, I barely made it out the door when a snap of electricity surged through me.

I fell to my knees, grunting with pain, and glanced over my shoulder, only to lock eyes with the man who held a tiny remote in his hand.

"I'm Ivan Petrov. Welcome to my realm, boy."

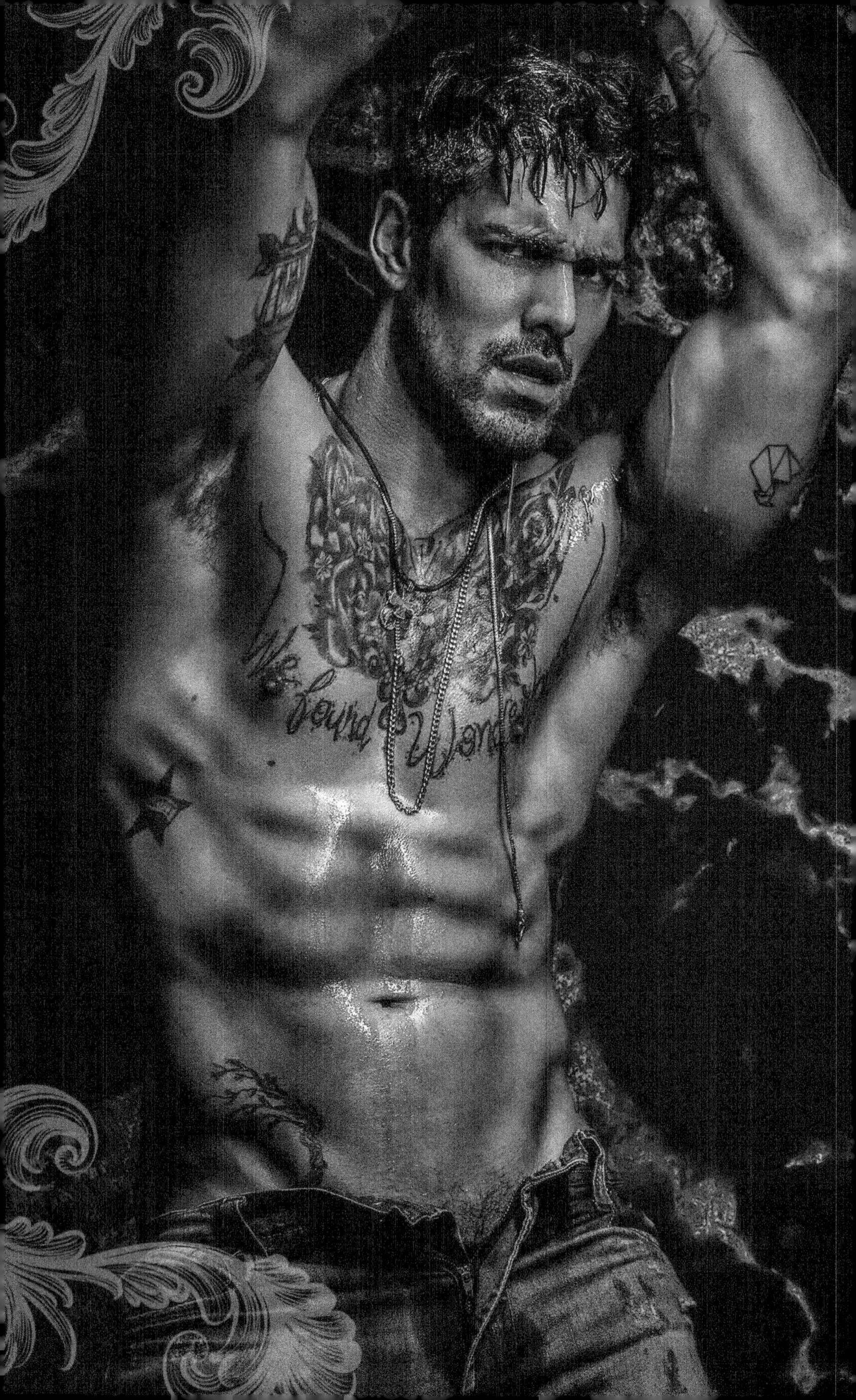
We found

Chapter 8
Kingston, 10 Years Old

Torture center.
 The only time I saw the light of day was when I was brought here to train. Snow covered the ground as far as the eye could see—even the trees in the far distance were cloaked in white.

Everything about this place screamed *nightmare*. Dark and damp castle walls. Ghosts roaming the halls at night, some of them laughing, others crying. Twilight had arrived once more, and longing slammed into me. I yearned to feel the breeze on my face. To smell the air that I knew would be as fresh as the snowfall. I'd even stand in the snow if I could.

It'd been two weeks.

I was brought to this godforsaken facility every day. Some of the boys called it the training center. Or *the death ring*. Ivan Petrov said it was a room designed for hand-to-hand combat and weapons training. The looks on the fighters' faces told me there was more to it.

I got my confirmation as I waited for my turn in the ring.

My chest clenched as I watched a guard carry out a dead boy's body. He had the mangled form thrown over his shoulder like he was taking out the trash. Would that be me next?

I cracked my knuckles.

"I hate this fucking place," I muttered to myself, then winced at the foul language that seemed to have sprouted in me overnight. My brothers would have my head if they heard me.

Something clogged in my chest, remembering the last time I saw them. It seemed like a lifetime ago. I missed them and my little sister. Was she okay? Or did these assholes get her too?

"Remember, boy." Ivan Petrov's snarky voice came from behind me. "Win this one and I'll let you know where your baby sister is."

You're a survivor, my little Kingston. You were born to reign in every life.

My mother's voice, which I hadn't thought of in so long, came back to me, renewing my strength. It didn't matter that I wasn't home. I would reign over this fucking arena and kill anyone who tried to end me.

Including my own father, who was the reason I was here.

He owed these criminals a debt that he didn't pay, so they'd gone after Rora. Instead, they got me. At least I *hoped* they'd only got me.

Without acknowledging the man, I made my way into the ring, determined to give them a show they'd never forget.

I stood at the center, my eyes locked on the boy at least five years older than me. Judging by his expression, he had something to prove. Not that I could blame him. Whispers claimed that he'd been born here and never knew anything or anyone but the people in this facility.

His cheek was bruised; his eyes blank.

At ten, I was bigger than the average kid, but this guy dwarfed me. I was weak. Unprepared.

The punch to my face came out of nowhere. I heard the crunch, then felt the searing pain in my skull as the blood gushed out of my nose.

Ignoring the blood, I cracked my jaw, keeping my attention on my opponent. Then I pulled back my fist and released it into the boy's ribs with all my might. I didn't stop there. Alternating fists, I punched nonstop. All the pent-up frustration and anger from the last two weeks boiled over.

The boy's eyes widened, his breaths coming in ragged pants, but I was too far gone to consider his fear. It was kill or be killed.

Fury surged. At my opponent. At this fucked-up place. At the vermin surrounding this wannabe-gladiator arena.

A crimson haze crept along the edges of my vision, pushing everything and everyone out, and leaving me alone with a boy like me. We were both victims.

Another punch and he fell to his knees, blinking in confusion before falling over. The dust cloud around him. Gurgling sounds filled the air.

I froze, my mind finally falling silent, as I stared down at the body. The red fog of rage lifted, and I braced for the consequences of my actions.

A man appeared out of nowhere with a black bag while I stood immobile, unable to comprehend what just happened.

"Punctured lung," a man muttered as the boy choked on his own blood, his eyes showing life for the first time in the two weeks I'd known him. He spit out blood, but something solid hit my boot.

I lowered down, wiping at the blood on my shoe, and spotted a tooth. I reached for it, along with a fistful of sand. As it moved through my fingers like an hourglass, his life slowly faded away.

That day, I became a ghost.

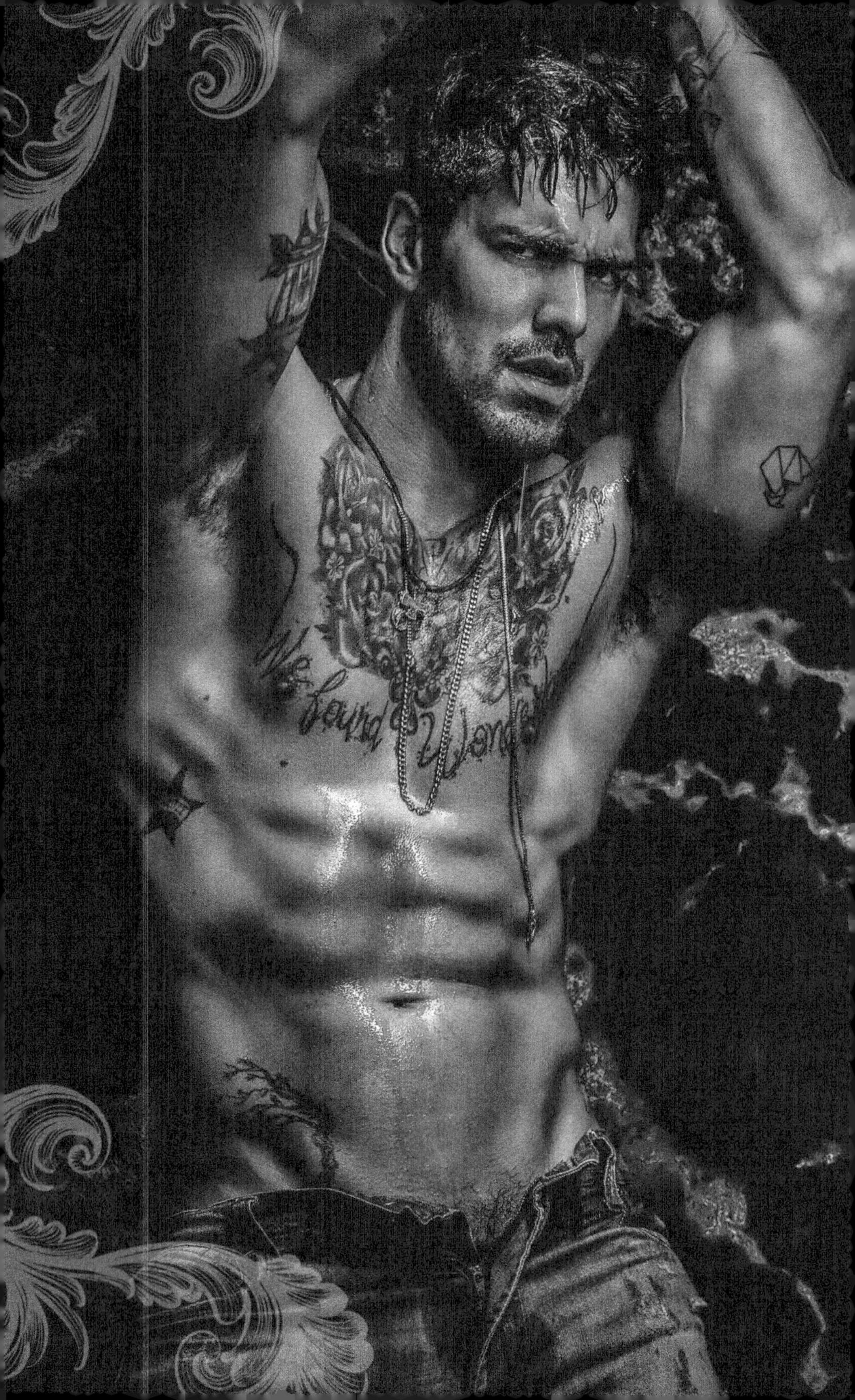

Chapter 9
Kingston, 11 Years Old

My defenses cracked like lightning across the sky. With each passing day, I descended deeper into hell. Every passing night, I slipped into madness. There were hours when breathing alone was intolerable.

I was desperate to escape this hell. The escape seemed impossible. My reality became a fight. Became another struggle to survive.

"You," the guard called out, and every fiber of me knotted. His eyes focused intently on me. Bile rose in my throat, my skin crawling with revulsion. But I hid it all behind a blank expression filled with nightmares.

I didn't want to go. I didn't want to stay.

The choice wasn't given.

Standing up, my legs unsteady, the snickers and pity drifted off the other boys, wrapping around my throat like a noose. If only it'd suffocate me. Relief shone in their eyes at not being the ones chosen, but that was how it went in this hell. Some days just weren't your day.

Eyes on Ivan and Sofia, I let myself imagine the day the life left theirs. I learned quickly who it was that ruled over this hell. Who was responsible for the life I was forced to endure. A life I didn't want, but was too much of a coward to try to end. So each day, I did what was demanded of me, taking the lives of other boys to continue "earning" my place in this hell.

Every muscle in my body tightened at the picture of me running into the knee-high snow. I wouldn't make it a hundred yards before being dragged back. I should know; I'd tried it more than once.

I closed my eyes, attempting to drown out the grunts and moans. The sounds were perverse and wrong in my ears.

"Come here, boy." A demon with a woman's voice. I moved on autopilot, the perfume invading my nose.

I shut my mind down, seeking refuge in a warm paradise where teeth, stained with the blood of those who'd dared touch me or had tried to kill me, hung on the wall as décor.

Chapter 10
Kingston, 12 Years Old

F ear was part of my every breath and each heartbeat. It shouldn't be, I needed to be braver, but I couldn't shake it off.

Two years, four months, two weeks, and twelve days. Eight hundred and seventy-eight days in a windowless, empty basement cell in the middle of the Siberian landscape. The only time I caught a glimpse of the outside world was when I was taken upstairs to fight.

The training didn't bother me as much as the killing. I tracked the number of lives I'd taken by the teeth I pulled from the corpses. They were just boys, not so unlike me.

One day, someone would probably rip my teeth out when they were done with me.

I leaned against the pillar as I watched a fight between two older kids, my racing heart hidden behind my well-worn mask. Days and months of torture did that to you.

Bright lights surrounded the arena, illuminating the strangers scattered all around it. They shouted, cheered, waved their money in the air with greed in their eyes. The walls behind me were painted red, just like the blood staining the sand in the arena. But that wasn't what captured my interest.

It was the only window in the room that stretched on the far wall, letting me see the clear blue sky. It didn't look cold, despite the snow covering the ground. If only the window would open, I'd jump out of it and try my luck at escaping again. I'd take my chances, even in these rags my captors called clothes.

I missed my brothers. My sister.

Their faces slowly faded in my mind, but I clung to them with all I had. Each night before I fell asleep, I cataloged everything I remembered about them. They were looking for me. I knew it in my heart. My father would abandon me, but not my siblings.

The only comfort in all of this was that my baby sister had been spared. It was one of the only things keeping me going, though I still remembered that day clearly. Her eyes full of terror; her chubby cheeks stained with tears.

A loud roar pulled me from my thoughts to where a boy twitched and bled all over the sand beneath the ring. He fought to breathe; he fought to live another day. But everyone knew he wouldn't. With each passing second, the light in his eyes dimmed until it was extinguished completely.

"Fuck, he didn't make it." A mutter by a boy behind me had me turning around. "The Killer is unbeatable."

His dark blue eyes were resigned. Tired. He looked the way I felt. Beaten and hungry. I'd seen him around, but I didn't know his name. After I was forced to kill the first friend I made, I never bothered to learn their names again.

"Louisa, stop this instant."

Sofia Volkov's voice interrupted the boys in their morbid discussion. She strolled in, glaring after the girl who'd escaped her control. Dressed in a fancy blue dress and holding the hand of another girl—a twin, by the looks of it—the pair looked crestfallen at being scolded so openly.

Reign of a Billionaire

So the rumors were true. Sofia Volkov had a weakness, and they were living under this roof.

My attention flickered to the one running into the arena on her chubby legs, wearing a ridiculously bright red dress full of lace and frills that looked out of place here.

"Call a doctor," she yelled, her hands frantically flying through the air and terror evident in her voice. The girl couldn't be older than seven.

I felt the breath rush out of my chest. She appeared fragile, almost too small for her age. She shouldn't be here. It was too dangerous.

Tears streamed down her face, her blonde curls bouncing with each step she took. But it was her eyes that captivated me. Big and golden with hazel specks. She fell down to her knees next to the dead boy, grabbing his cold hand into hers and shaking it desperately.

And all the while, she cried, her soft whimpers filling the deathly still arena that had only seen cruelty and death, nothing like this display of empathy.

Then suddenly The Killer snatched the girl, wrapping his bloodied fingers around her neck.

"Let her *go*," Sofia Volkov, the bitch of all bitches, hissed. I hated the woman—her puppet of a husband even more—but I didn't want the little girl hurt.

The tension in the air was so heavy I felt goosebumps rise on my arms. I didn't move, my focus remaining glued to the little girl with the most unusual eyes I'd ever seen.

"Nobody move or I'll snap her neck." The Killer tightened his grip, flashing his feral smile, while the little girl clawed at his hand. Her ivory skin was turning purple.

Ivan chortled. "You stupid boy. You're dead and don't even know it."

The Killer bared his teeth, and I watched in horror as the scene played out. Why wasn't anyone saving her?

I hadn't known men—or women—like this until I'd been forced

here. I'd never seen truly evil men inflict so much pain on others. A shudder rippled through my skinny body.

The Killer lifted the girl off the ground while gripping her neck, her black flats dangling in the air as she kicked her legs. Every muscle in my body tightened instinctively. Without moving my eyes from the scene, I shifted to the next pillar so I could sneak up on The Killer from behind.

Sofia Volkov's eyes turned black, and I wondered if she regretted creating this monster out of a boy. Blood rushed through my ears, the entire arena only background noise. I kept my eyes on the scene, inching closer.

I swallowed, waiting for one of Sofia's men to do something—anything—but nobody was budging.

I remembered the last time I saw my sister, two years ago. The fear in Aurora's eyes had stayed with me, and I knew that same fear was now rolling off this little girl.

Before I even understood what was happening, I jumped on The Killer's back, my arm wrapping around his monstrous shoulders. We all lost balance, falling backward. I grunted from the weight crushing me, but I didn't release my grip.

He gurgled. The girl whimpered. I scrambled to get the upper hand, and when I did, I squeezed the boy's neck with everything I had. Seconds ticked by. They felt like hours. His body twitched. Once. Twice. Then he went limp, and I peeled his hands off the little girl.

I took her in my trembling arms and shoved the slumped body to the side.

His blood didn't soak the dirt, but my sins did.

The sudden onslaught of noise finally hit me. The crowd pulsed as one, their eyes locked on me with disbelief. Then came the screams and cries of a little girl.

"Shhh," I murmured softly, in the same way I used to calm my baby sister down, as I rubbed her back gently.

Reign of a Billionaire

I was in so much trouble. They'd punish me for this. I clenched my jaw, preparing for the consequences that were sure to come.

I didn't regret it. Her little body no longer shook with fear. Instead, it clung to me like I was her life raft.

Sofia Volkov stepped forward, her eyes locked on mine. "Well, looks like I found a bodyguard and companion for my girls."

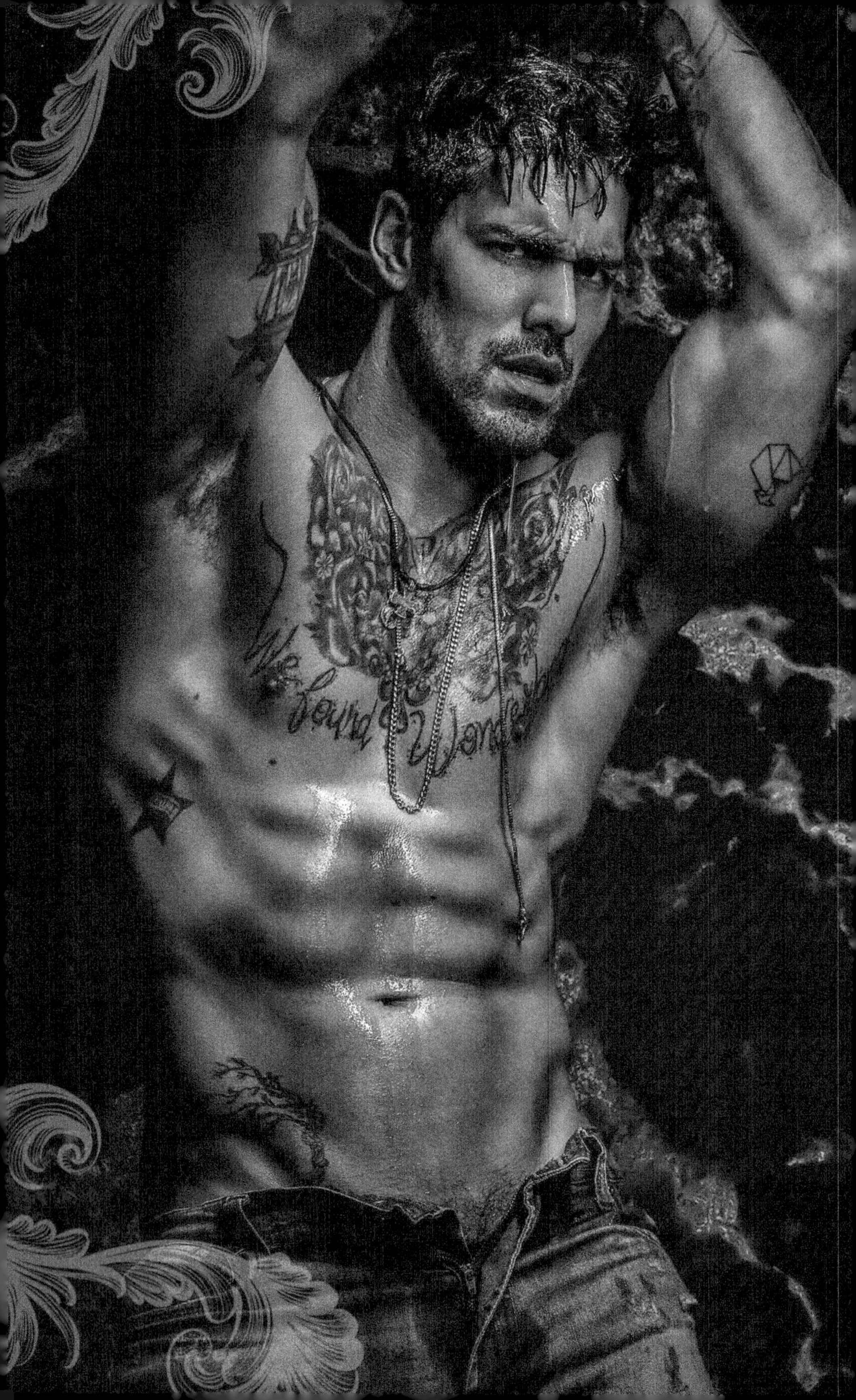

Chapter 11
Liana, Present

The next night, I watched the scene unfold in front of me while dread weighed heavily in the pit of my stomach, threatening to buckle my knees.

Yesterday, I sat at a table in downtown D.C. with these men. Today, I hid in the shadows. My mother loved to parade me around dinners and social events with these freaks, but when it was time for the deals and transactions to happen, she left me out.

I never complained. It worked for me. It gave me the freedom to do what I needed to do.

Like standing outside an ominous looking, abandoned building under the blanket of night. The sound of a ship horn came from the murky waters, signaling there was life around us. The wrought-iron gates surrounded the deserted construction area. Long shadows lurked in every corner, waiting to come out and adding to the creepy vibe of the place.

The wind howled, reflecting the storm raging inside me. The skies cracked with thunder as two of Cortes's men stood in the middle of the abandoned warehouse in Canton. My heart pounded in my chest, cracking my ribs.

Eva Winners

My mother stood there, indifferent and wrapped in her fur coat as she inspected her latest crop of goods. It was a lucrative venture that came with mortal consequences and stained even the most troubled soul.

I watched their exchange—two enemies who had a penchant for destroying people's lives. The Brazilian cartel. The Russian mafia. Two leaders who were willing to tolerate freezing temperatures, shivering under their heavy coats.

My mother remained a silent observer, her lips curved into her signature humorless smile.

The men stood by their leaders and kept their hands readied on their guns. They discussed business in hushed tones, making it so I was unable to hear the details. Weapons and alcohol were traded.

I didn't move—knowing weapons and alcohol were only the face of the operation. A disguise for what was to come. It was their next trade that kept me here, sticking to the shadows. These situations weren't a novelty to me. I had seen this exchange plenty of times over the past decade. I should be used to it by now.

I wasn't.

The doors of the shipping container opened and I inhaled a sharp breath. At least a dozen young girls lay there, unconscious, unaware of the dangerous men—and woman—standing mere feet from them.

The cold air whipped at my face, but I couldn't feel it. I'd weathered Siberian temperatures. I was used to the evil of humans. I had thick skin. I'd lived through loss. My twin. Ghosts I couldn't remember.

A life as Sofia Volkov's daughter had prepared me for a lot of things—crime, cruel men, manipulation. But never this sight.

Shaking off the distracting thoughts, I squared my shoulders. The cold metal pressed against my waistband, the knife digging into my thigh, which I found reassuring. Dressed in fleece leggings and a warm sweater, all black, I waited for one of the two most lethal mobsters of the underworld to leave.

Unaware of my presence in the shadows, the leaders exchanged a few more words and shook hands. And then, they headed away from the docks. My mother's men left along with her. Perez took only his personal bodyguards, leaving two behind to handle the cargo.

"Showtime," I whispered as I made my way through the construction site, keeping my steps silent and light. Cortes's men were too busy to notice me as I approached them from behind like a ghost in the night.

My heart clenched as I watched one of them cop a feel of a young, unconscious woman. The stifling sensation of hatred and despair surged through my veins. The failings of man floored me every time I witnessed it.

I gave my head another shake, refusing to be distracted by emotions. Those served me nothing. Instead, I focused on saving these women. If I was going to do this right, I needed to have a clear mind.

As I stalked toward them, I reached for my knife and pulled it out of its holster. I always preferred it over my gun. It got me in and out with less chance of detection.

By the time I made it to them, the icy wind pinched my cheeks. I inhaled a deep breath, every muscle in my body tense.

"Having fun, boys?" I asked, not bothering to mask the derision in my voice while my heart raced in my chest. The two men halted mid-movement, and before they could reach for their weapons, I made my move. I pounced, slicing the backs of their knees in fluid movements, and both collapsed onto the cold dirt ground.

They scowled at me, but before they could move, I straddled one's back, uncaring whether I cracked his spine or not, while at the same time stabbing the other one through his palm.

The second guy let out a scream when I grabbed the nape of his head and smashed his skull against the ground, blood splattering everywhere. His body twitched before going limp, his dead eyes staring at me accusingly.

It didn't bother me at all. I only wished I could have prolonged his horror a bit more.

"Geez, that was over way too soon," I muttered with a labored sigh. "The only rock in the whole yard and it had to find itself underneath his skull."

The asshole trapped underneath me grunted, scowling at me over his shoulder.

I pulled out my blade nailed inside the dead guy's palm and brought it to the other guy's throat, shutting him up.

"You crazy bitch," he growled, causing blood to sputter out the sides of the blade's puncture wound.

"You have no idea how crazy I am," I murmured against his ear. He stilled below me, fear trickling out of him like smoke. "I'm going to savor your pain so fucking much."

My knife pricked deeper into his skin, and he into the dirt.

"P-please," he begged, but his pleas meant nothing to me. The girls they kidnapped had begged too. Cried and prayed. These bastards reaped the benefits and forgot all about them.

"I wonder if you ever showed those girls any mercy." The disgust in my voice was unmistakable. "Give me one instance, and if I find it to be true, I'll spare your life."

As if. You played in this world, you died in this world. It was the unspoken motto, one he should know well.

He remained still, licking his lips nervously as his puny brain scrambled. He wasn't able to come up with one, to no one's surprise. The bastard couldn't even name one situation when he'd even *attempted* to spare these girls. Didn't even have the creativity to make one up.

My eyes flicked to the container full of unconscious girls as I wrenched him up and sliced across his Adam's apple. He shrieked, but the moment I pressed the blade harder, it turned into a gasp.

"Shut that door, *suka*," I ordered, tilting my chin toward the container while still holding the knife to his neck. "I don't want the girls freezing to death."

He crawled, pulling his body forward to shut the door with trembling fingers. My lips curled in disgust at his cowardice. These men were brave when it came to helpless women, but put them at someone else's mercy and they were crybabies.

Once he shut the door, his gaze shifted to me, considering me. I watched his fear slowly fade as he took all of me in. A petite young woman. I looked weak, but I wasn't. I'd been to hell and back, and I'd never let anyone overpower me again.

I could see the decision cross his expression before he lunged at me. I anticipated the move, taking a step to the right. My knife slammed into his shoulder, and a bloodcurdling scream pierced the frigid air.

He face-planted into the dirt, and I grabbed a fistful of his hair, slicing my blade across his neck with more force than before. His blood spilled into the dirt, pooling around him in fits of gurgles.

Maybe I should feel something, but I didn't. No remorse. No fear. *Nothing*.

I kicked his body and let him fall to the ground with a satisfying thud.

It was time to take care of the innocents.

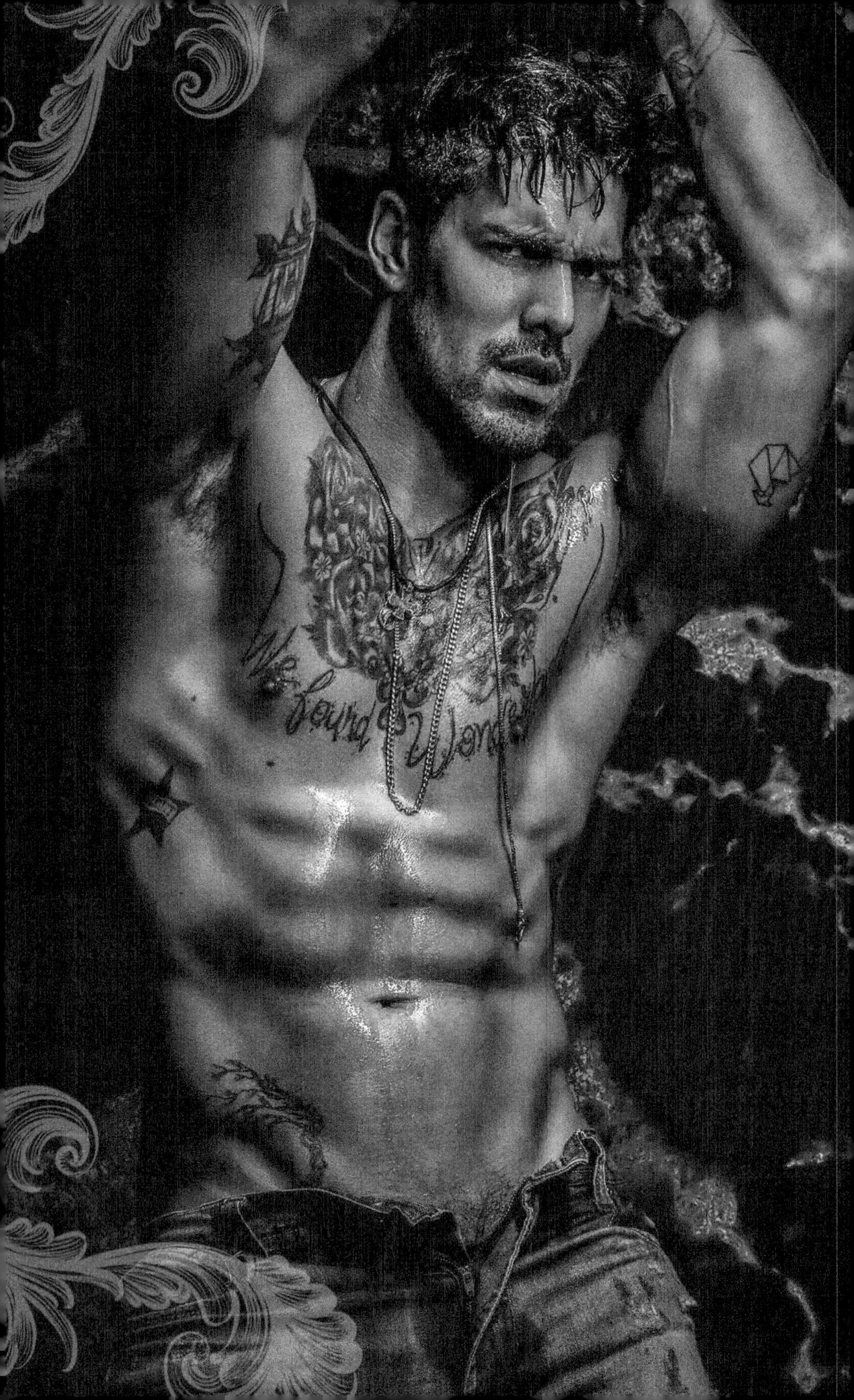

Chapter 12
Kingston

I stared ahead, stunned at the gruesome murder.
    It had been the last thing I expected to witness when I followed Liana from her hotel room. Was Sofia backstabbing Perez Cortes and using her daughter to make it happen? It was a plausible explanation, yet my instinct warned that wasn't it.
    Unless this was a spur-of-the-moment kill. No, it couldn't be. Liana came prepared. She waited for Sofia and Perez to make themselves scarce before she attacked.
    But then *what*?
    Liana Volkov puzzled me more by the day. When I walked past her in the restaurant, there was no recognition in her eyes. Yes, she seemed astonished, certainly a little curious, but it wasn't in line with the way a person reacted when they saw someone they used to know. A boy assigned as her bodyguard for years.
    Did she forget me? It seemed unlikely. I'd spent more time with her twin, but I'd known both sisters for years. It would be impossible for her to forget me, just as it was impossible for me to forget them.
    I watched in silence, sticking to the shadows as Liana staggered upright, glancing around, then fixed her blonde locks with clean

fingers. Her hand didn't tremble. Her expression was eerily calm. It was clear she knew what she was doing.

The more I watched her, the more I wondered whether *anything* was as it seemed. But I had no time to ponder it as she pulled out a cell phone, fingers flying across the screen. The moment the standard *whoosh* of a message leaving her inbox sounded, she tossed the phone across the yard. It skidded along the gravel until it fell over the side of the nearby dock and into the water with a splash.

She stared down at the corpses, grinning with satisfaction. A long-forgotten emotion pierced through me as sharp as a blade, her grin doing things to me I couldn't make sense of. That dull ache in my thigh throbbed, almost like it was a sign to look closer.

What did all this *mean*? Was Liana a friend or a foe?

I watched the petite woman stand over the corpses, and I wondered if she was waiting for reinforcements. Or maybe she was reflecting on her sins.

I didn't know. Liana's body might have survived, but on the inside, she was just as dead as Lou.

The sound of the engines approaching shattered the cold silence, and with a lethal efficiency, Liana opened the container door, ensuring the women were in plain view before disappearing in the nick of time.

Two vehicles and a bus came to a stop. The door to the first black SUV opened and a familiar figure stepped out—Nico Morrelli. The second stopped and another door opened to reveal Áine and Cassio King.

It was a known fact in the underworld that Áine King had an ongoing operation of rescuing victims of human trafficking. Nico Morrelli, with his real estate spanning multiple continents, ensured the women were safe and rehabilitated.

Their eyes landed on the dozen sedated women huddled in the container, and they quickly got to work.

"Do we know who sent the message?" I heard Cassio ask.

Nico shook his head. "It was an untraceable line."

Smart.

It would seem that Liana was very familiar with covert dealings.

If I'd learned anything from this display, it was that Liana Volkov had become a formidable enemy or reluctant ally.

I didn't know what motivated her, but I would find out. And then, I'd plow through. She'd never see me coming.

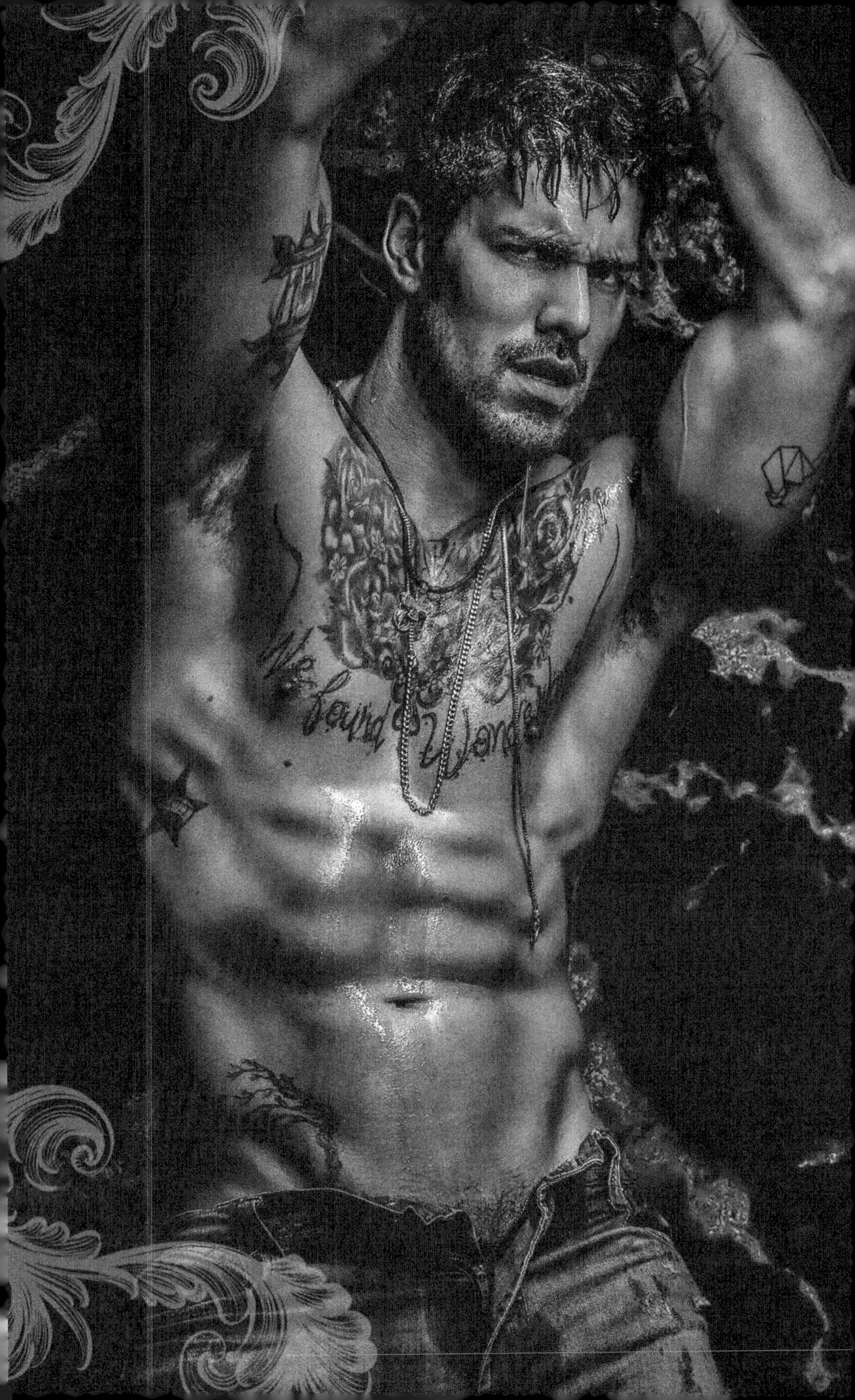

Chapter 13
Liana

I flicked the lights of my hotel room on and came face-to-face with arctic eyes.

"Where have you been?"

My stomach dropped at seeing my mother seated in the chair, the full ashtray next to her hinting at how long she'd been here. My heart stopped, then kick-started with a jolt, drumming painfully in my chest. I knew what would follow if I played my cards wrong.

"I needed some fresh air."

My voice was steady and my expression clear of any emotion.

"You've never been a good liar," she said angrily. "Your eyes... They're the windows to your soul."

I stilled. The words—I'd heard them before. I searched my memory, different puzzle pieces shifting yet refusing to come together. Why were there so many holes in my memory? Black, gaping holes that sent me spiraling into an abyss where nothing and nobody made sense.

"Why are you here, Mother?" I asked, my voice hard despite the tingling in my fingertips. "It can't be to discuss my eyes."

My palms began to sweat, and I knew the adrenaline from earlier was wearing off. I couldn't crash, not now. Not with *her* here.

"Do it." Mother's voice pulled me back. I watched as her eyes shifted behind me before I felt it. The prick of a needle. I went into fight mode, sticking to my training, but my vision blurred.

I blinked rapidly before everything went dark.

The stench of death filled my nostrils and blood pooled everywhere I looked.

Haunted screams. Evil laughter.

A scream bubbled in my throat at the sight of bodies sprawled over the filthy ground.

It's not real, a whisper in my ear warned.

Yes, it is, another mocked.

"Why are we here?" I shouted loudly, but the only thing that came out was a whimper.

The place was loud, the arena full of battered men and broken boys. Being here was a bad idea and I knew it, but I couldn't let my sister come alone. I reached a hand out for her, but all I got was empty air.

"I'm okay," she said faintly.

"Where... Why..." I choked, unable to articulate what I needed to ask.

"Find him."

"Find who?"

She pointed her finger and I followed, my eyes roaming the space until I found a stranger standing on his own. My brows furrowed. Why couldn't I see his face?

"You shouldn't be looking at him." Who, I wanted to ask again, but my words wouldn't form. "Not with all these eyes around," my sister warned. "If Mother catches you, it'll be bad. For both of you."

Reign of a Billionaire

My brows knitted and I swallowed, the warning unsettling. "You told me to find him."

"When you're alone. Not here."

The whole arena was unsettling, like I was walking through a haze and only parts of the scene were in focus. I shook my head, letting the thought go. Somewhere deep down, I knew she was right, yet my gaze darted back to the person she'd pointed out. There was something about him that seemed to call to me.

"Ghost and Drago are next." Mother's announcement echoed through the arena like a deadly whip.

I waited anxiously, watching as the faceless man readied to enter the arena with Drago. Fear slithered through my veins, but I couldn't understand why I was afraid. I wasn't the one going into the arena with Drago, a man known for his brutality. I reached out to touch my sister, to feel something real, but I couldn't seem to close the distance between us.

A movement caught my eye and I locked on Drago's back. I felt myself moving toward him, my steps so light I wondered if I was floating. All of a sudden, nothing mattered except delaying this fight. I stopped just in front of my mother, making sure to ram my shoulder into the beast.

I barely knocked him off-balance, but he whirled around, his fingers connecting with my neck and tightening into a fist.

My breath hitched and my heart slammed into my throat.

"What—" I gasped. I hadn't counted on Drago's vicious nature overruling his fear of my mother.

He snarled, his face hardening. I barely blinked before he slammed my body into the wall. The back of my head hit the cold stone, causing my ears to ring and my vision to blur. It cleared just as quickly.

As my body slid to the floor, he was wrenched off of me. The sound of crunching bones filled the air, followed by a howl.

Drago was sprawled on the filthy ground, groaning painfully as his eyes rolled to the back of his head. A commotion surrounded me, and I brought my hand up to my hair to feel for a cut or bump. Why *wasn't my head hurting? I felt the impact, but somehow I felt nothing.*

My sister grabbed me by the elbow. Mother hissed something, although I couldn't understand a single word.

All eyes were on us, but I kept staring at the faceless man before me. My savior.

"Take them to their rooms," Mother ordered. I glanced around, wondering who she was talking to. Her eyes locked on my sister. "Step out of line and you'll both be punished."

"Yes, Mother," my sister grunted, dragging me along as the boy followed behind us.

The moment we were out of sight, he reached for me. Something twisted in my stomach, something that shouldn't have been there.

"That was reckless." His tone was full of disapproval.

My sister let out a frustrated groan. "You fucking think?"

Her glaring eyes darted between us. In rushed steps, we sped up the stairs and down the hallway to the east wing.

"I'm sorry." I wasn't sure who murmured those words over and over again. Was it my sister? Or was it me? It was all mushing together, right along with this guilt that was gnawing at me.

We stopped by our rooms and she headed straight into hers, slamming the door with a loud thud. I turned to the faceless boy.

He didn't object, and I felt the emotions swirling around him like a dark cloud. "Don't ever put yourself in danger like that again."

I jutted my chin stubbornly, pressing my lips into a thin line. "You put yourself in danger every day for us."

He let out a warm chuckle. "What am I going to do with you?"

Butterflies took flight in the pit of my stomach as I stared at the face I couldn't see. I couldn't understand... Why couldn't I see him? Why couldn't I remember who he was? To me? To my sister?

I knew he was someone important. But who?

A splash of cold water yanked me out of the dream. I blinked my eyes open, black dots swimming in my vision and water dripping off my eyelashes. I tried to make sense of it all. Why was my mind showing me myself when I was 14 years old? I knew it was just a dream, but the images seemed so real.

Disoriented, I waited for the room to come into focus, and the moment it did, my heart froze.

"Please... No," I whispered. "Not again."

I squeezed my eyelids shut before opening them again, but the reality didn't change. The sweet haze from moments ago, filled with butterflies and warm hands, had vanished. I was in a tub now, my wrists and ankles bound. I studied the room. The bright white tile and walls blended together, their brightness magnified by the naked fluorescent bulb overhead. There wasn't a window, but the door was left open.

"Finally awake." Mother entered the bathroom, her stiletto heels clicking against the tile. "Did you get some rest?"

My lips thinned, refusing to answer. I hated when she did this shit. Even more, I hated that I didn't see it coming.

"Not enough," I hissed. "What are you doing here?"

"What have you done with the women?"

A shiver started at the base of my spine, the old me trembling with fear. Fear I thought was long since buried thanks to the days and weeks—maybe *months*—of torture I'd endured at her hands. I couldn't stand the cycle repeating itself. Thoughts rushed around in my head for the best answer.

I landed on denial.

"I have no idea what you're talking about."

Her eyebrows rose in surprise at my calm tone.

"Tell me the truth," she demanded, her jaw clenched. She wanted to believe me, I knew it. "This is a matter of life and death for all of us."

I scoffed at that. "It seems you've already decided on death for me."

"This isn't a joke, Liana!" My mother glared at me, her Italian accent thickening. It was always the harshest when she was scared. "You know what the Tijuana cartel did to your sister. Do you want them to do that to you?"

I clenched my teeth, my voice lowering. I'd seen the video of my sister's body dissolving into nothing. I'd tortured myself enough with it.

"Let them fucking come," I hissed. "And I'll end them just like they ended her." My mother gritted her teeth, hating my rebellious streak. Lou was peaceful; I was a tornado. Lou was good; I was bad. Lou was innocent; I was far from it. "How can you even stand to work with them, knowing what they did to my sister?"

The black rage in my mother's eyes couldn't be missed. It was venomous and hateful, reflecting exactly how I felt about her associates. Hers was directed at me.

"You could get my father to help," I hissed, my blood boiling. "He'd kill them all if he knew the truth."

But truth was one thing Mother withheld. She'd used him, used all of us. She was Ivan Petrov's wife but had fucked the Irish mobster, my father, Edward Murphy, with one purpose only. To get pregnant. Ivan couldn't give her children and was more than happy to agree to Mother's seduction plan. It put one more mobster in their pockets.

She wanted an empire; she got it. She sought revenge; she got that too, ten times over. This was her own cruel version of revenge against the world. Only, she was too blind to see that everyone—including her daughters—paid for it.

"Your father can't help." Something about the tone of her voice set my senses on high alert, but I didn't dare question her.

Had something happened to my dad?

I hadn't been able to get in touch with him for a while now, but that was nothing unusual. Sometimes he and Mother went through episodes of total silence. Growing up, they included us in their petty power plays, but my sister and I always had each other to lean on. It hurt that they couldn't ever put their differences aside for us, but it brought us closer.

I didn't have that anchor anymore. And I'd hardened that organ called a heart.

"It's just you and me, Liana." She dusted nonexistent wrinkles out of her Oscar de la Renta dress. "And I won't tolerate disobedience."

Her pruney fingertips reached for the faucet, twisting it. The pipes protested, and when I took my next breath, the rush of icy water came running out.

Minutes blurred, and so started my screams.

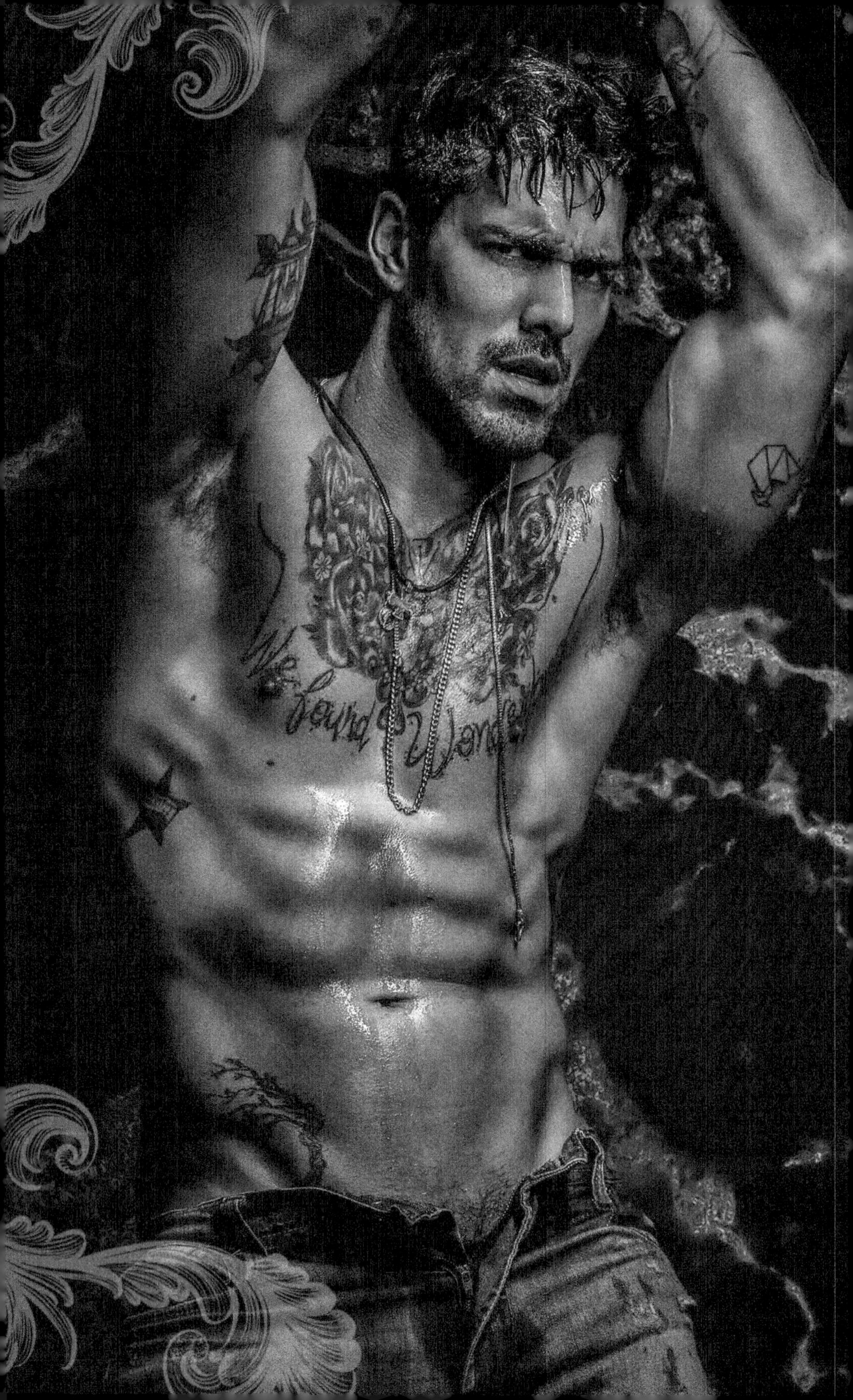
We found

Chapter 14
Liana

"You took her from me." Mother's blurry face was distorted. "I need her back. Understand me?" I nodded, despite not comprehending what she meant. "Very well, Liana. Let's start." The screams rang in my skull, refusing to cease. The shocks came, wrenching screams from my throat until it bled.

My body startled awake and I sat up straight, my ears ringing. I breathed heavily as sweat covered my skin, making my nightgown cling to my skin. I shook until I realized they were my own screams.

I brought my weak hands to my face, pushing drenched strands away from my forehead.

The ringing in my head made it difficult for my lungs to work, and I felt myself start to heave. Whispers that plagued my dreams, speaking faster and faster, taunted me.

You're too easy to break. You're too weak.

I squeezed my eyes shut, chasing the nightmares I didn't understand far away. *Memories.*

I shook my head and closed my eyes. They weren't memories, they couldn't be. That never happened. The cracks in my chest and my skull deepened while a dull ache drummed behind my temples, lingering for hours as I lay awake staring at the ceiling, trying to remember.

Trying to forget.

A week later, my mother and I were back in the motherland. My birthplace.

Exhaustion weighed heavily on me. I'd barely slept a wink over the past week, each night a new dream plaguing my sanity every time I dozed off. They didn't make any sense. There was no rhyme or reason behind their recurrence, but nonetheless, each one rattled me down to my core.

Frost settled into my bones, drawing a shiver out of me. Gosh, how I hated the cold and snow.

The first snow of the Siberian winter covered the landscape, stretching beyond what my weary eyes could take in. Ironic really, since every inch of Mother's property was drenched in crimson, the invisible blood of innocents coating every corner.

The metal gates of the mansion opened ahead, my mother's house—my prison—looming stark white against the gray sky. No matter how clean and pristine it looked, there was no hiding the sins beyond the property line.

My mother was the first woman in her family to sit at the head of the business. She was a Pakhan—well, to some. If you asked others in the underworld, that title belonged to Illias Konstantin.

I didn't know—nor did I care—who the rightful leader of the Russian mafia was. I wanted to burn it all to the ground.

I sometimes hoped my mother would come to her senses and see what her place in this world had cost us. I used to think my mother loved me. My twin and I had grown up wanting for nothing. We had the latest technology at our disposal, the latest fashion and gadgets and cars, but we never had our mother's love or affection.

Reign of a Billionaire

It was pretty early in life when both my twin and I learned that our mother loved only one child—Winter Volkov. Our father, on the other hand, wasn't much of one. He wanted to be, but Mother had him by his balls. Edward Murphy, an Irish mobster, couldn't do much but leave us at the mercy of the Russian underworld.

I couldn't forgive either one of them for my sister's sad ending. They were supposed to protect us, shield us, or at least cajole us into a false sense of safety. All they managed to do was break us.

The car pulled up in front of our home manned by four guards just as my mother's phone rang.

"What?" she spit out angrily. "How could you lose another shipment?" A heartbeat of silence before she spoke again. "Do we have any leads?"

Two "lost" shipments of flesh in such a short timespan were bound to raise flags and hurt the business Perez and my mother had going. Not that I gave two shits about it. My goal was to crumble their empire from within and let it burn as I held the matches and a gas can.

"I'm dealing with it."

A bead of sweat rolled down my spine, knowing exactly how my mother would deal with me. It'd be time for another one of her "sessions," and I wasn't sure how many more of those I could take. I hadn't broken...yet.

I clenched my jaw, resisting the urge to bolt out of the car. Instead, I folded my hands in my lap and begged my heart to stop thundering in my chest. I listened to one side of the conversation, my gaze trained out the window.

I sat upright, keeping my eyes trained on the guards waiting for the signal to open the door. It had to come from my mother.

"Does Perez know?" Her voice was steady, but I knew what she was masking. Could feel it in the space between us on the leather seats. She sounded calm, collected, and poised. "Keep it that way. See if we can organize a shipment for the Tijuana cartel."

Santiago was the head of the Tijuana cartel who worked with Perez and all the scum in the underworld.

My lip curled with disgust as she ended the call and gave a signal to the guards. The minute the gates swung open, I got out of the vehicle and started walking toward the front doors. The walls couldn't be seen from here, but I felt them.

They were slowly closing in, suffocating me.

I started to climb the grand staircase that I used to play on with my twin, taking the turn toward the wing where my rooms were. The old paintings stared back at me, frowning at my state of mind.

"Where are those girls, Liana?"

My mother's voice came from behind me. The memory of the dreams that plagued me lingered in the back of my mind. I wanted to remember the faceless man. I wanted to remember the details of my sister's death. But I couldn't ask her.

I knew enough to know I wouldn't get the truth from her. Over two and a half decades under her thumb had hardened me.

"I don't know what you're talking about, Mother." I kept my voice cool, nonplussed. "I'm tired. I'm going to—"

"What were you doing in the Port of Washington a week ago?" I ignored the accusation in her voice. She was fishing. She didn't know I was in the port. The tracker she thought she had on me had been removed a long time ago, and it now lived in my clutch. The one that stayed behind in the hotel room right next to hers in D.C.

I resumed walking, my mother's heels clicking behind me as she followed me down the corridor.

"I've never been to the Port of Washington," I lied, then feigned curiosity as I added, "Where is it?"

"Nowhere."

Stopping in front of the door that led to my bedroom suite, I turned to face her. "Why do you ask?"

My heart pounded as I locked eyes with the woman who gave me life. She was a bad mother, but an even crueler criminal. She protected us from her enemies, but not from herself.

Mother sighed. "Never mind."

I nodded. "Good night, then."

I entered my suite and shut the door firmly behind me, dreading sleep and my nightly visits with the ghosts that just wouldn't let me be.

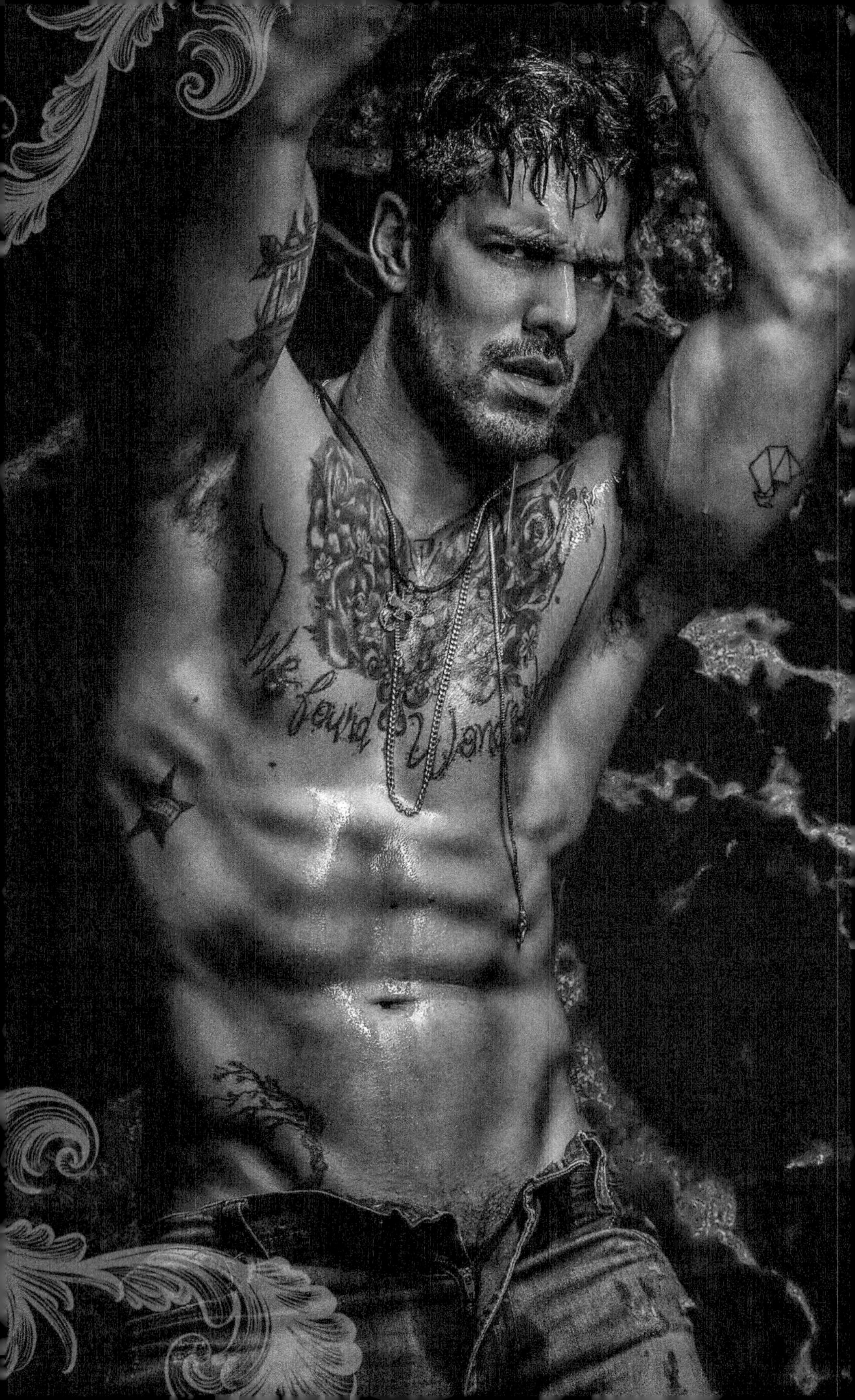

Chapter 15
Liana

My neck was stiff and every muscle in my body ached. My fingers flew across the keyboard and my eyes burned from hours spent staring at my laptop screen. For two days, I'd been trying to penetrate Nico Morrelli's walls. I'd tried every possible combination and hit a dead end every single time.

My sister had been better at this tech stuff than me. She'd taught me a few tricks, but I was always better at sketching. At art in general.

My chest tightened. God, I missed her. I should have been stronger. I should have done a better job protecting her. I should have—

There were so many "should haves" as self-loathing threatened to overwhelm me. I had to quickly put the lid on those emotions. It never boded well going down memory lane.

Instead, I focused on ensuring the women I saved were okay. So, biting my lip, I tried again. I searched for any crack in his firewalls before the screen blanked out on me.

"Dammit," I muttered, frustrated, my palms hitting the table. "I need to *know*."

I'd done detailed research on the man. He was a genius, and he was also a virtuous crusader. He funded Gia's—his housekeeper's—shelters, who had been a victim herself. For whatever reason though, I wanted assurance that these women were safe, that I hadn't endangered them further.

A message popped up on the dark web.

> YOU'LL NEVER BREAK INTO MY DATABASE.

"What the—"

I had not expected this.

My heart pounded wildly. It shouldn't surprise me that Nico Morrelli caught on to me trying to penetrate his network. While I debated whether to talk to the man or not, another message came up.

> WHAT DO YOU WANT?

"At least he's to the point," I muttered under my breath. Then, deciding I might as well get the information I wanted, I brought my fingers to the keyboard.

> ARE THE GIRLS SAFE?

> THEY ARE.

Relief washed over me like a cold stream on a hot summer day, except there was no sunshine here. I hoped those women would have theirs though. Another message came in.

> WHO ARE YOU?

My hands hovered over the keyboard. I wanted to tell him. I needed a friend. But trust was an expensive thing in this world. Misplacing it could cost you *everything* that ever mattered to you. Another message popped up.

> WE CAN HELP YOU.

Before I could contemplate my reply, my laptop pinged, warning of a counter trace, and I closed out of the software, slamming my laptop shut. Goddammit, that was stupid. Morrelli's reputation should have been enough for me.

I gritted my teeth, turning my face toward the window and gazing out into the dark night. A full moon glimmered over miles and miles of snow, and I inadvertently shuddered. Fuck, I'd had enough cold weather to last me a lifetime.

At the sight of the white landscape, a memory filtered in through my throbbing temples.

The castle—our prison—stood dark and ominous among the winter wonderland. I couldn't help but compare it to an evil surrounded by innocence. Ivan and my mother, and what they were doing here, were evil. The rest of us were innocent.

Or something like that.

"Sun's setting," my sister grumbled. "We have to go back."

Everything about this home unsettled us. I'd rather stay out here and freeze until the sun set over the horizon than go back inside. Out here, the shame could be temporarily forgotten.

My twin and I walked in silence, lost in our thoughts.

"Make sure you keep your distance from the basement," I warned her.

Fear slithered through my veins. Ivan and his goons had been gawking at us for months. It was only a matter of time before they made a move.

"So you noticed it too," she whispered, eyeing me. We looked identical aside from a slight variation in our eye color.

"I don't like the way he's looking at us."

She knew who I meant. Ivan was a cruel pig. I couldn't even believe Mother would marry someone like that. If that was what every marriage was like, I never wanted a part of it.

"Me neither," she muttered. "It gives me the creeps."

"Me too."

We waded between the trees, the temperatures plummeting drastically. "What if he tries something?"

"He's too scared of Mother," I grunted, stomping on a pile of hard-packed snow to release some of my irritation. "And that fucking bodyguard will rip anyone apart who tries to get near us." The first smile of the day passed between us. "Maybe we should stay out here," she said pensively. "Build an igloo."

I shuddered despite my warm coat, but my twin could be convincing, which was how we ended up attempting to build an igloo for the next hour, almost freezing to death.

A tear rolled down my face. I missed her so much. The talks we had. The hugs she gave me. She always had my back.

A throb started in my temples, and I pinched the bridge of my nose, hoping to get some relief.

My thoughts strayed back to the dark-eyed stranger from the restaurant whose burning eyes had caught me off guard. I had never experienced such loathing aimed at me, and that was saying a lot—I wasn't exactly a likable person thanks to my blood relations.

Yet there was something about that mysterious man. He knew me. I didn't know how, but I'd stake my life on it. I dug through my memory, trying to remember where I'd seen him, but the harder I tried, the more my head ached.

My eyes traveled aimlessly over the bedroom that'd witnessed my past, present, and possibly my future—however long it might be. Half-completed sketches lay across the bedspread—the faceless man plaguing my dreams, terrorized women haunting my waking hours, my twin. My chest tightened and my breaths turned shallow.

The despair. The shame. The disappointment. I'd been guilt-ridden over my sister's death for eight years, unable to move on. The video of my twin's torture had been tattooed into my brain cells, refusing to ease the pain.

I reached for the sketch of my sister's face with trembling fingers.

"I wish it had been me, Lou," I whispered, my voice shaking. I'd give anything to have her with me, to talk to her, to ask her questions. I loved her so much, and she loved me. The only person that ever did.

The grandfather clock chimed, telling me it was midnight. Once it stopped, the eerie silence of the house returned, sending chills up my spine. This place wasn't a home; it was a prison. I'd grown up in this manor, blinded by the horrors these walls hid.

No matter how many times it was cleaned and polished, or how shiny the chandeliers and furniture were, there was no hiding the evil that lurked within these walls and hid in the basement.

A knot twisted in my gut, and soon a sob escaped my throat, followed by many more. Each one lined with loneliness and regret. I cried for my sister, for myself, and something else that seemed to be missing in my life.

Was it a mother's love? My father's?

I gave my head a subtle shake. You couldn't mourn something you never had. Couldn't miss something you never felt.

Pulling myself together, I shifted my energy to the restaurant's surveillance. Something about that stranger with dark eyes wouldn't let me be. Once I was inside their security system, I honed in on the right day and time. My fingers flew across the keyboard, speeding up the surveillance until I saw him again.

I studied his expressionless face. Dark eyes. His features were angular and cold—sharp cheekbones, olive skin, a dusting of semi-silver stubble, and full lips in a hard line. He had the look of a man who was drowning. A man who mourned.

Like me.

But then his face tilted, like he knew exactly where the cameras were, and he stared right at me. The screen froze, and something in the pit of my stomach tugged at me, warning me that he was someone I should stay away from. Still, curiosity nudged me to look him up.

I ran facial recognition in the FBI database. Nothing. I tried the CIA's. Nothing. Then I tried the dark web. Still nothing.

I stood up abruptly and started pacing, agitated. Every roadblock and unanswered puzzle fueled my tension higher. I fought the urge to smash my laptop to bits before taking a deep breath and cooling my temper.

Eva Winners

My phone buzzed and I reached for it, taking a seat again and unlocking it. My brows knitted.

> Unknown number: You're welcome.

Frowning, I clicked open the message and found an attachment. A newspaper article. My brow furrowed further as I read through the old clipping. A picture of a boy appeared on my screen. He looked vaguely familiar, but I couldn't quite place him.

> Me: Who's this?

> Unknown number: For saving the women.

An incredulous scoff escaped me. *What an odd mobster you make, Nico Morrelli.* Forgetting all about him, I scrolled and began to read through an old article.

The Ashford family was hit with yet another tragedy. Kingston Ashford, age 10, has been kidnapped during a visit to the Washington Zoo.

In recent years, Senator Ashford's rumored activities have put a target on his family.

I had to pause and roll my eyes at "rumored activities." More like blatant involvement with underbelly criminals. I shifted in my seat and read the final line.

The youngest boy is the latest to pay the price. Let's hope his outcome isn't deadly like that of the senator's wife.

Bizarre.

Why would someone send me an article on Kingston Ashford? I'd never heard the name. It made no fucking sense. But then a thought occurred to me. What if this had something to do with my mother? I had witnessed the many boys who'd been subjected to the abuse and torture in this very house. The boys they pitted against each other in those gladiator matches.

A few keystrokes had me hacked into my mother's files. I

searched through them with a fine-tooth comb, wanting the idea of my mother being involved in a child's kidnapping to be just that. An idea. Surely she stood by *some* moral code.

Frustration had me dropping my face in my hands. My mother was too old-fashioned, her laptop practically empty. Maybe I was going about this all wrong though. Ivan had been on the progressive side. Yes, he was dead, but maybe my mother was still using his laptop?

"It would make sense," I whispered to myself. He would have had everything already set up on his device.

I shifted my efforts and was inside Ivan's database a few minutes later. *Bingo.* The folder was almost too easy to find. It took no time for information to start pouring in.

"Kingston Ashford," I murmured softly. The name on my lips sounded foreign.

I read through the information as it streamed in. He was born in Washington, D.C., and had four siblings. His mother was shot dead, and he was later kidnapped. Jesus, talk about bad luck! But that was where the trail fizzled out. Kingston Ashford was presumed dead until he resurfaced a few years ago.

There was a single photo in Ivan's electronic folder, and I instantly recognized the dark eyes. There was an unmistakable resemblance to the stranger from the restaurant, in the lines of the boy who had been turned into a ruthless man.

And deep down in my heart, I knew why. Otherwise, why would Ivan have information on him?

I wished my mother's late husband had kept more information. I was curious, although knowing what he and my mother put people through, I shouldn't want to know.

I released a shuddering breath, the hatred radiating off the man in the restaurant suddenly making sense. It would also totally explain that blank look. I often saw the very same in the mirror.

I shook my head and diverted to another site that might have more information. The one belonging to Nico Morrelli. I might not be able to penetrate his walls when it came to safeguarding the victims of human trafficking, but it shouldn't be the case with someone like Kingston Ashford.

I typed his name in and more information trickled in.

Connections to the Bratva, Cosa Nostra, Irish and Greek mafias, the Syndicate, the Omertà... The list went on and on. Jesus, maybe the Ashfords were in deeper than it seemed.

I read on, scrolling from screen to screen, when it went blank.

Dammit!

Frustrated, my palms came down on the keyboard, my laptop beeping in protest. I really had to up my game in the technology department if counter-tracing kept targeting my own barriers.

I shoved away from the table and stood up when the sound of clicking heels echoed through the hallway. The unmistakable sound of Mother's Jimmy Choos. I wiped my bed clean of sketches, shoving them underneath my mattress. She hated seeing my drawings, saying it was a reminder of my twin. I also shoved my gun and knife under my mattress, a habit my sister and I had developed living under the same roof as monsters.

I caught my reflection with puffy eyes and tearstained cheeks in the vanity and rushed into my bathroom, splashing my face with cold water just as a knock vibrated against my door.

Taking a deep breath in, then exhaling slowly, I padded barefoot across my cold floor and opened the door.

"Hello, Mother," I greeted her in a voice that hid all my turmoil. Stepping aside to let her enter my only haven in this building, I watched her strut into my room, her eyes roaming over every inch of it.

"I'm glad you're awake." I turned to face her, standing and studying her blonde hair, the same shade as mine. Except hers was dyed and there were grays hiding in her mane, indicating her age, which her face refused to show. She'd had so much plastic surgery done—albeit quality work—that she could pass for being two decades younger than she really was. Until you looked in her eyes and spotted the bitterness and loss that no amount of surgery could erase.

"I'm awake," I confirmed. "So are you."

She nodded.

"I know we just arrived, but I need to go to Moscow tomorrow." My eyes widened. It was unusual for Mother to share her itinerary or justify her activities. Unless... "I need you to come along."

"Why?"

My mother narrowed her eyes. "Do you have something better to do?"

Yes. "No."

"Then you're coming."

"We just got here," I protested. "Why can't you go alone?"

Whatever she was up to, I was sure her many victims were already shaking in their boots. Usually that was how it went. If you were in Sofia Volkov's sights, you'd better fucking run.

She sighed.

"Why do you have to make everything so difficult?" I remained silent, our gazes clashing. Something wasn't sitting right. Maybe it was the fact that she was here in my wing of the castle for the first time since my twin's death. Or maybe my sixth sense warned there was more to it than she was sharing.

"I'd like to stay," I repeated again, my eyebrows raised in defiance. I didn't love this manor, but I could use some time away from her. It was easier for me to plan my missions when I was alone.

"No." The single word had me reeling like she'd slapped me.

"What's going on, Mother?" I asked her, prodding. "What are you not telling me?"

Her jaw clenched and my heart pounded, waiting for her reaction. The last time I defied her, I lost a part of myself.

"Be ready first thing in the morning," she gritted out. "I'm not letting you out of my sight from now on. I won't allow history to repeat itself." She pushed her trembling hand through her hair, anguish in her plastic expression. "It always has a way of repeating itself," she muttered.

Then she turned around without further ado and left me staring after her, more confused than ever. *History is repeating itself.* The words echoed on repeat in my skull. What did she mean by that? She couldn't have been talking about my twin. Could she? She had to be referring to her firstborn, Winter Volkov, who was kidnapped by the Irish.

I remained frozen, staring after her, the wheels in my mind churning. My mother kept so many secrets, I was starting to wonder whether she was suffocating beneath them too.

She wasn't happy. I couldn't remember her ever being happy. Not even when she was with her lovers—male or female. She didn't have any friends. And she certainly wasn't happy with the sperm donor, as she called my father. To this day, I didn't know why my mother had chosen Edward Murphy to get her pregnant. There had to be something else behind it, aside from Mother wanting children.

There was no way that my father wanted to expand his family. The head of the Murphy mafia family had sons and another daughter. I'd never bothered to learn about them. I didn't want to know what I couldn't have.

My sister had been enough for me. Father certainly never attempted to save us from Sofia Volkov. Then my twin was taken. He didn't swoop in to save her, and I couldn't forgive him for it. Fuck, I couldn't even forgive myself.

Memories twisted in my chest as I made my way out of my bedroom. Mother had a separate wing where she handled business and personal matters. I rarely ventured there, but now, I had to get answers. She couldn't leave me in the dark. Not anymore. Not this time.

As I made my way deeper into the castle, the sound of thunder rumbled in the sky, almost as if announcing impending doom. This side of the estate was adorned in riches, all of the corridors filled with paintings of strangers. There wasn't a single portrait of our family to be found.

As I turned the corner and came up to the door of my mother's suite, I closed my eyes for a moment. My breaths were even despite my erratic heartbeat.

I sensed there were big things at play, and I didn't have the luxury of ignoring it. I'd done enough ignoring to last me the rest of my life. *No more.*

Thunder crackled outside, almost as though the skies agreed with me. Or maybe they were warning me to run back to my side of the castle.

My palms sweating, I raised my hand but froze mid-air, hearing the voices inside.

"It had to be an inside job." I recognized the accented voice of Perez Cortes booming through the phone speaker. "I've killed every man who knew about our shipment to ensure no traitor was left breathing. I expect you to do the same."

"I'll have the bodyguards killed," my mother replied. Just like that. Perez, just like my mother, didn't value human life.

"But not just them." Perez's voice clearly signaled no room for negotiation. "I expect your daughter to be part of that body count. Ghost is snooping around her, and I don't believe in coincidences."

Who was he talking about? A ghost?

"She doesn't know—"

Perez interrupted whatever Mother had been about to say. "It's an auction block, Marabella contract, or death for your daughter. Take your pick, Sofia."

There was a long pause while I stood in stunned shock, staring at the mahogany door. Had it really come to this? Me on the auction block? Perez, his Marabella arrangements, and his idea of high-prized girls being auctioned off should—*would*—be burned to ashes.

And who was this ghost they spoke about?

I let out a sardonic breath. Perez Cortes was threatening me, and I was worrying about a ghost.

"She's my daughter," Mother said again. "You will not touch her." I swallowed, hearing the protectiveness in her voice. I should feel relieved, but somehow it made the hair on my body stand. It only meant that Mother had a different plan. "I protected her from my husband"—Ivan Petrov was the shittiest husband a woman could have. He was cruel and evil, and thankfully not my problem—"and I'll protect her from you."

He laughed. "You really should have put a leash on that one a long time ago."

"Fuck you." The fury in Mother's voice was impossible to miss. "Only I decide her fate."

Bitterness thickened on my tongue. She was sparing me torture at the hands of others, but not her own. Punishment would come. It always did.

"She's dangerous, and you know it." There was another long pause before Perez spoke again. "And with Murphy's death, he's no longer around to protect her. From you or from me."

He's dead.

The statement ricocheted like a broken record. It shouldn't be a surprise. When you lived among evil, it tended to catch up to you.

Why didn't I feel sorrow? Pain? All I could focus on was that something was wrong. It wasn't just this fucked-up business relationship. It wasn't the death of a father I barely knew. It went a lot deeper than all this.

"Yes, she's a danger to you, but not to me," Mother hissed. "So you better watch the fuck out."

"Then get her in line, Sofia." *Click.* The line ended, the silence deafening before something thudded against the wall and the door opened. I stood there, our gazes locking, my hand still mid-air.

"What are you doing here?"

"I want to know what's going on," I demanded.

Mother stepped aside, opening the door wider. "Come in."

Slightly surprised but hiding it behind a calm façade, I walked past her, still barefoot, the door shutting behind me silently. Then she started pacing back and forth until she came to a stop in front of the window.

For the first time in a very long time, Mother looked alarmed, confirming that nagging suspicion I'd been having. But her expression told me she wouldn't divulge a thing. I waited in silence, unwilling to be the one to break it.

She took a seat in her lounge chair and stared up at me with lethargy.

"I have to tell you something." My heartbeat came to a screeching halt. A different memory filtered through. Ignoring the ache in my heart and ghosts that plagued me, I tried to focus on the here and now. I had to stay present.

"Are you listening?" Mother's voice whipped at me. The lump in my throat grew larger as memories of my sister flashed through my mind, choking me. The Tijuana cartel tortured her. Would I find a similar end under Perez? I wasn't sure when she left her seat, but suddenly Mother's hands cupped my cheeks, her icy fingers digging into my skin. "How much did you hear?"

I swallowed. "Enough."

"Perez won't get to you." I nodded, because there was nothing else to do. I wasn't scared. Maybe I should let him get to me and destroy his operations from within. It actually wasn't a bad idea.

"What... happened... to...?" I stammered. I should feel some emotion knowing Father was dead. It terrified me that I was becoming as heartless as my mother.

"Your dad?" Mother put into words what I wasn't able to. I nodded. "He's dead."

"What happened?" I whispered, resigned.

"Juliette DiLustro." The name didn't mean anything, but I'd find out everything there was about her. "It's been a while since he died."

Silence lingered, and I waited for her to say something else, when she didn't, I asked, "Who's the Ghost?"

For the first time ever, my mother's face lost all color, and her voice when she spoke was hardly audible. "Nobody important." I narrowed my eyes, and she let out a heavy sigh. "She washes money for Luciano Vitale." I stared at her in surprise. It wasn't what I expected. "In fact, she's his wife."

She had to be lying. That explanation made no sense. Why not tell me that right off the bat? Why the fear in her eyes hearing that word? The Ghost.

"Is that the truth?" There was a hint of challenge in my voice. It was my turn to draw surprise from her.

"Yes." Her gaze darted away, staring out the window into the dark night, and I knew it wasn't. It was a blatant lie. There was more to this ghost than Luciano Vitale and his wife. "You better stop, Liana, or—"

Or I'd have to pay the price. It'd be time for another torture.

My hands clenched into fists, and I turned to leave. Only once I was at the door, my hand on the doorknob, did I glance over my shoulder. My mother was still in the same spot, her face pale.

"I'm not going to stop until those who killed my sister are dead," I said quietly, closing the door behind me. I was going to find out exactly who the Ghost was and what their connection was to my mother's operations.

Because my sixth sense warned it had something to do with my twin.

Chapter 16
Kingston

She was in fucking Rossiyskaya Federatsiya. Russia.

It was the one country I'd never gone back to. I'd rather burn in hell for all eternity than step foot in that godforsaken country. Kingston Ashford died in Russia. In his place, Ghost was born.

I'd been beaten, broken, and torn down, only to be turned into a lethal assassin. During my physical combat training under Ivan and Sofia, I was an eager pupil so I'd become invincible. I vowed to myself I'd be the scariest man of them all so I could protect Lou. Then, in the blink of an eye, she was gone. When Alexei got me out of Russia eight years ago, there was nothing left of me. Nothing but a killer.

I utilized all that I'd learned to reinvent myself. Alexei offered me connections and a hand in kicking off my first business, but then I found my way into the Thorns of Omertà. It turned out I had a real knack for finding people and ending them. So, I became a sought-after assassin for powerful people—in and out of the underworld.

But nobody knew that. I hid it all behind my name. I'd learned to hide my cruelty and obsession with my victim's teeth from my siblings behind an unmoving mask.

Eva Winners

I carried a highly desirable last name, but unlike my brothers, I was only a shadow of the man I was born to be. My brothers constantly asked what happened to me. I couldn't voice the words to describe those years since my kidnapping. Raised among the bloodshed and violence, fighting to survive, I became violence. It was part of my DNA and every instinct in my body.

So even though I'd been rescued from hell years ago, there were times when it felt like I was still there, in that dungeon, in that fighting ring.

I couldn't close my eyes without remembering the days, the nights, and most of all, *her*. Sleep became impossible, the dreams too agonizing to bear. The memories haunted me. I roamed this earth without purpose even when I reconnected with my family.

Until I found her—them—again. So *of course* it would stand to reason that they were both in damn Russia, out of my fucking reach.

"You okay?" My brother-in-law's voice yanked me out of my head, and I turned to meet his pale blue gaze. Kostya, my nephew, stood next to him in an identical position, looking like his badass sidekick.

Alexei was the illegitimate son of Nikola Nikolaev and his mistress, Marietta Taylor. Nikola's wife was a jealous, psychotic bitch who had Alexei kidnapped when he was two years old and handed him over to one of the cruelest men in the Russian mafia. Ivan Petrov. The human trafficker who eventually got his hands on me. And just like that, two lives were ruined.

"Yes."

The party in Alexei and Aurora's Portugal home was in full swing, their green lawn sprawling with visitors from every criminal organization that all shared a common goal—ending human trafficking.

Aurora, my sister, stood within earshot, surrounded by her girlfriends and visitors. Holding her full champagne glass aloft, she pretended to sip from it, her eyes constantly seeking out her husband. My own eyes scanned the crowd.

Reign of a Billionaire

"If you want to disappear, I'll cover for you."

He knew I hated crowds. He did too. He tolerated it for his family, but I couldn't stomach it. The thought of someone accidentally brushing against me made my stomach roil. To this day, I had to be restrained when examined by a nurse or a doctor.

But if I left, what in the fuck would I do? I couldn't go to Russia, and I didn't want to relive the horrors of the dungeon in my dreams. So I observed all the guests, laughing happily and marveling at the emotion that had evaded me for the past eight years.

"I'm good," I deadpanned.

"Uncle Kingston?" Kostya looked up at me. "Is it true you have a house built from human teeth?" My eyebrow shot up in surprise. "Uncle Royce said if I'm bad, you'll pull my teeth out and add them to your house."

"It's true," I confirmed, letting my eyes wander around the lawn. "But tell Uncle Royce next time he threatens you with it, I'm gonna come for all *his* teeth. They're bigger."

"Promise?" I returned my eyes to my nephew, who was grinning happily. I nodded my confirmation. "When is he coming?"

"Not sure."

A booming laugh erupted, and all our eyes landed on the group where Luciano stood with his wife. They were with Vasili Nikolaev and his wife, Luca DiMauro, and Raphael Santos. The latter killed Santiago Tijuana Junior.

I stiffened, unable to fight the onslaught of memories from eight years ago. It might as well have been yesterday as fresh as the memories were.

The agonizing screams caused me more pain than all the torture I endured. They continued for seconds, minutes, hours until deathly silence followed.

I forced my eyes wide open and my brain to focus. Dread filled my veins like concrete. My mind was sluggish, and my eyes unable to focus. I blinked blood off my eyelashes, my gaze darting around, looking for the familiar golden strands.

Except she wasn't here. She was gone. The only thing that was left behind was the bloodstained floor and my hollow heart.

The door opened, but I was too broken to flinch. I knew more pain was coming, but I no longer cared. I'd barely hung on to my consciousness, eager to meet death.

Men entered, moving slowly. I heard whispers but couldn't make out the words.

"Kingston." A face with pale blue eyes swept down my mangled body. "We're getting you out." My lips opened. They moved. My vocal cords burned. "What?"

"Get—" Her. I prayed he heard me, understood me.

He looked around. "Who?"

Her, my Lou, I tried to say.

"We can't tend to his wounds here," someone said. "Grab him and let's get out of here."

Voices carried on around me, and my body shifted. The pain was excruciating, making my teeth rattle. I passed out and didn't wake up until it was too late.

I sought the end from that day forward, but it refused to come.

"Did you hear about Sofia Volkov?" Dante Leone's voice penetrated my memories, capturing my attention. The unhinged bastard looked like he was ready to go on a killing spree. "She has a daughter. Marchetti sent the news. We need to get that kid—"

"You won't fucking touch her." The threat escaped me, calm and deadly. Dante's eyes narrowed. "Or I swear to whatever God you believe in, I'll end you."

The air stilled around me. A thick tension filled it, too many criminals with weapons in one spot. My sister appeared out of thin air, stepping between me and Dante, while Alexei attempted to yank her back from the crossfire. Aurora, being who she was, refused to budge.

"You want to tell me why you're defending that bitch's daughter?" Dante scoffed. Aurora shifted on her heels, and I nudged her gently in her husband's direction and out of the line of fire.

"You knew she had a daughter?" Alexei asked, amplifying the

tension involuntarily. It was probably what everyone had been wondering.

Shrugging my shoulders, I let the anxiety roll off me and taint the sunny afternoon. It was so quiet, the nearby waves the only sound breaking the silence.

Without a flicker of emotion, I looked at my watch before making my announcement loud and clear.

"Anyone touches Sofia Volkov's daughter and I'll have their teeth decorating my mantel."

"You know we're on your side?" my brother-in-law stated in an even monotone.

My sister and brother-in-law must have decided a conversation was needed after the incident at their party. They'd changed, probably expecting a long night discussing something that was none of their business. Alexei was in his signature black cargo pants and black dress T-shirt while Aurora wore a modest quarter-sleeved dress that came down to her knees.

I pulled the door open to let them enter.

"Did you lose your kid?" I asked as they walked in.

"He's with Vasili and Isabella," Alexei answered as he sized up my latest real estate acquisition. Aside from his wife, there was nobody he trusted more than his half brother and half sister.

Aurora's radiant face and dark brown eyes studied me, the questions floating at the surface. There was no going back to the person I was before I was kidnapped. That part of me wasn't just repressed. It was extinguished.

My sister might keep searching for it, but she'd never find it.

"What is it, Rora?"

I rarely used her nickname anymore and her smile faltered for a second, probably reminding her of that fateful day when I was kidnapped. She still blamed herself.

She opened her mouth but remained silent, then shook her head. "Nothing. I just wanted to make sure you're okay after... You rushed out of there so fast."

My attention darted to Alexei, who stood emotionless, his hands tucked in his pockets. He was going to let his wife handle this on her own. He was just here for moral support—hers or mine, I wasn't sure.

I shut the door and walked toward the kitchen to get a drink. Both followed, taking a seat at the table while I poured myself and Alexei a glass of cognac and a glass of wine for my sister.

"You want to talk about it?" I raised a brow at my sister's question. "About her daughter."

I leaned against the counter, sipping my drink. "If I did, I'd go see a shrink."

Alexei rubbed his jaw tiredly while Aurora bit her bottom lip, peeking up at me from underneath her thick lashes. My sister was a badass, but the whole incident of my kidnapping had scarred her. Well, both of us—just in different ways.

I wanted to tell her that I'd blow the whole fucking world to ashes to keep her protected, but I wasn't the same person anymore. I wasn't as articulate. I had to hope she knew.

"How long have you known she has a daughter?" Alexei ended up asking.

I rubbed my jaw tiredly, debating how to answer that question as truthfully as I could without going too deep into the years of my imprisonment.

"I saw them recently in a restaurant." It was a half-truth. I'd known for a long time that Sofia had twin daughters. It was only a few months ago that I learned one of them was still alive. He nodded, choosing not to push.

"Is she involved in her mother's operations?" My gaze snapped to my sister, and her shoulders went rigid while her husband growled at me. I internally cursed myself for my sharp movement, and Aurora stared up at me with a wretched expression filled with guilt.

I forced a smile on.

"I'll deal with Sofia Volkov and her daughter," I stated calmly.

"Will you be able to kill her daughter if it comes to that?"

"Yes." No. Maybe.

My sister hesitated. "I don't like it, Kingston." My sister had been working at the FBI, her determination in finding my kidnappers and killing Ivan Petrov having led her there. Our brothers encouraged her career, knowing she needed closure, but lately, she'd been focusing her talents on ending human trafficking.

Unfortunately, they were like Hydra. You cut off the head of one, two more emerged from the shadows. Those fuckers had to be burned from within with a torch and gasoline.

"Don't worry, Rora," I said while checking my phone and plotting a war. A message from Nico Morrelli waited for me. I opened it and scanned the invite list. Tension rolled through me as I realized Liana Volkov was hard at work, getting herself added on the guest list as "Princess Leia," and those idiots in the Tijuana cartel hadn't even picked up on it. Slightly impressed, I let dry amusement fill me.

Why in the fuck would she want to attend one of Santiago Tijuana Senior's parties? They were sick and twisted. There was a reason Raphael Santos pushed him. Thank fuck I'd tasked Nico with keeping anything related to the Volkov family on his radar.

"Kingston, you know I'd do anything and everything for you," my sister said, her brows bunching together with worry. "But I don't have a good feeling about whatever it is that you're planning."

My smart little sister. Anything related to those cretins was bound to end in catastrophe. But I couldn't stop it any more than the moon could stop its rise in the sky every night.

"I got it all under control."

Aurora and Alexei shared a look.

Neither one of them believed me.

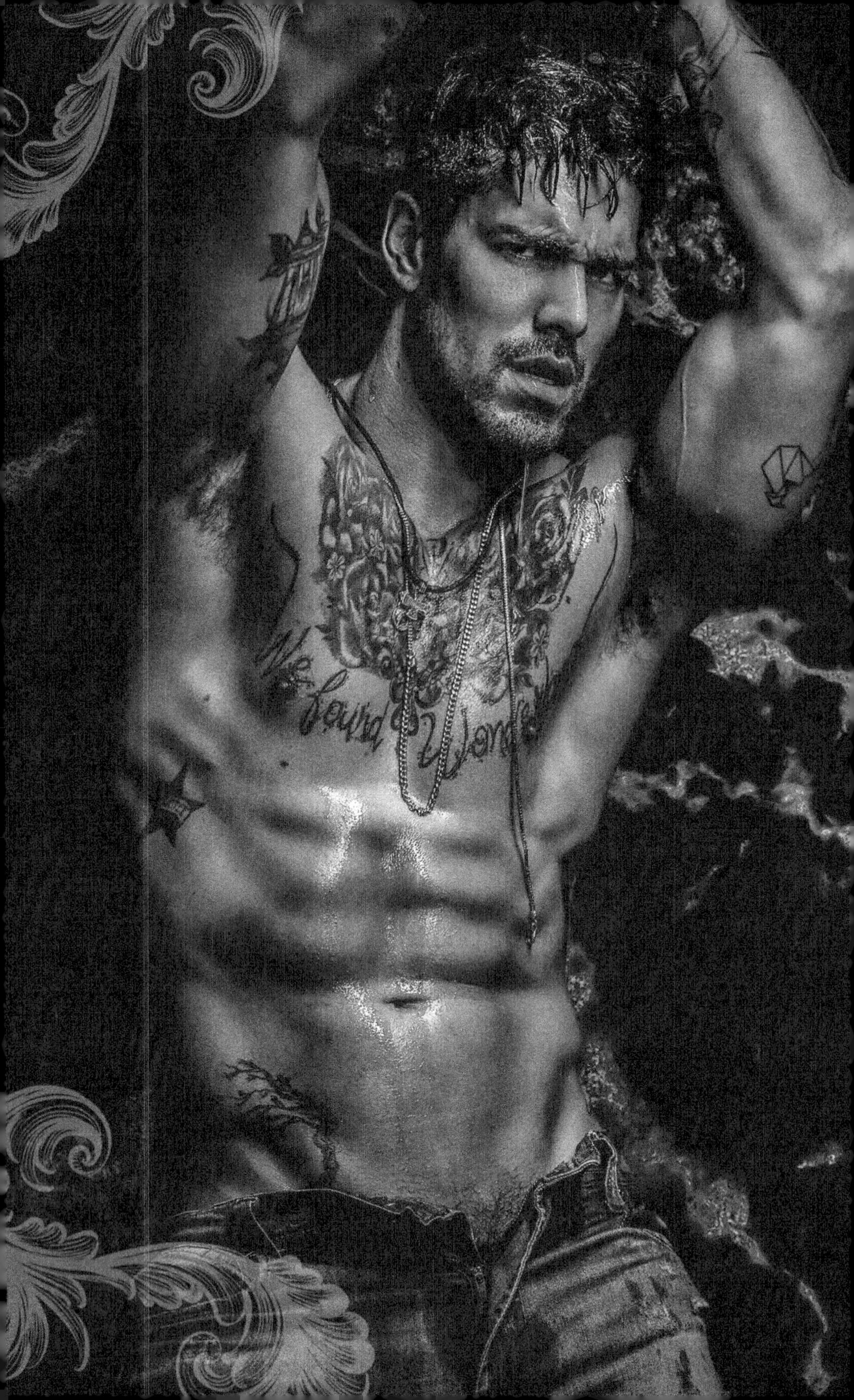
We found

Chapter 17
Liana

I shouldn't be here.
    The thought rang through my mind on repeat. I'd have liked to think I was a smart woman, but this was just plain dumb.

After our impromptu trip to Moscow and subsequent run-in with Mother's lover, Donatella—which I was positive wasn't accidental—I was able to lose the two women and the bodyguard who'd been following me like an annoying shadow.

It gave me the opportunity I'd been searching for to do my own thing. After shaking off my security, who wouldn't admit they'd lost me for fear of punishment from the terrifying Sofia Volkov, I found myself back in the States. I was able to get information on the deal that the Tijuana cartel was brokering. I was a street over from the Capitol Building in D.C. where human rights should be protected. Yet, here I was, witnessing the workings of criminals and corrupt politicians alike.

After hearing about my father's death and the mysterious ghost, I returned to my room and looked up information on Juliette DiLustro.

There wasn't much to find, aside from the fact that she was married to Dante DiLustro, who was one of the four Kingpins in the Syndicate. A search for Luciano Vitale and his wife didn't produce much more aside from a few photos in *Entertainment Weekly*.

The next search topic was even less productive. *Ghost*. I worked on my laptop, trying to uncover any clue as to who or what the ghost was. I'd been trying for hours when a message came in from a new unknown number.

I pulled out my phone and unlocked it, expecting it to be from my earlier mystery acquaintance. Frowning, I read the message a second time.

> If you keep looking for me, you won't like what you find. I wasn't one of the most lethal men in the underworld for naught.

I gave my head a subtle shake. There was only one explanation that fit. The Ghost must have sent this. But who was he? Was he even a *he*? I attempted to reply to the message, but it bounced back. Whoever sent it must not have known me well. Now I was even more curious. I hadn't been able to trace the line back to any of Mother's associates. It kept circulating on loop, never leaving the D.C. area.

I hadn't learned the source of the message or any details about the Ghost. However, I did learn about this event, meaning my efforts weren't completely in vain.

So here I was back in D.C., crashing a party in enemy territory, and there was no guarantee I'd make it out alive. Mother was busy who-knew-where with who-knew-what.

It was all the better, because it allowed me to pursue my own leads, which now put me in a favorable position in a casino owned by the Tijuana cartel.

It was stupid as fuck, but I couldn't ignore my sense of responsibility. It weighed me down like the excess baggage I'd carried around since my twin's death. Hell, maybe even since I'd learned of our family's sins.

Reign of a Billionaire

I glanced around the well-lit terrace, seeing faces that the FBI would run over each other to get their hands on. Criminals mingling without a care in the world, vacant-looking women on their arms. Mostly underage. Mostly under the influence.

Some database maneuvering secured my name on the list of invitees—not without a handsome fee, of course.

The scene made me sick. My fingers itched to grab my handgun and start shooting, but I had a target in mind, so I wouldn't let myself get trigger-happy.

The breeze carried the music through the terrace, the bass and sound of slot machines mixing into a rhythm that seemed to drive more than a few drunks to dance beneath the tacky strobe lights.

I stood in the corner, watching people and their ridiculous greed. For profit and power, while choosing ignorance over integrity. No matter though, because tonight, all these girls paraded around would be set free.

Cool air swept through the night and licked at my skin, fragrant with sex, alcohol, and sin. The sound of rowdy laughter drew my attention, and I spotted a gray-haired man in the northern corner of the terrace, surrounded by sinister-looking men.

I swallowed.

There was no need for introductions to understand who stood in the opposite corner. Santiago Tijuana, whose deceased son had gone after Sailor McHale after she married Raphael Santos. The idiot.

Santiago Tijuana Sr. was back to being the head of the cartel in Cuba, his rap sheet rivaling that of any dictator. His cold-blooded attitude and cruelty kept him on every agency's radar, but the man was too smart to be caught red-handed.

My gaze traveled over him and a tattoo on his hand caught my eye. It matched the one I'd seen back on the hand of the gorgeous green-eyed man at the hotel. The same tattoo had been carved on the stranger's left hand—a weird symbol in the mouth of a skull.

What were the odds?

It was then that I spotted that very stranger. He towered over everyone, his physique so imposing I wondered how I hadn't spotted him sooner. Taking a full step back into the shadows, I kept my gaze on him. If he spotted me, it'd be game over.

Who was he?

The answer was clear. He was a member of the Tijuana cartel. *Shame*, I thought, *I'll have to kill him.* I studied him, wearing a sleek gray three-piece suit. His muscular frame was attractive. His dark, slicked-back hair was styled to perfection, but it was his striking green eyes that would likely have women falling over themselves. And then there was his face, bone structure cut from steel and not a single emotion giving his thoughts away.

Discreetly positioning my phone, I snapped a photo, hoping the facial recognition program I'd built would help identify him later. If I didn't kill him today.

For almost thirty minutes, I watched the group of men without being too obvious and waited for them to move. When they left, the women who roamed the party would be ushered into their quarters and then presented to others for their pleasure. I'd only have a small window to rescue them, twenty minutes max.

Finally, the men dispersed, and I was on the move. I caught a glimpse of myself in the mirror. The slit in my long black gown was perfect for accessing the knives and handgun strapped to my thighs. I feared I didn't bring enough weapons, but it was too late now.

I made my way to the room I knew was in the south wing of this building, sticking to the shadows. I'd done my research and knew there was a servants' hallway that would allow me to get to my destination without being spotted.

My eyes darted around the area. Clutching the hem of my dress, I sped down the glittery hallway and took the first side door. Once in the hallway, I slipped my heels off and picked them up, making a run for it.

Reaching the south side of the building, I stopped and took a deep breath before pulling out my handgun. I'd sent a note to Nico

Morrelli via the dark web. He'd taken care of the last batch of women; I knew he'd take care of these.

> TRAFFICKED GIRLS READY FOR RETRIEVAL.
> FIVE MINUTES. EAST CAPITOL STREET.

I didn't bother waiting for a reply.

I reached for the doorknob, my heart pounding, and attempted to push it open.

"Fuck," I whispered. It was locked, but I'd anticipated as much. Reaching into my hair, I pulled out a hairpin. With a steady hand, it took me less than a minute to unlock the door. "Open sesame."

I pushed it open and looked around. Whispers and murmurs escalated, scared faces and tearstained cheeks littering the entire room.

"Hello, ladies," I greeted them. "Want to leave?"

Gasps filled the space, and as one, they all nodded. "Good," I murmured. "Leave everything behind—we don't have much time. Come this way and take the staircase on the left. Run like the devil is on your heels to East Capitol Street. First right when you exit this building. A team will be waiting for you and will take you to safety. Got it?"

Another round of nods, and then pandemonium erupted.

Just as the last girl turned the corner, disappearing from view, the visitor's door opened. It all happened in a split second. My back slammed into a wall, stealing the breath from my lungs. My left hand holding the gun was pushed against the wall, restrained by a tight grip, and a blade was pressed against my throat.

"Where the fuck are the women?" a man with a buzz cut and an earpiece hanging from his headset grunted.

The sharp tip of his blade pierced my neck, stinging. "How the fuck should I know?" I hissed, praying he wouldn't send an alert.

I needed to buy time, get this fucker off of me so I could blow his brains out and get out of here.

His grip on the knife tightened, his knuckles turning white. Fuck, just one nudge and I'd be dead. I used every bit of strength I had left to push him off.

He stumbled back and blinked, clearly not used to a woman with combat training. His surprise didn't last. In the next breath, he lunged at me. I attempted to kick him in the balls. He grabbed me by my hair, then slapped me across my face. Hard.

My cheek exploded. I let out a gasp, but before I could take my next breath, another slap followed. My lip swelled. Fury bubbled inside me as I stomped on his foot, then kicked him in his balls.

He bent over, letting out a whimper. Taking advantage of his temporary immobility, I flattened my hand on the nape of his neck and slammed my knee into his face. His nose broke on impact, the crack of his bones like music to my ears.

Pressing the barrel of my gun against his temple, I leaned closer, my face just inches from his ear. "Blowing your brains out will make my day," I purred in a cold voice.

"And here I thought there might be a damsel in distress in here." A deep, taunting voice startled me, and I whipped around, the man I was pummeling forgotten. Swallowing, I looked into the dark eyes of none other than Kingston Ashford. The image of the boy from the photo in Ivan's file flashed in front of my eyes, and I couldn't help but wonder what hell he'd gone through.

His hard, unrelenting gaze was in stark contrast to his casual pose. He was leaning against the wall, his arms folded and his eyes ice cold. My heart thundered in my chest but I ignored it, refusing to show fear.

"Clearly, I'm not a damsel. Now get lost, or I'll be cutting off two sets of balls today." I narrowed my eyes on him.

"Nice to see you again," he said, ignoring my dismissal. God, there was something about his guttural tone that was almost... seductive.

A whimper of my victim pulled my attention and I struck him in the temple, knocking him out, then turned back to the unexpected visitor.

"Are you stalking me?"

One meeting was a coincidence. Two, no fucking way.

"Now why would I stalk you?" Emotion played across his face and his eyes—blazing, almost like he'd seen a ghost. Just as quickly as it appeared, his expression shuttered into one of polite interest.

"You tell me." I licked my lips nervously. There was something about this man that was unsettling. I didn't like it. "What do you want with me, Kingston Ashford?"

Surprise flared in his eyes, his scruffy jaw hiding some of his hard face. "So you know who I am."

"I did my homework," I breathed.

"So you did."

A beat of silence followed, something about the tone of his voice not sitting well with me. His eyes lingered on my injured cheek, darkening. His jaw tightened, and he looked away. A shadow of something dangerous passed his expression, making my heart shudder and then speed up. For him.

"Why are you here?" I rasped. The darkness in his eyes unleashed something within me, chasing my rapid heartbeats and frying my nerves. I raised my eyebrows, tilting my head to the side and hiding this unusual reaction behind my stony facade.

"Morbid curiosity."

"That can get you killed."

Something flared sharply in his eyes before it was completely gone.

"Go for the jugular next time," he drawled, giving me pause, but then I remembered the grotesque scene I'd created around me. Clearly, he wasn't disturbed by it. "Slice him right here." He demonstrated on himself, a spot right under his jaw. "He'll bleed out like a pig. Then take his tooth. Didn't your mama teach you that?"

I blinked at him. Kingston Ashford was a nut job—there was no other explanation. But then his words sunk in and realization dawned.

"You know her?" Mother partook in Ivan's torture. Of course he would know her.

My breath caught in my throat as he pulled out a pistol and attached a silencer to its barrel. Before I could even blink, he pointed the gun at me and pulled the trigger.

My eyes closed, my mind silent for the first time in years.

Chapter 18
Kingston

The body slumped to the floor with a satisfying thud. Blood roared between my ears, muffling the noise of everything else.

The silencer still on, I shoved the pistol back in my holster and closed the distance to the dead body. I stared down at the unmoving corpse and blinked away the red fog that'd descended when I fired the bullet, then leaned over and pulled out a tooth with my pliers.

"What're you doing?" Liana's voice was distant, and I found her watching me with a blank mask.

The party was held for distinguished politicians, with its annual tradition of serving trafficked minors and women on a silver platter—one that went blissfully ignored. It was their way of gathering the evidence to hold against the honorable governors, senators, and others when they needed a favor.

The corruption was a wheel that never stopped turning.

"I need his tooth."

Her brows pinched in confusion.

"Why?" My molars clenched. It was a damn habit that I couldn't shake. It kept me sane. I needed to know how many lives I'd taken by the time this all was done. I'd known Liana since before her school years; she'd seen me collect teeth while I was Sofia's prisoner. "Do you need dental work?"

My frustration bubbled, reaching a new high and preparing to explode. She said she did her homework and knew who I was, but she clearly didn't remember me.

"No, I don't need dental work," I gritted, pondering why she didn't remember me. If she did, there wouldn't have been a need to do homework. Nico Morrelli gave me a heads-up—someone was poking and prodding around my identity. It had to be Liana.

I had so many questions of my own, but it was best I said nothing. For now.

Her lips parted, and that was when I cut her off, my anger reaching fever pitch. "Shouldn't you be running before I blow your fucking brains out?" I snapped.

Truthfully, I was surprised she didn't point her own gun at me. Instead, her arm remained hanging down her body, almost as if she were resolving herself to that fate and prepared to die. Her golden-hazel eyes searched mine, and I could see her mind working hard, leaving me to wonder who, in fact, this woman was.

She wasn't the Liana Volkov I remembered.

This one stirred strange feelings in my chest that I hadn't felt in years. The emotion spread to the rest of my body, and I hated her for it. I needed it gone. She was my enemy.

...Wasn't she?

She scoffed, smirking. "You can try to kill me, but you'll fail. Fair warning to your fragile male ego."

I'd spent over a decade being her and Lou's bodyguard. How could she not remember?

Unless shit happened to her after her twin died. I knew firsthand how vicious Sofia and Ivan could be when double-crossed. It could be that Liana was put through something so traumatic that her memory suffered. Or she felt Lou's agony. It would make sense. When one twin hurt, so did the other. When one was sad, so was the other. The twins shared a connection despite being very different personality-wise. Liana was ice and fire where Lou was ocean and sunshine.

"So bloodthirsty," I remarked warily, recognizing that the once-harmless woman had been turned into a very capable killer.

She shot me a heated look from under her lashes, then murmured in a low, bedroom voice, "And I haven't had my fill, so you might want to be careful, Mr. Ashford."

"Ghost." She blinked, confused.

"Excuse me?"

Jesus, did she remember fucking anything?

Ivan Petrov and Sofia Volkov had trained me into a lethal killer. And so much more. Those first two years in captivity were excruciating. Until I'd seen her—them. Life under Sofia and Ivan's roof was fucking hell until Sofia made me her daughters' bodyguard. The twins had been a beacon of hope for me at my most desperate hour. I strived to become the best killer, the best hitman, the best bodyguard.

Pushing it all out of my mind, I focused on the petite woman with an angelic face. Her eyes shone deceptively, full of innocence and lies that had cost her twin her life.

"I go by Ghost, not Mr. Ashford. Not Kingston."

Something flickered in her eyes. "I've been searching up the mysterious ghost," she said, her brows knitted. "So Ghost and Kingston Ashford are one and the same."

"Yes."

An eye roll followed. "I'll call you whatever I like," she shot back. "And it won't be Ghost. Now stop annoying me, or I'll kill you."

"Go ahead," I retorted.

Her lips thinned in displeasure, and our eyes locked, speaking in a language neither one of us could understand. Until she broke the silence.

"You know, I almost wish you'd try to kill me so I could slice your throat and end this annoying conversation."

My muscles tensed at her words, suddenly recognizing her thirst for self-destruction.

"Trust me, ice princess, when I try to kill you, I'll succeed." Her gaze flashed with open defiance, noting my choice of words. *When*, not *if*. But for some reason, she chose not to focus on that.

"Why are you here? And what's your connection to the Tijuana cartel?"

"I'm here to kill them."

Her eyes flashed in delight. "Me too. Can we join forces for tonight?"

Knowing it would be easier to go along than argue, I nodded my assent. And not a moment too soon. Four goons appeared, their gazes darting to the dead body. Then the bullets started flying. I yanked Liana through the opposite door, and we both covered a side. She was gripping her gun as I held mine.

"You take the two on the left, and I'll take the two on the right," she mouthed.

Without delay, we leaned, aimed, and shot. *Bang. Bang.*

The bullets punched their way through the men's necks, almost as if shot by the same person. Blood gushed and bodies fell to the ground.

My pistol still had a silencer, but Liana's didn't.

"Shit."

It was what happened next that shocked me to my core. Knives replaced the gun, and she started killing the guards one at a time. Screams filled the air, blood spurted the floors and walls like geysers. I watched in amazement as she sliced their throats, one at a time.

She stood over the last corpse, savage and vengeful, her chest heaving as she watched the life fade from her latest victim.

Her head lifted, meeting my gaze, and her lips curled into a feral smile.

The silence pierced the air between us, louder than bullets. I didn't move, and neither did she. Instead, she stared at me, her hands drenched with blood and her eyes distant. Blank. Somewhere along the way, this woman had been turned into an assassin.

And for the first time in forever, my dick was as hard as a rock. I'd never thought I could get turned on by a woman killing so savagely, but here I was, aching for *this* woman.

And I fucking hated her even more for it.

It was a betrayal to her sister. It was breaking a promise I'd made to myself. This lust ate at my flesh like poison, like a venomous snake, mocking my love for Lou.

Why the fuck did my dick ache when I looked at her?

This woman was only the echo of the one I'd once loved. There was too much history between us—granted she didn't seem to remember any of it—but with the way our pasts intertwined, maybe it was natural that my dick and my emotions would become traitors.

Her resemblance to Lou was fucking with my mind and body. Being in her presence was a form of self-torture, yet I couldn't help but crave it. Crave *her*. Those lips... that voice... those eyes that were so much like my Louisa's.

It was heartbreak all over again. A reminder of what I'd lost.

She leaned in for a kiss but stopped short, her expression shattering.

"What is it, sunshine?"

I might be a prisoner in this fucked-up castle in Siberia, but when Louisa was around me, I was free. She was my own personal ray of sunshine that took me to paradise, and all she had to do was stand next to me. But it was when she smiled that every one of my thoughts slid away. Only she had the power to numb the pain.

She averted her eyes, her face heating to a bright red.

"I've never kissed anyone on the mouth," *she muttered, embarrassed. Then her shoulders slumped.* "I've never kissed a boy."

Her hair was disheveled, her cheeks red, but it was her eyes that always captured me. Golden and warm.

"I've never been kissed either," *I admitted.*

Her eyes shot to me, shocked by my declaration. There was one subject we never broached—it'd break her. It broke me, too.

My cheek was hot and stinging. My ears rang. I didn't want to think about any of that when I was with her.

"Let's not talk about that."

She nodded somberly, the sadness in her eyes gutting me more than any other horror I'd witnessed. This world wasn't made for us, yet we found ourselves stuck in it, trying to survive and find light anywhere we could. It was taking a toll on all of us, but Lou the most.

Sofia called her weak. She wasn't. Lou was compassionate and caring, her soft heart wanting everyone to be okay. Her twin, on the other hand, was tougher and only had a soft spot for her sister. Everyone else, she detested.

I brought my fingers to her soft strands, the scent of sunlight and warm honey seeping into my lungs.

"Do you want to kiss me, sunshine?" My fingers trembled as I brought her hair to my nose, inhaling deeply.

She let out a shuddering breath. "Not if you don't want to."

I wrapped the length of it around my wrist. "With you, I do."

Her eyes and lips were so alluring when she smiled. It made my heart beat faster. "It'll be my first kiss."

"Our first kiss."

Lifting onto her toes, she tilted her head toward mine, offering herself up so generously. I bent to brush my lips against hers, and my chest fluttered. It *fucking* fluttered for her.

She pressed herself against me, her arms coming around me to kiss me deeper, both of our moves unpracticed and messy, our teeth clashing.

Breaking the kiss, she pulled away, breathing heavily. My heartbeat raced in my chest. For her. It was all for her. I could die a happy man now.

I ran my fingers down the length of her golden hair, marveling at its softness and all these feelings that she brought up in me.

"Is it supposed to feel like this?" Her soft whisper brushed against my cheek.

"I don't know, but it feels right." She wrapped her arms around my neck and buried her face into my throat.

"It does," she agreed, her lips moving against my skin. "I'm glad you're my first kiss."

I took her chin between my fingers. "Your first, your last, your only."

Her eyes found mine, heartbreak in them gutting me alive. "Forever." Her lips found mine for a whispered vow. "However long that may be."

"It'll be long," I rasped into her mouth, loneliness in her eyes screaming and pleading to keep us together. "I'll find a way out of here. For both of us."

"Kingston, if I don't make it—"

I brought a finger to her lips. "Don't say it."

She grasped my hand in hers as her chest rattled with a shaky breath. "If I don't make it, promise you'll protect my sister." She squeezed my hand with all her might. "She's stronger than I am, but not as strong as everyone thinks. Promise me you'll protect her."

There was nothing I could refuse Louisa. Fucking nothing. If she asked me to walk into a burning building, I would. If she asked me to burn the world to the ground, I'd only ask when.

"You know I'll do anything. So if that's—"

"There you are!" A voice, similar but so different, cut me off. I looked back over my shoulder, finding her twin fidgeting. "Mother wants to have dinner with us."

Fuck, I hated their mother. Everything she stood for and everything she was. How in the fuck did someone so evil give birth to someone as good and gentle as Louisa?

Louisa pulled away, and my fists clenched, fighting the instinct to hold on. It was as if I were born with it. Everything about her sparked the protectiveness inside me tenfold.

As she walked away, I didn't realize it would be the beginning of our destruction.

Her twin was the only thing left behind, a ghost of the woman I lost, but also a temptation. The urge to pretend for a moment—just one moment in this cursed life—that I had Lou back in my life was overwhelming.

I wanted Louisa; I was left with Liana. I vowed to protect Lou, but was left with the promise to protect Liana—even if just for this place in time, here at this fucked-up party.

Maybe Louisa knew all along what was coming? Her death. My lonely existence. The pull toward the wrong sister.

Whatever *this* was, I had to contain it before it spiraled out of control.

Chapter 19
Liana

T he Ghost.

Kingston Ashford was the man my mother and Perez were afraid of, one of the most lethal men in the underworld. And he aimed his attention on me. This definitely earned him some points in my book. Although, I didn't think I'd earned any in his.

I couldn't quite decide whether this man was watching me with disdain or admiration.

The drive to his apartment had been short. I couldn't go back to the hotel with splashes of blood all over me, and my accomplice in eliminating Tijuana's guards insisted I get cleaned up.

I pulled out my phone and checked in with my contact. At least one thing went well today. Nico Morrelli had all the women safely in the shelters.

Another shipment intercepted, I thought proudly.

Kingston's car came to a stop, and I didn't bother waiting for him to open the door. I reached for the handle, pushing it down, when a forceful impact had me falling back on my ass.

My eyes flared, fury bolting through me when dark eyes locked with mine.

"A gentleman opens the door," he remarked, challenging me to disagree.

I remained rooted to my seat, stunned. I couldn't remember the last time any man had tried to be a gentleman with me.

I let out an exaggerated sigh, although my insides roared with feminine appreciation for his manners.

"Then by all means," I said, relaxing. "Lead the way."

A heavy moment passed between us, my eyes finding his and drowning in his darkness. Why was there this familiarity to him that I couldn't shake off?

Hesitantly, he extended his hand. I eyed it for two heartbeats before slowly sliding my fingers into his warm palm. My breath hitched at the contact and my pulse skittered like the wings of a hummingbird, my eyes glued to where our skin touched.

No disgust. No panic.

I climbed out of the car, and he slid off his suit jacket and handed it over to me.

When I shot him a dubious look, all he said was, "It'll hide the blood."

My mouth curved into a silent "O" with understanding. I wrapped his jacket around me, his musky vanilla scent instantly surrounding me and cocooning me into a warm and protective hold.

Taking a step away to carve some distance between us, we made our way inside the building, the doorman already at the ready. I nodded my thanks, then continued toward the elevator with sure steps, my mind on alert. Kingston Ashford moved with the grace of a panther and surveyed the area with the attention of a predator.

Once inside the lift, he reached out and pressed a code on the keypad. The elevator moved swiftly up, and in the next breath, it pinged, the steel door opening directly into the penthouse.

Kingston motioned for me to go first and, taking a deep breath, I stepped into the spacious area overlooking the city skyline. The interior was large and bare, not a single item screaming *home*. It held an industrial feel, with the walls finished in various shades of gray.

He followed right behind me and the elevator doors slid closed, leaving us alone in this mysterious man's space.

My gaze flicked over my shoulder, intent on marking any obvious danger before continuing.

I caught the reflection of the two of us in the mirror and my breath was cut short. Splatters of blood stained my face and arms even though my dress appeared intact. More likely, the black hid it all.

My cheek was bruised and my lip was swollen. In short, I was a mess. Meanwhile, he looked like he'd just come from a black-tie event —which, I reasoned, was exactly right.

"Show me where I can get cleaned up, and I'll be out of your hair in no time," I declared, pushing my shoulders back and looking away from our reflections.

He tilted his head, indicating a door at the far end of the hallway. "That's a guest room. There are some spare clothes." I wrinkled my nose at the thought of wearing someone's sloppy seconds. "They're new."

He didn't wait for my reply. Instead, he turned on his heel and disappeared behind another door. His bedroom, I presumed. So many strange emotions warred inside me at the thought of what that room might look like, *smell* like.

I sighed, and with one last glance at the darkening skyline over the city, I made my way to the guest bedroom.

Once inside, I looked around. Simple. Just the barest of furnishings—four-poster bed, nightstand, dresser. Closing the door behind me, I rummaged through the drawers. They were empty, aside from some clothes that still had tags on them.

I walked to the bathroom, closed the door, and locked it behind me. The man might be helping me today, but tomorrow I knew he wouldn't hesitate to kill me. *When I try to kill you, I'll succeed.* His words rang in the back of my mind, promises of what I could expect from him loud and clear.

I leaned back against the door and closed my eyes. Kingston was underestimating me, and when he finally did try to kill me, I'd beat him to the punch.

I turned on the shower and waited for the water to warm up as I stripped my bloodied dress off. I threw a glance at the mirror, staring at my reflection.

I was covered in blood and looked... broken. *Just like him.* I reared back. I had no clue where the thought came from, but it was there. I was as sure about it as I was about my own brokenness. I wasn't a naive girl with hopes and dreams anymore. I had been born into this world of crime; I'd likely die in it.

There was no way out.

I stepped under the spray of water, letting it wash away all my sins, sweat, and grime from the day. I watched red-tinted water rush down the drain along with another small, innocent part of me. Soon, there'd be nothing of the old me left.

The events of the day rolled through my mind, but it wasn't the murders I'd committed that plagued it. It was *him*. Eyes ablaze, his control lethal and his strength unwavering as we tackled the enemy together.

And then there was this animalistic attraction to him. Something deep within me responded to the very essence of him. It was confusing me, throwing me off course.

A shiver ran down my spine even under the scalding hot spray.

I desperately tried to calm my erratic heart, but the longer I remained unmoving, the more unsteady my breathing became. My inhales and exhales were a fast, fractured rhythm. Then, in one jolt, a memory rushed to the forefront of my mind.

"*Kiss me, sunshine.*"

What was that? I'd never heard those words before. I fell forward, bracing myself against the white tile. I closed my eyes, but it wasn't enough to lift the spell. More words came crashing in, fuzzy images warring behind my eyelids.

"Kiss me like there's no tomorrow for us."

The voice was a little rough. The touch on my skin was a lot gentle. Lips dragged across mine, then kissed me deeply, devouring me.

It was then that the scent registered—vanilla, musky, and clean.

Like *him*. Like Kingston Ashford.

Chapter 20
Kingston

I carded a hand through my hair and pinched the bridge of my nose.

What the fuck was with me lately? It was stupid to bring Liana back into my penthouse. Reckless. Out of character for me.

I never brought *anyone* to this condo, yet here I was playing knight-in-fucking-armor for my enemy's daughter.

Promise.

Yes, that had to be it. I was just fulfilling my promise to Louisa.

I poured myself a glass of whiskey and gulped it in one go, then slammed the glass on the countertop of the bar. How fucking long would my pain hover around me?

I closed my eyes, images of Louisa flickering through my mind on a reel. Her face. Her smile. Her eyes.

Fuck!

The images of Liana and Louisa were starting to intertwine, confusing me. The same face. The same smile. Why didn't the memories hurt now that Liana was in my vicinity?

I heard the shower turn on, and I pictured Liana stripping her dress off. I couldn't help but wonder how soft her skin was... Goddammit! I had to get a grip.

Maybe I was weak.

Or maybe I was desperate to feel normal again, like I had with Louisa. I was her first and last. She was supposed to be my first and last.

Yet here I was thinking about her twin in my guest room. I wanted to touch her, lick her, bite her. First fucking temptation in years, and I was failing miserably.

I wasn't a good man, and I worked for many who were even worse. After my father fucked me over, I'd learned that the world wasn't about good and evil. There were so many shades in between, and I had to do what I needed in order to survive.

Louisa never held any of it against me—not the blood on my hands, not the number of deaths I'd been responsible for, not the darkness that consumed me.

Irritation flickered in my chest while a fire burned deeper, licking at my soul. Or whatever was left of it after Ivan Petrov and Sofia Volkov. For the first time in forever, I felt edgy. Irrational. Impulsive. I couldn't—shouldn't—jeopardize my peace of mind.

My phone rang and I answered it without checking the caller ID. "Yes."

"Where in the fuck are you?"

I groaned, cursing myself silently. The last person I needed to deal with right now was Dante Leone. His brand of crazy only made me crazier.

"On vacation."

An echo of silence. "Vacation?"

"Yeah."

"Vacation," he said again. Jesus, did he train a parrot to repeat my words?

"Yes, you should give it a try."

He snickered. "I don't like that idea *or* your tone."

I scoffed. "Ask me if I care."

"I need your help finding someone." Obviously, Dante's selective hearing was in full force because it went over his head.

"I'm busy."

"With?"

My heart beat faster, a vision of thick blonde hair and smooth porcelain skin and everything forbidden flashed before my eyes. My teeth clenched at this nauseating need for the wrong fucking twin.

"I'm busy being *on vacation*."

"Did you... Did you finally find yourself a woman?" The disbelief in his tone was evident. Not that I'd ever grant him an answer. "You did, didn't you?" I grumbled my annoyance, and he laughed. Loud and slightly crazy. "Why didn't you say so, *amico*?"

My mood soured and a sardonic feeling pulled in my chest.

"Good luck with Phoenix, Dante," I said, alluding to his obsession with Romero's daughter. The guy went as far as getting engaged with her sister to get to Phoenix.

I ended the call, the irony and similarities of our situations not escaping me—with one notable exception: both Romero sisters were alive.

I gave my head a subtle shake, then blinked, realizing I was standing in front of the guest room. I ran my tongue across my teeth, attempting to quell all these feelings bubbling inside me and failing.

I lost my first battle since running into Liana Volkov.

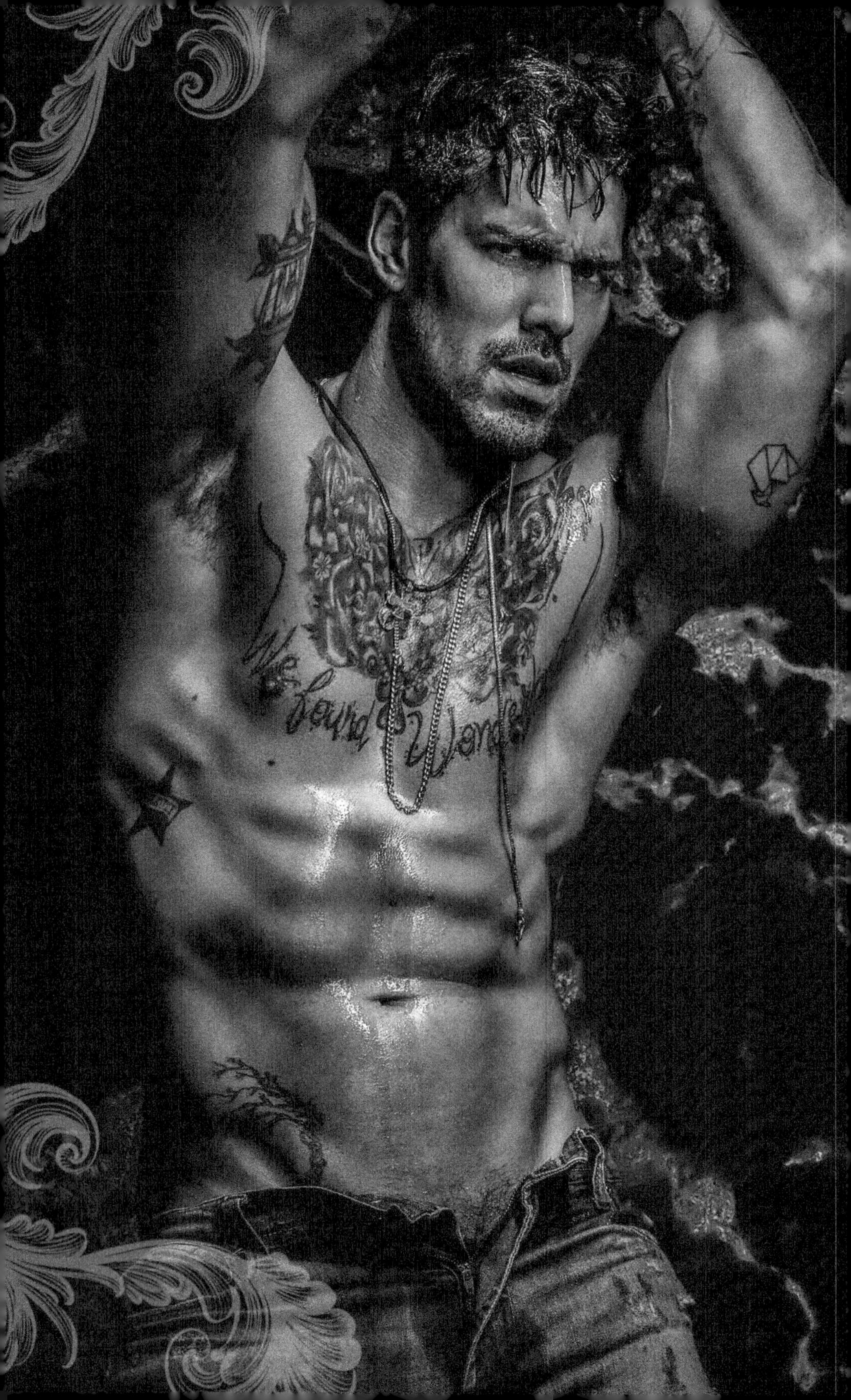
We found

Chapter 21
Liana

I staggered back and sat on the ledge of the tub, the memory that slammed into me with the force of a transport truck still lurking in my periphery. Closing my eyes, I tipped my head back, relishing in the soothing sound of the water running and trying to make sense of it all.

The magnetic pull that emanated from Kingston had awakened something deep inside me—that had to be it. A shiver ran down my spine as the hot water slid down my skin, my sex aching and throbbing.

Why was my usually comatose pussy coming to life *now*, of all times?

Rather than doing something stupid, I closed my eyes and slid a hand between my legs to find the skin sensitive and hot with my arousal. I imagined it was his big hand touching me, and my heart sped up. My nipples tightened.

Shaking my head, I couldn't understand my body's betrayal, yet I couldn't stop myself from picturing him. Owning me. Thrusting inside me. Touching me.

The realization slammed into my brain, driving my mind into havoc.

Touching me?

I yanked my hand away as if burned. I didn't want him to touch me. Why would I even want Kingston at all? *I don't,* I told myself. I didn't need or want any man. The scars made me self-conscious, despite the fact that reconstructive surgery had all but erased them.

A single tear rolled down my cheek, only to be swiftly washed away by the shower water. Like my scars. Like my broken heart.

"Kiss me, sunshine." The voice I kept hearing terrified a little part of me. Who were those words spoken to? *"I want to be your first, your only, your last."*

My mouth started to fill with saliva and I pressed my lips together, forcing my heart and mind to settle. What was happening to me?

I lifted my hand, tugging at my wet strands. I wished I could pull all my hair out and find the hole that had to be in my skull, letting everything that was wrong spill out. I was tired of the dreams I didn't understand.

I forced a lungful of air into my chest. Breathe in. Then breathe out. Again. Each inhale and exhale slowly soothed my mind and body back under control.

Ignoring the wretched commotion beneath my skin, I quickly washed my hair and rest of my body, before stepping out of the shower and wrapping a towel around myself and exiting the bathroom.

My bare feet froze, and I stilled at the doorway.

Kingston Ashford was in my—okay, the *guest*—bedroom, leaning against the wall casually and watching me with the dark eyes of a predator. His torso was bare, and I couldn't help admiring the ink on his chest. I couldn't quite make out the design, but it extended from his chest down his right arm, all of it connected with a complicated mashup of symbols.

Reign of a Billionaire

I didn't like that he was here. Especially not now, after the memory that left me feeling raw.

Vulnerable. Scared of the unknown.

"Ever heard of privacy?" My voice trembled, my heart drumming in my throat and my ears. He didn't answer, but for some reason, my body hummed with anticipation. My nipples pebbled, aching for something. Or someone. My gaze traveled down his jeans to his bare feet. It made sense, he was home, yet something about him half naked had me reeling. Did he expect something?

I lifted my head and locked eyes with him.

"If you think I'm sleeping with you—" Why had my voice become breathy? He must have taken a shower too because droplets hung off the ends of his midnight-black hair. My fingers buzzed, the desire to touch him shaking me to my core.

"Who ever said anything about sleeping?"

The insinuation was… tempting. Filthy. My skin pulled tight with an ache that was foreign yet familiar. Just like in my dreams. The space between us filled with my heavy breaths and his burning gaze.

"What do you want?" I breathed.

"Make yourself come and let me watch."

My mouth parted in shock. My cheeks went up in flames. He couldn't be serious. Something was off, but I couldn't figure out what. I opened my mouth to say no, but I couldn't find my voice. What was wrong with me?

When I remained silent, he continued in that sinfully deep baritone wrapped in sin and promises of carnal pleasure. "If it's any more appealing, I could do the same."

My eyes fell to the impressive bulge in his jeans and my mouth went dry. I licked my lips, my tongue darting over the cut. I hoped the sting would restore reason in me. It didn't.

I wasn't a virgin. I wasn't particularly shy. Yet something about letting another person watch me in the intimate, private time when I touched myself made me feel vulnerable. Exposed. Then there was the idea of anyone touching me and feeling those scars firsthand. I couldn't let that happen.

"No touching?" I blurted. "I can take almost anything else."

"No touching."

I shivered, mesmerized by my body's response to the possibility of seeing him jack off while I touched myself.

"I don't much like it anyhow," he stated matter-of-factly, surprising me with his admission. What were the chances? I thought I was alone in this predicament. "But something about you... I could bring myself relief while watching you."

He recited it like it was a business transaction. I didn't like it, yet I felt the slick moisture between my legs.

"So... we masturbate while watching each other?" He nodded, his face an unfeeling mask while his dark eyes were like flames.

My gaze darted to the comfortable-looking bed. "Where do you want me?"

I wanted to mentally slap myself, but the words were already out of my mouth. I might as well own them. He tilted his chin toward the bed, and I strutted past him like I was on a runway, swaying my hips. I had officially lost my mind.

"Lose the towel," he ordered just as I reached the bed.

Without meaning to, I obeyed. What. The. *Fuck?*

I had to redeem myself, so I retorted, "Lose your pants." I glanced over my shoulder and caught him staring at my ass. "Hey, eyes up here."

"What's that on your back?" he asked, not bothering to stop staring at my ass.

I stiffened. It was a faint scar that plastic surgery couldn't erase, but I wasn't going to tell him that.

"We agreed on watching each other whack off, not talk. Now pants off; otherwise I'm getting dressed and getting outta here."

His lips twitched, but the amusement never reached his eyes. Then, to my surprise, he unbuttoned his jeans and pushed them down his muscular, tattoo-covered thighs. God, he was a *specimen*.

Mesmerized by every naked inch of him, I got on the bed, my gaze never wavering from him as he sat down on the oversized chair that would easily accommodate me straddling him and—

I gave my head a shake. *No.* I didn't want to straddle this man.

"Lie back against the pillows," he instructed. "Half-upright position. Your eyes on me." His jaw was taut as he watched me follow his command. "Now, spread your legs and touch yourself."

His strong fingers wrapped around his cock at the same time my hand slipped between my legs. He started to stroke his dick, the muscles in his arms flexing. It was—I reluctantly admitted—the most beautiful sight I had ever seen.

A soft moan escaped my lips at the same time his sigh filled the space, enveloping us in our own private bubble.

"Let me see you work your clit."

I rubbed it faster, spreading the wetness around while obscene noises of his movements and mine vibrated through the air. I closed my eyes, teasing my swollen, slick pussy with desperation unlike ever before. My clit throbbed, and I thrust one finger inside my entrance.

"Tell me what you're thinking about."

"Your cock inside me."

My eyelids flew open at my words, shocked at my revelation. He sucked in a breath, his hand on his cock, still stroking. I couldn't tear my gaze away from his groin, watching him work himself. His fist squeezed the head of his cock and a bead of moisture appeared on the tip, which he smeared everywhere.

I wondered how he tasted as waves of heat rolled through my limbs, setting my core on fire. God, I was needy for his cock. I wondered how it'd feel inside me, but it was something that would never happen. Not if neither one of us liked to be touched. Plus, there was the whole *I work alone and he might kill me* thing.

"Your pussy would strangle my cock, would milk it." His voice, wrapped in sin, did things to me that he didn't notice because he was staring at my hand between my legs. My fingers moved faster, my pleasure climbing, expanding. "I want you on my face right now."

A visible shudder rolled through me. "I thought you didn't like contact."

"I want to lick your juices, suck on your clit until you're screaming with pleasure. I'd work you till you passed out."

I licked my lips as I stared at his erection, turned on beyond my wildest expectations.

"Fuck," I breathed, staring at his jutting cock, with its smooth skin and veins along the side. The head dripped with a pearly liquid, and I imagined that thickness pounding inside me, splitting me in half and filling me up more than ever before. My pussy clenched around my fingers, and I moaned.

"On my face," he grunted. "Now."

The word cracked off the bedroom like a whip. Without meaning to, I obeyed him, scurrying off the bed and coming to stand in front of him.

"How do I do it without touching you?" I breathed. I was trembling with eagerness.

"Your knees on the armrests," he said in a low rumble. I followed the instruction, my legs spread obscenely, my pussy on display in front of his face. My body hovered awkwardly above him when his next words had my legs shaking. I felt him slide down the chair slightly, so that he was positioned beneath me. "Sit that cunt down on my face. I want my face dripping with your arousal."

My body obliged immediately. My engorged clit throbbed with an achy need as his mouth closed around it.

"Ohhhh," I moaned loudly. Goosebumps broke along my skin. Heat bloomed in my pussy. His mouth worked its magic as he licked and sucked like his life depended on it.

My back arched and my body rocked against his mouth, needing more. I could hear the fleshy sound of his beating off—so fucking erotic.

I wheezed as I ground down against his face, my fingers digging into the headrest of the chair. My legs were shaking, my movements uncoordinated because of how turned on I was. How needy. I panted, my eyelids heavy as I watched him eating me out with a blissful expression on his face.

I writhed, rocked, and cursed. My orgasm was so close I could practically taste it. The pressure inside me wound tighter, coiling like an active volcano. He licked and sucked, his tongue penetrating my entrance, and I was convulsing, my vision going dark as the pleasure dragged me into the ether.

I shuddered against his mouth as he continued licking me, swirling all the slickness and juices, then fucking me with his tongue while I moaned incoherent words. He licked me with ruthlessness, until I began shaking, my hips rocking and chasing a second orgasm.

My body splintered into a million pieces while my mind was wiped. I screamed as wave after wave of white-hot bliss wracked my body, tearing me to pieces.

"You'll always be mine," he murmured, and my eyes snapped to him. His arms flexed furiously as he jerked his cock. His gaze locked on my swollen pussy, his movements rough, and my trembling thighs lowered just as hot jets spurted all over his hard abs and my throbbing pussy. "Louisa."

Ice froze my veins where lust and fire burned just moments ago at hearing the name I hadn't heard voiced in so long.

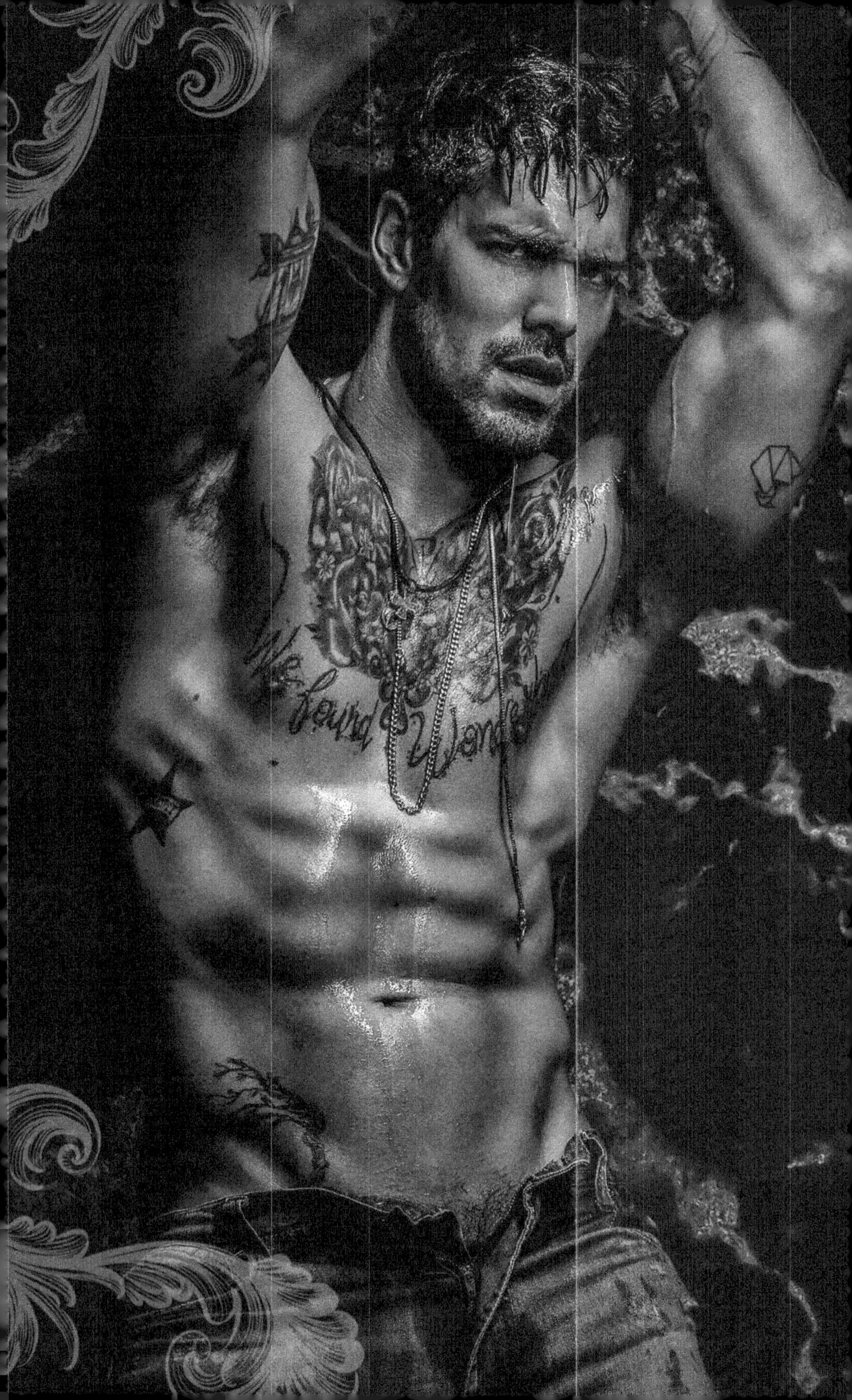
We found

Chapter 22
Kingston

She trembled, breathing hard.
    My cock pushed against her hot entrance, and I watched our bodies almost join. Hers, pure as fresh snow. Mine, marred from years of fighting.

"Are you sure, Louisa?"

She was so tight, so tense. The tip of my cock was barely inside her pussy, but I could already feel her walls clenching around it.

Her eyes found mine. "I'm sure, Kingston." Her lips peppered my flesh as she hung on to me tightly. My muscles trembled with the intense need to make her mine. "You wanted to wait; we waited. Now I'm eighteen, I want you. My first, my last, my only."

My hips jerked and I sunk deeper, drawing a gasp from those pretty lips. "Mine," I panted.

"Yours." Her gaze never wavered from mine. "I'm all yours, and you're all mine."

I slowly pushed inside, both of us glancing down, watching my dick disappear into her body.

She clutched my shoulders, her fingernails digging into my skin.

"Is... it... in?" she breathed, reaching her lips up to brush against mine.

My biceps shook, not from my weight but from all the emotions and self-restraint. I gritted my teeth and fought the urge to thrust all the way in, not wanting to hurt her.

"Almost." It was the only time I lied to her.

"I don't think we fit," she croaked.

"I promise, we fit." We were the only thing that made sense in this world. "Relax, sunshine." She squeezed her eyes shut. "You're taking me so well. Your pussy was made for me."

Her eyes opened, shining with pure, unfiltered love. She wrapped her arms around me, her fingernails digging into my back. Marking me, just the way I was marking her.

"And your cock... It's p-perfect." Her hips rocked against mine in unpracticed movement, her voice quivering. "I'll belong to you for as long as I live, but you also belong to me, Kingston."

"Always," I vowed, my hips thrusting forward until I filled her completely. Pleasure unlike anything else shot up my spine, and I groaned into her throat. "I'm yours until I draw my last breath."

She made a vow; I did the same. She kept her vow until the day she was killed; I'd just broken mine.

Self-loathing. Self-condemnation. Self-destruction.

Guilt. Rage. Bitterness.

Never again.

I wouldn't repeat the same mistake again, regardless of how beautiful Liana looked.

This time around, it'd finish me off.

With one shake of my head, I stood up. Her body slid off me and she fell on her ass with betrayal in her eyes as I strode away from her. But the taste of her, the scent of her, stained my skin.

I almost fucked her—not that what I'd done was innocent. It all went so fucking wrong. It took all my self-control not to grab her by that slim waist and slam her down, thrust inside her, and piston her until I emptied myself.

Reign of a Billionaire

The moment I was back in my bedroom, I realized I was still butt naked. Fuck! Pulling on a pair of pajama pants, I lay in bed awake, staring at the ceiling and wondering how I could have stooped so low. I pondered what the fuck could have happened for Liana to have changed so drastically.

The girl I knew didn't know how to slice someone's throat or shoot to kill. She didn't have her hands drenched in blood. Maybe my mind no longer remembered her. Them. Maybe somewhere along the way, my mind had broken.

Fuck, maybe I missed Lou so much that my mind conjured a small part of her in Liana desperate for just a moment when she was still with me.

"Kiss me, sunshine." My hands were in her soft strands, tilting her face up, her mouth a heartbeat away. "Kiss me like there's no tomorrow for us."

Her lips brushed against mine, soft at first and then harder. She whimpered, pressing her soft body against mine. My thumb swept over her pulse point in her neck, feeling her erratic heartbeat.

She wanted me despite the fact that I wasn't worth loving. She loved me despite how tainted I was. She needed me despite the fact that I was a killer.

And she... well, she was the easiest person to love.

She pushed onto her tiptoes, her soft hips pressing against my groin, and I grunted into her mouth. Her arms wrapped around my neck, fingers tangling at my nape.

"I love you, Kingston," she breathed into my mouth.

Click.

My eyes snapped open to find the barrel of a gun pointed at me. The woman I dreamt about had her finger on the trigger and a pissed-off expression on her face. No—not the woman in my dream.

This woman, I should keep my distance from. Although, judging by the way her nostrils flared and her chest heaved, it might be too late.

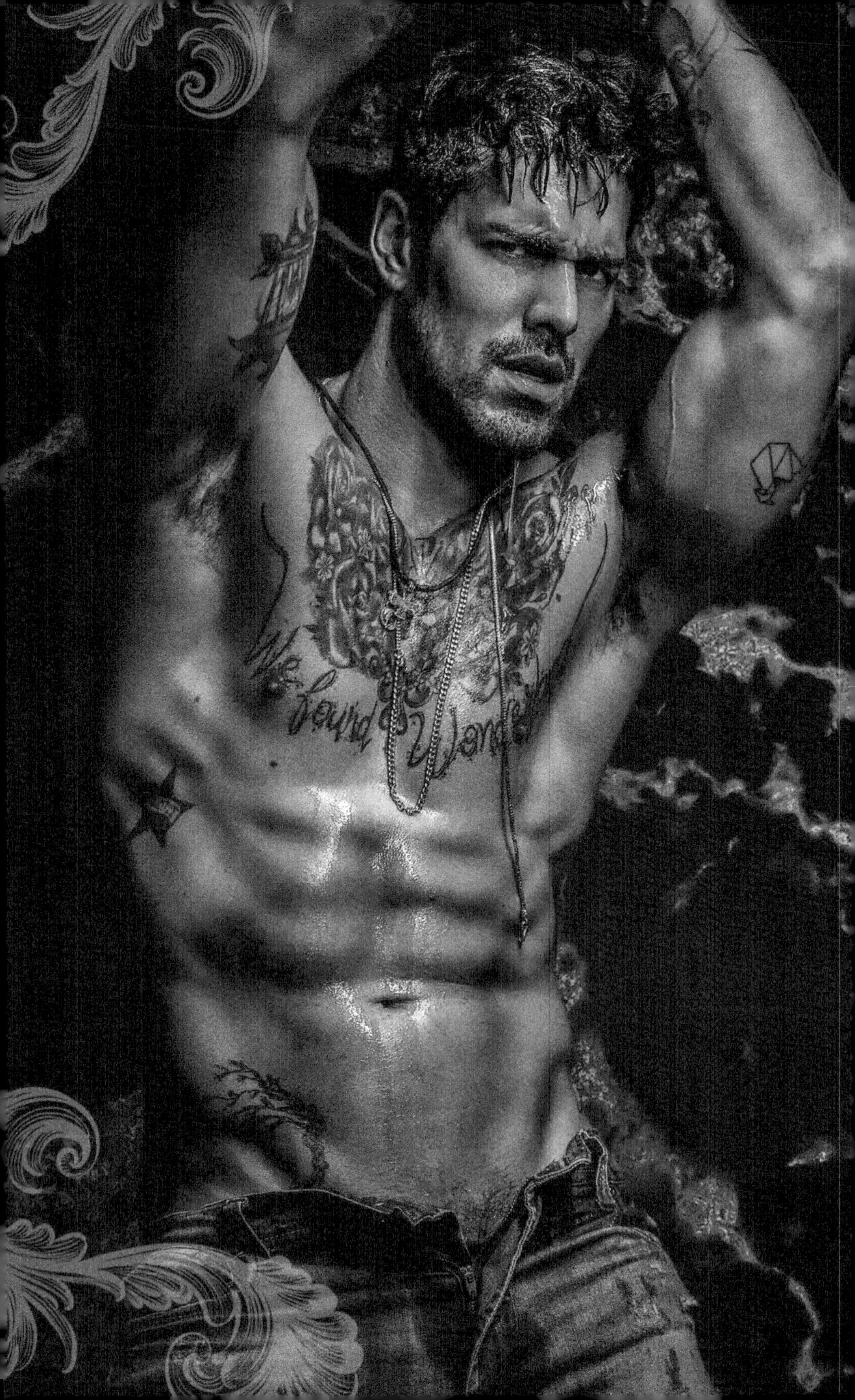

Chapter 23
Liana

Kingston Ashford was an asshole.

I should have sliced his throat while he slept, cut off his dick and put it in the blender, then forgot all about him. Instead, here I was, giving him a chance to fucking explain. His unaffected reaction to my gun in his face was enough to set me off all over again. Maybe I needed to try harder.

My lips curled into a smile.

"Name's Liana, dickwad," I said, compartmentalizing this pain in my chest. I gazed down at him, at his long limbs hanging out from his mussed sheets, and had to clear my brain of his intoxicating scent. "How did you know Louisa?"

I waited for an answer while debating how I'd end this man's life. Slow and painful, or quick and clean.

After he left, I cleaned up and got dressed in a pair of jeans and a shirt. There was no fucking way I'd remain under this roof after that performance. The dull roar between my ears made it hard to think, and it took several deep breaths before my pulse settled. He knew my twin, and then... did things to my body that made me feel alive for the first time in as long as I could remember.

Maybe that was his plan from the first time he saw me in the restaurant.

A shudder full of disgust ran down my spine.

My fingers itched to put a bullet into his skull or reach for my knife and plunge it into his neck so he'd bleed out—painfully slow.

"I asked you a question," I gritted.

"Did you?" The completely unruffled tone of his voice was starting to *really* grate on me now. Wasn't he scared? I could end him before he took his next breath, yet his eyes were devoid of emotion.

I shoved my gun into his temple, the cold metal meeting its target. "How did you know Louisa?"

My heart thundered with vengeance in my chest.

There was a beat of silence where he roamed his gaze over me chillingly. The man who I'd shared a brief moment of passion with was gone, not a single trace of him left.

"You should know," he said. What was this man *talking* about? We would be here all night at this rate. It suddenly occurred to me that I wouldn't get anything out of him. I should kill him, yet my hand trembled with the thought.

"If I knew, I wouldn't be asking you," I snapped.

He remained quiet, watching me in that unnerving way. I took one small step backward, keeping our eyes locked. *So I don't get blood on me,* I lied to myself with a sour taste in my mouth. Another step.

"Running already, ice princess?" His eyes glittered with something I couldn't understand or decipher, and I didn't like it.

Frustration bubbled inside me—at this man, at myself, at the gaping hole in my chest.

And I snapped.

I pulled the trigger, and the bullet lodged itself into the mahogany headboard, inches from where he was propped up. My heartbeats. His breaths. Animosity and confusion—his and mine—suffocating the air.

I couldn't stay here.

"You're fucking crazy," he gritted, his eyes turning dark as coal.

Reign of a Billionaire

I smirked, blinking innocently. "Oh, my bad. I was trying to flirt."

"Your flirting skills leave much to be desired," he muttered as he shifted, and my finger tightened on the trigger. "Don't you even think about pulling that trigger again. I'll come back from the dead and make you regret ever crossing paths with me."

I scoffed. "Too fucking late." Then I turned and ran.

Dread settled in the pit of my stomach, each step taking me away from him felt heavy, but I ignored it. On shaky legs that threatened to buckle my knees, I rushed down the busy D.C. street toward my rental car. I'd parked it strategically in an alley not far from where I fled the party mere hours ago.

The sun had long since set and the city flickered with lights while the cold bit at my cheeks. Kingston's guest room closet provided me with a change of clothes, even a pair of tennis shoes that were my size, but nothing warm, not even a hat or scarf.

I was such an idiot for going to his place. An idiot who let a handsome face lure me into his penthouse.

What was I even thinking?

I came out of the whole ordeal more confused than ever.

The flashing blue lights of a police car caught my eyes, but I ignored it as I rushed down the pavement. Loud laughter and party music pounded through the air, a nightclub nearby I imagined. People in various stages of intoxication passed me by, blissfully unaware of the misdeeds taking place around them.

"Louisa," called an unfamiliar voice, and my head whipped around, hearing the name that made my heart clench every time. A woman waved, and my brows pinched. I didn't know her. And, more importantly, I wasn't Louisa. Just then, a girl flew past me, almost knocking into me, and joined her friends. That familiar loneliness wrapped its invisible hand around my neck and I swallowed the lump in my throat.

Twice in the same night. What were the fucking odds?

Maybe it was the universe warning me of dangers that surrounded me. Mother. The cartels. My feeble attempt at saving innocents. But I couldn't stop. Not while there was a single breath left in my body. The fear in my gut twisted into the same fury that had kept me going since learning of my sister's death. It was poisonous and vengeful, a fierce determination driving me forward.

Another cold breeze swept through, and I clenched my teeth as a shiver skidded down my spine.

I'd seen too much death. Too much pain. In my past. In my present. I couldn't bear to think of a future that went on in this way. I'd been trying to make a difference, but instead I felt as if I'd lost myself. In bloodlust. Revenge. Hatred.

I shook my head, chasing all the ghosts away. I wasn't ready to deal with them. Not now. Not here.

"Hey, babe. You look like you need a man to warm you up tonight."

I ignored the shrewd comment. Men were pigs, thinking they could spin some lame line and get laid.

I continued on, my tennis shoes silent against the pavement. As I moved through the crowd of people, I had only one thing on my mind: escape. I needed to get to my car and leave this sick city behind. The street finally quieted down, but the hair on the back of my neck stood on end, and I looked around frantically. I spotted my car, and my step faltered.

I didn't park my rental all the way back here. It was a basic rule of safety—never put yourself in a position where you might be cornered.

Taking a deep breath, I looked up at the dark sky and exhaled. I needed to get back to Russia before my mother noticed I was gone. Christmas was days away and she never missed a holiday—no matter what crisis was unfolding in the world.

I started walking, my steps hasty and my senses vigilant, keeping my eyes on my surroundings. It was as silent as a graveyard.

I was in a full jog when I heard an eerie sound. *Beep. Beep. Beep.*

It was faint, but it might as well have been church bells. My gaze traveled over the car, realization forming in the pit of my stomach. Without wasting a breath, I turned to run back.

Reign of a Billionaire

But it was too late.

The ground beneath my feet rumbled. Heat seared my spine, and I fell to the ground with plaster and debris falling all around me. My face smashed into the hard pavement, knocking the breath out of me. I gasped, attempting to roll onto my back, when I felt a thud at my temple.

Then it all went black.

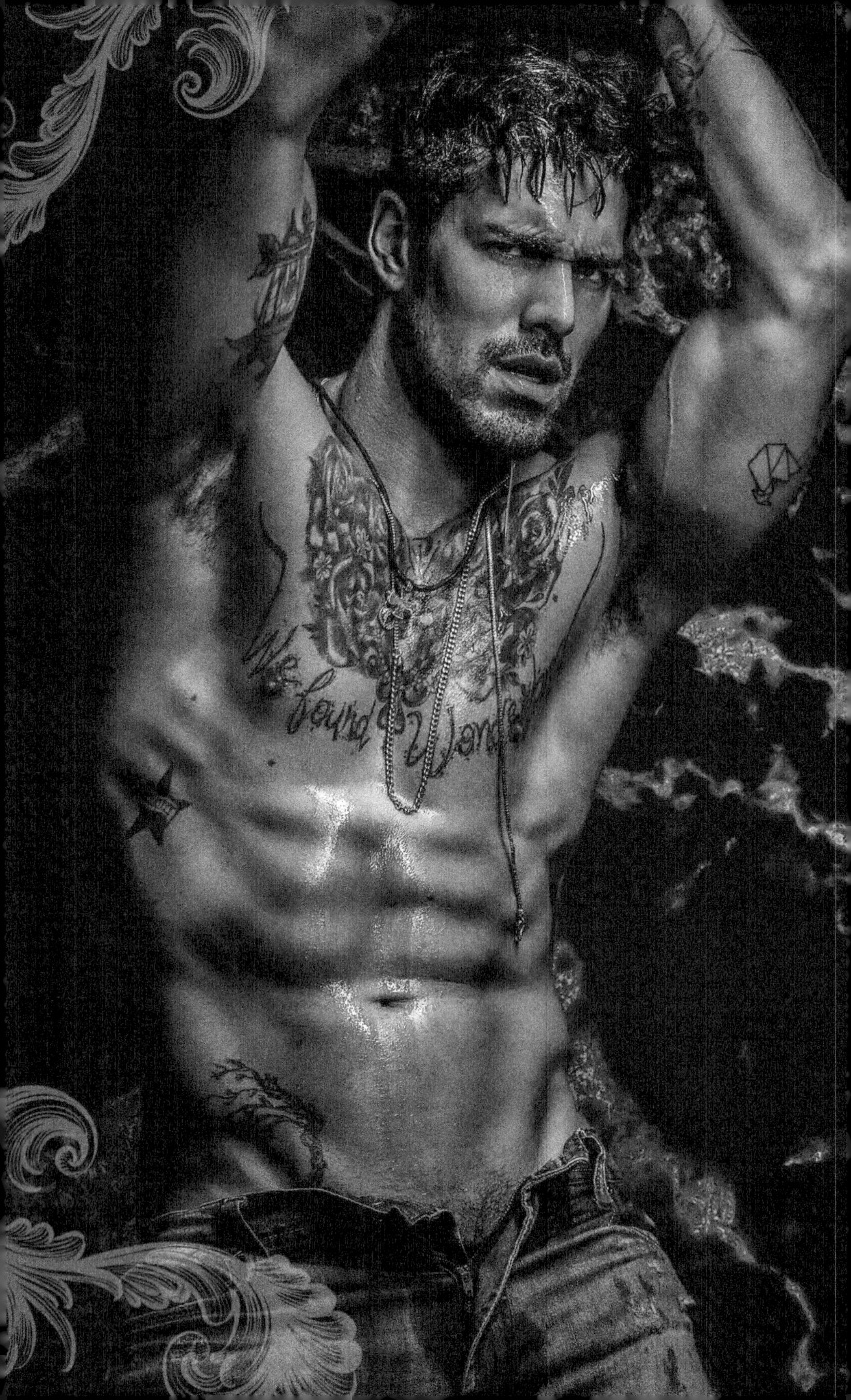
We found

Chapter 24
Liana

"**I**s that her?" I heard a man mutter. "If it's not, Perez will have our balls. Santiago doesn't give a shit as long as it has a pussy."

"It's her." A chuckle filled the darkness, making my heart gallop. "If it isn't, I'm fucking keeping her."

My eyes fluttered open, my tongue heavy in my mouth. I attempted to move, but found myself unable to. A cold sweat broke out across my skin as I was dragged toward a car, each movement causing my flesh to burn.

The fuckers sedated me.

In the next second, I was thrown onto a hard leather seat. The car pulled out and sped down the road, jostling me around on the back seat. A sharp turn had me rolling onto the floor, and a shooting pain exploded in my skull. Clearly they didn't care whether I made it to where we were going in one piece.

"Sofia Volkov will bring out the big guns when she learns another of her daughters has been taken."

I attempted to thrash, move, but it was futile. I had to settle down; I refused to let terror overwhelm me. If I did, I'd spiral.

Taking a deep breath in, I exhaled, focusing on slowing my heartbeat. Was this my end? No, it couldn't be. I still had so much to resolve. There were still things I didn't understand. My thoughts flitted to the man who'd been infiltrating my dreams. The faceless man. The similarities I found between Kingston Ashford and a ghost that kept hiding from me.

I had to survive this and get to the bottom of who and what Kingston Ashford was and why he bore similarities to the faceless man.

The car came to a sudden stop, halting all my thoughts and jolting me back into my body. The back door opened, and a set of strong hands scooped me off the floor. I peeked through my eyelashes and my breath caught. The hand wrapped around my waist had a skull tattoo on it. The very same one as the head of the Tijuana cartel.

The driver muttered a curse, then gritted, "Your uncle said to bring her to him. He and Cortes have an understanding."

"That's null and void." The grave, vaguely familiar voice belonged to a beast of a man who threw me over his shoulder and started walking. It wasn't long before he ascended the stairs. Nausea rippled through my insides—I'd never been able to tolerate drugs well.

Suddenly, the man holding me like a sack of potatoes stopped, took a left, and entered a room, throwing me onto the bed. My body bounced off the soft mattress, and I *hated* that I was so weak. I needed to find a way to shake the fog off.

My flesh crawled at the thought of him—anyone—touching me. I tried to roll off the bed, but this damn weakness refused to give way. I swore to God, if he touched me, I'd slit his throat.

"Relax, I have no intention of touching you."

My nostrils flared and I cleared my throat painfully. "What?" I croaked. "Too good to touch me?"

Okay, that was dumb. I blamed the drugs. I forced myself to shift on the bed as the drowsiness began to wane.

"If you want me to touch you, just say the word," he drawled with

Reign of a Billionaire

a smooth smile. The tightness in my chest loosened, and I released a long breath. "But we'll wait for the drugs to leave your system."

I wasn't fooled by his handsome face. His hair was perfectly styled, and his jaw was freshly shaved. The olive skin accentuated his green eyes. He was dressed sharply, and I wondered if he normally kidnapped women in a custom suit or if this was a special occasion.

"Who are you?" I asked, unable to keep the animosity from my voice. Years of hostility toward any man in the mafia had become part of my DNA. Besides, the Tijuana cartel was responsible for my twin's murder. That alone was enough to have hate simmering through my veins.

"Giovanni Agosti." He made an exaggerated bow while flashing me a smile.

I rolled my eyes. "Let me guess, you're single."

He flashed another smile, even as his green eyes narrowed. "How did you know?"

Running out of patience and pissed off that I'd let myself get taken, I ran through what I knew of the men in the mafia. I didn't recall hearing of Giovanni Agosti, but couldn't shake off the feeling that I should have.

"Mateo Agosti," I blurted. "Any relation?"

"My uncle."

My brows furrowed and I gritted my teeth. "He runs the Italian mafia in Boston," I remarked. "How is he connected to the Tijuana cartel?"

"He isn't." He watched me like a hawk. "I am. Santiago Tijuana's my uncle." I nodded but didn't say anything else, not knowing what to say or ask without exposing how little I knew about the Agosti family and their criminal empire. He chuckled softly. "You aren't going to ask me for details? After all, it's a well-kept secret."

I tilted my chin, watching him pensively. There were so many damn secrets in the underworld; I'd stopped asking questions a long time ago. At the end of the day, it came down to right and wrong, and *our* choices. Our lineage wasn't something we had control over.

Finally, I shook my head. "No. I have enough of my own crosses to bear. What do Perez Cortes and your uncle want with me?" I asked instead, studiously observing him.

"You caused my uncle quite the headache. Do you even know how much he would have made from those women?"

"*Innocent* women." I gritted my teeth, not seeing the use in denying my involvement. They had me—the jig was up. "Some underage."

Giovanni sighed, pushing his hand through his hair. "If you would have waited, I'd have taken care of it."

My heart stilled as I stared at him, my eyebrows shooting to my hairline. "Elaborate," I demanded.

He waved his hand in dismissal. "It's a moot point now. My uncle was going to punish you." He didn't need to elaborate for me to understand what he meant. Like I said, men were pigs. "Then he was going to hand you over to Perez Cortes for his upcoming auction."

"Auction?" I repeated flatly, not trusting him enough to reveal what I knew. This auction topic had been thrown around a lot lately, and I was sick and tired of hearing about it. Then there was the whole thing of me being tossed on the chopping block.

"He's been collecting notable daughters of prominent figures, mafia princesses from families that have fucked him over." The unspoken word hung in the air. He knew I fucked Cortes over, rescuing innocent girls from his trafficking ring.

My hands curled into fists. I wished I could get my hands on Perez Cortes and wring his neck. Destroy his whole operation from within.

And this was my chance. Possibly my only chance.

I squared my shoulders and looked up to find Giovanni Agosti watching me, his eyes hard, dangerous. But still, something told me he wasn't anything like his uncle.

"Are you involved in human trafficking?"

"I'm not. There are plenty of women who *want* to work in that industry, why would I go through the trouble?"

Reign of a Billionaire

I pulled my arms across my chest and jutted out my chin. He wasn't wrong, and I had to hand it to him for acknowledging a woman's right to choose how to live her life. "Now, Giovanni Agosti," I started with a smug expression. There was no way in hell I'd be going back to Russia to deal with my mother now, and I was done being a puppet. "How would you like me to kill your uncle and, in turn, you deliver me to Perez Cortes?"

"That's an interesting proposition," he remarked, his eyes flaring. If he was surprised, he wasn't letting it show. "Tell me more."

And that was how the most unlikely of alliances was made.

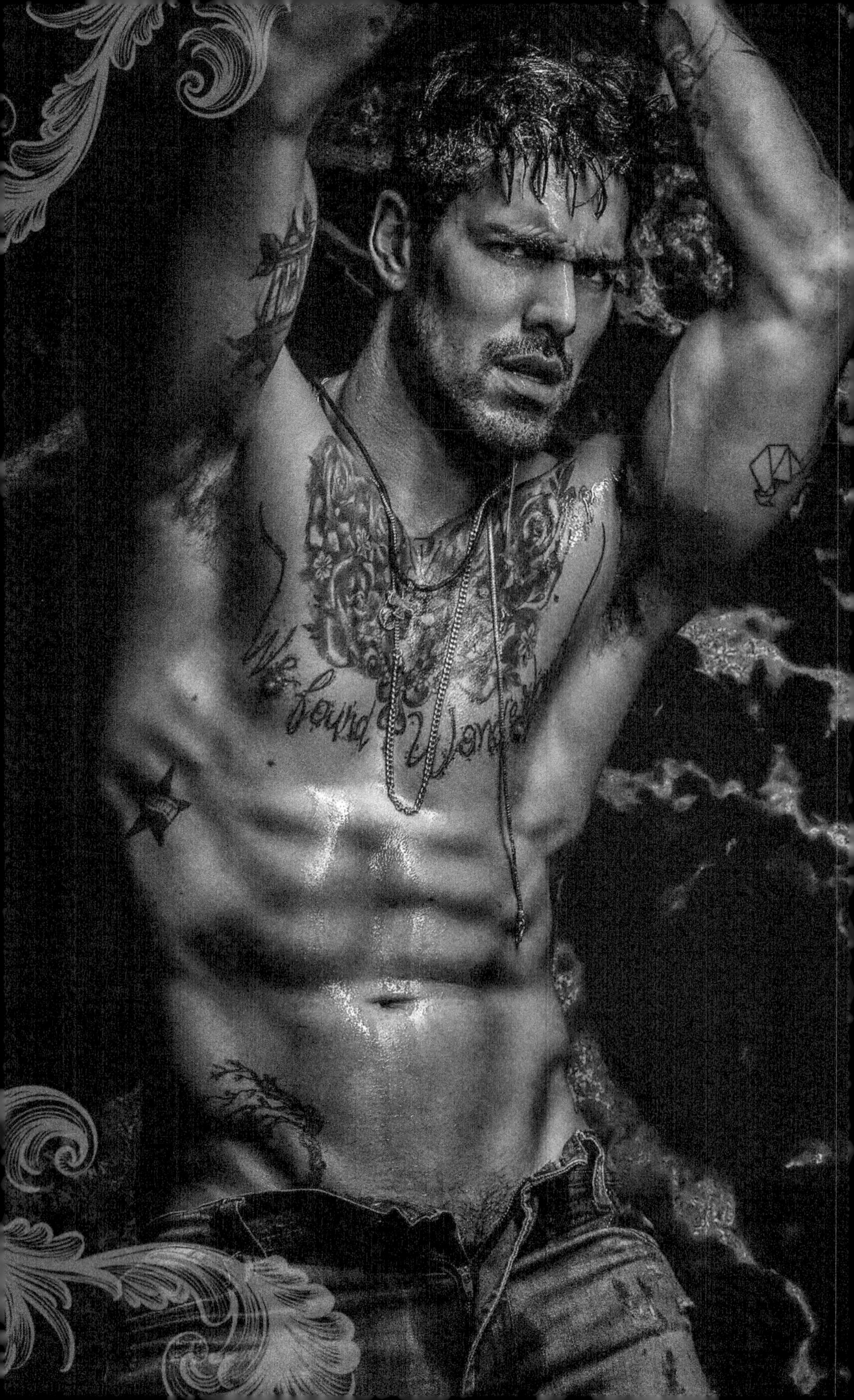

Chapter 25
Liana

G iovanni had parked his Land Rover in front of the Georgetown manor that was bought on the backs of human trafficking victims. Literally.

"Stop smiling," Giovanni reprimanded.

I rolled my eyes, raising my bound hands. "Relax, freak. This will work."

His eyes blazed with annoyance. "Not if you're smiling like you're happy to be here," he growled.

"Would you rather I cried?"

"No. But at least act scared so he's not suspicious."

My "captor" didn't seem to have a rich imagination. Giovanni liked my plan but didn't want me executing it. As if he could ever be the one to do it. First, he had a dick. Second, Santiago was his uncle.

Case closed.

"Just get me in," I muttered. "I have a knife tucked under my shirt. Once I'm alone with him in the bedroom, you get rid of the guards."

He shook his head. "I cannot risk him—"

I cut him off with an exasperated breath. "He won't rape me. I'll never let it get that far."

My voice betrayed none of the anxiety I felt inside. I'd gotten good at hiding my emotions. From the looks of it, Giovanni was an expert too. I could practically see his mask slide into place, his face all harsh lines and hard angles.

"Once you end him, take the servants' stairs. There's a door underneath that will lead you to the side street. Wait for me there."

I rolled my eyes again. "You've got to learn to say please."

Without answering, he exited the car, slammed the door, then came around. I bit the inside of my cheek, my heart reeling with so many emotions. Santiago Tijuana was the last man to see my sister alive. He owed me an answer and a life.

Today, we'd settle the score. I only wished I could take my time and make him wail like a pig for days on end.

The passenger door opened, Giovanni's body hiding me, and I opened my mouth so he could gag me. There's a first, I thought drily. He was lucky I was desperate to get my hands on his uncle.

"This better work," he muttered under his breath, barely moving his lips while securing the gag.

I blinked, communicating to him that it would. It had to.

Giovanni threw me over his shoulder—the man had some serious caveman energy—then made his way to the gate that surrounded a charming little mansion with a monster inside.

There had been guards all around, but nobody reacted to seeing me manhandled. It would seem this was a regular occurrence.

Showtime.

I started kicking, my muffled protest barely audible as I fought against the man who was delivering me to the cartel that killed my sister. God knew my mother played the video enough times while torturing me.

As my phony captor made his way into the manor, my half-assed attempt to struggle against Giovanni convinced the guards that I wasn't here of my own free will.

This plan would work.

"Boss's nephew is here," one of the guards spoke into his earpiece. "Alert him."

Yes, alert him, I thought smugly while adrenaline pumped through my veins. We needed the fucker present and accounted for.

Giovanni strolled inside, up the staircase, and through the hallway until a voice shattered through my erratic heartbeat. A set of doors opened with a loud bang, and I twisted around, seeing my target at the threshold of his bedroom suite.

He looked like a twisted '70s porn star, wearing a robe and slippers with a gold chain around his neck. I decided, right there and then, I'd strangle him with it.

"You brought her to me." Fuck, even his voice was putrid. "I thought you might still be mad at me. That you'd want to keep her for—"

Giovanni cut him off. "I told you that was water under the bridge, Uncle."

My eyebrows hit my hairline. What was Giovanni mad at his uncle about? Aside from human trafficking, obviously. But before I could ponder it further, Giovanni was inside the ridiculously gaudy suite of Santiago Tijuana, throwing me on the mattress. For the second time in one night.

Motherfucker.

He turned his back to me and stood there, blocking me from his uncle's view and giving me a chance to grab my knife. I hid it between my bound wrists and let the rope glide over the blade. Once. Twice. I left the third one for my final act.

"You can go," the old fucker dismissed him. "I have to teach this one a lesson."

I sensed more than saw Giovanni stiffen. Then, he strode out of there without a single objection. The door closed behind him, his footsteps fading with each second.

Dreadful silence, eerie and disturbing, filled the space like poison.

"You're pretty." His voice slid over me, but I remained still. "We're going to play now," Santiago purred, tracing his hand down my spine. I fought disgust at being touched, forcing myself not to react too soon. "You know why you're here?"

I shook my head, my fingers closing around the knife and gripping it hard. The old Santiago ground against me, his blunt bulge rubbing against the curve of my ass. Bile rose in my throat, feeling his hands on my body. Anticipation wrapped around my throat like a vise, cutting off my air.

But my mind remained clear. It was amazing what years of training could do.

"Fuck, how is it that you're prettier than your sister?" Lead settled in my gut. I wanted to lash out. Slice him into tiny pieces while he was still alive, so he could feel the pain. Instead, I waited. "She fought like a wild cat. Bled like a pig."

Blinding fury roared to life, causing my chest to heave and blood to rush in my ears. No more waiting. It was time to avenge my twin. It was time to make this bastard pay.

I shifted around, and with the last glide of the blade against the ropes that bound me, I was free. In one swift move, I twisted myself up to straddle him and brought my blade to his throat.

"Scream and I'll bleed you like a pig." Gripping a fistful of his hair, I shoved his face against the mattress. "Now let's play, old man."

"You stupid bitch," he spat. "You'll never get out of this alive."

"Oh, but I will," I drawled. "You though, old fucker, you're going to die." I dragged the tip of my blade, cutting the skin on his neck enough to bleed but not enough to slice into his artery.

The bastard didn't know how far I was willing to go.

"Even if you escape me, you won't escape him." He attempted to fight me, gasping for air. "Perez will end you. Just like he ended your sister."

I froze, my heart stopping before jumpstarting into turbo mode. Santiago shifted his bulky form, but I tightened my grip on him. First, I needed answers. His death would come soon enough.

Reign of a Billionaire

"You ended my sister," I hissed. "I've seen the video."

He attempted to fight me off, but the fucker was too out of shape and too old to stand a chance. "It wasn't me."

Blood dripped against his crisp white sheets. He bucked against me, and I moved the blade to the base of his neck. "Utter one more lie," I gritted, "and I'll make you bleed, nice and slow, so you can feel every drop of blood as it leaves your body."

He stilled, fear clouding around him like a disease.

"It's true. She didn't die while under my care. Perez took her, then sold her using one of his Marabella Mobster arrangements."

Images flashed through my mind. The video of her screaming while her body dissolved in a tub.

"Liar!" Fury surged through me, the room suddenly enveloped in a red haze. "I saw her body disintegrate with my own eyes. The video originated from your compound."

The man laughed. "Stupid bitch." I shivered from the fear and hope invading my entire being. Should I wish my twin alive or dead, I didn't know. "It was doctored."

My eyes welled up with confusion, but also hope.

"So she's alive?" I ignored the way my voice cracked. It had nothing on the way my heart splintered. He laughed again, making my rage burn hotter. "Is. She. Alive?"

"Maybe. Maybe not."

Hope and despair were at war in my chest. All these years, I'd never envisioned the possibility of her being alive.

"My mother..." My voice betrayed none of the turmoil inside of me. Unshed tears burned in my eyes, but I refused to let them fall. "What does she know?"

He shrugged. "Why don't you ask her?"

Mother lied to me, I realized with a new level of hatred. I always knew she was twisted, but this... this was a new low, even for her. My twin had a chance at being saved, and Mother did nothing. Fucking nothing!

Fury, hotter than ever, burned through me, making me see red.

Clenching my teeth, I pressed the blade farther into his flesh. "I'm asking you, suka."

"My guess is she knows it all," he gritted.

"You're lying," I said, desperation leaking into my voice.

He turned his head and smirked. "Am I?" Through the fog of pain, I knew he had to be taunting me. Stalling. "Your best bet is Perez if you want to find out where she is." Is! Present tense. Before my hope could ignite further, he added, "Dead or alive."

A tight band of anger wrapped around my ribs, turning my breaths shallow. This fury was directed at my mother. At the entire shitty underworld that used and abused innocent women.

In a sudden and precise move, I sliced his neck wide open. I slid off of him, careful not to get his blood on me. Instinctively, he reached up to stop the bleeding, but the gash in his neck was too deep. I took a step back, watching him gasp for air.

Blood soaked through his fingers, turning them crimson.

I didn't move, not until the last flicker of life faded from his eyes.

As I stood there and took in my work, I decided that I would never go back to my mother. I'd find my twin—dead or alive—and take her where she always wanted to go.

Chapter 26
Kingston

The church was brimming with people who came to mourn —or celebrate—the death of Santiago Tijuana Sr. The man was a piece of scum who had it coming, but that didn't stop people from putting on a whole dog and pony show.

There were slimy politicians, leaders of various criminal organizations, and any other gutless criminal with ties to the underworld. Human hypocrisy always amazed me.

But then, I was here too, along with Enrico Marchetti, Kian Cortes, Giovanni Agosti, Lykos Costello, and the Callahans. Of course, Perez Cortes wasn't here—not that anyone expected him to be.

"Are you ready to take over the Tijuana cartel?" Enrico asked Giovanni, the latter in a piss-poor mood since he stepped foot into this church. Nobody wanted to be here, but he seemed particularly eager for an out.

"You weren't the one who killed him, right?" Aiden was the more reasonable Callahan. His brothers—reckless twins—apparently had a bet going that Giovanni had been the one to finally end his uncle.

"No."

"What's the problem, then?" demanded Enrico.

Giovanni's jaw clenched and his green eyes flashed angrily. "No problem at all."

"Do we have any other information on Sofia Volkov's daughter?" Marchetti's words had my full attention.

"I do." My eyes narrowed on Aiden. He better not be stalking my target, or I'd pull out all his fucking teeth and make him look like a ninety-year-old man. My darkness was tempted by hers, and while a sane person would reason it was a recipe for disaster, I wouldn't argue. "I haven't validated the source yet." Awkward silence surrounded our pew. Most men here wanted to end Sofia Volkov and anything she represented, including her kin.

I, on the other hand, had an entirely different revenge plan in place—one that needed Liana alive.

"Well, don't keep us in suspense, dear brother," one of the Callahan twins muttered.

"There was an explosion a few days ago in D.C., a car bomb apparently. A setup by Perez Cortes targeted at Sofia Volkov."

The news hit me like a sledgehammer, my chest twisting painfully while I kept my expression blank.

"We need to get our hands on her daughter," Marchetti gritted. He'd had a chip on his shoulder—much like the rest of us—ever since Sofia tortured his wife. "And I don't want my wife knowing about it."

"It would give us leverage," Aiden agreed. "Except she's dead." When everyone's eyes snapped to him, he explained, "A burnt body was found in the explosion, identified as Liana Volkov."

Tense silence followed, but it had nothing to do with the holy establishment we were in.

"Why would Perez want her dead? He had a business relationship with her mother." Kian voiced the question everyone was thinking. Except I knew the answer: Liana tampered with Perez's business. Sofia might have refused to admit it, but Perez clearly saw the truth.

Guilt squeezed my chest, tightening my throat. I should have grabbed Liana the minute I saw her alive and breathing, careful planning be damned.

Aiden shrugged. "No idea."

"That doesn't make any sense." Kian's brow creased. "Just twenty-four hours ago, he announced a flesh auction with Liana Volkov being presented for sale. If the fetched price isn't adequate, he'll use the Marabella Mobster arrangements." My eyes sharpened and a red alert shot through me. Perez wouldn't be so stupid. "Why would he rally buyers if she was dead?"

"If she's alive, we need to get our hands on her," Marchetti hissed. "I want leverage on her bitch mother."

I jumped to my feet and left the church without another word, then typed out a message to my brother Winston.

He promised me his jet months ago. I was about to take him up on it and disappear again.

The moment I entered my flat, I really wished I hadn't.

My brothers stood around my space like judges, juries, and executioners. And they wasted no time descending on me like goddamned flies. The only one who stood casually, taking no part in this, was Alessio, my eldest, illegitimate brother. In fact, he looked like he'd rather not be here at all.

"I hear you have a girl," Royce blurted out, grinning like a fool. "An actual girl, not a blow-up doll."

I side-eyed him. He might have some freaky tendencies, but I didn't. "I don't," I deadpanned, flicking a glance at Winston.

"I didn't tell him a thing," he grumbled.

"It's true," Royce agreed. "It was Aurora." I would need to have a conversation with my sister about details that should never be shared with my brothers, especially Royce. "And I saw the warning you made public, saying a certain woman is off-limits."

Because I made a promise, I thought silently. There was nothing more to it. That little moment of shared passion was insignificant. *Liar!* The devil and angel on my shoulder called bullshit.

"I'm really worried about you," Byron interjected, always the protective big brother. "You shouldn't go after Sofia Volkov alone. She's dangerous, and we don't want anything to happen to you. At least let us help."

"I work better alone." It was the truth. Besides, I'd done unimaginable things while my brothers killed for our country. Well, except for Alessio. He'd endured some shit too, but I didn't know him well enough to accept his offer of help.

"You think you could figure out who this belongs to?" Royce asked, ignoring my non-answer and pulling a bloody bag with a body part from his pocket.

"What the fuck?" Winston growled. "Is that a finger?"

Alessio shook his head. "You're a sick motherfucker, Royce."

Byron looked at his watch. "Well, Royce. You started this shit, getting us all to come here. Now say your piece, and do something with that bloody finger so we can all get back to our lives."

"I was in Venezuela for a business trip." My eyebrows shot up, but I didn't say anything. "On my last day there, I found this in my hotel fridge."

"Jesus," Byron muttered. "Why didn't you call the local police?"

That would make sense for my brothers who were, for the most part, law-abiding citizens, but nothing Royce did made sense. "And the local police is corrupt as fuck there."

Without a look in Royce's direction, I asked, "And you thought you should bring it to me, *why?*"

"Because it was addressed to the Ghost. Or Kingston Ashford."

The tension amplified, something shifting in the air. I reached for it and made my way to the freezer. Once I threw it in an empty spot, I turned around and faced them all.

"Next time, write an email. And don't bring me body parts," I snapped. "Unless they're teeth."

"Jesus, here we go," Winston grumbled. "Just don't do it in front of Billie. She's still scared to be around you." Byron leaned against the wall, not in any hurry to shut Royce up. "But if you want to end our crazy brother," Winston continued, giving a pointed look at Royce, "I'll help you bury the body."

"I won't need help," I said, my words reverberating off the walls.

Royce grinned. "You wish you were that good."

"I am." There was no boasting in my voice. In order to survive under Sofia's and Ivan's thumbs, I had to become the best in everything. I had to become a living nightmare.

Strained silence reigned for a moment, then Royce's booming laughter filled the space. He was the only one who saw humor in everything. It was enough to drive anyone insane.

"Body part aside, what are you all really doing here?" I asked.

"Why is there a bullet in the headboard of your bed?" Byron changed subjects.

"Why were you in my bedroom?"

"Royce was convinced you were hiding from us," he deadpanned.

Disbelief had me angling my head and crossing my arms. "In the bedroom?"

Sometimes having brothers sucked. They were so fucking nosy. I didn't even know how they'd gathered this latest information. It was the reason I rarely stayed in D.C. and had properties around the world that nobody knew about.

My expression blank, I let my eyes roam over each of my siblings. "Want to check out my bathrooms too?"

Winston folded his arms and declared, "Too late, Royce has already been there and done that."

"Privacy must be an unfamiliar concept," I deadpanned, narrowing my eyes on my brother. "When I agreed to getting this place, you all promised me my privacy," I reminded them. "The keys I made for you are for emergencies only."

"Most of us didn't go snooping around your penthouse." Alessio regarded me with a dry expression. Then he narrowed his eyes on Royce. "Only the guy with the finger in his pocket did."

"Nobody was snooping," Royce corrected him. "We wanted to clean it for you."

"Would you shut the fuck up about the snooping and cleaning?" Winston drawled, rolling a cigarette between his fingers.

"If Kingston has a girl, we have to vet her." Royce made no fucking sense sometimes. "And if she's shooting at you—" He slid his hands into his pockets, rocking back on his heels. "Yeah, we can't have that."

"I. Don't. Have. A. Girl." My teeth were clenched so hard, my molars were about to crack.

"Ohhh... okaaaay," Royce appeased with a drawl, rolling his eyes.

My gaze flicked to Winston, who shrugged his shoulders and raised his hands in surrender. "Don't look at me."

"Who's this girl?" Byron stared at me, nothing but genuine interest and concern in his eyes. "We just want to meet her."

I headed past them, making my way to the bar. If my siblings were planning on lingering, I'd need a stiff one.

I poured myself a glass of whiskey, then glanced over my shoulder. "Help yourselves."

Winston shook his head. He gave up alcohol for his wife. Alessio and Byron poured themselves drinks, and Royce went for a beer.

"You know, baby brother, if she's trying to kill you, you might need to let her free," Royce stated, circling back to the previous topic. Unfortunately. "This girl might not be the right one."

"I don't have a girl," I pointed out again. Clearly, he was slow to grasp. "You've made a wrong assumption. Again."

"It's not what I'm hearing," Royce muttered. "That bullet in your headboard says star-crossed lovers heading for tragedy."

"It worked for Romeo and Juliet," I deadpanned.

"They ended up dead," Byron pointed out.

I shrugged. "We all die one day."

"Morbid, but true," Alessio agreed. "Is there a reason your girl would want you dead?"

I didn't answer. There was no easy way to explain it. Or maybe there was, but I wouldn't give it to them.

"Do you want us to *take care* of her?" Royce's words barely left his mouth before I was in his face.

"You get anywhere near her, I'll fucking kill you." The threat slipped through my lips effortlessly. It was a big fucking slipup. "She's mine to take care of."

Over my dead body would I let anyone—including my own brothers—touch Liana. If my promise to Lou ended up broken, it would be because I did it.

Someone in the room let out a low whistle, but I kept my eyes on Royce. My brother stared at me for a heartbeat before breaking out into a full-blown grin.

"You really like her." After a long moment of silence, he slapped my shoulder. "I guess we're gonna have two mad killers in our family."

"How do you know she's a killer?" Winston questioned.

"Nico Morrelli," Alessio answered.

"Word is that Sofia Volkov's daughter has been working behind her mother's back," Royce supplied.

It was the single topic that had been avoided like bullets in our family since I resurfaced. The name hovered in the air, stained with filth. Yet today, it was thrown around like candy.

"Was the finger the reason for your sudden interest?" I demanded, watching Royce like a hawk.

"Yes," he admitted. "I wanted to spare you."

"And you thought you'd learn who that body part belonged to... How?" Winston asked incredulously.

Royce just shrugged. "People talk."

"What does she have against you?" Byron asked, ignoring Royce, who was obviously full of shit. "Why is she shooting at you?"

I shrugged, unwilling to admit her sister's name slipped through my lips after I'd come into my hand like a teenage boy. It would require more explanation, and I wasn't willing to go there with them.

"Maybe if you show her the old you..." Winston watched me as I stilled. My brothers still looked for that Kingston—unwilling to come to terms with his metaphorical death.

My life had become tightly intertwined with the underworld. I could cut all ties, but even then, I'd forever be the ghost. The killer. The boy who fought to survive.

"Do you want to kill her?" Royce joked, sipping his beer with a smirk. "Or want us to give you pointers on how to win her over?"

"Jesus, don't take any advice from Royce," Winston muttered. "You're gonna lose your woman before you even get her."

"Just tell us what help you need from us," Byron offered, picking up on my silence.

I downed my drink in one go and locked eyes with Winston. "I'm gonna need that jet, big brother," I reminded him. It was something I'd lined up with him almost a year ago. Of course, I never thought it'd take this long to get my hands on *her*.

He nodded.

"Are you sure it's smart to fuck with anything related to Sofia Volkov? Anyone with a will to live would keep the fuck away." Alessio's question was warranted, but I wasn't just anyone, and my will to live was extinguished eight years ago.

"Except she isn't with Sofia," I said. Once she was in Cortes's clutches, it'd be harder to get her back. If she was about to be put up for auction, he'd be damn sure to make her life hell. "Perez plans to use her for a flesh auction, or the Marabella arrangements if he doesn't fetch the right price."

My brothers' eyes on me, I suddenly knew without a doubt that—with them on my side—nothing could stop me.

"I don't follow." Alessio cleared his throat. "Are you going to participate in the auction?"

It was my last resort. "I made a promise a while back. Sofia's daughter is part of that promise. Besides, it'll be killing two birds with one stone. Sofia will go nuts, and I get to keep my promise."

Understanding washed over their expressions.

"What do you need us to do?" Royce asked.

"It's best you don't know where I go, and don't look for me while I'm gone," I said seriously. "Once I have her, I'm going to disappear for a while."

And the Omertà wouldn't find us.

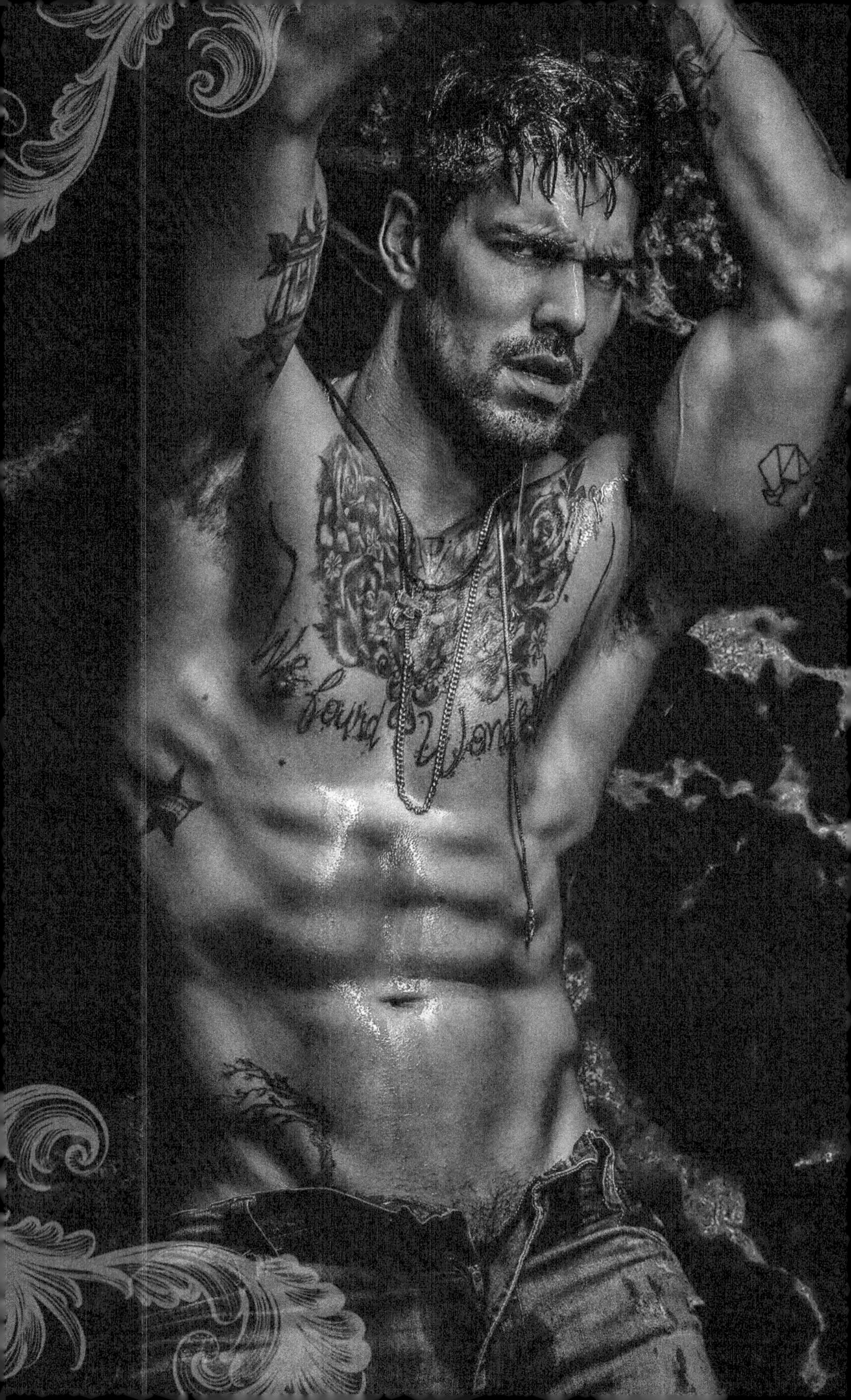

Chapter 27
Liana

The sound of shattering glass woke me up.

I jolted upright, my eyes landing on the bedside table. I blinked as the digits came into focus. It was almost eleven in the morning. I gasped, realizing I'd slept for almost twelve hours straight. I hadn't slept that long in... forever.

"Who in the fuck puts a glass on the edge of the counter?" came Giovanni's irritated voice.

I winced, knowing full well I was the culprit. Giovanni didn't have maids, and I was too accustomed to someone cleaning up after me. During the past three days, it had become obvious to me that Giovanni was a happy bachelor. He didn't like people in his space, but he insisted I hide in his penthouse. It wasn't the ideal cohabitation scenario.

The world thought I was dead. My phone—all of my purse contents, actually, were destroyed in the explosion. But here I was, lying low and plotting.

My throat tightened for a moment, remembering all the times my sister and I had drawn up escape plans growing up. Even when we were little and could be easily distracted from what went on in the dungeons of our estate in Russia, we were always looking ahead at a life where we'd be free of our mother and Ivan.

And here I was now—free of my mother. Lou would be so excited at our prospects.

God, I missed her. I hadn't been there to save her. To protect her. *Why*, dammit? For the life of me, I couldn't remember anything but what my mother told me. However, after the comment by Giovanni's uncle, I was starting to suspect my mother's words had all been lies. Except, what was the truth?

All of this was slowly driving me insane.

But if I stayed the course and let Giovanni help me, I'd take everyone responsible for my sister's destiny down. Some parts of the plan were finally unfolding, and my lips curled into a smile remembering how we ended the old Santiago Tijuana, making him scream like a pig.

Exhaling, I wiped a hand over my eyes. I'd be lying if I said I hadn't enjoyed the sound of his agonizing gurgles. He deserved it. Perez would get to taste my wrath soon too.

But none of it compared to learning that my sister—my other half—could be alive.

"Don't get your hopes up, Liana," I rasped, my voice barely above a whisper. The likelihood of any woman surviving eight years of hell was slim.

The door to my sanctuary suddenly opened and Giovanni stood there, wearing a black suit. Tucking all my turmoil behind a mask, I flashed him a reserved smile.

"How was church?" I asked, sliding out of bed. I didn't reveal the conversation I'd had with his uncle. Trust was a lesson I didn't need right now. All I needed to know was that Giovanni, as the head of the Tijuana cartel, wouldn't continue human trafficking. That was where our relationship started and ended.

"Very preachy."

I snickered. Stretching my arms wide in the air, I continued, "It didn't go up in flames with so many sinners in one spot?"

Reign of a Billionaire

The ridiculously large clothes hung off me, making me appear like a damn kid. But it was all Giovanni had, and I was thankful not to have to sleep in my undergarments. I didn't trust anyone that much.

"It didn't."

I let out a sigh. "That's a shame." I flipped my hair out of my face and smiled savagely. "I kind of hoped it would. Burn all those motherfuckers to ash."

I didn't care that it implied he'd get swept up in the fire. We were reluctant, temporary partners *at best*. There'd be no love lost, and he knew it, so why pretend?

He let out a sardonic breath. "I can't decide whether you're reckless or just crazy."

I flashed him a too-sweet smile.

"Maybe a little bit of both." Our gazes locked, and I thought back to the first time I saw him. "What was the deal with you and my mother back at the hotel lobby?" I asked, referencing the coded conversation that was impossible to follow.

He shrugged. "I was delivering my uncle's message." My eyebrows knitted as he continued, "I had to play my part in his schemes."

"What schemes?"

"His human trafficking deals with your mother."

I stiffened. "You supported it?"

"No. I've been slowly dismantling it, but the fucker was paranoid and kept a lot of information to himself."

That sounded about right, and it reminded me of my mother.

He pushed his hand through his dark hair, and it was only then that I noticed Giovanni's eyes glazing with fury. "What's the matter?" I demanded.

His jaw clenched before he ran his tongue across his teeth, flicking his gaze to the side before bringing it back to me.

"Perez wants me to hand you over today."

My heart skipped a beat and I clapped my hands in delight. "That's good. It was our goal all along."

He shook his head. "That was *your* goal. Not mine."

I scowled, my senses on alert. "Explain yourself."

"It's not safe, Liana. I don't like this plan one bit." There was no fucking way I would give up now, not after hearing that Perez had information on my sister. I needed to find out who he sold her to, and then I'd kill the motherfucker.

"You cannot go back on our agreement," I growled in a rush. "I need to destroy his human trafficking ring from within."

"We can do it together," he reasoned. "The safe way."

My fingers twitched with an urge to murder him if he refused to follow through. I was sick and tired of men thinking they knew better than me. My heart tripped over itself, realizing this was probably how my mother became who she was today.

Her firstborn—the most precious—daughter was taken from her and she vowed to become the most powerful and ruthless woman in the underworld.

Shoving it all into the dark corner of my mind to deal with later, I locked eyes with him.

"No." It took all my willpower not to reach for my knife. "You're now the head of the Tijuana cartel. You'll hold up your end of the bargain and deliver me to Perez with a fucking bow, smiling all the way through it."

I was committed to this vendetta. I needed to get close to Perez now more than ever. I needed to know where my twin was. If she was alive, I needed to save her.

He sighed tiredly, and I knew I was close to winning.

"Hold up your end of the bargain," I continued. "It will prove to Perez and the likes of him that you can be trusted. Then get the list of anyone involved with it, and destroy them from the inside."

"You're too bossy," he said in a begrudging tone.

"So fucking what?" My palms came to rest on my waist, ready to battle him. The stupid sleeves hung half off, somewhat hindering my pissed-off image. "If I were a man, you'd acknowledge it's a brilliant idea."

"Jesus," he muttered, blowing out a breath. I'd never had a big brother, but I imagined if I had one, he'd be just as annoying and overbearing as this man in front of me. "Perez is a psychopath. You'll be at his mercy, and more vulnerable than ever."

"I can handle myself." My teeth clenched. "Unless you forgot, I killed your uncle," I pointed out.

"Perez will have a whole fucking army around him. Especially now that you single-handedly killed off my uncle and all his guards." I killed Santiago, but I wouldn't have been able to get near him without Giovanni's help. Not that we'd share that tiny bit of information with Perez.

"Like I said, I can handle myself."

"Liana, don't be reckless. You won't help anyone by getting yourself killed."

"The world thinks I'm already dead."

"But you're not." He took a step forward. "You know, this could be your chance to start fresh. Away from everything and everyone in this world."

My fists tightened until I felt my muscles burn. I flashed him my most punishing glare, then jammed a finger against his chest.

"Not until I make those responsible for my sister's death pay." *Not until I find her—dead or alive.* "She was half of me." My voice sounded far away, even to my ears. Pain and adrenaline buzzed through my veins. "Can't you see, Giovanni? I can't move on. I'm not okay." My voice trailed off as I tamped down a sniffle. "I'll never be okay, not while those responsible roam this earth."

Each heartbeat was more painful than the last.

"You won't find closure. Only more questions." Giovanni's calm voice ripped through the chaos in my chest and my mind. I met his green eyes. He sounded collected, but underneath the surface, I sensed something else. Something familiar.

"What are you saying?" I whispered.

"You know, probably better than anyone, that nothing is simple in our world. I don't know what happened to your sister, but even if she's alive, she won't be the same person you remember."

The vivid images from the night my life shattered around me played through my head. My broken body. My broken mind. If my twin survived, she'd be in worse shape than I ever was.

I didn't have a choice but to go after answers. She'd do the same for me.

Chapter 28
Liana, 18 Years Old

My mother's screams rippled through the air, but I could barely hear them. It was like I was underwater, drowning.

I opened my eyes, the blurry outline of my mother swimming above me, and I realized I *was* drowning. I tried to resist, flailing my arms and kicking my legs, fighting against her hold.

My eyes widened, staring at her through ripples of water. I opened my mouth to ask why, but only bubbles came out. Gurgles. Burning my lungs. Seeping into my muscles.

Somehow, someway, even through the fog of pain, my brain was urging me to fight, but my arms were getting weaker. My lungs were failing.

And then I was yanked out.

Screams rang in the air. Not my own. Not my mother's.

A video played in the background. "You killed her," Mother hissed. "Your actions led to your sister's death." Water dripped off my eyelashes. I blinked desperately, trying to understand. What was happening? "You might as well have been the one to end your sister."

"Why?" I whispered to the woman who gave me birth.

It hurt to breathe. It hurt to move.

"This is why," she screamed, pointing to the screen behind her.

My teeth clattering, I found the strength to sit up. The burning in my lungs flared, but I ignored it. I had to see what she was talking about. It was then that my eyes zeroed in on the screen, the scene sending horror through me. Every fiber of my being shredded into atoms that would never be the same.

"You're too weak." My mother's voice was breaking my heart. "Too soft. You cannot survive like that in this world." Tears ran down my cheeks, not understanding. "The strong daughter can survive this underworld. The stronger daughter will take it over when I'm gone."

I panted, confusion wading with my terror.

Another scream tore through the air, and she looked away. My gaze followed and locked on the source.

The sharp inhale of breath. A tortured scream. Deafening silence.

Chapter 29
Liana, Present

Giovanni Agosti's tall frame, encased in a three-piece suit, seemed overdressed for a meeting with Perez. But hey, who was I to argue with an Italian?

Meanwhile, he studied me where I stood, clad in black jeans and a white shirt, with undergarments that would turn off a sex addict.

We'd been in the guest bedroom arguing for the past twenty minutes. One thing was clear, this man was as stubborn as a mule. It was annoying as fuck, and I already felt sorry for whatever woman fell for the man's bedroom eyes. Because they were the only thing going for him.

"You're sure I can't convince you not to do this?" he asked in an aggravated tone. He was pissed off, his jaw clenched and eyes trained on me as if he were seeing me for the last time.

"*Ya uverne.*" When he gave me a blank look, I added in English, "I'm sure."

It wasn't often I spoke Russian. It hadn't felt right since... Not since I'd lost my twin.

"I didn't know you spoke Russian."

It was my turn for a blank stare. "You do know I'm Russian, right?"

"You do know I'm Italian, right?"

I rolled my eyes. Giovanni Agosti screamed Italian, despite his connection to the Tijuana cartel. But his Italian heritage was a hard thing to miss, even without his last name. With a smooth smile on his face, I couldn't help but notice that he was a beautiful man. With bronzed skin and dark hair, his Mediterranean heritage shone through.

"You don't say," I shot back, snickering. He flashed me an easy smile, even though his green eyes regarded me warily. "Where does the Tijuana connection come from?"

There was a silence for a heartbeat, and just as I thought he would ignore me, he responded. "My father had an affair with a cartel princess and forced my mother—" He broke off and cleared his throat, his eyes hard and dangerous before continuing in a dry tone. "Pardon, my *stepmother* to raise me as her own. They kept it a secret for a while."

The coiled knot in my chest tightened with sorrow for him. That must have been difficult to come to terms with. It would seem all of us in the underworld were damaged in one way or another.

"I'm sorry. We can't pick who our parents are, but we can decide who we want to be." Better people. Better friends. Better siblings. Then, because the silence was stretching like a rubber band ready to snap, I shifted subjects. "Hit me."

Giovanni blinked in confusion. "Excuse me?"

He sounded offended, and I let out a frustrated breath. "Hit me," I repeated. "I sure as fuck cannot be delivered to Perez looking like I just walked out of a spa."

"I'm not hitting you." He huffed in disbelief. "You're crazy."

"You won't be beating me," I explained. "It's just business."

He slid his hands into his pockets and rocked back, watching me. "Well, the deal is off, then. I'm not hitting a girl."

"I'm not a girl." I rolled my eyes. "So typical, women have to do all the work." He wasn't falling for it. I could see it in his raised eyebrow, in the way he watched me with an expression that said he was on to me. "Fine," I gritted. "I'll do it myself." I shook my head. "What do you think Perez will say if I turn up looking like a pampered princess?"

"Your lip is already somewhat busted," he reasoned.

I rolled my eyes, annoyed. It was practically healed. I'd have to take care of this myself. I made my way to the door and gripped the handle, but before I could slam my head against it, I felt a pressure on my shoulder. On instinct, I grabbed Giovanni's wrist and twisted, drawing a grunt out of him, but to his credit, he didn't even attempt to defend himself.

"No, don't do that." I narrowed my eyes, but before I could say anything else, he added, "My uncle would never damage his merchandise." I glared at him. "It was how he viewed women, not me. Anyhow, he'd never leave a mark on a woman, because it would reduce her resale value."

Understanding—and disgust—dawned on me, and I exhaled. "Very well. No marks on me, then."

"Finally she sees reason," he muttered. "Once I hand you to Perez, how do I ensure you're safe?"

I tilted my head pensively. "The easy way would be if he shows up and we eliminate his guards, then use him as a bargaining chip to secure intel on the location of his compound."

"That would be way too easy," he remarked. "But we can hope." He pushed his hand through his hair, muttering something that sounded suspiciously like *Way too optimistic.*

I waved an arm in the air. "I'm still here."

The corner of his lips lifted. "You don't fucking say. Once you brush out that wild hair and cool your temper, meet me in the kitchen and we'll talk."

"Have the fucking coffee ready," I called out to his retreating back.

His answer was flipping me the bird over his shoulder, but his chuckle didn't escape me.

As I made my way into the bathroom to get ready, I stared at my reflection and couldn't help but begrudgingly admit that it felt good to have a friend—however reluctant.

Chapter 30
Kingston

Perez Cortes was one paranoid motherfucker. Who the fuck voluntarily stayed in the fucking Amazon? Sick, sadistic human traffickers, that was who!

The black Land Rover traveled through the rough terrain of the Amazon jungle for hours before we disembarked and made our way on foot. Sweat collected on my brow as we trudged through the jungle. Alexei was on alert, wondering what my angle was.

"I need to find Perez's compound," I said as we climbed over a particularly dense pile of rotten shrubbery. Endless green stretched wide, but I could see signs of a coastline up ahead, as well as distant buildings and planes flying overhead.

"Why?"

The auction was happening in Porto Alegre, so logic predicted that Perez's compound wasn't too far. I needed to get to Liana before that auction. There was no fucking way I'd let anyone else touch her.

"He has Sofia Volkov's daughter."

Alexei never missed a step, traversing the forest floor with sure steps and using a machete to break down fallen trees in our path. The birds chirped in overtime, warning of a foreign presence.

"I see." Typical of Alexei not to judge me, ignoring the fact that Sofia Volkov had wreaked havoc on so many families, including his own. "Have you asked Kian or Marchetti for the location?"

"Marchetti wants to get his hands on her daughter to draw Sofia out," I answered reluctantly.

"I see."

I suspected he did. I loved my brothers, but the fact of the matter was that I couldn't let them get near the shit I was involved in. Alexei lived and breathed this kind of risk, and he hated Sofia's husband, Ivan, as much as I did. There was nobody I trusted more than him.

The fact that he kept his word and didn't tell a single soul—including his wife—of our plans or where we were told me he'd have my back through any storm we weathered. All these years, I still wasn't sure why he thought he owed me.

"I never thanked you," I said, the gratitude long overdue. "For saving me eight years ago."

His pale blue eyes found mine, and he nodded. The shadowy expression that I used to see in the years following my rescue had changed since he married my sister.

"I fucked up your life," he finally said. "It's the least I could do."

I looked at him, and the puzzle piece fell into place. He'd been blaming himself for my capture even though he was never the reason it happened in the first place. He was a victim of circumstance, being Ivan's prisoner during his childhood. The day of my capture, it was Alexei who followed my sister back to our house and ensured she made it back safely, and for that, I considered us even.

My father, on the other hand, was a different story. His arrangements put a bullseye on his children's backs. *He* was to blame.

"You didn't deserve that fate, Alexei. None of us did." I let my eyes roam the jungle's planes. "Our parents are to blame. Not us." I glanced his way. "We just have to do better with the next generation."

"Yes, we do," he muttered from my side. "Do you want to talk about her?"

Her. Liana. Louisa. The twins I failed. Did I want to talk about it? Where would I even fucking start? I swallowed the lump in my throat, keeping quiet. I felt detached from everything apart from this strange sensation when it came to the twin I wasn't supposed to care for.

"No," I finally answered, but Alexei must have read something in my expression because his lips lifted.

"You're whipped."

"Fuck off, asshole."

Alexei looked out at the cloudy sky, staying silent for a beat. "Sofia's daughter or not, if she's the one, go for it."

I shrugged. "It's complicated."

"What relationship isn't?"

I looked at him in surprise.

"Who are you and what have you done with Alexei Nikolaev?" His lips twitched as he flipped me the finger. "I never thought you'd be offering relationship advice."

It was his turn to shrug. "Your sister's teaching me a lot."

I stayed silent for a beat. "I'm happy for you. For both of you."

He nodded his thanks, then pulled out his binoculars from his pack. I followed his line of sight, and when he handed me the pair, I homed in on the docks, streets, and alleyways corrupted and controlled by Perez Cortes. Dusk had started its descent over the drug- and human-trafficking-infested gateway city.

"Bidding at the auction might be the way to go," Alexei stated matter-of-factly. "No one's ever been able to find Perez's compound. It's how he's managed to survive all these years. Kian's the only man who's left that place alive."

Kian Cortes, a friend to the Ashfords, made it his business to track down men—and women—who didn't want to be found. We had quite a bit in common, though we'd never officially worked together.

"Nothing's impossible."

"True," he agreed. "But do we have months to scout every inch of this jungle to locate his compound?"

We both knew the answer to that. A week with the likes of Perez Cortes could feel like eternity.

The rancid taste of unease lingered in my mouth, warning that I might have to go against my principles and fatten the motherfucker's purse at his auction. But I had to trust my instincts here. They had saved my life way too many times, and right now, they told me he'd break Liana beyond repair once he had her in his compound.

That was where his torture really began.

The hum of the engine was the first thing we heard. The headlights came next. We both reached for our weapons, aiming them toward the incoming lights. One Jeep. Two. A fucking caravan of them.

I shared a *What the fuck have we gotten ourselves into?* look with Alexei.

"This'll be fun," he muttered as they all came to a stop, surrounding us. If only we could lure them off this cliff.

"Clearly our definitions of what constitutes fun don't line up," I retorted dryly.

Four armed, uniformed men jumped out. Fuck, if they were locals, they worked for Perez. More flooded the area until a familiar figure stepped out.

"What the fuck?" Alexei's voice portrayed the surprise I felt. Of all people, Kristoff Baldwin, Byron's buddy from his military days, was the last person I expected.

"I didn't expect to see *you* here," I deadpanned. I'd used Kristoff over the years to broker properties around the world.

If he was working with Perez, we were fucked. In fact, the entire Ashford line would be doomed. He was intimately aware of family secrets and hidden assets related to my brothers which could easily ruin them.

"Ditto," he said brusquely.

"What are you doing here?" I asked, my voice colder than Siberia.

"Looking for my daughter."

The stillness of the jungle reflected the dread in his eyes. The eerie *swoosh* of leaves resumed, matching the storm in Kristoff's expression.

"The one who refused to answer your calls?" I questioned, recalling his comment from when I last saw him.

He nodded.

"In the jungle?" Alexei asked.

The fatigue in his eyes was glaring. So was the fear. He reeked of it.

"She got into hacking." My brow furrowed at the odd explanation. "Apparently, she wiped Perez's bank account." Alexei whistled, clearly impressed. "Please spare me the kudos," he said, pushing his hand through his already unkempt hair. "First year of college and not a single month has gone by without some sort of trouble. Larson, intoxication, getting arrested for breaking and entering, and now getting kidnapped."

My lips twitched, part of me already liking the kid, whoever she was.

"Don't forget theft," Alexei added, a hint of amusement in his usually cold voice.

Kristoff shot him a murderous look, clearly not appreciating being reminded of his daughter's extra-curricular activities.

"You say that in front of my wife, and I'll have my daughter wipe *your* accounts clean," he growled. Alexei's expression remained unflinching. Kristoff's eyes filled with conflicted uncertainty as he looked away. "Jesus, I'd give up every penny of my own just to get her back. I can't go back without her."

"Why Perez Cortes?" I asked him.

He shook his head. "Fuck if I know. I'm gonna be bald by the time all my kids wrap up their tantrums."

"Let's get her back, then," I said. "Although, I think you could pull the look off. Unlike Byron." My phone buzzed and dread filled my stomach, saliva pooling in the back of my throat. "The auction date has been set."

It would seem we'd both be restoring Perez's bank accounts soon.

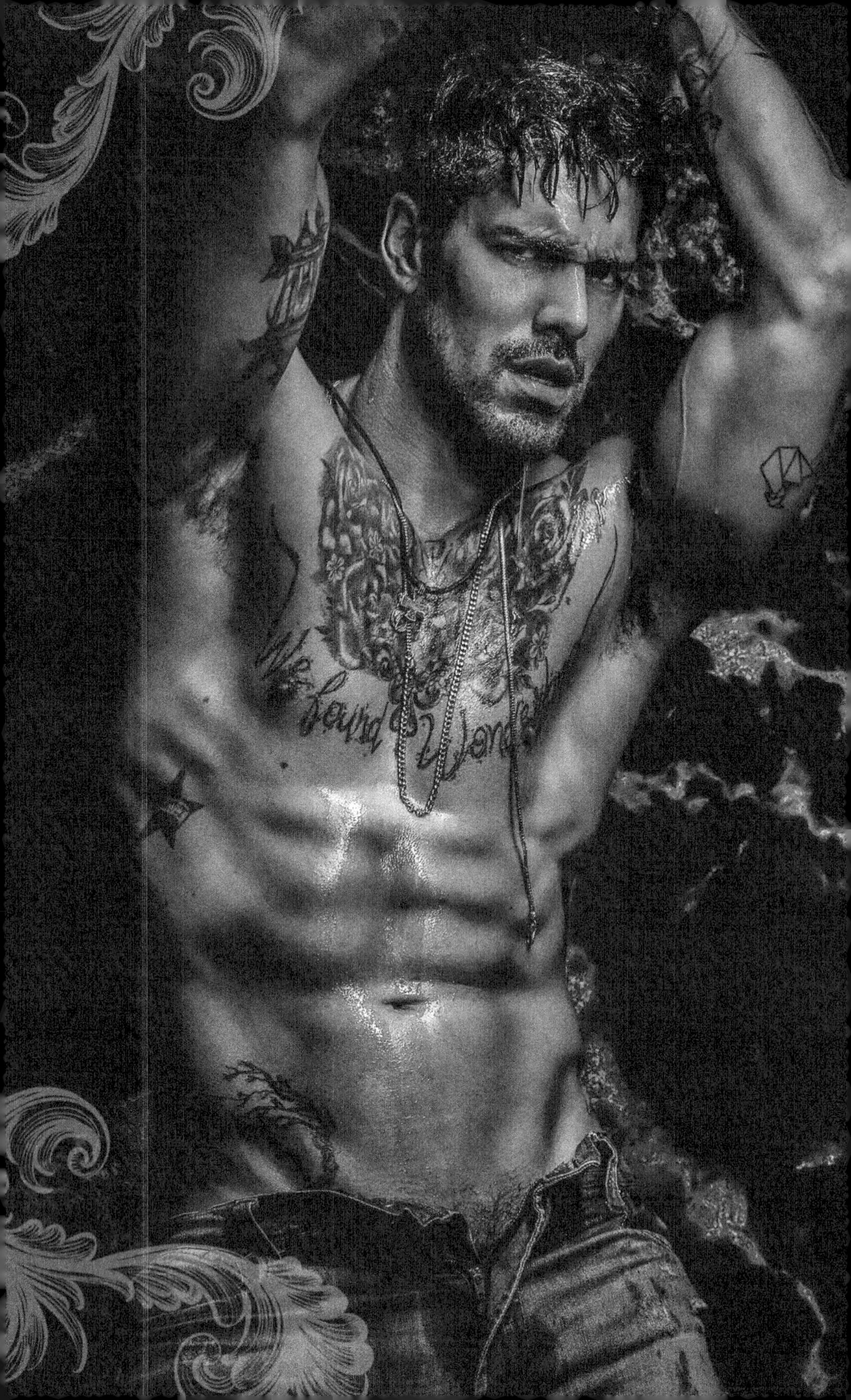

Chapter 31
Liana

My wrists and ankles bound once again, I sat in the chair and tried to reason with my nerves. I shook my head to clear it—my plan *had* to work. There was no room for failure, and any panic would just get in the way.

"You okay?" Giovanni asked out of the corner of his mouth.

"Yes."

Surveying the room, I noted the yellow walls, wooden floors, and randomly placed pillars, with large doors providing a view of the water and the boat slowly approaching.

"It's a warehouse," he explained. "That's just a tender to pick you up and take you to the larger ship."

I swallowed. Not exactly ideal, but it was the only way to get to Perez.

"Maybe he comes to pick me up personally and we snatch him," I murmured, the hope in my chest a vicious bitch. After all, he personally handled a transaction with my own mother not too long ago. Maybe he'd want to do the same now.

The boat docked, and it didn't take long for two men to make their way to us. One was heavyset, and the other skinny with dark sunglasses.

"Fuck, no Perez," I hissed.

"I should kill them and end this," he muttered.

"No," I gritted. "I need Perez."

Not taking their gazes off me, the two men swallowed the distance between us.

"Agosti," the heavyset man greeted. "Congrats on the promotion." Giovanni didn't answer, just nodded tersely. "This the bitch?"

Giovanni's growl vibrated behind me, and I had to act quickly before he gave up the ruse.

"Who are you calling bitch, you pussy?" I snapped, struggling against the ropes and giving as convincing a performance as I could manage. "Untie me, and I'll show you how much of a pussy you are."

"Jesus fucking Christ," groaned Giovanni.

The two men laughed, sharing amused glances.

"Feisty bitch," one man said as he pushed his glasses up his nose. He took a step forward, bringing his face closer, the scent of tobacco and motor oil invading my space. I held my breath, waiting. One more inch and... *Bam!* I headbutted him with all my strength.

He staggered back, clutching his nose as blood seeped between his fingers.

"This fucking *bitch!*" he screamed, raising his hand to slap me, but before his fist could connect with my face, Giovanni stepped in front of me and intervened.

"No marks on the woman." A collective chill spread between us all. It was so quiet I could hear each drum of my heart. *Bum... bum... bum.*

The men stared at each other, Giovanni's face reflecting not a flicker of emotion. Strained silence reigned for a moment before the other man broke it.

"You're right," he growled. "Perez wouldn't be happy with damaged goods."

Reign of a Billionaire

I gritted my teeth, fighting the urge to smash these two morons' heads with my hands tied behind my back.

This would be too easy.

Not a single sick bastard I'd killed in the past compared to the assholes on this ship. However, I found one thing advantageous. They considered me to be easy prey, and I planned to use that to my benefit.

It took less than sixty hours for the pigs who were taking us to Perez Cortes to strike. The smoke. The laughter. The fumes of their filth. The other women were huddled in the corner, sleeping, but I lay awake.

I'd been keeping an eye on the women and tracking a roach crawling along the filth-covered floor. The bug kept walking in circles, bumping into hay, but remained determined to get to its destination. Kind of like me.

God, I was tired.

I needed rest in order to keep my wits about me, but then who would ensure these girls were safe? It was up to me to protect them.

My anxiety had me wide awake now, and I counted the seconds it took for the roach to finally give up. The dull pain in my temples seemed to grow with each passing day, and I was beginning to think it had something to do with the conditions of my living situation here, not to mention being on edge twenty-four seven. Confusing thoughts invaded my brain, and I could no longer distinguish between memories and dreams.

You killed her.

I wanted to ask who, but I had nobody to ask. My lip trembled, my heart aching for *her*—whoever she was.

I didn't know, but judging by this coiled knot of emotions in my chest, I felt it was important. It hurt. So fucking much, and I didn't know why. The only time I'd ever felt this pain was when I let thoughts of my sister filter in. Could that be a clue?

Eyes stinging, I blinked rapidly, years of training still firmly in place. My mother beat and electrocuted that weakness out of me.

Kiss me, sunshine.

Goosebumps rose on my skin. The voice in my head sounded authoritative, important. So *why* couldn't I remember him? The squeak of a metal door traveled through the air. A light gust of a cool breeze broke through, sending a shiver down my spine.

I remained still, keeping my breaths even, and waited.

As I listened for footsteps, I once again thought about how goddamn predictable men were. With their dicks and their greed, they never failed to disappoint. The jingle of keys. Another door creak.

Peering at the figure through my eyelashes, I watched as Bill—the short guard who'd been drooling over the girls since I arrived—trailed his meaty, disgusting hand up one of the girls' thighs while she slept.

Disgust clogged my throat, but I remained perfectly still with my jaw clenched. A soft, sleepy whimper came from the girl, and nasally breathing rumbled from the soon-to-be cockless man. The groper's hand inched higher up, and I went for the holstered knife hiding in my very unattractive granny panties.

Fury surged, filling my vision with a red haze. My fingers closed around the knife, and without a sound, I was behind him. Reaching around, I pressed the blade against his throat with my left hand and gripped his hair with my right.

"Make a sound and I'll slice your throat," I warned in a hushed tone, careful not to scare the girls. When he didn't respond, I pressed the knife into his throat, piercing his skin. "Understand?"

"Yes," he rasped. "But you won't get away with this."

I ignored his warning. "Step away from the girl and move out."

Slowly, he did as he was told, and the moment we were outside the door of our prison, I cut him with precision and watched him fall onto his knees, gurgling.

"Psycho... bitch."

I came around him, my lips curled into a sadistic smirk.

"Well, you got one thing right tonight," I said coldly.

The man struggled for breath, his chest heaving and his hands clutching his throat. But there would be no mercy for him. I stood there, watching him choke on his own blood. Then I stepped over him without a second thought and made my way to add a few more kills to my list.

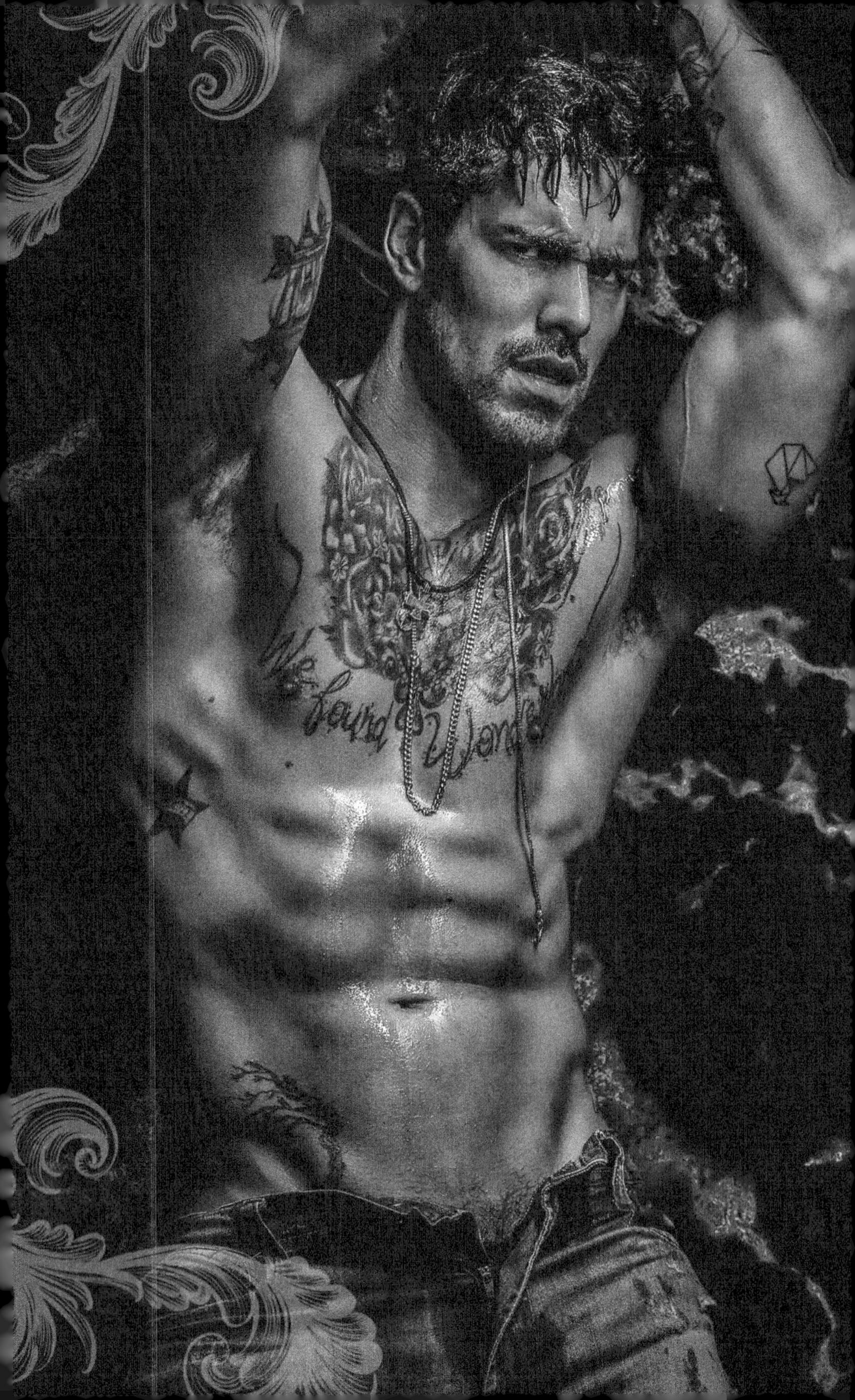
We found

Chapter 32
Liana

"We were born to die," I whispered, my breath fogging the air. I tried to be brave, but fear rattled my bones every time I stepped foot in this arena. Mother and Ivan called it a training center. It wasn't. This was where death found its mark.

"Everyone's born to die." The dark timbre of his voice soothed the tremors slightly. "It's just a matter of when."

"I hate that you... That she makes you fight."

This was the only spot where nobody ever found us. There was irony in finding safety where the horrors took place.

Clutching the pencil between my lead-stained fingers, I looked up to find his beautiful face. Only... the shadows hid it from me. Each time I shifted, they followed, shrouding him in darkness. How strange, I thought to myself. I clutched the pencil until it hurt, desperate to anchor myself to something that felt real.

I parted my lips to say his name, but the moment I did, the sickening crack of bones echoed through the air. Blood dripped... Drip... Drip... Drip... Until my fingers were soaked with blood.

His blood. My blood.

My heart twisted with agony as the same words repeated on a loop in my head. I can't lose him, I can't lose him, I can't lose him.

"It's okay," he whispered, his words broken and disappearing into the air around us. Just like my fragile heart. "You're not hurting me."

Another crack of the bones. More blood gushed out.

"Nooooo!" My shriek pierced through my skull.

My eyes snapped open, and I bolted upright. My panting filled the space as I gasped for air. For a second, I was disoriented. I looked around, expecting to find blood. Instead, all I found was a group of women huddled together, and I remembered where I was.

I pushed a long breath out. This scenario wasn't much better, but I'd take it over my dream. My fingers were still shaking, but I willed them to stop.

The innate need to lash out—at my captors, at destiny—struck me, but I knew I had to keep a cool head. I was *so close* to finding out what had happened to my sister.

Since I had been taken, it'd been one cage after another. One ship. Then another.

The security had been doubled after my first murder spree. No matter though, because the guards got the message: Stay the fuck away. There wouldn't be any sampling while I was on this ship.

The last two weeks in this godforsaken cargo ship were maddening as fuck. Christmas had come and gone. So had New Year's. I killed a solid number of guards only for them to be replaced with new ones, along with another unconscious, frail-looking young woman.

Reina Romero.

I felt a sort of kinship toward her, and stood guard over her while she lay unconscious in her drugged state. She'd murdered several guards, and I had thoroughly enjoyed the show. I decided right then and there that I liked the girl.

My eyes traveled over the sleeping girls.

Helpless. Vulnerable.

Their fathers, brothers, and husbands had either double-crossed or were indebted to Perez, and they were expected to pay the price. It disgusted me and frightened me at the same time. What would become of the captive girls?

In the past two weeks, I'd attempted to teach them some form of self-defense. Even if by some miracle they were all saved when we arrived at our destination, they'd need it eventually. It was only a matter of time. Some of the lessons stuck; a lot of them didn't.

The howling sounds started, like a haunting lullaby, signaling another day had passed since we had arrived in this hellhole.

It'll bring me closer to the truth, I reminded myself. Anger at being manipulated and lied to simmered, shooting the adrenaline I needed through my veins. For eight years the video of a woman's body disintegrating into nothing tormented my mind and soul. Now, I wasn't sure if it was my sister or someone else. Either way, my revenge wouldn't stop now, regardless if the woman in the video was my sister or not. Meanwhile, I held on to this tiny flicker of hope. What if my twin was alive?

My mother must know the truth, and I hated her for leading me to believe whatever she needed me to believe. Maybe I'd been young and naive enough to trust it, but she wasn't.

Soon I would face the evil that orchestrated my abduction and sold my sister. It was all going according to plan—as much as was possible anyway.

A cough pulled me from my thoughts, and I scooted over to Sienna, an eighteen-year-old girl who'd been here even longer than me. She had a horrible case of seasickness, and I didn't envy her one bit. She'd been throwing up for weeks, barely able to keep anything down. I would have blamed it on the unappealing food, but the rest of us weren't sick from it.

"I hate ships," came her weak voice as she rolled over to face me, her eyes fluttering open. "My stepfather's yacht never made me *this* sick."

I gently pulled her up into a seated position.

"It doesn't help that you're not eating," I said, handing her a piece of hard bread. She wrinkled up her button nose at the unappealing sight. "I know, it's disgusting."

I finally coaxed her into taking it, and she forced herself to swallow with a painful-sounding gulp.

"I've had better," she muttered.

"Me too." I'd also had worse, but there was no sense in bringing that up. "How did you end up here?"

"Fuck if I know." She winced. "My mom would flip if she heard me cursing this way." My lip twitched at that, and it gave me a glimpse of what she might be like if she weren't despondent and shaking like a leaf, the strands of her honey-colored hair slithering across her shoulders. Lifting her head, her eyes met mine with stubborn defiance. "This only happened because of *him*," she spat, accusation clear in her voice.

"Your stepfather?" I asked tentatively. Her gaze darted around at the sleeping girls before returning to me, eyes misting. "Who's your stepfather?"

She waved her hand weakly. "Kristoff Baldwin."

I tapped a finger to my chin. The name sounded familiar, but I couldn't place it. "What does he do?"

She shrugged, then winced and rubbed at her shoulder. She was weak, days of throwing up and sleeping on the cold, hard ground taking a toll on her body. "Real estate shit. Construction something or other."

The name finally fell into place. "Baldwin Enterprise," I blurted, my brow furrowing in confusion. "Your father owns Baldwin Enterprise?"

"Stepfather," she corrected, wiping her mouth with the back of her hand. "My mom married him when I was a teenager. My sisters think of him as their dad. And then of course, he's the twins' real dad." A hint of bitterness underlined her words. "I'm not jealous if that's what you're thinking. Besides, Kristoff certainly knows how to behave like an overbearing father."

She was lucky in that regard; it was more than my sister and I had.

"What does he have to do with any of this?" As far as I knew, Kristoff Baldwin didn't get involved with the likes of Cortes.

She swung her bruised eyes to me, her face ghostly pale. "And what is *this*?"

My stomach lurched. If her stepfather had no dealings with the underworld and they went after her anyway, it meant there was no rhyme or reason behind the girls being snatched. Nobody was safe.

"Nothing," I muttered, handing her a dry piece of bread. "Try to nibble on this."

She took it from me gingerly, tears flowing freely from her face now. She brought it to her lips but didn't bite into it. Her hand hung in the air as she gulped once, twice.

"I fucked up," she whispered, shaking her head. "It had to be that stupid program I wrote."

"What program?" I asked, intrigued.

She sniffled. "I did it during one of my coding classes at college. I wanted to prove to Tyran Callahan that I—" Her voice broke and my blood ran cold. "I meddled with Perez Cortes's bank accounts."

My eyes blew wide. "Why would you do that?"

She swallowed hard. "Tyran kept saying I was too young for him." I tried to recall how old Tyran Callahan was and failed. All I could remember was that he was a twin like me. "So he said when I could hack into Cortes's personal files, he'd take me out." She moved to stand, waving away my attempt to help her. "I'm starting to think that my roommate was right."

"About?"

"Tyran might've just been trying to bait me," she muttered, shame filling her expression. When I gave her a blank look, she explained. "As in 'I'll go out with you when pigs fly,' but for some stupid reason, he went all specific."

Poor girl took Callahan's rejection as a challenge. She had yet to learn that men were idiots of the finest class.

But instead of saying all of that, I smiled. She didn't need me pointing out the obvious; she was already beating herself up over it.

"You showed him, didn't you?"

A sardonic breath left her. "I sure did. Look where it got me." She was too young and too naive to be involved in this corruption. "Who is Perez Cortes anyway?"

"Put it this way, he's not the best person to steal from," I said softly.

"I'd never even heard of him." Despair laced her voice. Of course she hadn't, she hardly looked old enough to be a college student.

"He's not a good guy." And that was putting it mildly. There was one thing that my mother did right, and that was educate me on the who's who in the underworld. It didn't matter how big or small someone was, she drilled everyone's names into me.

This girl clearly had no clue our world even existed. If I got out of this alive, I'd whoop Tyran Callahan's ass for giving her hope where there was none.

"I'm going to need therapy when all this is said and done."

"Maybe," I agreed, wondering if therapy wouldn't be such a bad thing for the women and men caught up in the underworld. "Until then, are you up to learning some self-defense?"

She still had the will to live, a burning fight in her eyes despite her weak state.

"Bring it on." Her gaze darted from me to Reina's sleeping form in the cage next to ours. "I want to become as nuts as that lady."

"Alright, then, Sienna. Let's kick some ass."

Her lips curved into a soft smile despite the despair in her eyes. "Don't cry to me when I puke all over you."

"Don't cry when I kick your ass."

Reign of a Billionaire

Reina Romero gripped my hand as we were pushed across the dock, up a flight of stone steps, and into a filthy courtyard. We were shuffled around like cattle, and all the while, I kept my eyes trained on the girls.

"Don't make eye contact," I warned Sienna and Reina in a soft whisper, shuffling them both deeper into the moving crowd. Both were shell-shocked, their faces white as a sheet. I tugged them along to the podium and led us onto the stage.

Sienna's gasp captured my attention, and I found her staring at the rows of men. To my surprise, she was smiling, tears glistening in her eyes. I followed her eyeline but didn't see anyone aside from the leering faces of those eager to witness our degradation and humiliation.

"What is it?"

"That's my dad," she whispered, her lip trembling. "My... stepdad."

A pinch of relief hit me, knowing this girl would be okay. Her parents—unlike many others—had come to save her.

"Dim your happiness," I murmured in a hushed tone. "Keep your expression stoic, and don't let on that you know him."

Her eyes found mine, confusion clear in them. "But—"

I took her hand and squeezed it tightly. "Trust me. And stay away from that douchebag Tyran. I'll take care of him for you."

Something in her eyes flared, strength I sensed in her all along hitting me head-on. "Don't. I'm gonna make him pay myself."

I smiled proudly. "Good girl."

A guard came behind her, pushing her forward, and I gave her a reassuring nod. I watched with bated breath as the bidding for Sienna Baldwin started. With each number thrown into the mix, the tension in me grew, and it wasn't until she was escorted toward her father that I took a full breath.

Until it was my turn.

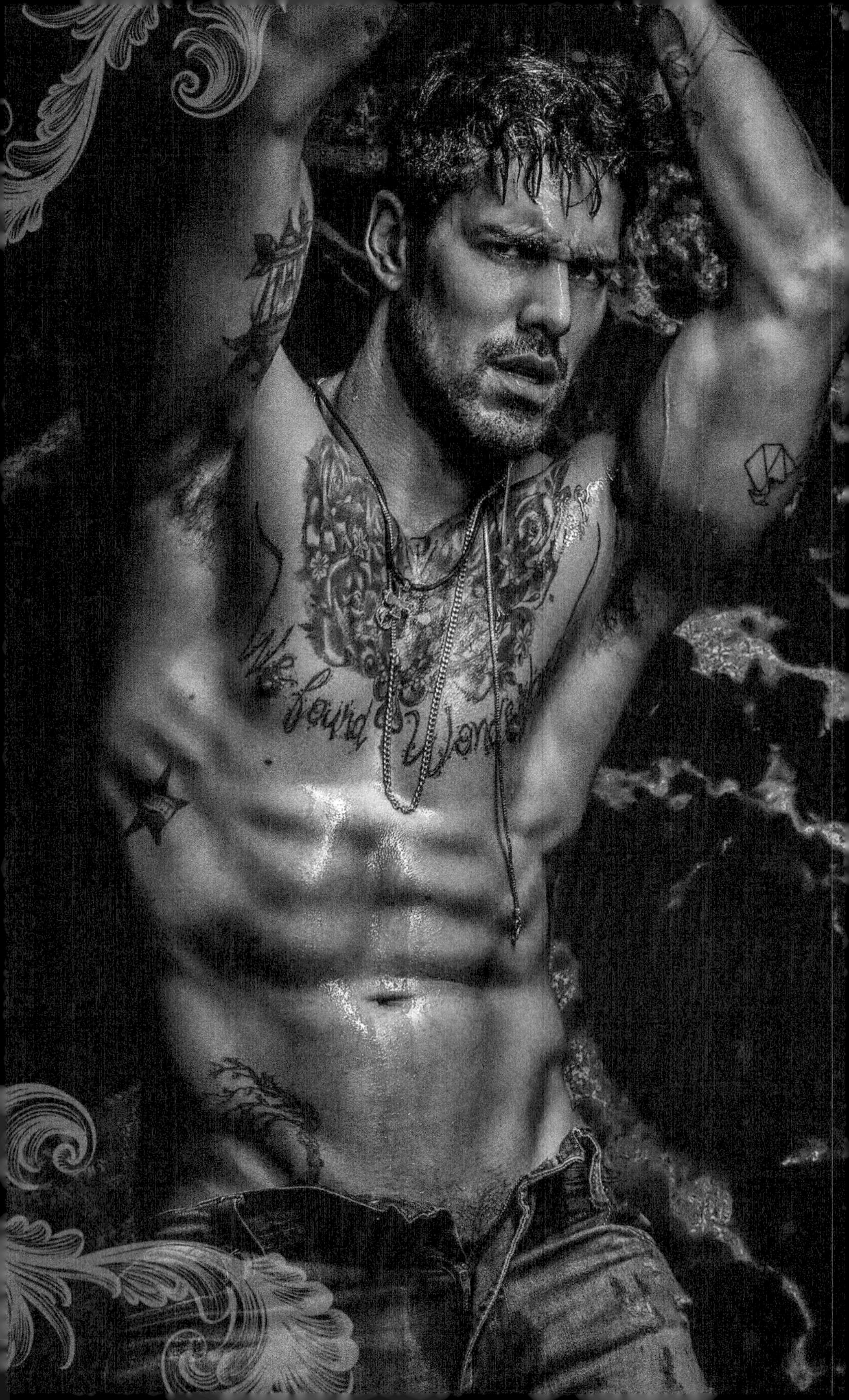

Chapter 33
Kingston

Life was an abstract concept. It was what you made of it. The perfect one was an illusion that could be shattered in the matter of an afternoon at the zoo. Or a betrayal that you never saw coming.

Every human on earth had an agenda. We were all waging our own wars. Some were losing and some winning. I'd had enough of losing—my family, my friends, the one person who'd helped me see the light in my darkest moments, and later, her sister.

Louisa made me vow to keep her twin safe.

So whether it was my excuse or simply my way of getting back something I'd lost, at that very moment, I knew my mind was made up.

Liana Volkov would be mine.

I stared across the square at her defiant expression, and I started to see it. Not the enemy. Not the facade that she thought she'd mastered. It was the face of a lioness protecting the innocent. It was the girl who'd been broken by the loss of her sister. Just like me.

Standing among the square in Porto Alegre in Brazil, I watched women being auctioned off, one by one, and kept a gaze on the only one who mattered to me. She hadn't noticed me yet, all her focus on the girl by her side.

My stomach churned watching the terrorized women being sold in this creepy-as-fuck portside town.

The cobblestone square reeked of brutality, despair, and death.

I glanced at Kristoff Baldwin as he bid for his daughter, hot fury emanating off him. Another notch and he'd set this entire place on fire. The tic in his jaw alone announced it to the world, but thankfully, these greedy motherfuckers were too blind to see.

Finally, he won the bid, paying a pretty penny for his stepdaughter. As if she understood the wordless warning, she kept her expression blank as she was shuffled to him. Kristoff's hand rested on his weapon, ready to fight if need be.

"Here's your bitch," one of the armed guards spat.

Kristoff caught her as she stumbled forward, eyes never leaving the man.

I read his lips as he reassured the girl. "It's okay. We'll talk about it on the plane."

He slowly slid his gaze to me and, with a terse nod, disappeared from this fucked-up place. My attention was quick to shift back to the person I was here for.

Liana Volkov.

I clenched my teeth, noting the flimsy material of her white nightgown that revealed too much yet not enough. Her curves were fucking centerfold-worthy. Her hair was long enough to wrap around my fist twice.

But it was her fierce expression that burned through my skin and straight to my dick. I had to look away though, because it hurt to look at her. I flicked a disinterested glance to the second-to-last girl on the stage clutching Liana, and was taken aback in surprise. Reina Romero stood in line, next up on the butcher's block.

My mind worked at lightning speed. The girl looked like she'd been to hell and back. Fuck, Reina wasn't part of my plan, but I couldn't leave her.

The guard yanked Liana by the arm, dragging her to the front. My jaw clenched and my teeth ground down, earning me a few curious glances. It took all my restraint not to lunge forward and kill all these motherfuckers. But if I did that, I'd risk the lives of others too.

I pulled out my cell phone, scrolling through my contact list for Dante Leone. He could get the information to his brother and figure out the best way to rescue Reina.

Fuck—*no signal*. They must have jammed the servers.

I attempted his brother, my brothers—all four of them—to no avail. It seems Perez Cortes owned the cell towers around here too.

Goddammit. This was the last thing I needed right now.

A movement on the stage caught my attention, and even though Liana refused to let her fear shine through, I could still note her pale face and stiff posture.

Someone threw an egg, but she was quick to duck, so it landed on a guard behind her instead. The woman had impressive reflexes. Another thing that set her apart.

The bidding started. One hundred thousand. Two. *Three*. It was time I ended it all. I raised my hand, flashing a two and six zeros.

"Two million to the man in the back!"

Everyone's eyes turned my way, half of my face hidden behind aviator glasses. Not that too many people would recognize me. There were benefits to being a ghost and sticking to the shadows. Nobody ever saw you coming.

Liana's eyes snapped to me before widening. It was the only reaction she let slip before freezing her expression. The rage burning through her golden eyes told me she wished she'd put a bullet through my head when she had the chance.

My cheek twitched.

I was going to enjoy her banter.

A part of me froze, realizing I was looking forward to spending time with her. Yeah, one taste of her pussy and she'd rewired my brain. Goddammit!

I stood, waiting for her to be brought to me, and with each step closer, her expression turned icier. She glared at me with deep malice, as if I'd murdered her entire family. I hadn't, but I might. Sofia Volkov had it coming.

The moment she was near me, she hissed, "What the fuck, you sick bastard. Give me back to Perez."

What was she talking about? Didn't she know Perez was a million times worse than I could ever be?

"No." My jaw tightened underneath my practiced smile. Her face flushed and blotchy red marks traveled down her neck and under her flimsy nightgown. "You're mine now, ice princess."

I always collected my debts—usually in the form of teeth. And I always kept my promises.

Chapter 34
Liana

My bidder towered over the crowd. Dark hair. Aviator glasses that hid most of his face, but it was impossible not to recognize him. Those tattoos that lurked underneath that white polo shirt. That darkness that spun around him like the second layer of his skin.

When I looked up and saw Kingston Ashford standing among the crowd of bidders, my gut twisted with the fury that'd been keeping me going for years.

I'd been putting my entire being into saving innocents behind my mother's back, and now with a fierce determination, I was going to make this man regret ever fucking meeting me.

"What the fuck, you sick bastard. Give me back to Perez," I hissed.

My goal was to get back to Perez and question him about the Marabella arrangements. I needed to know where my twin ended up.

"No." He leaned in closer so we were nose to nose, his shrewd eyes assessing me while gripping my forearm, his fingers squeezing like shackles. Then he was stupid enough to call me "princess."

Oh yeah, this fucking man just earned himself an expiration date.

I'd kill him and enjoy every fucking moment if he didn't release me. I needed to hunt down Perez's compound and question him. He had information I needed.

"You motherfucking *prick*. I'm going to slice your dick off and feed it to you unless you take me back."

His eyes glowed.

"You're a foul-mouthed little wench." A muscle in my jaw pulsed. My control shook like flimsy branches weathering hurricane winds, but I managed to stay calm. But then he had to go and taunt me. He yanked me closer, his body flush with mine, his voice low and threatening. "Let's get one thing straight. I bought you. You do what I say, whatever the fuck I demand."

"Fuck. You." I met his gaze with mutiny.

He reached up to toy with a strand of my hair, wrapping the blonde locks around his thick fingers. When he tipped my head back, I gritted my teeth, letting him see the full scale of my hatred.

"There'll be plenty of that, don't worry."

The guards snickered, and I knew they'd heard Kingston's threat. Adrenaline rushed through me, making the hairs on the back of my neck prickle.

I reacted.

Reaching for the first guard's knife, I took hold and shoved it into his gut, effectively cutting off his snickering. Before I could stab the next one, a pair of strong hands scooped me up and threw me over his shoulder.

"Put me down."

He slapped my ass. Fucking. Slapped. My. Ass.

The indignation and rage exploded in my veins as I started to pound my fists. He didn't even flinch.

"I should have put a bullet into your skull," I seethed. I meant it too. First chance I got, this fucker was *done*. "Asshole," I added for good measure.

The cold air brushed up my nightgown, sending goosebumps down my thighs. My fists hurt from pounding against his solid back, but what hurt more was having to admit how well his jeans hugged his gorgeous ass.

What? I never claimed to be a saint.

"Kingston... This is... This is so wrong."

"So is shooting at me in my own home, but you don't hear me complaining about that."

"You're so fucking dead," I gritted. The further he took me from the auction, the harder I fought him. "Better hope your affairs are in order because you're a dead man walking."

"How cliché," he said flatly, slapping my ass for emphasis. *Hard.*

"You're one to talk, Kingston." No answer. Obviously I needed to work harder at my insults. "Listen, you seem pretty desperate for a girlfriend, but I'm not it. I'd sooner put bullets in your head than fuck you. So, do us both a favor and take me back."

"Okay." He turned left, and my heart shuddered with hope. "No."

I blinked, confused, but before I could say anything, he threw me into the back of a car. Thinking on my feet—or ass, in this case—I jolted forward, my hand landing on the driver's shoulder.

"I'll give you fifty thousand—"

My words were cut off when Kingston's hand yanked me back. The driver looked over his shoulder, a pair of arctic, pale blue eyes slamming into me.

"He's not here to help you." Kingston shut the car door, settling next to me and offering me a placating smile. "Watch this one. I have to go back and bid on another."

The driver's expression remained impassive, but I could have sworn I saw disapproval flicker in them. Kingston shut the door and took off in a jog. The silence that followed was deafening, or maybe it was the adrenaline coursing through me, tampering my hearing.

"I'll give you a million dollars," I whispered. "Just open the door and—"

"No."

What was it with these men and one-word answers?

The car door opened after what felt like ten years later and I jumped in my seat. Kingston slid into the seat next to me. "Let's get the fuck out of here, Alexei."

I searched my memory for the significance of the name, but I was so frazzled, my brain refused to cooperate. Whoever this driver was, I was certain he was part of the underworld. His freakishly blue gaze flickered in the rearview mirror, and Kingston grinned like a damn fool. What I would give to punch that smile right off his face.

"I don't remember the last time I saw you smile."

My head snapped to Kingston. Alexei's remark struck me as odd, but I had no time to ponder on it. Reaching for the door handle, I yanked hard.

"It's locked." Kingston scowled, his hawk-like attention on me, watching me like I was his next meal... or kill. Fuck if I knew.

"Well, unlock it," I gritted, continuing to pull as if by some miracle it'd open. This was going nowhere. Feigning giving up, I leaned back into the seat with a sigh and locked eyes with Kingston. "Listen, any other time, I'd be flattered that a guy would go through all this trouble for me." He shot me a dubious look. "I would," I assured him quickly. Too quickly, probably. "It's the most effort any man has ever put into getting with me."

"Don't be too flattered." Kingston's voice dripped with sarcasm. "Your ego's too big as it is."

"Jesus Christ," Alexei muttered while I shot him a glare. I really wished he would drop dead.

Returning my attention to Kingston, I caught his gaze measuring me and shivered. I hated this reaction, especially now that he'd disrupted my plan.

"Don't cry to me when I kill you." I glared.

"I'll try not to."

His voice dripped with sarcasm, and that pissed me off even more. He handed me a bottle of water. I snatched it, trying to calculate how much further this whole charade was putting me back in my quest for answers.

Reign of a Billionaire

My vision fogged with red rage. It clouded all my senses until I couldn't breathe. I threw the bottle back at him, letting out a blood-curdling scream.

You could've heard a pin drop in the silence that followed. I blinked, my breathing chopped and heavy. I inhaled. Then exhaled. I repeated it again and again, until the world came back into focus. Two sets of eyes watched me warily as if I had lost my mind.

My eyes drifted around while my pulse thundered in my ears. I hadn't even realized that dusk had fallen and that we'd been driving through the jungle.

The car door opened in front of a helicopter, and I knew it was now or never.

With my wrists still bound, I bolted out of the car, my heart thundering in my ears. I didn't pause to look behind me, but I could hear Kingston's curses, demanding I come back. Ignoring rocks and sticks digging into my bare feet, I kept running.

Unsurprisingly, Kingston's footsteps fast approached. I felt him gaining on me, and could almost smell his vanilla scent.

Suddenly, strong arms wrapped around my waist and lifted me off my feet.

I let out a string of curses, kicking my feet in the air.

"Stay away from me," I said between ragged breaths. "You're ruining everything!"

"Calm down."

It had the exact opposite effect. I swung my head, headbutting his nose with the back of my skull.

"*Fuck.*"

It was the last thing I heard as I was dragged into unconsciousness.

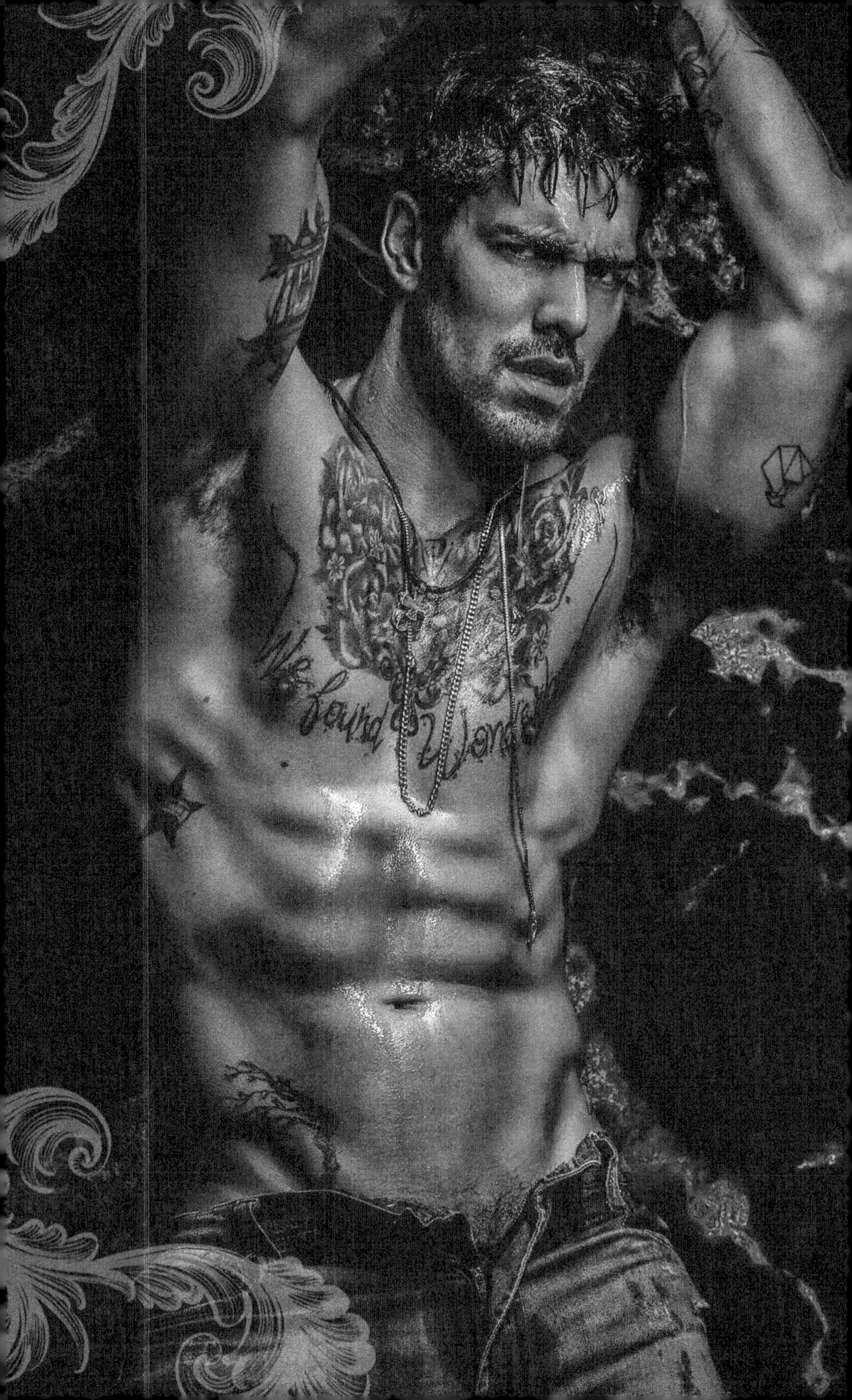
We found

Chapter 35
Kingston

Thank fuck I had the tranquilizer with me.

I wasn't expecting her to thank me on her knees, but I certainly didn't expect her to lose her shit and attempt to run back to Perez. This goddamned woman went full savage.

Alexei handed me a handkerchief, and I wiped my bleeding nose.

By the time I'd gotten back to bid on Romero's daughter, the auction was finished. So, dialing in to my brother's broadband satellite, I quickly got a message to Kian Cortes and dropped our location pin. He'd get it to the Leone brothers, who would ensure she was rescued. Nobody knew Perez's ways and location better than his own brother, Kian.

My primary focus had to be getting Liana out of there before Sofia Volkov showed up. In fact, I was surprised she hadn't swooped in yet.

"Want me to take her?" Alexei offered. A muscle in my jaw flexed, something about any man getting near an unconscious Liana rubbing me the wrong way.

"No."

He nodded. "You sure about this?"

I lowered my gaze to her sleeping face. Like this, she looked young and untainted. The picture of innocence.

"Yes."

"If you need anything else, you know how to get in touch with me."

"Thank you." I turned to face him. "And tell Rora not to worry."

The corners of his lips lifted. "No promises there." His eyes lowered to Liana's slumped form. "She looks nothing like *her*."

Her. Sofia Volkov. The woman who'd brought so much misery to so many people.

"She doesn't," I agreed, shoving the bloody handkerchief into my pocket and heading toward the helicopter.

There was more to Liana than met the eye, and I needed to peel back her layers to understand what had happened to her. I needed to fulfill my promise. And most of all, I needed to understand this attraction.

I strapped her in, fastening the seat belt across her chest. A soft moan snatched my attention, and sneaking a look at her face, I froze as the old pain slashed through me. Her curls. Her soft, full lips. There was something there. She looked so fucking *familiar*.

She's her twin, my reason scoffed. Logic didn't do much to assuage my guilt and confusion. In fact, my hopeful heart wanted to remain blind.

Another breathy moan, and my dick twitched.

I rubbed a hand over my face.

Why was it that both my heart *and* my dick were in the business of fucking me over?

I'd purchased this island in the Mediterranean through Kristoff Baldwin.

If I didn't want to be found, I wouldn't be. The estate and

surrounding land weren't listed publicly. Unless you were fifty miles out and knew exactly where to look, the white Roman-style home on the hill would remain incognito. And if you were on the island, you had to wade through thick jungle, shrubs, and rivers to even reach the stream that snaked around it protectively.

The dense foliage hid it from curious eyes on the local fishing boats that often ventured close to the island. Even the gardens were designed with privacy in mind. And then there was the high-tech security installed across the island that would make it hard for anyone to infiltrate if they happened to find themselves on its shores.

It was a perfect hideout, a lonely place befitting the desolate and dark feelings in my chest.

After a visit to a doctor who checked over Liana to confirm her well-being—and her glaring at her the entire time—I was assured her bruising would fade. She was malnourished so I had ordered a generous supply of food with the couple who maintained the house when I was away. The fridge would be stocked and the house clean by the time I got there, and the staff would be nowhere to be found. It was the way I preferred it—being alone.

Except this time, Liana would be with me.

After I took another short helicopter ride, I used my brother's jet to get the rest of the way. Liana slept for the entirety of the trip. I checked her pulse several times, worried about the dosage I'd administered, but her heart beat strong and steady.

It must be her exhaustion from weeks of captivity and the trauma of being on that grimy stage yesterday.

Now, with sunset imminent on the opposite side of the world and the chirping of birds quieting down, I crossed the stone bridge with Liana in my arms, a long-forgotten feeling slammed into me. *Home.*

I'd been here many times, but this feeling rarely struck me. It had eluded me since Lou's death, and hardly resurfaced. Confusion swirled inside me as I lowered my eyes to the precious cargo I held.

Could it have something to do with—

I firmly cut off that train of thought. This had nothing to do with

Liana and everything to do with the fact that I had Sofia Volkov's daughter at my mercy. That I'd kept my promise.

"Home sweet home," I rasped, the pain in my chest as strong as ever. I could almost pretend that Louisa was here with me, that we got what we'd hoped for—a life together away from the underworld, reigning over our own domain. Just the two of us.

My body went cold, knowing full well that could never happen, and my chest tightened with unspoken grief. I knew it was time to let those memories go. Or at least try to.

My footsteps rang against the bare stone of the empty house, and my eyes locked on the wrong sister.

Even though she was dead weight, she weighed next to nothing. I climbed the stairs two at a time, my gaze reluctantly falling to the slope of her nose, the apples of her cheeks. She was different from what I remembered of Louisa.

Stronger. Frailer. *Older*, naturally.

The suite we stopped in front of was large and airy, mahogany furniture with dusky rose accents everywhere. It was Louisa's favorite color.

I laid her down on top of the linen covers, her blonde hair fanning over the pillow. I studied her face, those harsh cheekbones she'd inherited from her mother. Her skin was almost translucent, making her full pink lips pop.

Liana's arm dangled limply, her eyes twitching behind closed lids, looking at once both an angel and my waking nightmare. I wondered what she was dreaming about. Did she think of her sister? Did she regret not showing up that night we were supposed to run away?

For a moment, I considered taking her nightgown off and replacing it with a clean one, but then decided against it. Her arms were bruised, and so were her bare feet. I wasn't sure what she endured during her captivity, but there was no need to add to it.

She curled into herself, and her eyes blinked open.

For several moments, she only stared before she said, "Where am I?" Her voice was soft and raspy. Then furious. When I didn't answer, our gazes locked in a silent battle and she added, "I'll kill you if you cost me my sister."

My muscles tensed at her words. The drugs must have made her delusional. I pulled a blanket over her and headed out of the room.

"I'll have food and drink brought up to you, ice princess." My hand on the doorknob, I glanced over my shoulder to find her glaring at me. "Want some ice cream?"

She stiffened. "I hate ice cream."

My brows furrowed. Both twins dreamt of a day when they'd be able to have ice cream every day. Their father fed it to them once, and Lou fell in love with vanilla. I couldn't remember which flavor Liana liked, and I regretted it now.

"If you change your mind, there's ice cream."

"I want to murder you," she snapped.

"You can kill me after your belly's full."

At that, I sauntered through the doorway, not bothering to lock her in.

There was no way off this island.

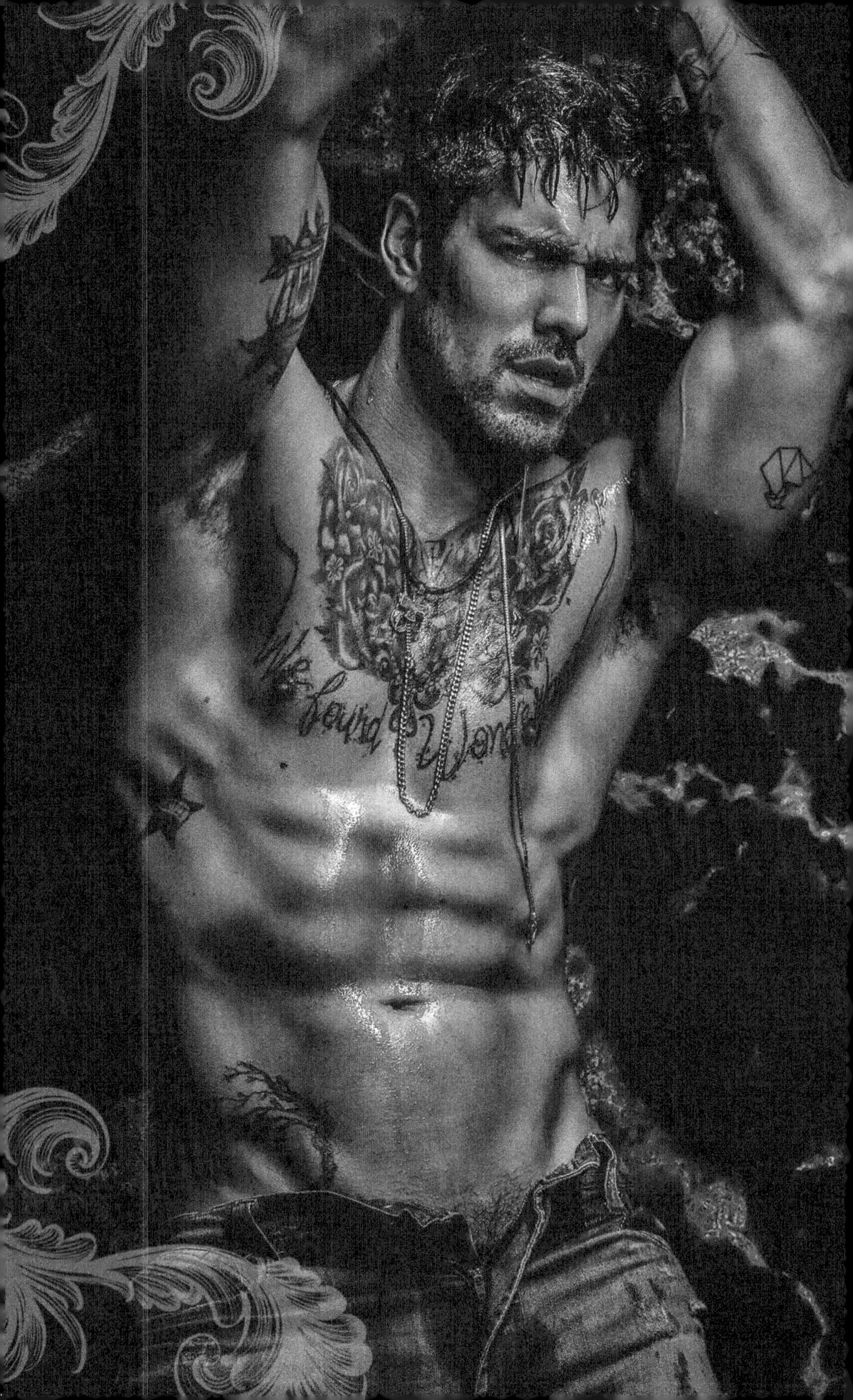

Chapter 36
Liana

The rising sun set fire to the horizon, inch by inch, lighting up the sky in the most beautiful colors I had ever seen.

I lay in bed, my gaze locked on the patterns thrown across the shutters.

A shadowed figure came into the room last night, leaving behind a food tray. I didn't want to eat it, but the delicious smell wafted through the air, prompting an answering growl from my stomach.

I ate everything off my tray before grogginess overtook me.

When I woke up next, I found another tray with fresh eggs, bacon and toast, and orange juice. The works. Sitting up in the soft bed, I stared at the food, trying my damndest to resist it. But weeks of stale bread had made me weak, and I was like a bottomless pit.

Shoving the bacon aside, I grabbed a piece of toast and the eggs. I couldn't eat fast enough, scoffing it down so I could make room for more. As I ate, I took in my bedroom in the light of day. It had arched ceilings with cream walls and various pink accents everywhere.

My favorite color.

My brows furrowed. No, it was *Louisa's* favorite color. Mine was green. I blinked repeatedly in confusion. Dozens of hazy memories pounded inside my mind, making it difficult to sort through them.

Colors don't matter, I told myself. It was an easy mistake to make. My twin and I had a lot of similarities. For most of my life, it was hard to decipher where one ended and the other began.

Instead, I focused on the food. An appreciative moan slipped through my lips as I savored it, all but licking my plate clean. I'd need it to give me strength for what I was about to do.

Kill Kingston Ashford. Escape this fucking place. Get back to Perez Cortes.

Before I was ready to do any of that though, I needed to sort myself out. So, I snooped through the room. Much like in his penthouse, he had dressers and closets stocked with new clothes, and the bathroom with toiletries.

I stopped in front of the mirror and gasped in horror. My skin was a canvas of blue and purple bruises, the black circles under my eyes telling the story of so many sleepless nights. My hair was a tangled, matted mess. My face was filthy, and so was the white nightgown I'd been forced to change into when I first boarded the ship.

Locking myself in the bathroom, I started the hot water and peeled off every piece of fabric. My nose scrunched in distaste as I picked up a whiff of my own stench, surprised that Kingston didn't spray me off with a hose.

I'd have done it to him.

I stepped into the shower and let out an exhale, closing my eyes. Hot water had never felt so cleansing.

It was the small pleasures that made everything better, made our childhood bearable. Whether it was sneaking ice cream in the middle of the night or tucking ourselves into a quiet corner and letting our imaginations take us away from Mother's hellscape, we had each other. And then it was snatched from me.

My fingers curled into fists, fury coursing through my veins. It was her fault my twin was dead as much as it was mine. Yet, for some reason, she'd made me suffer alone.

Reign of a Billionaire

I turned off the water with unsteady hands, then wrapped a towel around my body.

Why did Mother despise me so much? As her *treatment* became more and more brutal over the years, I hoped my father would come to visit me and he'd see how much I was suffering. I hoped he'd see the error of his ways, and we'd join forces and destroy them all—Mother and the Corteses and Tijuanas of this world. Together.

I waited... and waited, but he never came.

Instead, Mother turned on me. Every time I deviated from the carefully constructed prototype she wanted me to become, she made me endure another session. My memories and those torture sessions had left me broken and scarred, despite the plastic surgeries.

Bile rose in my throat before I swallowed it down. Moving methodically, I dried off, hoping to scrub away from the past and focus on my plan.

Dressed into a pair of jeans, a light pink crewneck T-shirt, and a pair of Converse, I made my way out of the room and through the hallways, peeking inside each room. Multiple bedrooms in different shades of aqua, green, and blue.

My steps faltered at the blue bedroom. While the last two had been clearly vacant for some time, this one was occupied. A floor-to-ceiling window showcasing the breathtaking view of the crystal blue water. What in the fuck was this place?

Glancing around, I ventured inside.

A pair of military boots discarded at the foot of the bed. A wallet on the nightstand. An odd-looking bracelet with... My eyes locked on a revolver, bracelet completely forgotten.

Bingo!

I couldn't believe my luck. I snatched the revolver and checked the chamber. One bullet.

I couldn't resist a snicker. What kind of idiot left a revolver with a bullet in the chamber out in the open?

The clanging of pots from somewhere in the house startled me and I spun around, almost expecting someone to catch me red-handed, touching something I shouldn't.

But the space was empty.

Gripping the gun, I followed the sound down the stairs. There was nobody in the dining room or living room. Another crash. I walked around until I found the kitchen.

And my captor.

To my amazement, Kingston was cooking—eggs, waffles, and pancakes. My stomach growled, despite woofing down my breakfast merely an hour ago.

He flicked me a glance, never pausing his movements.

"Good, you're still awake." His eyes fell to the gun in my hand, but his movements never faltered.

He was wearing jeans that hugged his ass like a second skin and a white T-shirt that revealed inky swirls. Despite his shortcomings, Kingston was a beautiful man.

"Obviously." It pissed me off that I noticed anything about him. I should just put this bullet in his skull and end him.

Kingston didn't appear bothered as he moved around his kitchen. And, since I was already noticing things about this man, I took note of his choice of design once more. Similarly to the upstairs rooms, this one boasted a wall of windows that led to the patio outside. For someone with such dark moods, this place seemed too cheery in contrast.

"Are you going to shoot me?" he prompted. My stomach growled again. Damn bodily needs. It was the last thing I needed or wanted right now. "Better hurry up and get it over with, then." He nodded to the spread he'd laid out.

He raised his eyebrows, waiting for me to say something.

"I warned you," I muttered. "I warned you that I'd kill you."

"Go ahead." The air vanished from the room at his cold tone, something about him unnerving. "But hurry up so we don't starve to death."

I remained in place, taken aback by the nonchalant tone of his tone.

"You ruined everything," I gritted, keeping my aim on him and my finger on the trigger. "Now, I'm going to make you pay."

"Are you going to hold that thing all day, or can you help set the table?"

I refused to move, and with a sigh, he moved to the cupboards and pulled out dishes and utensils. I let out a sinister chuckle. Watching him do such domestic things after witnessing his lethal side was a trip. Maybe the man had a split personality.

In no time, the table was set and food was on the table. Two plates. Two glasses. Two sets of silverware.

He sat down and picked up a crispy piece of bacon, and my lips curled with disgust. His eyes flared with surprise and his jaw tightened. But then he got up, scooped up the bacon onto a small plate, and walked over to the trash can, throwing it out.

"Why did you do that?" I asked as he placed the empty plate in the sink.

He sat back down, eyes sweeping over my face.

"You don't like bacon," he said simply. The sound of his voice was deep and gruff, something about it getting to me every time.

His words sunk in. "How do you know?"

He shrugged. "Could be the way you scrunch your nose." Those lips curled into a cruel smirk. "Either shoot me, Liana, or sit down and eat."

Something about his nonchalance pissed me off, and I fought the temptation to grab a pan off the stove—preferably still sizzling—and throw it at his head.

"I don't want to eat." I tightened my grip on the gun and glared at him. "I want to kill you."

He lifted his shoulder, looking at me in an unnerving way. "That revolver has been sitting in the same spot for years and hasn't been cleaned once."

"Why would you have a revolver with only one bullet on your nightstand?"

"Maybe I wanted to end it all." I gaped at him, unsure whether he was serious. Maybe he was toying with me. "Want me to save you the trouble?"

I pursed my lips at his comment. He knew I was teetering on the edge, yet all he did was egg me on. He raised his brow in challenge, and I glared at him as my senses sharpened.

"Then a game of Russian roulette," I declared, pleased with my quick thinking. "Since you're so eager to end it all."

I saw something flicker in his eyes. He took a bite of his food and swallowed before replying. "You can sit down, enjoy the food, and play the game at the same time."

He behaved like a distinguished gentleman one second and a savage criminal the next. It was confusing as fuck.

Gritting my teeth, I stomped my way to the table and sat down, still holding the revolver. I wouldn't eat, but I'd let the man have his last meal. What could I say? That shower must've done wonders on my humanity.

"Here, happy?"

He reached for his glass and took a drink of his orange juice, then raised his eyebrow. "Hardly."

He watched me intently, his lips twitching, but he didn't smile. It was as if he knew something I didn't. This man was as annoying as he was handsome, and I didn't like it.

I stared at him as he ate, the smell of eggs triggering a pang of hunger. Again. I really needed to reevaluate my priorities.

He pushed his plate my way. "Here."

"There's a plate in front of me," I snapped.

"Yes, and you haven't touched it."

"Well, maybe you poisoned it." Agitation climbed up my spine. We both knew he'd scooped eggs from the same pan, although he didn't point it out.

One point for the kidnapper.

I pushed both plates away with the tip of my gun, ignoring another protest from my stomach. "If you're done, let's play."

"I love games." His voice darkened, and something about it had me thinking all kinds of sinful, carnal things.

"And I hate hearing you talk." He slid his intense gaze to me. "I want you to explain how you know so much about me."

And my sister, I added silently.

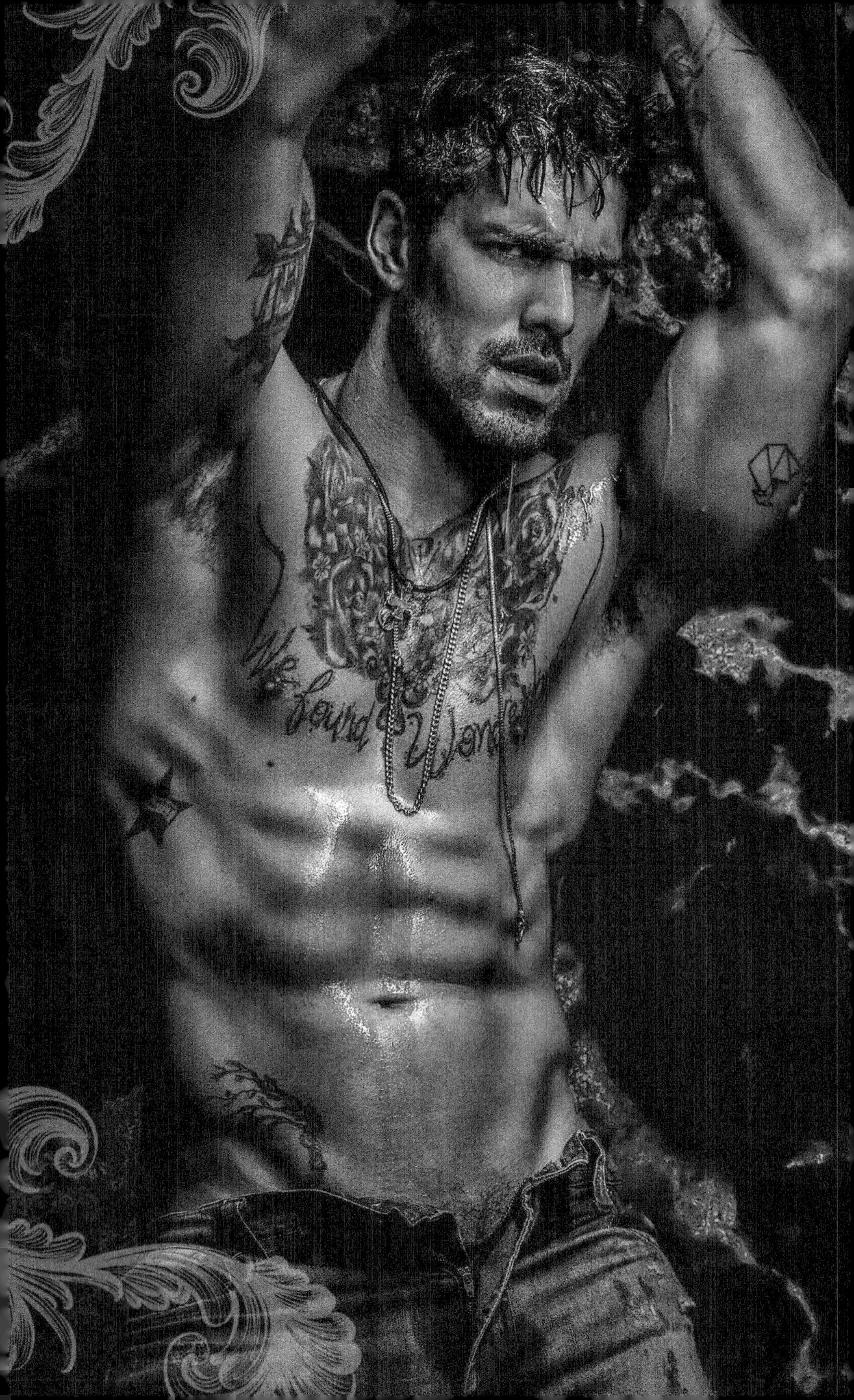

Chapter 37
Kingston

My brows pulled together at how enraged she sounded, leading me to one conclusion. Liana truly didn't remember me. What else had she forgotten? And, more importantly, what secrets was she hiding?

I intended to unravel every single one of them, starting with her absurd desire to be taken back to Perez yesterday.

"I'm waiting," she spoke again.

"I was your bodyguard once upon a time."

I heard her sharp inhale. "You're lying."

"Your memory can't be *that* bad," I drawled while she scrutinized me.

"I guess you weren't significant enough to remember." *Ouch.* She waved the gun around, and it made my tongue feel like sandpaper. I'd seen firsthand the kind of skilled shooter she was, but like I said, it was a rusty piece. There wasn't much stopping her from accidentally shooting herself. I decided to keep her distracted.

"You don't think ten fucking years were significant?"

She winced as my words settled around her. After a few seconds of silence, she spoke again. "The years are. You're not."

Double fucking ouch.

"Or maybe someone brainwashed you," I pointed out calmly. More doubt danced in her eyes. She was doing her best to hide it, but I'd spent years studying her and her sister's expressions. Being observant was a matter of life and death for some.

"Please stop talking. The sound's giving me a rash."

Jesus Christ. I saved her, yet she'd been giving me nothing but grief. I rested my hands on the table and leaned back in my chair.

"Instead of throwing insults, you should be thanking me."

If looks could kill, I'd have dropped dead on the spot. "I didn't need a rescue, you... you... *svoloch*." Luckily for me, her stuttered "asshole" rolled right off me. She'd called me worse—in English *and* Russian—though it was starting to appear she didn't remember that either.

"What would you have liked me to do? Let you be sold in the auction to Cortes?"

She opened her mouth before immediately closing it, her lips thinning.

I placed my elbows over the edge of the table and rested my chin in my palm while I stared down the barrel of the gun. "My turn to ask a question," I said with a calm I didn't feel.

She scoffed. "I don't think so."

"I thought you knew how to play the game." I reached for her just as she readied herself to bolt, forcing her back into the chair. My palm engulfed her small one holding the revolver, forcing her finger against the trigger. "Pull it," I taunted as I spun the cylinder and then clicked it back into place.

"I will when I'm damn well ready," she shot back, shooting daggers at me. "I have more questions."

My hand wrapped around hers. *Click.*

She let out a wheeze, her eyes wide with shock as they darted back and forth between me and the gun. I removed my hand from hers, her glare burning a hole in my chest. So fucking odd. Nobody had ever had such an impact on me.

"My question," I reminded her. "And I won't even hold the gun to your head."

She rolled her eyes, although the light tremor of her bottom lip didn't escape me. "I'm not even holding it to your head."

"Not literally," I agreed, amused.

Her fingers twitched over the trigger, her nerves practically seeping through her pores. I waited several heartbeats before I went for the jugular.

"Where were you?"

She blinked, her expression filled with confusion, and after a second of drawn-out silence, she finally asked in a shaky breath, "Wh-what do you mean?"

"Louisa was going to run," I said. "The only reason she didn't follow through with it was because you never came."

Tense silence filled the air. "You're wrong," she whispered. "The Tijuana cartel got her. Perez—" Her voice cracked as she shook her head, staring at me dumbly. "I don't know what you're talking about."

"We had a plan," I gritted out.

I could feel her carefully built armor cracking, disintegrating into smoke.

"What plan?"

Had guilt gnawed at her to the point of impacting her memory? Was that the reason she willfully forgot the price her twin paid? Or was she play-acting?

"She wouldn't leave without you. Not even for me."

Her delicate brows pulled up in confusion.

"For you?" I closed my eyes and pinched the bridge of my nose. Her confusion was grating on me. "What do you mean?"

Reliving this was a bitch. I felt responsible for not saving her. For not protecting her. Our secret love turned into a tragedy.

"She loved me. I loved her."

I anticipated Liana's move, but not the savagery in her eyes. She practically flung herself across the table. Pressing the barrel of the revolver against my forehead, her other hand wrapped around my throat, those golden eyes—so fucking familiar—glared at me.

"If you loved her, why didn't you protect her?" she hissed. "I should kill you."

The same guilt that had been eating at me for years stared right back at me through her eyes. Liana had been broken and put back together, but deep inside, those cracked pieces were in no better shape than my own.

"You should," I agreed evenly, my hand on hers, holding the pistol in place. "But you should also question why you have such gaps in your memory."

"Fuck. You." Her voice trembled with fury. "I remember everything worth remembering."

"Except for me and large chunks of your sister's life."

Chapter 38
Liana

"Time to die," I gritted, the anger returning with a vengeance and flooding my system. It didn't matter that this man had given me the most mind-blowing orgasm I'd ever experienced. It didn't matter that he made me feel all these things I'd never experienced before.

The need to finish this made my hands tremble. The only problem was, I physically couldn't pull the trigger. And judging by Kingston's expression, he knew it.

"Go ahead," he urged.

His grip remained on my own, the slightest pressure of his finger on the trigger. Silence dominated the space between us. Every single cell in my body itched to carve this man's heart out. If only I could give in to the darkness and let it happen.

Why? Haunted whispers clawed at my skull, piercing my temples and wrecking me from within. *Why can't I kill him?*

My mind was trapped in a maze, unable to find a way out, and this man was to blame. So many emotions and thoughts burst through me, and I didn't have what it took to process them all. I wasn't coping, and what mattered most in this moment was keeping this man from witnessing it.

So I closed my eyes. I could feel tears burning. Each breath I took suffocated my lungs instead of breathing life into me. The metal became unbearably heavy, and my hands shook with every passing second.

"Do it, Liana." More force on my trigger finger. My eyes snapped open, meeting his dark gaze. I yanked my hand away, then aimed. Terrified at what I'd find if I let him in, I pulled the trigger.

Bang.

And missed.

The gun slid from my fingers, falling on the ground, the thud of it loud in the silence of the aftermath.

"This was your last chance at shooting me." His voice held a dark edge to it. "Fair warning, though. The next time you aim a gun at me, it will be the last thing you ever do."

Oh God.

So many confusing feelings washed over me. Kingston Ashford was the only man I'd ever hesitated in killing.

I... was losing my mind. What good was I if I couldn't even kill my captor? Bile rose in my throat and suddenly the food I'd eaten churned in my stomach. A sharp, piercing pain shot through my temples.

Images of Louisa broke loose. Me. Our faceless bodyguard.

That last memory hit me so quickly, I clutched my head from the pain of it.

"Stop sketching him." *My sister seemed agitated as I finished another drawing, smiling dreamily.* "Mother will lose her shit if she finds it."

I chewed on the tip of the pencil, ignoring her and the faraway noise signaling Mother and Ivan's gladiator games. Each time we attended, their brutality resulted in fresh nightmares.

"I'll burn them before I go to sleep." *I flicked her a glance. She sat at the bottom of my bed, legs crisscrossed, as she typed frantically on* the laptop she'd smuggled in two hours ago. We wore identical pink-and-black pajama pants with MIT sweatshirts. We still hoped Mother would let her attend college in the fall. And if she went, so would I. Anything to get the fuck out of here and be a normal teenager for a bit. Maybe I'd finally get to do things that normal kids did—attend a concert, maybe even go to a party and make bad decisions.

"What are you doing?" I asked.

She lifted her head. "Trying to get into Ivan's computer."

I scrunched my brows. "Why?"

There could be nothing good on our stepfather's laptop. That man was a sick pervert and needed to be taken out. If only someone were brave enough to do it.

"So I know when the Tijuana cartel is coming."

"Mother told him no," I whispered. My stomach churned with nausea and my fingers clenched the pencil until it snapped in half. Frustrated, I flung the pieces across the room into the fireplace.

"I know," she soothed. "I just want to make sure Ivan doesn't try something behind her back."

I nodded, but my mood had already soured. Getting off the bed, I gathered all the sketches and made my way to the fireplace. I hated burning them, but it had to be done. One day, when we were far away from here, I'd store them in a safe place and maybe share them with people. I watched them slowly disintegrate into ash, as if they'd never existed.

Crawling back into the bed, I lay down.

"What are you doing?" My sister's eyes scrutinized me. "It's only eight o'clock."

I shrugged. "It's going to take me forever to fall asleep with all that noise."

You'd think I'd be used to it by now growing up in this fucked-up place, but I wasn't.

She let out an amused chuckle. "Want me to hold a pillow over your head?"

I rolled my eyes, not at all amused. I was terribly claustrophobic, and she knew that. "Want me to break your face?"

She shut her laptop, staring at me as silence stretched, before we collapsed into a fit of giggles. That night, we slept holding each other and dreaming of a better tomorrow.

My eyes welled with tears as I whirled around, rushing out of there and into the bathroom. The face that greeted me in the mirror was pale, eyes hollow and terrified. The face that was familiar yet all wrong.

"Why can't I remember him?" I rasped to my reflection.

There were clearly gaps in my memory that were alarming. The more I tried to remember, the worse my headaches were. I struggled to find bits and pieces of me that were missing, and I didn't know how to get them back.

Wiping my tears from my cheeks, my muscles quaked with silent sobs. I wrapped my arms around myself in comfort, holding myself together as I headed back into the bedroom and crawled underneath the covers. I closed my eyes, and for the first time in a very long time, I let myself weep.

For the girl I used to be and the girl that I'd become but no longer recognized.

The scent of vanilla teased my senses, slowly pulling me from sleep.

I lay still, my eyes blinking in the dark until a figure sitting in the corner registered. I sat up on the bed suddenly, pulling the covers to my chin and staring at the shadow.

"Why are you so creepy?" I rasped. I didn't have the energy to argue with him.

The silver hue of the moon projected the only light through the windows, throwing shadows across his sculpted jaw. Something about him seemed scarier now. Like he'd unleashed the full spectrum of his fury after our little battle of power yesterday.

"What did you dream about?" he asked, and I blinked at him, confusion taking center stage. I remained silent, our staredown stretching for seconds, minutes, until he broke it again. "I asked you a question, ice princess."

There was a harshness to him that could easily suck the essence from my soul. Everything about him was honed for danger, and it had everything to do with my last name. Some of my memories were hazy, but it didn't take a rocket scientist to figure that part out.

"I don't remember," I answered truthfully. And suddenly, I realized. For the first time in years, I'd slept without waking up drenched in sweat.

"Interesting," he commented ever so casually, but there was that tension you couldn't miss. It was in the strain of his long fingers resting on the armrests. It was in the way his legs were crossed stiffly at his ankles. His jeans should have made him appear casual, but failed. The top buttons of his shirt were undone, revealing the ink on his collarbone and up his neck.

"You didn't answer my question," I retorted. How long had he been sitting here? "Why are you so creepy?"

"Technically you're in my home, so you're creepy for sleeping in my bed." I opened my mouth but then closed it, appalled at his ridiculous answer, but you couldn't reason with lunatics, so I let it go. "Are you hungry?"

"No."

"You have to eat."

"Well, I don't want to," I snapped. "I lost my appetite waking up to a creep in my room." Everything about this man rattled me so much that my knee-jerk reaction was to fight him. "In fact, it's best if you get used to it. I plan on making you regret ever bidding on me. And if you were hoping for sex... Well, don't. Touch me, and I'll slice your dick off."

He didn't seem concerned about his dick. Instead, he placed his elbows on his knees and leaned forward, steepling his fingers. His dark eyes bore into me, unspoken messages in them leaving a sharp tang on my tongue.

"It appears you might be delusional." Was this fucker purposely provoking me? "You're my property now. That means you have to do everything I say."

I scoffed. "Hold your breath on that one."

"It's my job to keep you safe now." The fierceness of the words was a juxtaposition to the cool threat in his voice. "And I'll do it by any means necessary." I remained silent, glaring at him, and a small smirk tugged on his lips. Fucker found this amusing. "Now you're going to join me downstairs for dinner and tell me why you insisted on being taken to Perez."

My eyes darted to the window and he followed my gaze.

"It's too late for dinner," I retorted wryly.

"It's only eight, and Europeans prefer later dinners anyhow." It would seem Kingston had all the answers. He rose to his feet, and my grip on the covers tightened. He must have noticed it because I saw the hint of a smirk around his lips. "Be downstairs in five minutes," he ordered, then headed out of the room.

It wasn't until he was gone that his words sunk in. Europe! I was on an island in freaking Europe.

Chapter 39
Kingston

As we dined, the tension was so thick it could've bounced off the wall.

I took a sip of my sparkling water, needing all my wits about me as I dealt with this woman who managed to surprise me at every turn. She wasn't the Liana I remembered.

"How's your food?" I asked.

"I hate steak," she growled, candlelight flickering across her face. "I hate mashed potatoes, and I hate corn."

"Too bad, it's my favorite meal." I enjoyed all fine food, but I found the freedom of being able to grill my own food extremely gratifying after spending years being fed slop by her mother and stepfather.

I cut through my steak and shoved a piece into my mouth, then chewed it slowly as I studied her. I usually preferred solitude, but for some reason, I wanted this woman around me. So I forced this dinner.

Something inside me kept driving me to figure her out and understand this pull she had on me.

"A gentleman would ask what a lady's preferences are," she hissed.

"Good thing I'm not a gentleman."

"I forgot." She waved her fork in the air. "You're a creep." She wasn't far off. When my restlessness got the best of me earlier today, I went to her room and watched her sleep. It wasn't until I heard the soothing sound of her breaths that I calmed down. "I'll be sure to return the favor," she said, interrupting my thoughts.

My fingers tightened around my steak knife. I should warn her it would be unwise to sneak up on me. In fact, I'd killed people in the past who'd done just that.

I pushed my plate away and leaned forward.

"If you come into my room, I'll consider it an invitation," I said without a hint of emotion.

She sat opposite of me, her body rigid and her knuckles white. Every so often, she shot me a glare, and I imagined she was probably picturing all the ways she could slice me and dice me with her cutlery. I made a mental note to only give her butter knives going forward, although my instinct warned she'd probably find a way to end me using those too, which wouldn't bode well for her. There was nobody on this island, and the only way off of it was by plane or boat. Neither of which she had access to.

"Invitation to what?" she asked, her tone hesitant.

"To fuck you into oblivion."

Her cheeks flushed a delicate shade of pink and she gazed up at me through her thick lashes, making my heart twist. It reminded me so much of Louisa.

"You're a fucking deviant," she said, her voice breathy. She must have realized it because she clenched her teeth. "If I come into your room, you'll be dead before your dick has a chance to get hard."

And there was that.

Since Louisa's death, my cock hadn't responded to a single woman. I grieved my sunshine, then turned to celibacy with the full intention of dying that way. Until this one crossed my path. I didn't know what it was—her resemblance or her fire—but suddenly my dick decided to play. And it was wrong on so many levels.

The rest of our dinner resumed in silence despite many questions that needed answers.

I sat in my office attempting to handle a few emails and pay some bills. My mother left me a chunk of her inheritance and the empire she'd inherited from her father, but it came with responsibilities. And so did my own wealth I'd built on blood. My skills of tracking down people were highly sought after in the Omertà.

When the grandfather clock chimed midnight, I found myself staring at the laptop connected to my surveillance feed, watching Liana in the library like it was my sole purpose in life.

My heart thumped at the sight of her, and a yearning ache spread to my chest. I needed to understand this growing obsession with Liana, but this—having her nearby—would have to do for now.

I watched her cuddled up on the sofa, her legs folded and a blanket over her lap. She was beautiful, still wearing the same delicate clothes from dinner. Her hair tumbled down her slender shoulders in a cascade of sun-streaked waves. Her smooth skin radiated under the warm gleam of the roaring fire.

Holding the pad with her right hand and using the pencil with her left, she sketched. What or who she was drawing, I had no idea, but every once in a while, she'd throw a bundle of paper into the fire. Both twins drew, but Lou was always better at it, and judging by the way Liana watched her sketches burn with her eyebrows knitted together, hers hadn't improved.

She'd been in the same position for the past two hours, sketching and then discarding. Switching the pencil between her left and right hand, massaging her left wrist every so often. I'd claim she was pathetic for not giving up on the hobby that her sister excelled at, but I realized I was even more so.

Fuck, this was so goddamned stupid.

I shouldn't be spying on her through the camera, soaking in every expression that passed her face. I moved to close down the feed, but like each time before it, I stopped at the last second.

She started to hum, the tune distant and faint but enough to make my chest shudder. I wanted to march down the hallway and burst into the library, snatch her up, and carry her off to bed. Then I'd own her noises as I drove into her tight, wet heat, listening to her pleas for *more*. I wanted to torment her and make her pay for making me feel this way.

Clenching my teeth, I finally exited out of the program and shot to my feet. Again, I found myself bursting with restless energy.

Fucking hell.

Maybe bringing her to my island where there was nothing and nobody to distract me from her wasn't such a good idea after all. The effect of her presence grew more desperate by the hour, and every dark, primal instinct inside of me taunted me. I wanted to take her, bend her over, and claim her. My balls ached, eager to be buried deep inside her.

I jumped to my feet, walked out of the office, and blindly followed the path to the library. I needed to talk to her, hear her soft voice.

My legs brought me to my destination in record time, and I stalked inside, the door to the library slamming into the wall from the force of my urgency. Liana jumped to her feet, her eyes darting around as if expecting someone else here.

"What the fuck, Kingston?" Lightning bolts blazed in her eyes, and her décolletage blotched crimson. My gaze wandered to her breasts. Her next words told me my discretion lacked finesse. "My eyes are up here, *zasranets*." Jackass. She really loved cursing at me in Russian. "Or would you like me to dig out your eyeballs?"

I closed the door to preserve the heat in the library and leaned against it, tucking my hands into my pockets.

"Have you done it before?" I asked her casually.

She blinked, her cheeks burning red. "Done what?"

The corner of my lips twitched. Someone's mind was in the gutter. "Dug out someone's eyeballs," I clarified.

She fell silent, her expression darkening before she masked it.

"I have," she answered, her voice distant and flat. "I've stabbed a man in both his eyes and then watched him bleed out for hours."

The words were like a punch in the gut. Liana had always been the stronger twin, but never psychotic or ruthless.

She sighed, and the heartbreaking sound tugged on the strings of my blackened heart. She wasn't Louisa, but there was a part of me that craved to protect her and erase all the bad things she'd endured to become this ruthless version of herself.

But then just as quickly, she wiped her expression and narrowed her eyes on me.

"You need to do something about this library," she grumbled.

"What do you mean?"

"There isn't a single romance novel to be found."

My brows furrowed. "There is a whole section with Agatha Christie novels," I pointed out.

"Yeah, I know." *Someone* had made themselves comfortable. "But I wasn't talking about murder mysteries, was I?"

My molars clenched. There was nothing like going from one extreme to another.

"Why do you want to go back to Perez?" I said instead, focusing on the answers I needed from her.

"None of your business."

"I'm trying to help you." She gasped as though insulted and turned her head to stare at the fireplace. "Whatever you're trying to do, you need resources."

She glared up at me like a lioness ready to pounce for daring to point out the obvious. I bared my teeth, the sadistic part of me hoping she would. I was so up for a challenge.

"I don't need anything or anyone. If you want to help, release me and take me back to Brazil."

"No can do." Her eyes filled with fire. Some would say we were headed for a disaster. I'd argue whatever this was could be an ingredient for something more. "Unless you know how to pilot a plane or navigate a boat."

Her shoulders sagged for only a second before optimism filled her features. "I'm sure I can figure it out if you provide me with an operating manual."

I clenched my fists. Jesus, the woman was willing to kill herself to get back to Brazil. I pinched the bridge of my nose. It was clear she wouldn't be sharing anything. I could attempt torture, but hurting girls didn't sit well with me. I suspected this pretty little psycho wouldn't tell me anything even if I did.

"Sure, I'll get you the operating manuals for both," I finally relented. "If you manage to get either of them going, you can leave."

But first, I'd make sure to remove the ignition cables. Then we'd see how far she made it without the help she so adamantly refused.

Chapter 40
Liana

I'd been on this fucking island for a goddamned week.

And the only conclusion I'd come to was that Kingston Ashford was a pain in my ass. The only reason he'd given me the stupid operating manual was to shut me up.

It was my fault, really—I didn't specify *how* the machinery was delivered to me. As in, the fucker sabotaged the engines.

"Grady White top of the line, my ass," I muttered as I shut the deck floorboard with enough force to make the boat rock.

"You seem cheerful today." I'd recognize that smooth-as-silk voice anywhere. My limbs ached from all the climbing up and down this stupid boat and I wasn't in the mood. Despite the winter months, the temperatures during the day were warm enough to strip down into a bathing suit—or get a sunburn—which led me to believe we had to be somewhere in the far south of Europe. The Mediterranean climate was one indication; the numerous fruit trees, olives, and shrubs of lavender were others.

I slowly straightened up and found Kingston lounging in the shade in bermuda shorts and a white T-shirt, his ink somewhat visible beneath the stretchy material. He tossed me a bottle of water, and my traitorous eyes locked on his flexing bicep.

In my distraction, I barely ducked in time for it to miss me and hit the captain's chair.

"Drink." I glared at him, but before I could complain, he added, "And don't bring up the whole gentleman thing. It's getting old."

"You almost hit me with it," I fumed.

"Drink," he repeated. "I can't have you fainting."

I snatched the bottle off the deck, gulped down half of it, then pointed my finger at him.

"You did this on purpose," I accused.

"Did what?" Amusement flickered in his eyes, his voice dark with humor. "You're going to have to be a bit more specific. I do many things every day."

Nerves vibrated through me. I really disliked my body's reaction to him. I'd give my left tit to get rid of it. It was so fucking wrong. First, it was clear he was in love with my twin. Second, his morals were questionable. There couldn't be two of us with questionable morals—it'd be like feeding a serial killer more victims to murder. And lastly, if I didn't capture his attention before, when he apparently spent ten years as my bodyguard, it was clear he only saw my twin in me now.

"You let me have the manual because you knew it was no use. Damn you."

A quirk in his cheek. "I did."

"You fucking—"

"Better think twice about what you say next." He drew out each word, causing my nostrils to flare. He thought he could threaten me and I'd cower? He was dead wrong. I'd learned from my dear mother that nobody was to be trusted.

Everyone was out to hurt you, and this man was no exception. My goal was to hurt him first.

"It's not right to give me hope and then take it away." I breathed

Reign of a Billionaire

heavily, sweat dampening my temples as I wiped my palms against my tiny denim shorts. "It's cruel actually."

He watched me for a beat, his eyebrows pulling tight.

Dinners this past week had been frustrating but... somewhat amicable. Of course, that didn't keep us from lashing out at the first opportunity. Like now.

"You're right," he rasped. "I'm sorry."

My eyes widened. I tilted my head, studying his expression, but found nothing except sincerity in his eyes.

I dove off the side of the boat into the cool, crystal blue water that only came up to my knees, I waded through and made my way to the shore. The sand felt warm underneath my feet as I made my way to Kingston.

I stopped ten feet in front of him, the air crackling as we stared at each other. I often wondered what he saw when he looked at me. Just a broken woman? My twin? His enemy's daughter? Or maybe *I* was his enemy?

Whatever it was, it set me on edge.

"I have a surprise for you." His dark eyes cut through me. Something fluttered whenever he so much as glanced at me. I had to pull myself together.

"You're going to fix this boat and get me off this island?" I asked, squeezing the excess water from my ponytail.

He cleared his throat as he followed the movement of my hands. "You're smart enough, you don't need me to answer that." He stood up, towering over me, and then turned. "Are you coming?"

"Do I have a choice?" I couldn't help defying him. It was like my mouth moved independently from my mind.

"No."

My thoughts came to a halt when Kingston stopped, glancing at me over his shoulder. His lips slowly tugged in a smirk, and I hated how it frazzled me.

"I could throw you over my shoulder and carry you," he said, his tone goading. Was he... Was he flirting with me?

"Fine. I'm coming," I whispered, shaking my head and averting my eyes.

The rest of the way back to the estate, I followed in silence, careful not to step on sharp stones or branches. To my surprise, he led the way toward the library. The second I entered, a gasp left my lips.

"What—" I shook my head, at a loss for words. "How?"

Barefoot, I padded toward the south wall. Sometime over the last week, Kingston had rearranged one entire wall with floor-to-ceiling shelves. A ladder in front of it, carved ornately from solid wood. And the best part? It was stocked with a wide variety of romance authors—Jane Austen, Charlotte Brontë, Barbara Cartland, Eliza Haywood, Maria Edgeworth.

I turned to find Kingston watching me, propped against the wall with his hands shoved in his pockets. His stare was edged with something heated and dark—something that battled with my resolve.

"I found them stored away in the attic." He pushed off the wall and made his way over to me. It felt as if I'd forgotten how to breathe with each step. His long, graceful fingertips brushed over the frayed spines. "There are traditional titles, and some more..."

He cleared his throat, drawing my attention to his face. Was Kingston *blushing*?

"More what?" I pressed.

"More scandalous."

"Where?" I blurted. Heat rushed to my cheeks, and every inch of me grew hot, realizing I just admitted my love for dirty romance novels.

His eyes fell to my cheeks, and then he laughed. It was an easy sound, one that I didn't think he was accustomed to making.

Warmth curled low in my stomach.

He ran a hand through his dark hair, and before I knew what was happening, he closed the distance between us. His hand wrapped around my nape, and I waited with bated breath. I didn't know what I was waiting for, but something told me I was about to find out.

Kingston's mouth found mine, and I shivered. His kiss was

intense, stealing my oxygen and emptying my mind from rational thought. My curves molded to his hard body, burning everywhere he touched me.

He angled my head back, ravishing my mouth with an intensity and hunger that matched my own. It was as if he couldn't stop, and with every heartbeat, we lost ourselves to the sheer insanity of it.

Until he pulled away, leaving me unsteady on my shaky knees. His dark gaze clashed with mine as a storm brewed around us, and I knew he'd just altered the course of our lives.

"Enjoy your books," was all he said as he walked backward away from me, away from the puddle he'd just reduced me to.

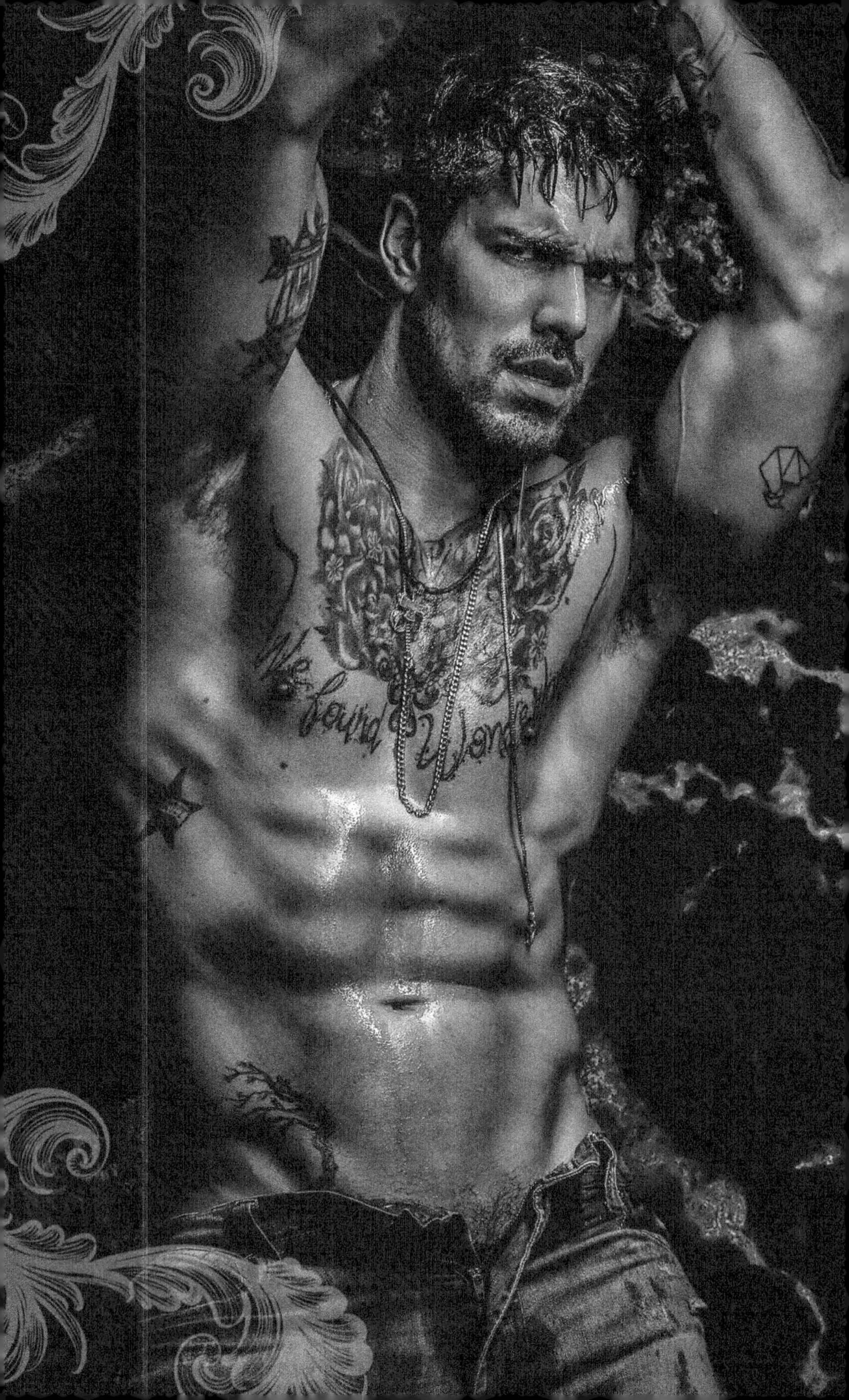
We found

Chapter 41
Kingston

Something had shifted—altogether steadily and slowly—over the past week. Or maybe I could pinpoint it to when I first saw Liana saving those women from the shipping container in D.C. Either way, it was confronting.

Liana Volkov had me in knots. I ached for her. I craved her presence all the fucking time, and that was unacceptable. Maybe this—whatever this was—was an ingredient for a happy life.

She wasn't supposed to be the one for me, but for whatever reason, I couldn't even go an hour without seeking her out. Our paths had converged, and we'd both been left fighting this sizzling attraction. If I wasn't sure before, I certainly was now. Our little foray across enemy lines just about set the fucking island on fire.

It was wrong; I knew that. But damn had it felt good.

I took a deep breath and took a seat in my office, staring out at the ripples in the sparkling water. Louisa always dreamed of a secluded place, somewhere warm with a beach all to ourselves. She never got it, but her twin did.

It wasn't fair, but I had neither the energy nor the courage to fight it anymore.

My phone buzzed and I flicked a glance at the screen. "Hello, Winston," I said into the speaker.

"You doing okay?"

"Shouldn't I be?" I retorted dryly.

"Consider this a heads-up." My shoulders tensed. "Illias Konstantin reached out to Byron. Apparently the Thorns of Omertà want your location."

"Who specifically?" I gritted. The underworld could always get in contact with me, but they never could locate me. It was by design— trust was a bitch that got you killed.

"Enrico Marchetti." Fuck, I knew he wouldn't let it go. The moment he learned Sofia had a daughter, he wanted to get his paws on her and make her pay for the torture his wife had endured.

Yes, I worked alongside the Omertà. Yes, I killed with them and for them. But I wouldn't allow them anywhere near Liana.

She was mine and mine alone.

"Tell him you have no way of getting in touch with me," I deadpanned.

"You got it." I could almost hear the smirk in his voice "How's my plane?"

"I had to take it apart."

"What?"

"I'll have it in shape before it's returned." Obviously I knew she'd never be able to fly a plane, but I wanted her to see for herself how futile working alone would be. And maybe I wanted to teach her a lesson at the same time, sue me.

"She's quite the woman, huh?"

"She is," I agreed, then steered the conversation away from Liana. "Any chance you know of someone who's capable of DNA tracing?" I asked, changing subjects. "That sliced finger I left in my freezer back in D.C. I want to know who it belongs to."

"Hmmm." Silence thrummed over the line for a moment. "I might. You okay if I have someone grab it from your penthouse? I'm in Paris with Billie."

Billie was my brother's wife, and considering the two had just spent six years apart, I understood his reluctance to leave her.

"How about I have it delivered to you once I'm back in the States?"

"Better that it goes directly to my friend Tristan Bennetti. He knows of an excellent forensic pathologist."

"Send me the address."

Once the call ended, I pulled up the surveillance and found Liana in bed, asleep, and a book pressed against her chest. I zoomed in and read the title: *Sex on the Beach*.

I got to my feet and made my way to her room, pushing my way in soundlessly. I found her in the fetal position, her brows furrowed as if she battled demons even in her dreams. A cool breeze swept through the cracked window. The moonlight cast a faint glow across her face, and my chest stirred at the sight. Her lips were slightly parted, and her breaths came out even and shallow.

I dropped to my haunches next to her and watched her sleeping face.

I used to tell the twins I could spot the differences in their facial features. I could no longer say that.

I skimmed a thumb across her cheekbone, glad to see the meals I'd been preparing for her were filling them out a bit more.

I stepped away and dropped into my usual seat in the corner. I knew it was wrong, but there was no way I could go back to sleeping alone. Not when I knew she warmed the sheets just doors down from me.

Whimpering noises dragged me from my slumber.

I blinked, adjusting my eyes to the dim room, and spotted the sun barely below the horizon. A crick in my neck and the stiffness of my spine told me I fell asleep in a chair. Again. My head groggy, I leaned back into the seat and adjusted so I was on my side, closing my eyes once more. It was when another whimper sounded that I jolted my eyes open.

At first, I couldn't find her. The bed was empty, but I could hear her sharp breaths. My eyes darted around, and I made out a body curled up in a ball on the floor. I sprung into action, taking the five steps to close the distance, then crouched over her.

Another whimper.

Her body shivered and her shoulders spasmed, her delicate hands wrapped around herself for protection. Her blonde mane blocked her face from my view.

"Please... No..." she whimpered. I pushed her hair aside to find her eyes screwed tightly shut. "N-not again."

"Liana." She didn't even stir. "Liana, wake up."

Her eyes fluttered open, but it was almost as if she looked through me. She was stuck in a trance, unseeing.

"Please," she whimpered. "Stop... Please stop."

"Shhh..." I whispered as my protective instincts shifted into place. "You're safe." I ran my fingers through her hair, combing her soft, golden strands. Her eyes found mine, but they were still glassy. "Shhh, I got you. No one's going to hurt you."

The startling realization of how sincere those words were hit me square in the chest. I slid my arms around her back and scooped her up. She snuggled into my hold, her body shaking as she continued to murmur her pleas.

I tucked her beneath the covers, and as I went to move, a whimper tore from her lips, her hand grabbing mine.

"Don't leave me." I froze. "Please."

"I won't," I promised. Her body relaxed and a reassuring sigh left her lips as she fell back asleep.

I climbed onto the other side of bed, resting atop of the covers, and laced my hands behind my head.

The more I got to know this woman, the more puzzled I became. It felt so natural and effortless to be in her company.

Don't leave me.

Those were the very same words I'd whispered to Louisa once upon a time. Unaware, Liana had struck a nerve, her words etching into my mind like the scars her mother had etched into my skin. Such a simple phrase, but it cracked my already broken chest.

I shouldn't get close to her, no matter how hard she pulled me into her orbit. It was a betrayal to Louisa, to myself... and to Liana. She deserved better.

So then why did my numb heart bleed at the thought of giving her up?

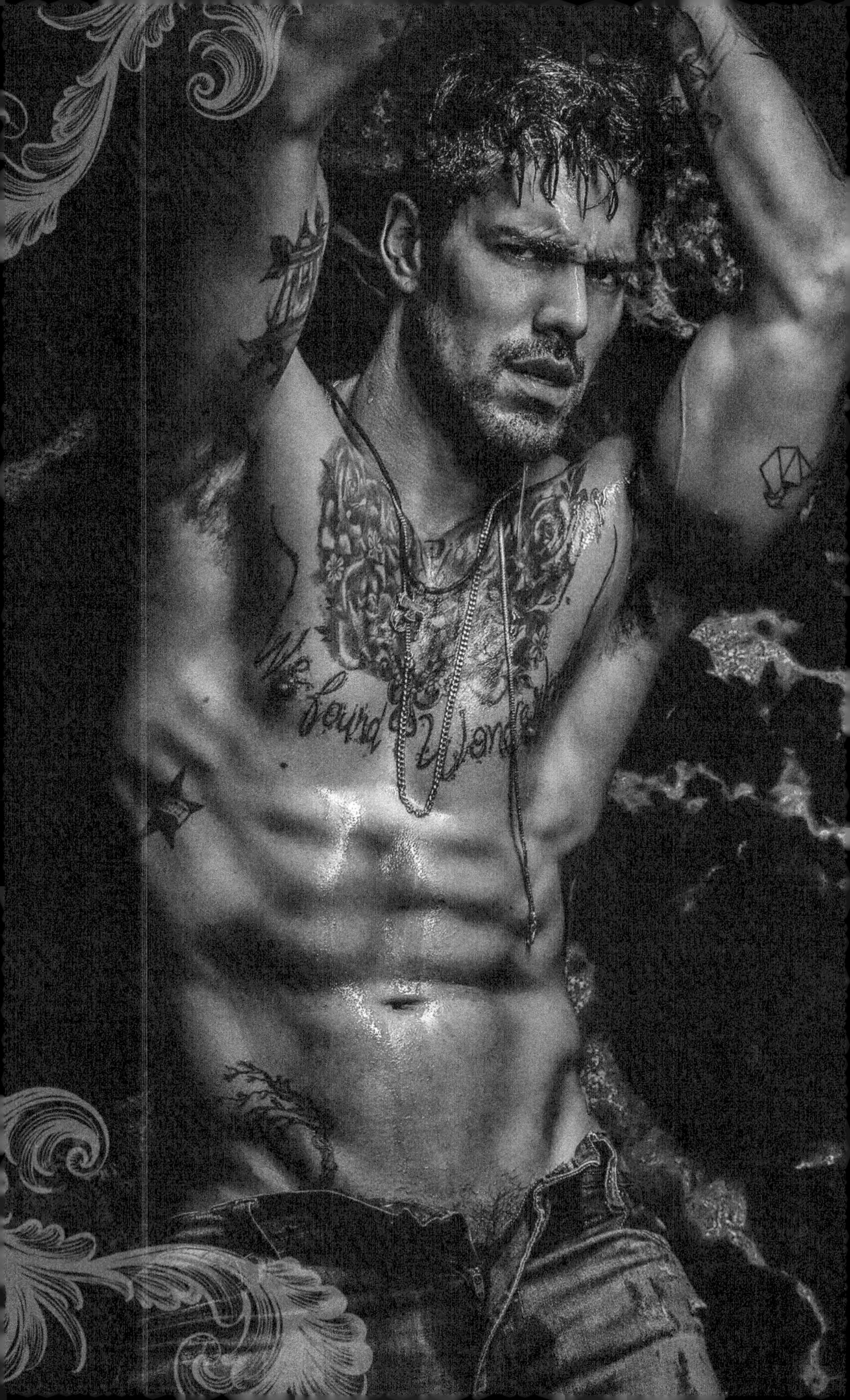

Chapter 42
Liana

Something smelled delicious, like warm spiced vanilla. I wanted to nuzzle into it and never wake up.

I opened my eyes and yawned when my gaze landed on the body next to me. I looked up, up, up and straight into a pair of dark eyes. I scrambled back from him, my heart racing in my chest, and fell right off the bed and onto my ass.

"You alright?"

"Why are you here?"

"You asked me to stay." He sounded offended, although I couldn't fathom why. He was in *my* bed.

"Why would I ask you to stay?" He shrugged. "We didn't—" I gestured frantically between us, sick with the thought that I might have had sex with him and not remember it. "Oh my God, please tell me we—"

I pushed my hands into my hair, nails scratching at my scalp. A set of bare feet appeared in front of me as Kingston slid out of bed and joined me on the hardwood. He took my chin between his slim fingers.

"You had a bad dream and asked me to stay," he repeated. "Nothing more; nothing less."

Finding the truth in his eyes, I let out a relieved breath, then shifted to stand. I got to my knees and froze, eye level with his crotch area, where an obvious tent had sprung in his sweatpants. The images of us fooling around in his penthouse danced through my memory—his spiced-vanilla scent, his hard and uneven breathing, his mouth on my pussy.

A shuddering breath left me and goosebumps broke over my skin.

My pulse throbbed between my legs, aching to feel a human touch shaking me to my core. This man was the only one I wanted to touch me, and now, I craved to feel his hands and lips on my skin.

"Eyes up here. And get up off your knees." I startled at the sound of his voice, jumping to attention like an Olympic gymnast. "Whoa there, easy," he rushed to say as I almost lost my balance, his eyes coasting over my legs and hips like he was thinking of ways to steady me. "I've never seen you move that fast outside of killing men."

Turmoil restarted in my chest. He knew me, but I didn't know him. And if everything he'd told me so far was true—which I suspected it was—then I should.

It was really too early for all this. "Don't give me any ideas."

Maybe he's scared of me, I thought proudly, then released an exasperated breath at the notion, mentally berating myself. Kingston—the Ghost—was one of the most lethal trackers and killers in the underworld.

He let out a derisive snort. "Touché."

Our eyes locked, and the roaring in my ears intensified. In his dark depths, I glimpsed a spark of something that sent heat curling through me. My nipples hardened and my skin flushed with arousal.

"Thank you," I murmured, the words leaving my lips without my permission. He stared at me but didn't move, and I shifted my weight from foot to foot, restless in the silence. It was a novelty to have someone not take advantage of me when vulnerable, especially after the weeks I'd spent waiting for the auction and Cortez. "Thanks for staying with me through my nightmare."

Dammit, I sounded vulnerable, but also husky and breathless. He felt like a physical force drawing me in, and the sensation had me taking a half step back on wobbly legs. His jaw flexed as he watched me retreat.

"How about some breakfast?" he offered, his voice soft despite something dark and savage lurking underneath his stony front.

"That'd be great, thank you."

He nodded. "Meet me on the terrace, ice princess."

My shoulders slumped, and I felt all the energy that had just been coursing through me trickle out. I was exhausted. *He* exhausted me. "Stop calling me that," I muttered as I turned away, not sure why that nickname bothered me.

I felt him hover by the door, his gaze hot on my back, before he walked out without another word.

Twenty minutes later, I appeared on the terrace, feeling fresh after my shower and wearing a thin-strapped dress—pink, *again*—with a white cardigan draped over my shoulders. Kingston already had breakfast cooked and the table set. He pulled out a chair for me, and I couldn't help but feel like a girl on a date. Not that I'd ever been on one.

"Do you always cook?" I asked curiously as he removed the dome-shaped cover from my plate.

He stood over me, waiting for me to take a seat, his crisp black shirt molding to his toned body. All he had to do now was flex those ink-stained biceps and I'd be a goner.

"I do."

The birds chirped, the sound of the waves in the distance soothed, and the breeze calmed as he sat opposite of me. The man had to be the epitome of efficiency because he managed to shower, change, and cook all while I was getting ready.

"Do you enjoy it?" I was impressed my voice was even, hiding this attraction I felt toward him. I blamed it on that fucking scent of his. Vanilla and spice.

"I do."

"Why?" Supposedly I'd known this man for at least a decade, yet I knew absolutely nothing about him. Maybe he could help me fill these gaps in my memory—without realizing it, of course.

He shrugged. "I like food."

"So do I," I remarked. "You don't see me slaving over the stove."

He snickered. "You're too busy killing."

"And you're not? You're a killer for the Omertà and you fucking collect the teeth of your victims."

He froze, looking like a mannequin for a moment, before he resumed eating. Instant regret slammed into me. This man might look like a monster straight from my nightmares, but he wasn't. Deep in my heart, I knew that. Considering his indoctrination by my mother and Ivan at such a young age, I was surprised he wasn't more insane.

"I'm sorry," I apologized. "That was uncalled for."

It didn't matter who he turned out to be or how many he killed. He was just trying to survive, just like anyone forced to endure the underworld.

He lifted his head, his eyes roving over my face before dropping to my lips. There was a look in his expression that told me he still silently suffered.

I picked up my fork and started eating. Scrambled eggs, almond croissant, blueberry pancake drenched in syrup. No bacon in sight.

We ate in silence for a while until he spoke. "Apology accepted." My shoulders slumped with relief. His gaze flicked up, heavy and emotionless. Yet a storm brewed underneath his darkness, changing the temperature in my heart from cold to hot. Talk about extremes with this man. "On one condition."

I scoffed. "This should be good."

His eyes coasted down my body, leaving a trail of ice and fire in their wake. I shifted in my chair, suddenly self-conscious. I hated these newfound feelings of insecurity. That wasn't who I was.

Impatience stared back at me. "Take it or leave it."

Unable to resist my curiosity, I said, "What's the condition?"

"You answer some questions," he drawled.

My eyes narrowed. "Fine, but I reserve the right not to answer."

"Fine."

"And I can ask you questions too," I amended quickly.

"Fine, but I reserve the right not to answer." He threw my own words back at me with indignation. "Although, I wonder what you'll possibly think to ask since you don't even remember me."

You and me both, buddy, I thought with a huff.

"Okay, now's your turn to wow me." I smirked. "Ask your question."

He let out a sardonic breath. "You're asking for trouble, aren't you?" I shrugged my shoulders and rolled my eyes before he continued. "Why didn't your mother save you when you were taken in D.C.?"

"Maybe she thinks I'm dead," I countered. I didn't think I was going to like this game.

"You were mentioned on the dark web. There's no chance she would have missed it. Perez has had an eye on you for a long time."

Somehow it didn't surprise me, but it still sent a pang through my heart. Not that I wanted to go back to that crazy bitch. It was more about the fact that I'd never experienced motherly affection.

"Then I must no longer be of use to her," I said, glad that my voice didn't portray my inner turmoil. I'd known for a long time my mother wasn't a good person, but she was still my mother. Even that was barely enough to try to forget the years of torture and dangerous living conditions. She only defended me when it suited her needs, and that was impossible to ignore now. "My turn."

I pondered how to phrase my question without having to bring up the horrors that haunted him.

"Why did... How did you end up with Ivan and..." *My mother*, I thought but couldn't utter the word.

"My father fucked him over on a deal, and Ivan decided to go after my sister. He got me instead."

He sounded detached, yet the meaning of his words ghosted a shiver down my spine. Just like me, he was a pawn in his parent's fuckup.

I swallowed a lump in my throat. "I'm sorry."

"How long have you been working for your mother?" He didn't want apologies. He wanted answers.

I thought back to when she first started pulling me into her business, training me in her signature ruthless way. I couldn't put a finger on exactly when it was, especially not with how unreliable my memory was. An ache resounded between my brows as I tried to remember, but with each probe into my memory bank, the pain intensified.

"A few years," I finally answered.

Maybe he saw the struggle painted on my face or maybe he was just impatient, but he let my non-answer slide. "Ask your question now."

"What's the deal with the teeth?"

His expression remained unmoved. "It's so I can keep track of the people I kill. Whenever I look at them, I'm reminded that my soul can't be saved."

I reared back in my chair, shocked at how easily the words rolled off his tongue. He genuinely believed he was tainted, undeserving of all the good in the world.

"Your soul doesn't need saving, Kingston. You were a *child*." My voice was barely a whisper as it hit the air and met his darkness. "Whatever we've done in this world, we did it to survive. It's them"— all the ruthless and cruel *ublyudoks* in the underworld—"who are beyond saving. Including my mother."

He let out a sardonic breath. "When did your outlook on life become so upbeat and positive?"

I shrugged. "I need something to keep me going." *To get to those who'd held the faith of my sister in their hands*, I didn't say.

"Your turn," I said before I could veer too far toward the rabbit hole.

"What do you want with Perez?"

There it was. "I'm not answering that one."

"You realize he'll kill you," he pointed out, as though the risk wasn't the most obvious thing in the world.

"Not if I kill him first."

He ran his hand across his jaw, pulling my gaze to his mouth. "I believe you mean that too."

I lifted my gaze to his. "I do."

"You won't be able to kill him on your own."

"I've done a lot of things on my own," I declared proudly. "I only have myself to depend on."

He ran his tongue across his teeth, deep in thought. "For a very long time, I believed so too. But I'm slowly learning I can let some people in. You will too."

Frustration rose in me. Or maybe it was jealousy? It was hard to decipher. I'd never been very good at regulating my emotions. All I knew was that I used to have my sister, and now I had nobody. Mother kept me too close to her to allow me the chance to grow close to anyone. Each time I did, we were ripped away. Giovanni was the exception, but still, I couldn't believe in it with the same conviction as Kingston. It seemed too good to be true.

"I'll take your word for it." Fuck, was it my turn or his to ask questions? This man rattled me down to my core, and it was starting to affect my ability to stay vigilant. Fuck it—I was just going to throw it out there. "When will you let me go?"

The silence was deafening as he stared and stared *and stared* at me.

"When your mother's dead and no longer poses a threat to you."

My mouth parted, his jet-black expression leaving no room for discussion. My stomach dropped like lead. I didn't want to imagine exactly how long he thought that would be.

"What if she finds us first?" I asked. I hoped she wouldn't. I had no doubt that Kingston was capable of defending himself, but if she brought her goons with her, it'd be hard for the two of us to fight them all, especially Drago. Now that I was free of her, I didn't want to go back to her poisonous bubble.

"She won't."

"You seem overly confident."

I opened my mouth to say something else, but he beat me to it. "What's your favorite ice cream flavor?"

I froze as the darkness morphed into a mirrored nightmare haunting my every dream. Flashbacks of my mother's torture shot through me as fear crept into the corners of my mind. Her questions—much like this one—sent terror into the marrow of my bones. These were trick questions, they had to be, and pain always followed because I never answered them right.

My fingers curled into fists. It was like his words had tipped my world upside down, and I had no idea why. Would there ever come a day when I'd be free of these mood swings? "I like them all."

His brow rose. "That's not an answer."

"It's my final one." I glared at him.

He leaned back into his seat. "You have a favorite flavor," he deadpanned. "But for an unknown reason, you refuse to say it."

I scoffed with a bravado. "And how would you know that?"

"Your eyes."

"What about my eyes?" I snapped.

"They're the windows to your soul." My heartbeat tripped over itself. Where had I heard that before? "They tell me when you're lying, when you're sad or scared, when you're excited."

My cheeks heated, and I inhaled slowly.

"It's my turn," I rasped, my words tumbling from my mouth on a tremor, eager to move the topic away from myself.

"Then ask, ice princess."

I gritted my teeth at the nickname. Answers first. Kill him later.

"What was the deal with you and Louisa?"

"I won't be answering that."

Frustration chafed beneath my skin, but it wasn't as if I could call him out on it when I just did the same.

"Where were you when my sister was taken?" I asked, my voice cracking.

His cool gaze slid to my neck, probably squeezing invisible hands around it.

"I was right there, dying alongside Louisa." He shot to his feet abruptly, causing me to flinch. "Where in the fuck were you? We talked about leaving for ten fucking years. Where were you, Liana?"

Then he turned around and left me staring after him. It had become a pattern—one of us was always leaving.

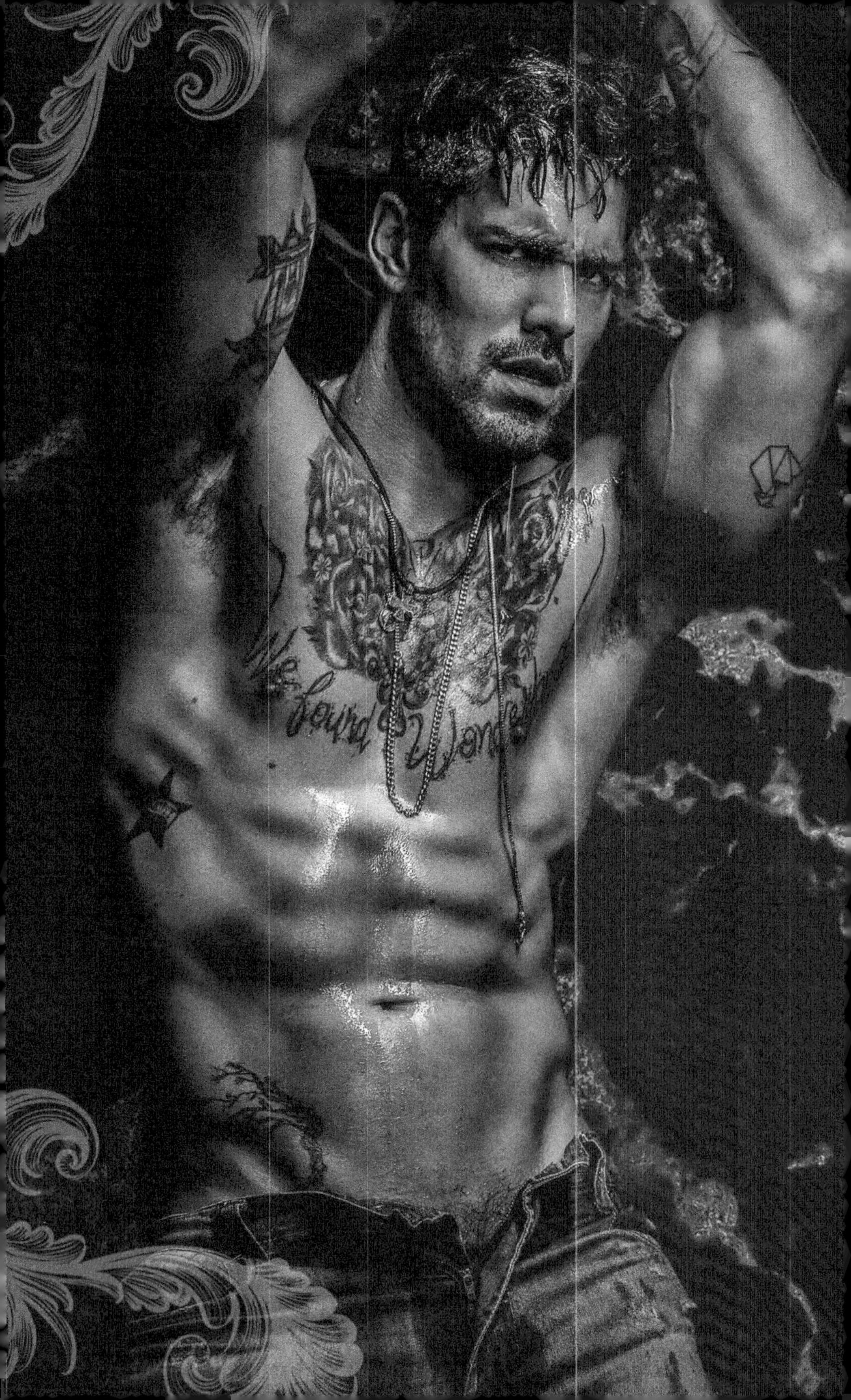
We found

Chapter 43
Liana

T en years. Kingston Ashford was our bodyguard for ten years, and judging by his tone, he blamed me for her death. And I... I couldn't remember him. *Except maybe in my dreams.* I shook my head side to side. No, that couldn't be him. Not if he was my sister's lover.

My heart only ever thundered like this when I dreamt about the faceless man or was with Kingston.

Being here, effectively stranded on this island, I was faced with the fact that my mother was at the epicenter of my life's worst moments. I'd known this for years, but the way she'd weaponized my loneliness made it second-nature to overlook. But I wouldn't run from it—from *her*—anymore.

The great Sofia Catalano Volkov.

I brought my cold fingers up, rubbing my temples and closing my eyes for a moment while flashbacks I couldn't piece together sliced through my mind.

My sister. The video of her torture. Santiago Tijuana's words giving me hope. The man I dreamt about whose face I never saw.

Could that be Kingston's face? It would line up with his time under my mother's control but... How was it possible that I didn't remember him? Or the events he spoke about? Could I trust him? Jesus Christ, was I attracted to my sister's man?

I couldn't stay here. I couldn't go home. Damn my mother. Damn this man who'd snatched me. All I knew was that if there was even the slightest chance I could save my sister—that she was alive for me *to* save—I had to try.

Rain streaked across the large windows, blurring my view of the ocean.

I loved the smell in this space; it had become my safe haven. Leather, firewood, and cigars. After sifting through the books and being unable to focus on a single book, I took a seat on the windowsill and stared at the horizon.

My breaths were quiet but my thoughts were loud. I couldn't forget Kingston's words, the accusations. Somewhere in the corners of my mind, warning bells went off, but I couldn't understand them.

Maybe I was going crazy.

I propped my head against the cool glass and closed my eyes. My body trembled as I was dragged back to the broken images playing in my mind.

I stared at the bowl of ice cream in my hands and let out an exasperated sigh. "Will they ever get this right?"

"Probably not." *I looked up to find my sister already handing me hers.* "Do you prefer vanilla sex?"

"Hey!" *I glanced around to ensure nobody heard us.* "Bring your voice down a notch."

"Jesus Christ. It was a joke."

I rolled my eyes.

"A bad one." *She shrugged, studying me. We both sported high ponytails. It made it easier to fuck with guards who couldn't tell us apart.* "This is exactly what I was saying—you need to focus on what matters. Be ready to leave."

"Are you sure?" *Worry was etched on my twin's face, and it had the desired effect of snapping me into seriousness.* "If we get caught, there'll be hell to pay."

"She won't catch us." *Did I say those words or did my sister?* "I'm not leaving without you."

"I'll be a third wheel."

"Never." *My forehead rested against hers, our hearts beating as one.* "Mother can't be saved," *I whispered.* "We both know that. Papa said so himself."

"He's not much better," *she spat, bitterness lacing her voice.* "He left us with her."

My lungs squeezed and my hands holding the ice cream bowl became clammy. "You know she threatened his life. His children's lives."

"We're his children too, and he had no issue abandoning us." *Distress on her face clawed at my chest.* "Why are they more important than us?"

My stomach churned with nausea. Of course she was right. Papa had sons and one other daughter who lived a life of being loved and cherished while we witnessed horrors and lived in fear of Mother's men, husband, and enemies.

"They don't matter," *I said, trying to calm her down.* "And when we're far away from here, we'll forget them all. It'll just be you, me, and—"

The rumbling sound of thunder beyond the window startled me awake, my mind grasping at straws. No, no, *no*. I was so close! You, me, and *who*? Was it Kingston? I wasn't sure, but if they were together before she—she... And after everything he revealed about wanting to run away before she died... God, I was unraveling, and it only felt like the beginning.

I was still no closer to trusting him. After all, he'd purchased me at an auction like I was a slab of meat. He yanked me away from Perez, taking away my chance to find out what happened to my sister.

I hugged my hands around my waist, studying my surroundings, but the library was empty. I slumped against the window, the dream still fresh in my mind.

Agony licked at every fiber of me as I dug through the memory. I had every reason to believe it was a real memory—the images of my sister so vivid it made my heart hurt.

I wiped my sweaty hair off my forehead and heaved a sigh. This was the most I'd remembered since her death. We were talking about running away. *Just like Kingston said.*

Peering through the fogged-up window, I noticed the remnants of the storm were finally clearing. I watched the clouds slowly drift away—for minutes, maybe hours. I couldn't help but feel envy; they came and went, enjoying their journey, while I remained stuck here. Confused and troubled.

Sliding off the windowsill, I quietly made my way out of the room. The hallway was empty, the home eerily quiet as I made my way down the stairs.

I clutched the handrail for balance, almost expecting for Kingston to jump out from the shadows like a ghost and push me to my death. Or back into my room. The jury was still out on his intentions.

Once at the bottom of the stairs, I swung the front door wide open. The birds chirped, calling me to freedom. I followed the call, and as soon as I crossed the threshold, my eyelids fluttered shut in bliss.

Freedom.

It might be fleeting, but it felt so good. I tipped my head back and relished in the sensation of the sun on my skin, the salty air on my tongue. I could hear the waves crashing in the distance, and a jolt of happiness shot through me.

I started walking, then running, faster and harder, my muscles screaming from the effort. Sweat rolled down my back, the jeans I wore too hot for this. But I ignored it all.

It felt like hours of running, although it couldn't have been more than five or ten minutes when I stopped abruptly.

White sand greeted me and I stepped onto it, my shoes squeaking. The sun cast a beautiful shade of bubblegum pink in the sky, its reflection bouncing off the smooth surface of the water. It was a picture-perfect sight.

The fingertips on my left hand zinged in that old, familiar way, eager to grip a pencil and sketch, immortalizing this view. I brought my right hand to my left wrist, wrapping my fingers around it as I twisted it in a circular motion, a habit I'd picked up somewhere over the years.

I kicked off my shoes and unbuttoned my jeans, pushing them down my legs. Left in my panties and T-shirt, I walked down to the water. I waded up to my thighs, reveling in the salty water lapping at my legs.

The cool water felt refreshing and relaxing, my tension slowly seeping away. A prickling sensation traveled down my spine, and I looked behind me. Dark eyes were trained on me, making my breath catch.

Kingston.

His presence hovered over the beach like a dark cloud as he studied me. Slowly, I waded out of the water, holding his gaze until my feet touched the sand again.

"You're ruining my sunny day."

No answer, just that heated gaze touching my skin.

My blood thrummed in my ears, our last encounter still fresh in our minds. Something in his gaze held me captive. I could still feel his hands on my body, his hard body pressed against mine. A bead of sweat rolled down my spine despite the cool water and light breeze caressing my exposed skin.

I realized it wasn't my best move to be caught with my pants down—literally—as one of the most lethal men in the underworld aimed his attention on me.

"How about some privacy?" I asked, reaching for my discarded jeans.

"It's too late for that. After all, I tasted your pussy. Privacy is a moot point now."

I rolled my eyes.

"Nonetheless, I'd like some now." I held my breath, waiting for him to move. Or to at least acknowledge me. He didn't do either. "Fine, stare away." I rolled my eyes. "I shouldn't be surprised you're not averting your eyes like a gentleman."

I held his eyes as I discarded my wet panties and put on my dry jeans. To his credit, his gaze didn't dip lower. He folded his muscular arms over his chest, his dark tattoos on full display, and his eyes locked with mine.

Ever since that game of Russian roulette, I'd been captivated by this man, and it turned out he might be just as nuts as I was.

"I'm not."

"You're not what?" I said, tilting my head to the side.

He studied me for another second before speaking, his voice deep. "I'm not a gentleman."

"You could have fooled me," I remarked wryly.

He tilted his chin toward the sea. "Isn't snow more your thing?"

I shrugged. "Isn't hell more yours?"

A ghost of a smile appeared on his face, and something fluttered in the pit of my stomach. I didn't like it. The things I was feeling were disturbing and unwanted. Yet, controlling it was as futile as swallowing oxygen underwater.

Chapter 44
Kingston

She hadn't tried to kill me despite the toll my questioning had on her. Yes, some of her questions enraged me, but if I was honest, it was more self-directed. Every second of Louisa's torture that I had to witnessed flayed me to this day.

Liana was right, I should have saved her. Neither one of us should be here without her. And yet...

I looked out the window only to find Liana, a mere faded version of my past lover, roaming the grounds. It would be so easy to forget that Louisa died and pretend she was here with me, but I knew better than to think that would work for Liana.

The woman was infuriating, beautiful, and cunning.

Sofia had made her into a femme fatale killer, but she had also lost control of her daughter along the way. Liana used her skills to protect herself and the innocent people who crossed her mother's path.

I trailed her movements as she headed to the gazebo. She kept kicking up rocks with her sandals, and the image reminded me of what she and her sister used to do when they had nothing else to entertain themselves with.

Eva Winners

When Sofia first assigned me to be their bodyguard, the twins were wary of me. After all, they'd witnessed me murder a man in cold blood. But as the months went by, slowly but surely, we became fast friends who shared a common dream: escape.

As if she could feel the weight of my gaze on her, Liana lifted her head and eyed my office window. Her brows drew together, huffing a breath of frustration.

"Stop staring," she mouthed.

I slunk back behind my blinds.

For years, I'd suffered, refusing to be open with anyone. And now, for the first time since Louisa's death, my heart was beating steadily and my soul was a little less scarred.

I stood from my seat, ready to go join her outside because it would seem I was unable to keep away from the woman, when my phone buzzed.

> Alexei: Sofia has been spotted in Montenegro.

I frowned. What was she doing there?

> Me: Do we know why?

Alexei's response was instant.

> The word on the street is that she's looking for the Popov guy.

I read the message several times. Barely a year ago, I'd helped my brother Winston rescue his wife from Danil Popov. Danil was a criminal, but he didn't seem like the type of man who'd engage or work with Sofia Volkov.

> Me: Danil Popov?

> Alexei: I'm guessing. Know him?

Reign of a Billionaire

> Me: Know of him.

I dialed up my brother, the ringing on the other end of the line the longest I'd ever heard, but it wasn't my brother's voice that picked up. It was my sister-in-law's.

"Hello, Kingston."

"Billie." I didn't waste any time getting to business. "I need Winston."

"Ummm, he's talking to Danil right now."

Surprise, surprise. Winston had made an unlikely friend in Danil, not that I understood it. Personally, I'd have gutted the man and then pulled out all his teeth.

"On the phone?" I asked.

"No, face-to-face." My jaw clenched. Winston would have already given me the entire fucking story by now, but instead, I was having to drag it out of Billie. I knew I made her nervous, so I tried to be considerate, but there were times—like now—where it'd be easier to just have her step aside.

"Where and why?" I needed to know whether the lead on Sofia was reliable. "Actually, tell him it's urgent, and it concerns Danil too."

"Huh?"

"Billie, put. Winston. On. The. Fucking. Phone."

Fuck, Winston was going to be pissed off when he learned about this. To Billie's credit, she just huffed, and I could hear her faint voice through the headset as she spoke to Winston.

"*Kingston wants to talk to you. And he's being a cranky bitch.*"

I let out an exasperated breath. Time to stop handling my sister-in-law with delicate gloves. It turned out she'd grown a set of balls sometime over the last year.

"Kingston," Winston greeted me.

"Watch Danil's expression," I instructed. "And put me on speakerphone."

He didn't hesitate. "You're on speakerphone, Kingston."

I got straight to business. "Danil, are you meeting or have you already met with Sofia Volkov?"

His response was immediate. "Fuck no. That bitch is crazy."

Just as I suspected. "Why am I hearing rumors that you're meeting with her in Montenegro?"

Two heartbeats passed before he flung out a string of curses. "I'm going to kill that motherfucker when I get my hands on him."

"Care to elaborate?" I demanded.

"My father's in Montenegro." Clearly he wasn't happy. "Don't worry, that meeting won't happen, because I'm going to murder them both."

I considered his words for a second before saying, "This could be our chance to set Sofia up."

"Are you saying let it happen?" Winston chimed in just as Danil's phone sounded, signaling a sent message.

"Yes."

"I don't know if I can let it happen. My father's dabbled in human trafficking in the past, and I'm certain it's the reason behind this meeting. I can't have that connected to the Popov family name."

Fuck!

"How long has he been involved?" I asked, debating whether it'd be wise to fly to Montenegro and try to corner Sofia myself.

"I'm not sure. I've only learned about it in the recent years," Danil admitted. "It's the reason I had him removed. He was doing it behind everyone's back."

Just as I ended the call, my phone buzzed again and I glanced at the screen.

> Alexei: You in?

A reflection of golden locks caught the corner of my eye and my decision was made.

The next day, with Liana by my side, we were parked on the outskirts of Budva Riviera in a black van. A large oak tree and the night's crescent moon provided us with decent cover.

Alexei's intel was that Danil's father and Sofia were meeting here —a state-of-the-art warehouse with a soundproof basement, according to blueprints we managed to get our hands on. Whoever our source was, they didn't want to be found.

Danil claimed he'd never heard of the building and insisted that his father wasn't en route to Montenegro. In terms of Sofia, we hadn't gleaned any additional information on her whereabouts, so it was possible she was already here.

"Why would Mother be in Montenegro?" Liana questioned, her eyes darting to Alexei, who sat sandwiched by two of his men. Clad in all black—jeans, T-shirt, and combat boots—she was in her element and ready to fight. "Are you sure your intel isn't fucked up?"

Alexei's expression remained unchanged. "I'm sure."

"But I've never heard any talk of—"

"I. Am. Fucking. Sure."

She glowered at him. "Don't get all pissy with me. I'm just telling you, Mother stayed away from the Balkans."

"Well, she's not staying away anymore," he snapped.

Her pretty features twisted into a scowl, but I had to agree with Alexei here. Was Liana the best judge of character when you took into consideration her relationship with her mother as well as her overt lapses in memory?

"Jesus, iceman. Relax." Folding her arms over her chest, she inadvertently pushed up her breasts, drawing my eyes to them. "I need a weapon," she declared.

Fuck, this was so fun to watch. I wouldn't mind some popcorn to go along with it.

"Over my dead body," Alexei retorted.

She shot him a scowl. "I'll be happy to arrange that."

I ran a hand through my hair, pulling on the ends. I was starting to question my decision to bring her along. She was a bit too eager to draw blood. None of this seemed to worry her. The woman was reckless.

Alexei's gaze flicked up, catching Liana's, heavy and emotionless, as if he were looking straight through her.

"You can try to die in the process."

Her features turned sour. "Listen, you might have been the shit twenty years ago, but now you're just an old man." Her eyes slid down his body, and jealousy raced through me. I didn't like her looking at another man, even though this one was madly in love with my sister. "Is that the beginning of a beer belly I see?" My lips twitched, glad to hear she found him lacking. "Besides, I don't see a single surveillance camera on this building," she pointed out. I'd noticed that too—a clear red flag. "I can see it on Kingston's face, he agrees."

She was really egging him on now.

He grunted. "I'm going to shut you up before we go anywhere."

My nostrils flared at his tone despite the fact that it wasn't exactly unwarranted. Alexei must have noticed it, because surprise flickered in his gaze.

His phone vibrated. "Okay, time to move."

I pulled out my spare handgun, handing it to her. "Don't shoot one of us by accident."

She smiled sweetly as she took it in her expert hands. "I'll try to exercise restraint."

"Jesus Christ," Alexei muttered under his breath, reaching for the door and shaking his head in disapproval. He exited first, then his men, followed by Liana and myself.

I grabbed her forearm, the softness of her skin suddenly making me forget why I stopped her in the first place.

"What?" she hissed, glaring at me.

Reign of a Billionaire

"Stay close."

She rolled her eyes. "I work better alone."

I was certain she was doing this on purpose, just to drive me crazy.

"Liana," I growled. "Promise me."

"Fine. I promise. Happy?"

An instant later, our feet pounded against the pavement. Gloomy silence hung heavily around us. We stopped behind a big metal door, and I motioned to the hidden camera.

We checked our weapons, Alexei's already aimed at the only window in the warehouse.

"Why are you so stiff?" Liana's question cut off my focus. "It's like you've got something jammed up your ass."

"Why are you looking at my ass?"

Alexei flicked his eyes up to the sky in a silent prayer.

"Something's off." Liana tilted her head to the warehouse's industrial doors. "Nobody's around."

"Tell us something we don't already see," Alexei grumbled. I'd never seen anyone get to Alexei like this. It'd be entertaining if our lives weren't on the line here.

"Maybe they were tipped off," I said, looking around for anything amiss. "Danil didn't want whatever his father's deal with Sofia was to stain their family name."

A heavy silence fell over us, and I sensed when Liana stiffened. "What is it?"

Her delicate brows furrowed. "I... I think I heard someone cry out."

Alexei cocked a brow. "Are you sure?"

She held her breath, pressing her back against the building. "There it is again," she said hurriedly, her eyes darting between us. "You guys should have your hearing checked."

Alexei rolled his eyes.

"Okay, let's head in," Liana announced in a clear voice. "I'm tired of you babies slowing me down."

"Dumb ways to die," I muttered.

Alexei shot us both a glare that said he'd love to make us hurt.

Man, this expedition was so much fucking fun. Even if it failed and Sofia Volkov walked out alive, I didn't think I'd be forgetting it anytime soon.

Chapter 45
Liana

Alexei Nikolaev was a killer.

I recognized one when I saw one. After all, I grew up surrounded by them. His tattoos screamed *Don't fuck with me*, but I was inclined to poke the bear. Maybe I'd developed suicidal tendencies somewhere along the way.

In his black uniform that hugged his muscles, you could say he was beautiful in a lethal kind of way. But one look into his eyes and game-fucking-over. Those were Medusa eyes that could freeze your heart and soul.

And it was exactly that which made me recoil.

I recognized the brokenness and darkness that stared back at me. I saw the same in Kingston's eyes. And every time I looked at my reflection. I refused to back down, watching my own nightmares play in that pale blue gaze of his.

"Okay, you two," Kingston interrupted. "Stop this bickering and get moving." I huffed and Kingston stepped forward, unapologetically invading my space. "Are we going to have a problem, Liana?"

The rhythm of my heart sped up as our gazes clashed, but there was a hint of fire brewing beneath the surface of his dark eyes.

"For Christ's sake," Alexei muttered. "Save the foreplay for later."

My spine straightened as a blush crept up my neck, so I glared back at him. "Stop being a pervert."

But before he could respond, a loud *boom* echoed in the air, shaking the ground beneath our feet.

For a moment, I was frozen. Time stood still as my life flashed before my eyes, but the images were so distorted and confusing. My sister. Me.

Where's Liana? I thought I heard my mother's voice in my ringing ears. *Who's Liana?* I thought I was dying. All my dreams were dying right alongside me. *Louisa died.*

And then someone grabbed my shoulder, pushing me to the ground. My knees hit the hard pavement and my chest followed, knocking the breath from my lungs.

I turned my head—left, then right—then registered Kingston's body covering mine, and Alexei's savage grip on the back of my head. I tried to lift my head, but he refused to let up. My breathing was labored, my ears were buzzed, and I started to shake.

"I can't breathe. I can't breathe." The words left my lips on a chant while my eyes burned from the smoke.

Alexei loosened his grip finally, giving me the illusion of freedom, and it was all I needed.

"Breathe, Liana." Kingston's deep voice penetrated through the noise in my ears and panic in my mind. The shrill sound of terrified screams invaded my head. *Where's Liana?* I was helpless. *Who's Liana?* I was broken. *Louisa died.* She died because of me. "Fucking look at me."

I turned my head to meet his eyes, finding safety in them. My lips parted, and I inhaled a big gulp of air. My body was shaking so hard I found it impossible to stop.

"Another breath." His command was impossible to refuse. "Good, now another." My chaotic breathing evened out, and his gaze never let go. "Better?"

I held on to him for dear life, needing his strength. I swallowed and closed my eyes until slowly but surely, I regained control of my breathing.

"Yes, thank you."

He nodded, and we both turned to find Alexei watching us with those eyes that would make the glaciers of the Arctic jealous. Kingston shifted off me, then helped me to my feet. It was only then that the chaos around us came into view.

Alexei's men were fine. So was he. But the debris and smoke around us would make it hard to get back to our vehicle. The warehouse was on fire, so we needed to get as far away as possible.

"We better put some distance between us and this place," Alexei instructed.

He went to move and I reached out, grabbing his sleeve.

"But there's someone in the basement." He looked at me, then lowered his gaze to my fingers clutching his sleeve. Startled and surprised at myself, I released him. "Sorry, I... don't usually do that."

"Don't what?"

I cleared my throat, something stuck in it. "Freak out. Or... touch people." Not unless I had to kill them, but it was best not to say that.

"We need to get to the basement," Kingston stated calmly, as if hanging out at a bomb site was an everyday occurrence. "They wouldn't be blowing this shit up if there was nothing to hide."

"Or maybe it's a trap," Alexei pointed out.

I inhaled another deep breath and met their gazes. "I'm not leaving here if there's a chance there's someone in that basement," I said with a note of frustration. "Dead or alive."

Without another look their way, I tramped through the debris and smiled to myself when I heard their footsteps behind me. Something told me they'd never allow me to go inside alone, and the thought filled me with a warmth I hadn't felt in so long.

I wasn't alone. Not anymore.

The farther we moved toward the warehouse—or what was left of it—the more I could hear it. *Whimpering.* I looked over my shoulder.

"Do you hear it now?" I whispered, Alexei and Kingston right behind me and the other men a few feet back.

They silently nodded and I continued forward, my boots heavy on the torn-up gravel. If there *was* someone here, we weren't sneaking up on them.

A muffled scream traveled through the air, and I stumbled. *Are we too late?* I thought, my pulse skittering.

"It's coming from the basement," Kingston said. "There has to be a way in."

"*Blyad*, it's always the fucking basements," Alexei muttered. He looked over his shoulder to one of his men. "Go back to the car and be ready to circle back for us." Another scream met us. "Definitely the basement," Alexei hissed.

I focused on the task ahead, following the sounds to the left, then right, until I heard metal clanking.

Breathing heavily, I fell to my hands and started pulling at the debris piled in my way. My fingernails hurt and so did my lungs, but I ignored it all. Whoever was screaming was suffering more than me. Alexei and Kingston followed suit on either side of me.

"There," I exclaimed in a whispered breath. "It's a trapdoor."

Alexei disappeared, and I flicked a glance at Kingston. "Is he okay?"

"He doesn't like confined spaces."

I nodded in understanding.

"I don't like to be suffocated," I muttered, shoving pieces of rock and metal aside.

"Not many people do."

A choked laugh escaped me. "True. I meant..." I trailed off, trying to find the right wording. It wasn't like I could tell him what my mother did to me. I didn't need his pity, and I was sure he'd endured much worse. "I don't like to be restrained."

"Here." Alexei was back with two saws, saving me further explanation. "Let's try cutting around the frame."

Handing Kingston a saw, the two of them got to work as I

watched on. To my amazement, the door popped open within minutes, and my mouth parted.

Wails and shouts streamed up through the hole. Without waiting for the two men, I headed through, feeling my way down the dark stairs. I raised my gun as I descended the last step.

I gasped when my vision corrected and they came into view. Five girls were huddled up together, wearing nothing but oversized T-shirts and metal collars. The terror on their faces was like a punch in my gut.

"Those fucking bastards," I hissed, my nostrils flaring.

They flinched at the harshness in my voice, and I lifted my palms, gun in one. Their eyes immediately locked on it and I cursed myself, quickly tucking it in my back pocket.

"It's okay," I whispered. A light switch caught my eye and I flipped it on. "I won't hurt you." They were in bad shape. Filthy. Bruised. "I won't hurt you," I repeated softly.

"Jesus fucking Christ." Kingston's voice held a fraction of the fury I felt.

"Were these girls part of Sofia's deal?" Alexei asked. The girls cowered in response, and I knew it had everything to do with my mother's name. Shame swallowed me like a sinkhole. My mother did this.

The girls looked downright terrified now. They shuffled to the corner, wrapping their arms around each other as they watched us, terrified.

I had to let go of my anger and help these girls out.

"We won't hurt you," I whispered as they started to shake, their soft cries echoing against the bare basement walls. "We'll get you out. Okay?" A flicker of hope reflected in their gazes. "Can I get closer?"

At their hesitant nods, I made my way to them, keeping my feet light. Crouching in front of the one closest to me, I whispered, "Can I touch your collar?"

There was a moment of stillness before she inhaled sharply.

"Okay," the girl with gray eyes answered.

"I'm Liana," I said, reaching for her collar but keeping my movements fluid and slow.

She lowered her lashes. "Visha."

"That's a beautiful name," I said, flicking a glance to the other girls with a soft smile. "What about yours?" I asked curiously.

"Delilah. Mae. Adira." I waited for the last girl to say her name, but she simply stared at the wall.

"Louisa. She's the youngest," Visha answered for her. "She's... they... hurt her."

My hands froze on Visha's collar, my pulse quickening. *It's a coincidence.*

"Liana." Kingston's voice frightened the girls, sending them scattering into the corner. But it was what I needed to get my wits about me.

I turned my head, glancing at him over my shoulder and giving him a look that said, *It's okay, I'm okay.* "Stay there."

I couldn't battle my demons now. These girls mattered more.

"How long have you been here?" I asked, brushing my fingers over the collar.

"Two days."

"Where are the others?" I rasped, hoping beyond hope that these girls weren't being used as bait.

Those anguished eyes gazed up at me. "They left two, maybe three days ago."

My adrenaline surged at the realization that they'd been collared and then abandoned like animals. My eyes darted around. No food. No water. Nothing.

I turned to look at Alexei, who seemed to pale underneath all his tattoos. "Think you can find some cutters in this mess?" He disappeared up the stairs, and I turned back to my girls. "We'll try to cut these and get you out of here."

"I want to go home," the girl with brown eyes cried. "I miss my mom."

Reign of a Billionaire

My eyes burned, and I smoothed my hands over my pants. "Let's get you out," I rasped. "Then we'll find your mom and get you home."

"You... you won't sell us?" The green-eyed girl assessed me suspiciously, her lip swollen.

"No. I will find who did this to you and kill them," I vowed.

"Then it's Sofia Volkov you have to kill." And there it was. Not that I didn't suspect it already, but hearing it spoken aloud, from the mouth of a bruised and battered girl no less, put a nail in my mother's coffin.

Alexei returned with cutters and... clothes. But before I could question him, he approached us with Kingston.

"It's okay," I soothed. "I'll hold it away from your neck."

The girls didn't move, their breathing stilled as Kingston snapped the metal, one by one, and Alexei handed them each a jacket. I recognized them as the ones his men had been wearing, and I lifted my head, mouthing my thanks.

"Ready to go?" The girls stood up, their frail bodies trembling. The girl with brown eyes, who'd been quiet and staring out absently, stumbled on her feet. My hands shot out to steady her. When I managed to get her standing, I saw the whip marks on the backs of her legs. Fury welled in my chest, but I kept it out of my voice as I offered my hand. "We'll get out of here together."

Her trembling fingers met mine and we started our climb out of the basement.

Straight into the DiLustro gang, the Kingpins of the Syndicate, and the Irish pricks—my half-siblings.

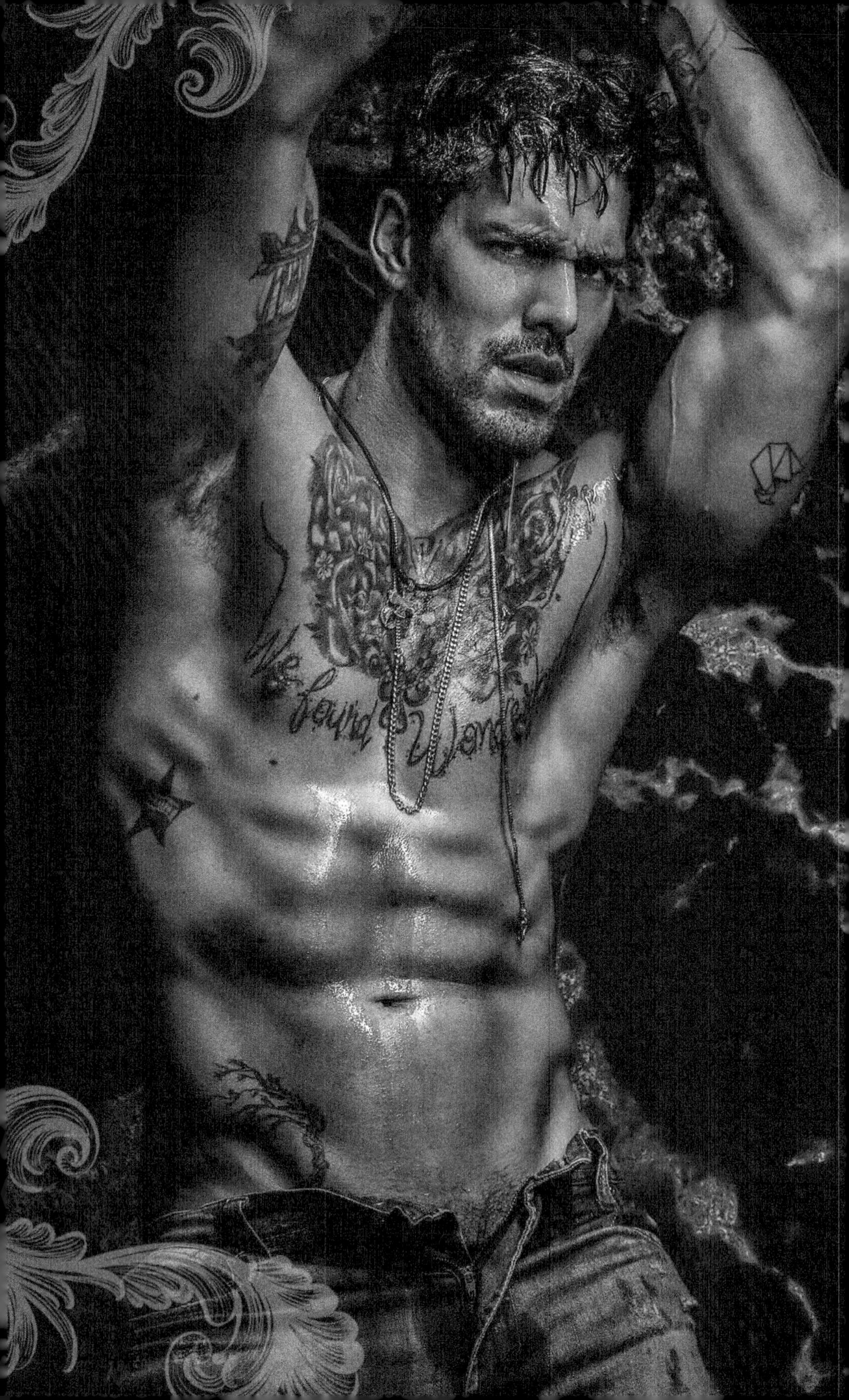
We found

Chapter 46
Kingston

This wasn't going to plan. Not at all.

We'd anticipated a trap, but never the Kingpins of the Syndicate. Even less Murphy's Irish mafia.

My mother came from the DiLustro line, so they certainly weren't strangers to me. Dante DiLustro stood with his wife, Juliette, both armed to the teeth. Basilio, his sister, Emory, and cousin Priest had combat gear that wasn't any less impressive. The only one who stood out was Ivy Murphy, who didn't have a single weapon on her. It was probably good she wasn't on this job alone because the girl would get herself killed.

And then there were the Murphy brothers, who ran a section of the Irish mafia, armed with weapons of mass destruction. They would happily level a whole continent without ever losing sleep. Someone had to get them under control, and fast.

They eyed our rescued girls, with the exception of the one clinging to Liana.

I flicked a glance at Liana to find her frozen, her eyes locked on Ivy and her bottom lip wobbling ominously. My chest tightened as realization dawned on me. It was probably the first time she'd seen her in person. Ivy was her half sister who was raised in a protective home while Liana and her twin had to survive Sofia and Ivan.

It was what we had in common. I was the youngest Ashford brother, but surviving the shit I had, it aged me tenfold. Maybe not to the naked eye, but my soul sure as hell was old as fuck.

It was the reason I reached out and gently squeezed her forearm, bringing her focus back to me. Her eyes met mine for a brief second. A terse nod, and she turned back to the group she probably considered her enemies.

"You better have a good reason for being here." Alexei broke the silence.

"The Kingpins and Murphys together," I stated coldly, my eyes roving over them. "Something's afoot."

"My intel indicated Sofia Volkov would be here," Priest responded.

"So you brought an army," I snickered. "Sofia's not here."

"It appears your intel was all wrong, DiLustros and Murphys," Liana snapped, clutching her weapon in one hand and holding the shivering girl protectively with the other. "Now get lost."

Basilio chuckled. "You must have some balls on you. How about you start with introducing yourself?"

"Fuck. You."

"It's only fair," Dante chimed in. "Since you seem to know who we are."

"I'm Kingston," I answered. "And this is Alexei."

Priest scoffed. "We know who you two are. Who is she? And what's with the girl hanging off her like she's Mother Teresa?"

I was just about to tell him to fuck off when Liana beat me to it. "I'm Lilith," she answered. "And I'm going to kill you all if you don't move out of our fucking way. We have somewhere we need to be."

Not a single muscle flexed on Alexei's face, and my own remained an impassive mask. The world knew that Sofia Volkov had daughters, but not too many knew the details. It was best to keep it that way.

"Badass," Juliette commented. "I'm impressed."

Liana's jaw clenched, her eyes flashing with fury.

"Sofia Volkov killed my father," Ivy Murphy chimed in, but Liana didn't spare her a glance. It was as if she purposely avoided it. Not that I blamed her. Liana only ever considered her twin a sister. Ivy and her brothers were Liana's half-siblings, but her paternal bloodline was where their connection began and ended.

Liana's eyes locked on Juliette DiLustro. I knew exactly what was coming.

"No, she didn't. The person who killed Edward Murphy is standing right there next to you."

"What—"

"How—"

The commotion broke out instantaneously, and Liana smiled ferally, never losing sight of the girls behind her. Protecting them.

"Didn't you know?" It was at that moment I realized I would never want Liana for an enemy. Her face could fool you into forgetting she was an untamed killer, but she spared no mercy when going for the kill.

"What do you mean?" Ivy's voice shook.

"Juliette DiLustro killed *your* father, Ivy." Liana dropped the bomb, going straight for the jugular. "Now, if you'll excuse us..."

Alexei shook his head. "Listen, we have to get these girls to safety. It's our priority. You guys figure this shit out."

Liana, Alexei, and I started moving, keeping the rescued girls surrounded, when Liana glanced over her shoulder.

"By the way, Sofia's not yours to kill. She's Kingston's." Her gaze met mine, and I pretended not to feel the squeeze in my chest. "So back the fuck off, or you'll answer to me."

There was heartbreak on her face, but also fierce determination. It was what made it impossible to resist her.

Liana

In all the years that I'd known about my half-siblings, I'd never hated them. Yes, there was always an underlying tinge of resentment, but at this moment, I fucking hated them.

Once we were in the van with Alexei's guy behind the wheel, the rescued girls squeezed close. When I turned, I found Kingston and Alexei watching me.

"What?" I hissed, keeping my voice low.

"Why did you lie about your name back there?" Alexei asked, his voice so cold it gave me chills. "It could've been a big happy family reunion."

My eyes flicked to Kingston as I asked, "What did you tell him about me?"

"Nothing." It was curious but not exactly surprising. He struck me as a private man. After all, there had to be a reason they called him Ghost.

"How did you know who my father was?" I asked Alexei.

"Secrets aren't kept for very long in the underworld. As you well know."

Alexei was right. No secret was safe. It was why my twin and I had always wanted out. Surviving wasn't the norm, it was the exception.

Sitting on the floor in the back of the van, my knees pulled to my chest, I stared out the tinted windows. I missed having a sibling. But Ivy, through no fault of her own, would never be that to me.

The sun crested over the horizon, bringing with it another day. Another nightmare. Another fight.

"I had a sibling, a twin, and she died." I turned my head and met Alexei's gaze. "My father left us with our mother, knowing exactly what she was. He went back home to his sheltered children, and he left us at the mercy of the wolves." I swallowed, glancing out the window. "So no, I don't want to get to know her. I don't want to know about her childhood and how it could have been ours, if only our father had had the balls to do something about my mother."

Kingston didn't comment, but he reached out his hand and I

followed his gaze to the weapon I still held, reminding me I was still his prisoner. Although it didn't feel like it, and to my own amazement, it never occurred to me to shoot him or Alexei during our little mission.

I handed him my weapon, and the rest of the trip was spent in silence.

Once the girls were safely situated in a women's shelter in Greece—courtesy of Lykos Costello—Alexei headed back to Portugal and Kingston and I got on a helicopter that would take us back to Kingston's island. And I was so very willing to go back, which was ridiculous. Stockholm syndrome at its finest.

"You sure there aren't parts missing in this helicopter?" I asked sarcastically as he leaned over and buckled the seat belt over my chest.

Kingston remained still, so close that his T-shirt brushed my bare arm. So close that I could count his eyelashes. So close that there was barely half an inch between our lips. Taking a deep breath, his aftershave seeped into my lungs and my entire body hummed with anticipation.

My reason demanded I pull away. My heart urged me to close the distance. And my body... It implored that I ravish him and feel all the things I'd not felt since the last time he kissed me.

He made the decision for me, skimming his lips over mine as he said, "Once we go down that road, there's no going back. I won't let you go."

Every touch seared through my skin, setting my heartbeat into a wild rhythm while electricity crackled around us like sparklers.

"What if I don't want to go back?" I breathed, brushing my lips against his. There was a haze inside my mind. A lungful of air I couldn't seem to inhale. "I don't want to be alone anymore."

My heart drummed in my ears, and a part of me hated feeling so vulnerable. The other, more dominant part of me just wanted to let go, knowing he'd catch me.

His eyes were dark and his hand slid up my neck, fisting in my hair. He traced my lips with his thumb. Fire and adrenaline shot through my blood while he watched me.

Like I was *everything* he wanted. Like I was the only thing he needed.

The press of his lips against mine made my blood sizzle. My lips parted, welcoming the heat of his tongue, and when he nipped at my bottom lip, then licked it, an explosion of fire burst inside me. A moan traveled up my throat and he swallowed it, sliding his tongue inside my mouth.

My hands came to his shoulders, not to push him away but to pull him closer. The warmth of his chest against mine sent a tremble through me, my nipples tightening. The heat of his body alone stole my breath away. My body melted against his, like he was a piece of me that had been missing forever. He deepened the kiss and my fingers curled, digging nails into his shoulders. I panted against his lips while his mouth traveled down my neck, nipping and sucking at my throat.

Then, without a warning, he pulled away, his eyes on me, full of promises.

"Let's go home." His rough voice blazed a path down my spine, his words soft and desperate like my need to feel him inside me.

Home. Somewhere along the way, his prison had become home.

Chapter 47
Liana

Twenty-four hours had gone by since that searing, unforgettable kiss.

To my dismay, once we got back to the island, Kingston didn't scoop me off my feet and ravish me. In fact, he acted as if nothing had happened. It left me no other choice but to behave the same.

I'd rather die than beg a man—even one as hot as Kingston Ashford—for attention.

And then there was the guilt that gnawed at me. Kingston was Lou's love, not mine. So why did it feel so right? I pulled at my hair and groaned. It might be for the best that we didn't stoke the fire.

Although, it didn't stop me from lounging here on the beach, gawking at Kingston's muscled forearms, unable to tear my gaze away. If he'd only discard his swimming shorts, he'd be gloriously naked and my eyes could have their fill.

My thighs tightened and my skin flushed. It wasn't a hard fantasy to come up with—even to someone as inexperienced as me. His muscular body would cover mine, giving me toe-curling pleasure as he fucked me... if that kiss and our hook-up in his penthouse were any preview.

Good Lord in heaven. I should have looked away, but I physically couldn't. His tanned, olive skin rippled. He had not an ounce of fat on him. His broad chest was inked with tattoos that begged to be explored. And then those six-pack abs...

But it was the ink on his strong forearms that always held my interest—almost like an angel wing wrapping its feathers around his forearm protectively.

My breath caught, and every part of me was suddenly in flames. My mouth parted and I discreetly checked to ensure I wasn't drooling. Thankfully, I wasn't that far gone. *Yet.*

It should be forbidden for someone that good-looking to walk around in swim shorts. He should be made to wear a full bodysuit to ensure every woman's safety.

You're the only woman here, dork, I reminded myself. I dropped my head, hoping he didn't see me staring. He shook his head, droplets from his hair sprinkling my skin and doing nothing to cool me off.

"I don't remember you having a staring problem."

"I don't," I snapped, my voice too breathy. "Maybe I'm not the only one with a memory problem."

"Uh-huh."

My gaze shifted back to him without my permission and my belly pooled with warmth, catching his eyes exploring my nearly naked body. I exhaled a shuddering breath and looked away again, but not before seeing the flash of a smirk on Kingston's face.

He was an enigma, and I wasn't quite sure why. Maybe it was this gaping hole in my memory, or maybe it was something else.

He sat beside me, not even bothering with a towel, and I couldn't resist. "The sand is going to be up your ass."

He flashed me a smile, taking my breath away, before he lay down and tipped his face up to the sun. His face, stoic even when sunbathing, tugged at my heartstrings. I stared at him, deciding whether to bring up our kiss and short conversation about not turning back.

"Still not done staring?"

I swallowed, my need to lash out and raise my walls insistent. It was a necessity around my mother and her associates, but around Kingston, I didn't want to be like that. Some habits were hard to break though.

"Why do you have so many tattoos?"

He didn't move, but his body stiffened. He didn't open his eyes. "They invoke fear. Scars draw pity."

I froze, unable to even breathe.

"Did my mother and Ivan..."

My voice cracked. The words were lost. My thoughts scattered in the wake of the violent hatred that flowed through my veins like lava. For a long moment, we remained quiet, our bodies almost touching.

"I'm sorry," I whispered. I swallowed the lump in my throat, too much of a coward to turn and look at him. "When I lost my..." My fists clenched and unclenched next to my otherwise still-as-death body. "Losing my sister killed me. Her screams have never left me." My jaw clenched as my voice broke.

"Me neither," he admitted quietly.

For a moment, there was nothing but our breaths, the sound of the waves against the shoreline and the sun against our skin.

"Mother..." My palms started sweating, the noises in my head louder with every uttered word. "She held me responsible."

"She's responsible." The wind swept through, touching my burning skin. "If she needed anyone to blame, she should start with the bitch in the mirror. You're a victim too."

I swallowed, needing to hear those words for so long, yet relief didn't come. Instead, my chest grew heavy and my heart pounded to the rhythm of a drum.

"It doesn't make it any better," I whispered. "The scars... I had them too." It was the first time I had admitted that to anyone. "Cosmetic surgery can do wonders," I finally said, clearing my throat.

"Is that the reason you don't like to be touched?"

"Yes."

My body started trembling. Memories, moments—history, written and unwritten—stuck between us, and I wasn't sure where it'd take us. All I knew was that I was coming undone, every fragile thread of me ripping apart, bit by bit, losing myself and my twin.

Silence.

The air shifted and a soft breeze caressed me. His cologne wrapped around me, sending a shiver down my spine. His warm, strong arms scooped me up, and it felt like my heart stopped.

"It's *not* your fault."

I brought my palms to his hard chest, his body hot like the sun. I didn't dare open my eyes. Not when his soft lips brushed against my cheek. Not when they met my own. My fingers curled into his chest, as if I could claw my way through him and bury myself deep inside.

I parted my lips and he captured my bottom one, sucking it lightly. Savoring my mouth as if memorizing every dip and curve.

Before he *bit* me.

My eyes snapped open to find his brimming with an inferno. The air between us crackled, electricity sending my heart into overdrive. At this rate, I'd end up with a heart attack at the tender age of twenty-six.

"I thought you didn't like to be touched?" I rasped.

The fire faded from his eyes, turning into sharp black diamonds. His grip tightened on my hips, and then he dropped me, my butt hitting the soft sand.

He left me without another glance, and as he disappeared from view, I couldn't help but note the irony.

I was the one left with sand wedged in my ass.

Chapter 48
Kingston

I wasn't going to last long with Liana in a tiny bikini. The image of her like that was now seared into my brain, and there was no cure for it.

I thanked all the fucking saints there were no other humans on this island, or I'd have to blind a lot of innocent people. And that would make a hypocrite out of me.

Slowly but surely, Liana was getting under my skin.

It caught me off guard. Or maybe I saw it coming a mile away but was unwilling to admit it. Every passing hour around her made me feel hot and edgy. It started with our rendezvous in my penthouse, the taste of her arousal, a drug that had me needing more. And then that kiss happened. The library kiss was an innocent preview, but yesterday was a game-set-match for her.

And she didn't even know it.

I ran my tongue across my teeth. Now that I'd touched her, tasted her, and seen a glimpse of the woman she was underneath her perfect femme fatale exterior, I couldn't resist her. I wanted to go find her and fuck her, *now*.

The real Liana was tormented by ghosts just like I was. She was vulnerable, yet a fighter. Soft but also strong. It was impossible to resist her.

But guilt was a powerful thing. I made a promise to Louisa and, by God, I didn't want to break it. I loved her; I still did. So how did I move on from it?

I poured myself a glass of whiskey. I didn't particularly care for alcohol, but since Liana had come back into my life, it would seem I resorted to it more than I cared to.

As the bitter brown liquid trickled down my throat, a memory rushed forward.

"I'm a wimp, Ghost," Louisa cried, her head resting against the table. *"I think I need more of that numbing cream."*

I chuckled. "Sunshine, you can't possibly feel the needle at this point. It's all in your head."

It was just the two of us in the safety of her bedroom as I inked the tattoo on the nape of her head—one to match the design on my forearm. It was the only spot that nobody here would notice, with the way she usually kept her hair down.

"I wish those tattoo stickers were permanent."

Unlike her sister, Louisa didn't handle pain well. It was the reason I gave her a strong painkiller and cream to numb her skin.

"Maybe I'll invent them if we get out of here," I mused as I picked the gun back up and started working on the shading.

"When."

My sunshine—always an optimist. "When," I mimicked, teasing.

After a few seconds of silence, she spoke again. "Kingston?"

"Yes, sunshine?"

"If you ran alone, I could keep Mother and Ivan off your scent."

I stopped and turned her chin so I could see the left side of her face. "Freedom without you is meaningless." Her lip trembled and I leaned over, brushing my lips over hers. "I'd rather have a few seconds beyond these walls with you than have to suffer a lifetime without you."

"Will you love me forever?" she questioned, her insecurity wrap-

ping around my throat. "Maybe when we're free, you'll see that I'm... nothing."

I let out a sardonic breath. "Sunshine, you are everything." I smiled hearing her exhale. "I'll love you when the sun stops rising. When the planets stop spinning. And when death comes for you, I will hold your hand and follow right along."

A soft sniffle filled the space between us. "I love you, Kingston."

"I love you more, sunshine." I continued with her tattoo, lost in thought. We'd make things right in this life, we'd be free to live our truth together.

"Don't let them take me," she whispered over the whirring of the tattoo gun. Gripping it between my fingers, I lifted it off her skin. She was staring, eyes half-lidded, at the wall opposite us.

"They won't take you," I promised. The Tijuana cartel was our biggest threat. There was no way to defeat them if Sofia and Ivan were willing to sell her, but I'd make sure we got out. "We'll be gone before they ever arrive. I'll keep you safe."

"Liana too, right?"

"Yes, your sister too," I agreed reluctantly. Liana was a wild card. She wasn't exactly eager to leave the underworld behind.

I quickly quashed the memory, but it was too late. Everything came crashing down. The control I exercised at all costs. The ghosts that haunted me. Those few stolen kisses. We never made it out of the compound together. I left Lou behind, and she wasn't something I thought I could ever leave behind. Dead or alive.

My fingers clenched around the whiskey glass, bitterness coursing through my veins.

Liana was innocent too. Her story—spoken and unspoken words —gutted me. I was confused as fuck. I loved Louisa, yet Liana had started to feel so goddamn right. Had she put a spell on me? Or was I so fucking weak that I gave in to the first true temptation that came along?

I slammed the whiskey glass on the table, disgusted at myself, and let out a hollow laugh.

I bolted out of my bedroom and tore down the halls to her room. My body was tense with suppressed hunger. It made me furious—at her, at myself, at the goddamned world. It poisoned me down to the marrow of my bones.

She and I... We couldn't end well. We *wouldn't* end well.

It was a recipe for self-destruction. Liana loved her sister; I loved her sister. Every touch, every kiss was a betrayal to Lou. It hovered over us like a fog, clouding our judgment. And still I couldn't stay away. Like a moth to the flame, I went.

The ghost on my shoulder warned that it'd only settle me temporarily, and once this lust dissipated, Liana and I would be left with bitter regret. But goddammit, this maddening lust tasted so fucking sweet, tempting us with its promises.

I stormed into her room, slamming the door into the wall in the process. Liana whirled around, wearing nothing but a red lace bra and matching panties. Fuck, she was beautiful. Her creamy skin. Her soft hips. Her perky breasts.

My heart drummed in my ears as those golden eyes met mine.

So warm. So light. So fucking right.

"What are—"

"I need you." I practically snarled the words, kicking the door closed with my foot. "And I think you need me too."

She let out a soft scoff, but nothing could hide the way her cheeks turned crimson. "I don't need anyone." Always so brave. So determined. "Besides, I can take care of my own needs, if you catch my drift."

Her lips curved into a sinful, seductive smile, and the images of her touching herself slammed into my mind. My dick stiffened in my jeans. It had been impossible to forget the images of her on my bed, rubbing her clit while her lust-filled eyes watched me jack off.

"Show me," I demanded.

Liana's fingers clenched into small fists and her shoulders tensed. Maybe I'd misread all the signs and she really did hate me. I didn't know anymore. I promised my love and fidelity to Louisa, and here I was begging her sister to touch herself in front of me. I wasn't in my right mind, that was for sure.

She glanced around me, almost as if expecting someone to save her. No, that couldn't be right. She didn't need saving. She was probably looking for a weapon to kill me with, but finding nothing, her gaze traveled back to mine.

"Jesus," she muttered, her slender shoulders relaxing a bit as she made her way to the chair. But she couldn't hide the traitorous tremor of her body. She wanted me too. "You're becoming obsessed with me." She sat on the armchair like a queen, a secret smile on her lips. Did she think about the night we shared all those months ago as much as I did? "But let me warn you, I have no intention of staying here, so you'd better not get used to this."

Her fucking mouth would be the death of me.

"Take off your bra," I ordered, tugging on my own shirt and sliding it over my head. Her eyes landed on my chest, and goosebumps peppered her skin.

"I don't like your bossy tone." Her tongue swept across her bottom lip. "Say please."

Her nipples tightened under the thin material of her bra, and her fingers trembled as she reached for the hook in front, but she didn't move to unclasp it. Instead, she waited with a raised brow and a challenge in her eyes.

"Drop the act, Liana," I said, my voice so deep and thick I barely recognized it. "I can smell your arousal. And the wet spot on your panties tells me you're drenched. Now take off your bra so I can see your tits."

Her chest heaved before she finally did as she was told. Discarding it onto the floor, her breasts spilled out and all the blood rushed to my groin. Her fingers came down to her armrests, clenching around them.

"Show me how you touch yourself."

She rolled her eyes, although the blush staining her porcelain skin told me she was enjoying the attention. "You already watched that show once, Kingston. This is going to get boring fast."

This maddening woman. I unbuttoned my pants, discarding them in one go.

"The sooner you stop talking, the sooner you get relief," I gritted. "Take off your panties so I can see your pussy."

"Don't go romancing anyone with that mouth of yours," she breathed, her eyes lingering on my tattoos and the scars they hid. Could she see them? Her gaze traveled lazily down my body to my cock, and I watched with satisfaction as she flushed.

I liked that she didn't look away, instead she watched me palm my length and tug on it. Once. Twice. She gasped, her breasts heavy and swollen, her nipples puckering tight in the cold air.

"Touch yourself, princess," I rasped, and the plea in my voice would have embarrassed me if not for how turned on I was.

Her eyes flitted to mine before lowering again. In a decadent, sinful motion, she hooked her right knee over the armrest and inched her hand between her thighs. The first brush of her fingers had her quivering.

Fuck, she was so fucking beautiful. Spread wide open in offering, I could see her arousal, her wetness sliding down her inner thigh. The scent was fucking *intoxicating*.

For the first time in a long time, I wanted to fucking touch and caress and devour. I wanted to feel her flesh against mine. Yet, it felt like such a betrayal to Lou's memory. It was her I loved. This woman in front of me was just a faded, fake replacement.

So I'd have to keep my distance. There wasn't anything romantic about it. This was just blowing off steam.

Her fingers delved between her thighs, parting her folds, and I watched her thumb circle her swollen nub, rubbing it with her slim, graceful fingers. Her breath hitched and her whole body tensed, the sound of her wet arousal, the musky scent of her desire, and her breathing the only things I could concentrate on.

Liana slid a finger inside her core, her back arching and her lips parting with a soundless whimper. She was pink and wet, clenching and inviting. Her gaze lingered on my cock, her movements synchronized with my own. I watched as her hips started to move in rhythm with her finger, chasing her release.

"What did you think about when you touched yourself on my bed the last time?" I asked, my voice rough to my own ears.

"The man in my dreams," she breathed, a moan slipping past her naturally pink lips, her thumb circling her clit with frantic need.

I surged forward, curling my arms around her waist and pulling her up. I should have been smarter than this. I should have been more in control, but my cock took over my brain, and it no longer mattered that Liana wasn't my Lou. I was acting on impulse, like a starved beast about to pounce.

Her hands slammed into my chest, her wet fingers splaying over my abs, and for a moment, we stood still. Her lips were inches from mine. Eyes shining like gold.

Fuck, those eyes! I loved and loathed that color. I loved and loathed that *face*.

I dumped her on the bed and she bounced with a gasp. My jaw clenched as I fought my body's urges that were tearing me apart from within.

"Are we watching each other or are you fucking me?" Her body trembled, betraying her brave words.

"On your hands and knees," I snapped, angry that she was thinking about someone else while getting off in front of me. Furious at myself for wanting her. Confused at all these conflicting feelings that made no goddamn sense.

She scrambled up, and I shuddered at the view. Jesus fucking Christ. I wasn't a saint, but the sight of her naked body, needy and beautiful, would have anyone falling.

With a growl, I fisted myself, squeezing my erection from tip to base, and brought my shaft against her wet folds. Her back arched and I curled an arm around her hips, holding her still, and with one forceful thrust, I drove myself deep inside her.

"Fuck," I hissed, and she let out a strangled moan, adjusting to my size. Her tight cunt stretched around my thick erection, spasming around it, and I feared I wouldn't last long. She was as tight as a fist and her core pulsated around my length.

Liana's golden mane blocked her face from my view. Gripping her hip with one hand, I brought my other up and wrapped it around her hair, tugging gently. She turned and gave me a glimpse of her beautiful profile.

Her body trembled as she arched against my groin with a soft whimper.

"Fuck me, Kingston. Finish what you started." My lips curled with satisfaction as I pulled out, leaving only the tip inside her entrance, before slamming back into her tight pussy. "Oh... Fuck..."

The sounds she made were my undoing. I lost all semblance of control. I fucked her hard, pumping into her fast and deep. Her fingers clawed at the bedsheets, welcoming each thrust and milking me of everything I had left. Her hips rocked backward and filled the air with our grunts and moans as her arousal dripped between our bodies.

"You're gonna wreck me." My chest rattled with a growl, and each one of my thrusts brought us both closer to the edge. "But you're coming with me."

I plunged into her like a madman. Her knuckles gripping the bedsheets turned white. She pressed her face into the duvet, muffling her moans of pleasure. The way she milked my cock and whimpered my name brought me closer and closer to release.

A groan vibrated from my chest as I drove into her hard and stayed rooted there, the tip of my cock brushing against her inner walls. Liana quivered as a rush of wetness dripped onto the mattress. She moaned through her release, grinding against my cock. That was all it took to send me flying. My balls tightened, and I came with a roar, my seed spurting into her.

We both shuddered through our release, and then Liana collapsed onto the bed. My body on top of hers, my mouth on the back of her neck. We lay there like that for what felt like eternity, lost in the fog, until the pleasure wound down and—

I saw it.

My brows furrowed. I blinked, thinking my eyes must be deceiving me. Maybe I had finally lost my mind. I tried to breathe, fighting against the need to believe it and being too fucking scared to trust it was real.

"Kingston?" Her voice sounded far away. I pulled out of her, my cum dripping down her thighs. Liana sat up, but I gripped her hair. "Ouch. Let go of my hair," she yelped.

Goddamn it. All this time... What could this... FUCK!

"Why didn't you tell me?" I managed to say.

She turned and her eyes met mine. She attempted to push me away, but my grip on her hair was too strong. She winced, and a visible tremor rolled down her spine.

"I don't know if this is some weird after-sex shit, but I'm not into it," she growled. "Let go of my hair, psycho."

My fingers curled around her silky strands, and I lifted them one last time. My heart came to a complete stop, the blood pumping through my veins.

Time slowed. My eyes landed on the marking I'd tattooed with my own hands all those years ago.

My legs weakened and I stumbled back from the bed, dropping to my knees.

All this fucking time, Louisa was with me.

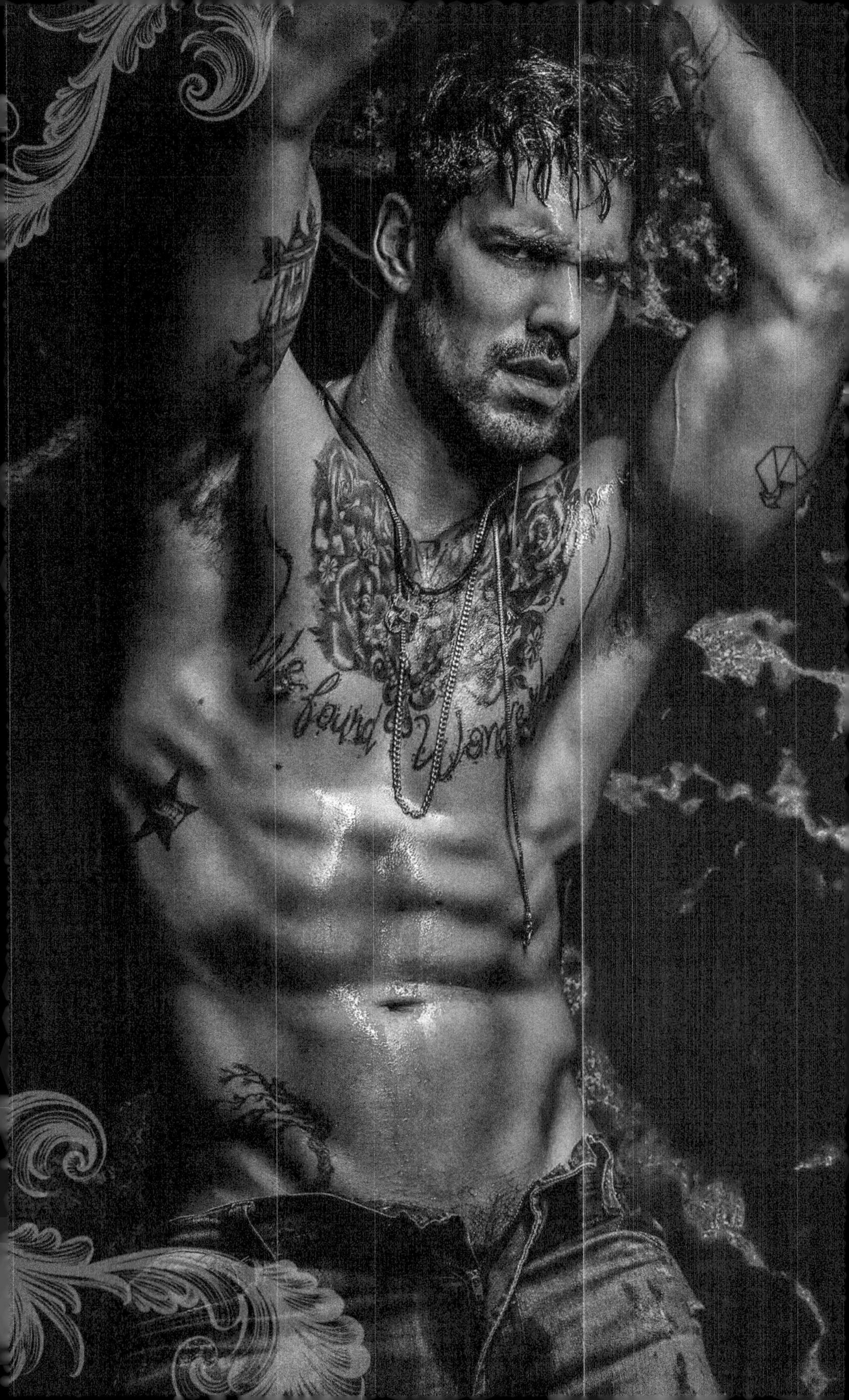

Chapter 49
Liana

I stared at Kingston on his knees, and before I could question him, he jumped to his feet and bolted out of the room.

My throat tightened as I stared at the empty space, immediately followed by an anger so deep I saw red. I gritted my teeth, my brain reasoning with me to let it go, but the vendetta brewed in my chest.

Pulling on a pair of shorts and a tank top, I stomped out of my bedroom and made my way toward his. I hammered on the door, then decided *fuck this*, and gave him the same courtesy he'd given me by barging in.

He was sitting on the side of the bed when I marched in, wearing nothing but pajama pants, his head in his hands and his gaze on the floor. A dangerous haze permeated the air, but I was too angry to heed its warning.

"What is your *deal*?" I snapped. "Every time you touch me, you leave me staring at your back—usually after you've dumped me onto the ground. I'm sick and tired of it."

He didn't look up.

My gaze roamed his bedroom, a bracelet of teeth dipped in silver and gold catching my eye. I narrowed my eyes as the whispers in my mind grew louder, but I quickly shut them down.

We'd settle this once and for all.

"Go back to your room," he croaked, shadows moving in his eyes.

Silver rays from the moon filtered through the open windows, illuminating his half-naked body.

"Is it me?" I asked, my voice cracking. No answer, only heavy silence. "When are you finally going to tell me what I did? I'm sick of you speaking in riddles, I want real answers."

Suddenly, I knew, this moment was it. This would determine the rest of our lives.

"It's not—"

I cut him off. "If you give me one of those *It's not you, it's me* lines, I swear to God, Kingston, I'm going to murder you."

He looked up at me then, and what I saw on his face was a brand-new emotion. The turmoil and warmth in it made my breath catch.

"Come here."

My body didn't even hesitate to obey the command.

I felt vulnerable as I padded toward him, every inch of me trembling with anger and anticipation. He parted his legs, and I stepped between them.

"I'm sorry," he murmured, his hands skimming up the backs of my thighs with a featherlight touch. "I didn't mean to upset you." Who knew such simple words could hold such weight. "Will you forgive me?"

"You..." I inhaled a deep breath. "You confuse me." He looked at me like he was waiting for me to catch up. "Don't make me... sad."

His fingers tightened on my thighs, digging into my flesh. "Do you regret it?"

I inhaled sharply. "I thought it was"—*Incredible.* My fingers laced through his dark hair—"intense."

His jaw clenched. "But do you regret it?"

"No." Maybe it made me the bad, selfish sister, but I didn't. "Not even for a second."

He let out a tense breath and pulled me closer, pressing his face into my stomach. A shudder erupted beneath my skin, warm from his soft touch.

"You're mine. Fucking *mine*." He bit the outline of my nipple through my shirt. "I'll slaughter anyone who ever puts a finger on you again."

"You're not a good man."

"I'm not."

"Good. I don't need a good man." My heart pounded at an awkward rhythm, wisps of a memory creeping into the corners of my mind. "I don't want to sleep alone," I croaked, my voice too raw, too desperate, as his face blurred through the mist in my eyes. I straddled him and his fingers grew firmer on my thighs, the fiery heat of his palms burning through my skin.

"I have to remove the weapons from under the mattress," he rasped, bringing his lips to mine. Our lips touched, but this kiss was... It was tender and lingering, *blindingly* passionate. A shiver skated down my spine like a lit match as he traced his lips along mine, his hot breath fanning my mouth.

This kiss was the kind you felt down to your toes. The kind that romance authors wrote about and schoolgirls dreamt about.

"I sleep with weapons too," I breathed against his lips. "Back home, anyway," I added, hoping my reminder that he was keeping me here as a pseudo-prisoner didn't kill the mood.

He smiled against my lips, and I slid off his lap.

It took a minute to clear out the weapons, and another minute for us to settle on the bed. Then I slid under the covers next to him and pressed my head against his chest, listening to his strong heartbeat. I listened to him breathe and found comfort in it.

"I like how you smell," I murmured against his chest, his constant petting soothing everything inside me. "My favorite flavor."

He stilled for a moment, then let out a soft breath. "You, sunshine, are my favorite flavor." My brows furrowed at the change of the nickname.

"No more ice princess?" I asked, tremor lacing my voice.

Tension radiated from him, every muscle in his body pulled taut. His fingers trembled as they brushed over my hair. "No more."

I felt his lips against my forehead, the gesture so simple after the earlier encounter, but it had every fiber of me trembling with so many feelings. My fingers traced over his ink, his muscles flexing under them.

I loved how big and strong he was. I even loved that he was a morally gray man. It was exactly what I needed. His gaze touched me everywhere, like he was seeing me for the first time. I couldn't wrap my head around it, but I loved his attention.

His hands brushed over every inch of my skin, then he shifted and I let out a soft protest. "Don't go anywhere."

He let out a sardonic breath. "Nobody, not even God himself, will tear me away from you," he rasped as he reached for my left wrist and hooked the bracelet around it. "This is yours."

My brows knitted, studying the delicate jewelry made of teeth dipped in real gold. It didn't bother me though. In fact, it felt as if it belonged there all along.

"It's a weird gift, Kingston," I murmured softly. I brought my wrist close to my chest and cradled it, that familiar throbbing there. "But I like it. A lot."

I nuzzled into him, my eyes locked on the shining metal. Why did it feel *right* to have it on?

"I still can't believe it," he whispered so low that I barely heard the words.

I lifted my head. "Believe what?"

He shifted us over, his body covering mine. I slid my arms around him, those scars that his ink hid rough under my fingertips. The truth was, I loved them, because they screamed he was a survivor. It made me feel safe with him.

"That you're here with me."

Bliss hummed beneath my skin as his weight covered mine. "So you won't be leaving me anymore after we... kiss?"

There was vulnerability in my voice, and I was sure he was able to see it in my eyes.

He ran a rough palm across my cheek and his lips brushed mine. "I'll never leave you again."

The promise seared through me like a romantic song and my heartbeats slowed to nothing.

"Ditto," I vowed, realizing I fully meant those words.

It might have been wrong, but my possessiveness over this man roared to the surface, and I'd hold on to him until my last breath.

His mouth trailed over my neck before he buried his head in my nape.

That night, we held each other all night.

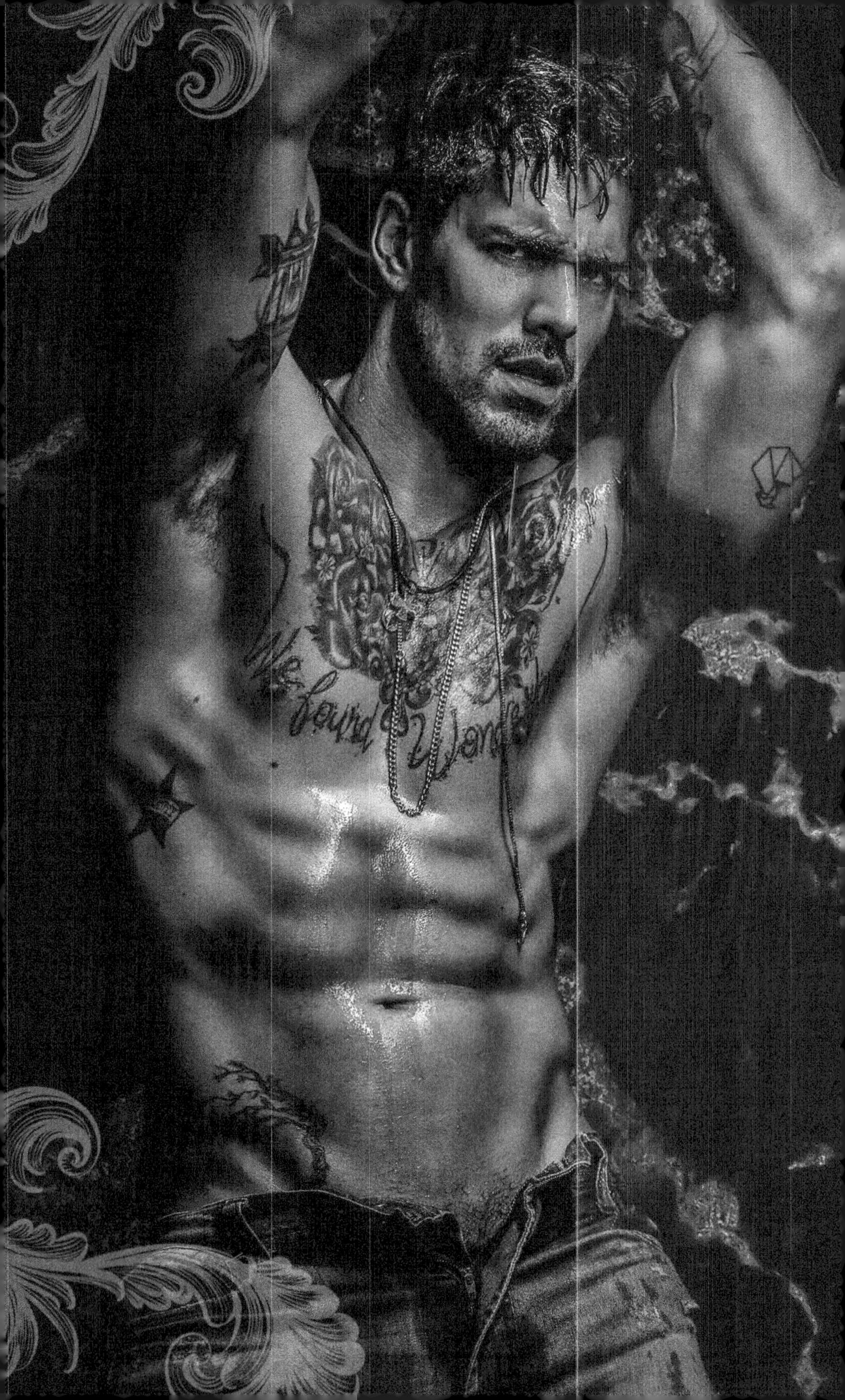

Chapter 50
Liana

The skin on the back of my neck itched as the cries of torture traveled through the castle. I looked at my twin and reached for her hand, interlocking our fingers while my other hand gripped the bracelet. It gave me strength. It kept me safe.

He'd given me a new one for every birthday. My twin didn't like it. She found the hard enamel and rugged dents gross, but she appreciated the strength I drew from it.

My twin squeezed once, then pulled away to rest her chin on her knees and wrap her arms around her legs, staring into the fire. Winter months in the Siberian manor were brutal, especially when Ivan Petrov was here. I shouldn't complain, especially knowing that I wasn't the only one suffering. Mother and Ivan's prisoners had it worse—a lot worse.

My legs shook while my mind chanted over and over again, "Where is he?"

I pressed my eyelids together as "Born To Die" by Lana Del Rey played in my head on repeat. I'd started to wonder whether our finish line would be death. It would seem our entire lives had led us to this *point. To die. Our road to freedom had been unending. It couldn't fail us now... Could it?*

I pushed at my temples with closed fists. Everything about the lyrics made me want to cry, and I knew there was no time for tears.

My palms pressed into my skin, my fear a white-hot current. He wouldn't hurt us. Mother was here. She wouldn't let him. But then where was she? Where was Kingston?

I hid my face in my lap to smother my cries. Please, please, please. I just wanted him. I wanted my—

The door crept open, and my sister and I whipped our heads up. I tasted her fear like it was my own, just as I knew she could sense mine. We scooted back, pressing ourselves into the dark corner.

Liana's breath fogged the space between us. Or maybe it was my own. I rocked, mouthing to myself, *I'm not scared. I'm not scared.* Eventually, I'd believe it.

The footsteps were getting closer. The hardwood creaked, piercing through my eardrums. Tears ran down my cold cheeks, searing a path down to my lips. My twin's hands gripped me hard.

He was getting closer. He was...

I jumped when a hand touched me. My back slammed into the wall and pain shot into my shoulder.

A scream pierced the ice-cold air.

I launched up off the floor and jumped onto the broad back, ignoring the shaking fear that gripped every fiber of my being. In the next breath, I was thrown off effortlessly, my limbs coming down hard on the stone floor.

The world tilted. My vision blurred. Pain surged through my temples.

Even with my head buzzing with adrenaline and pain, I tried to move, but my body refused to listen.

But then reality filtered in through the horror.

My eyes widened. A large hand covered my mouth while the other roamed down my body, lower and lower, until it reached my crotch. I bucked and kicked, my screams muffled and the back of my head hitting the floor again. The stench of tobacco and cheap cologne assaulted my senses.

My eyes roamed the room frantically, watching as my sister fought off another man. Disgust and despair clogged my throat.

"Stop fighting," he rasped. I could feel my energy waning, but I couldn't give up. Not now. Not ever.

Suddenly, his dead weight slumped onto me, suffocating me. Blood splattered my face and neck, coating me in crimson. My pulse roared in my ears, disorientation and confusion thick in the air as I blinked repeatedly.

I looked up to find my vengeful ghost looming over me.

"I'm sorry I'm late, sunshine," he said, extending his hand to me, his other already offered to my sister, who looked just as gruesome as I did. But his eyes remained on me, chasing my fears away and lending me his strength.

"I-it's... okay." My teeth clattered, but I almost melted with relief.

He kneeled for a brief moment, pulling a tooth out of each man's mouth, then straightened up. I met his eyes, harder and darker than ever before, flickering with fury.

He still held his knives, blood dripping on the hardwood. One more atrocity added to his plate. When would I be the one to protect him?

"Where were you?" my twin cried, accusation clear in her voice.

"It's almost time for another bracelet, sunshine," he told me, ignoring my sister. He pocketed the teeth, watching me with an impenetrable mask.

Kingston—my protector—had been our bodyguard, keeping our virtues intact and protected, only for the highest bidder to buy it like we were a pair of prized horses. Except he was so much more than that.

He was everything to me.

My eyes fell to bruises on his neck and his busted knuckles, and I couldn't help but wonder—how much did our virtue cost him?

My heart pounded in my chest. My ears rang. My vision dimmed.

I was too late to save her. I was too late to save him. A scream tore through the air. The world went pitch-black.

"KINGSTON!" I bellowed, my eyes snapping open. My damp hair plastered against my forehead, my chest tightening and making it hard to breathe.

Next to me, Kingston startled awake. "What's the matter, sunshine?"

His fingers brushed my damp hair while I squeezed my eyes shut, the distorted and confusing memories about my twin and me flashing behind my closed lids. My temples pulsed, a throbbing ache piercing my skull.

I wrapped my arms around my stomach, rocking back and forth. Shivers racked through me, nightmares that I didn't understand plaguing me.

Turning on my side, I rocked back and forth, soothing myself the only way I had for the past eight years. Kingston's fingers traced my nape, circling around gently as if following invisible lines.

"W-what... are you... doing?" My teeth chattered, making it hard to speak.

"Tracing your tattoo."

My eyes found his over my shoulder with knitted brows. "I... d-don't have... a tattoo."

"You do," he assured me, his voice warm and soothing. "I'm touching it right now."

Gasping for air and overcome with emotions, sobs took over. My gaps in memory alarmed me with each passing day. I should remember getting a tattoo. I should remember Kingston.

"What's happening to me?" I croaked through sobs, images that made no sense flashing through my mind.

My stomach churned with nausea. I brought my fingers to my temples, pressing them while shivers racked through me. I wheezed, trying to ground myself. I struggled to breathe. *Inhale. Exhale. In and out.*

"Louisa, look at me." Kingston's arms wrapped around me.

"It's... It's Liana," I stuttered, unable to control my tremors. "I'm... Liana," I wheezed. It all became too much. Or maybe I was losing my mind. Blood pounded between my ears, a shrill ringing sound growing with each heartbeat, making it impossible to grasp my thoughts. My eyes found his and I cried, "C-can't you see it, Kingston? I'm Liana, not Louisa."

His lips brushed against my temple, whispering words I couldn't understand through my panic attack.

"Just breathe, sunshine."

He pulled me into his lap, rocking me back and forth, and I buried my face in his neck, crying until sleep pulled me under.

Nothing made sense anymore. Or maybe it was that everything finally did.

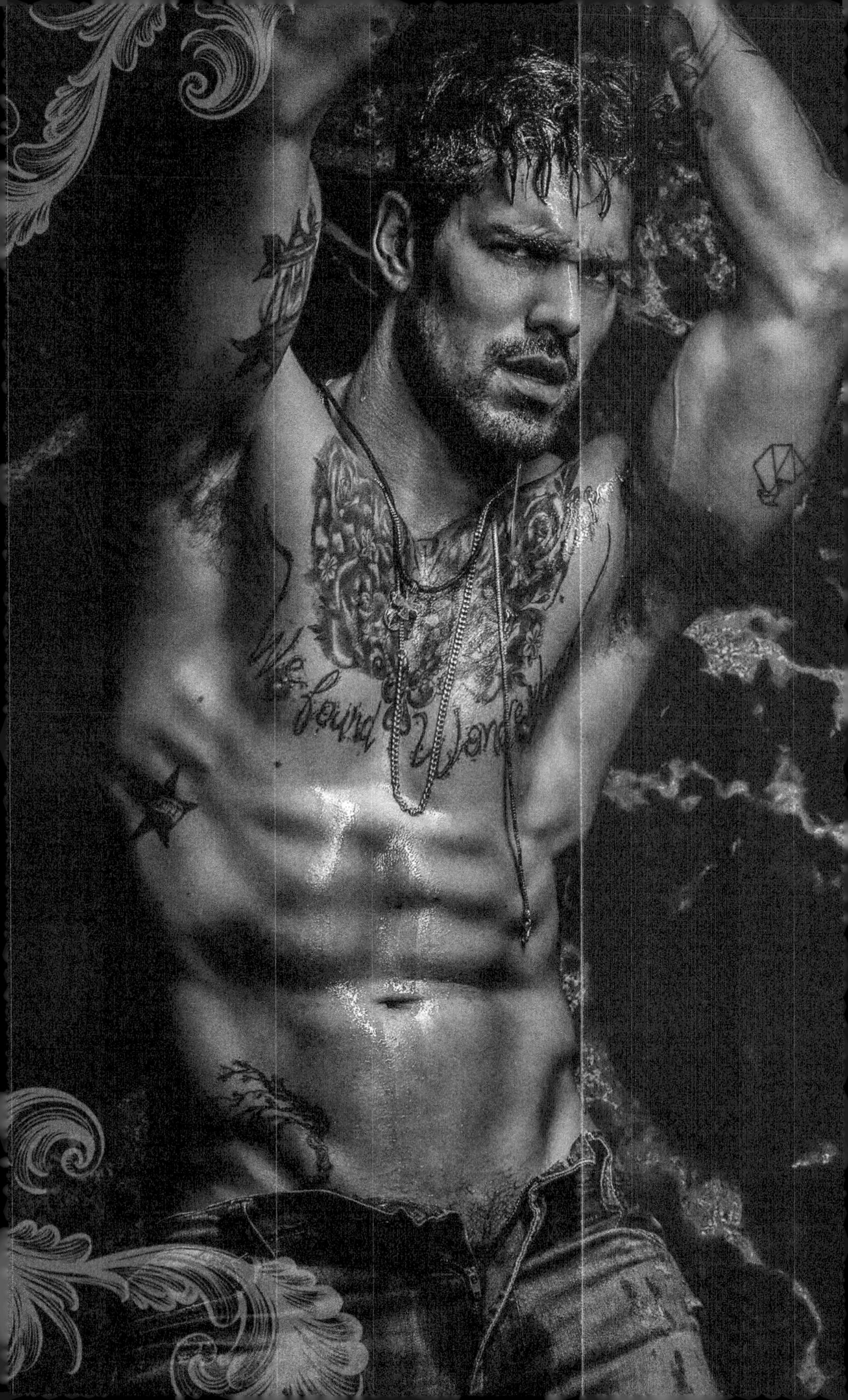
We found

Chapter 51
Kingston

Louisa fell back asleep in my arms, her mouth tight and her breathing shallow. I smoothed a hand over her brow, still not believing she was Lou.

My Lou.

All this time, she was alive and breathing. So she didn't remember me or our shared past, fine. I'd help her remember—someway, somehow. The main thing was that she was here. With me. In my bed.

Her sick mother must have put her through some extensive torture for her mind to be so damaged. Her trauma, combined with Sofia's brainwashing, had convinced Louisa she was her twin. Did that mean Liana was dead?

There was no telling what torture Sofia put Lou through. She might have injected Lou with so much guilt that her mind snapped, and the only way Lou could cope was by convincing herself she was Liana.

My jaw clenched.

Guilt gnawed at me at the realization that I'd failed her, not once but twice. I couldn't protect her in the dungeon, and then I left her at her mother's mercy. It didn't matter that I thought she died in front of me, witnessing her brutal torture at the hands of Sofia and her men.

I ran a hand through my hair and pulled on the ends. What the hell should I do? I could tell her she wasn't Liana, that she was my Lou, but I didn't think she was in any state to hear it.

Reaching for my phone on the nightstand, I quickly typed a message to Dante Leone, a member of the Thorns of Omertà, the organization I usually did bidding for.

> Me: I need the name and number of your therapist.

His reply was instant despite the time of night.

> Dante: I don't have a therapist.

I rolled my eyes.

> Me: Just send me the name and number.

> Dante: Are you finally dealing with your shit? I'm proud of you.

Dante Leone could be such a prick. Fun to hunt and kill pricks with, but thoroughly annoying.

> Me: Stop wasting my time.

> Dante: Why did you ghost us?

> Me: Are you sending me the fucking name and number or not?

> Dante: Don't get your panties in a twist. Coming right up.

The next message was a shared contact. Dr. Violet Freud, PhD from Harvard. I didn't waste any time booking Lou for an immediate session.

By morning, I'd talked the shrink into flying out here—well, I made her an offer she couldn't refuse that involved many zeros, but that was neither here nor there.

Careful not to wake Louisa up, I slid out of bed, showered, then got dressed and made my way to the helicopter pad. The sun was just rising over the horizon, and no matter how many times I came to my property in the Mediterranean, the sight never failed to impress me.

Today, it meant more than ever. This was what the two of us dreamt about. Living on the beach where the cold would never find us. Away from the world. *Safe* from the world.

The rich tang of the slightly salty air swirled around me. I loved this island. It had become the only place I considered home, now more than ever.

I heard the helicopter before I saw it. I watched Alexei, the only man I trusted with the coordinates, land the bird on the helipad. The moment it touched down, Dr. Violet Freud emerged.

"Mr. Ashford," she greeted me. "Next time you pull this shit, don't expect me to come running. I don't care how much you offer me, I don't appreciate being strong-armed." Alexei came up behind her, and she shot him a glare. "And don't send scary people like him to pick me up."

Putting my hands behind my back, I dipped my chin. "I'll take that into consideration."

"You do that," she snapped, pushing her gold-rimmed glasses up her nose and meeting my gaze. "Now tell me more about the patient."

"Louisa seems to be struggling with some sort of deep memory loss." From my periphery, I saw Alexei's body lean forward, his expression curious. I gestured for the doctor to walk ahead, then steered us in the direction of the house. "She has." I cleared my throat before continuing. "*Had* a twin. She seems to think she's her."

"Identical twins?"

"Yes."

"How long has she thought this?"

I pushed my hand through my hair, forcing my feet to keep moving. "I don't know." I pretended all this wasn't cutting through me. "Until last night, I thought Louisa was dead."

Dr. Freud reached for her glasses, her hand shaking. She must feel out of her element, but to her credit, she hid it well.

"Are you certain she's the twin you believe her to be?"

"Yes, damn it."

"How can you be so sure?" My jaw clenched and it took everything in me not to snap. "After all, you believed her to be the other twin until yesterday. It's easy to confuse identical twins."

"Because she has the tattoo I gave her." I held on to my cool. I couldn't afford to lose the only shred of hope Lou had. "Nobody knew about it. Not even her sister."

I stopped and took in the shoreline, the crystal blue water shimmering with rays, and fuck if it didn't give me hope.

"I'm confused why you didn't recognize her right away, then," she pointed out.

"I saw her die... I *thought* I saw her die in front of me." The memories of her torture shredded through me, tearing my fucking chest to pieces all over again. "She was beaten and tortured."

My voice cracked. I'd never gotten over it. Louisa was my soulmate. As children, we started as friends. I was her rock and she was mine. Our friendship grew right along with us.

"It sounds like she's dissociating, Mr. Ashford." Somehow, it didn't surprise me. After all the shit I'd seen and survived, I knew our minds dealt with trauma differently than our bodies. "From what you're telling me, she endured trauma and abuse. It's possible she's blaming herself for her twin's death."

"How do I get her back? How do I stop her from believing she's her sister?"

"You can't." She stressed the words, narrowing her gaze on me. "She needs to do that work on her own."

"That could take years." My hands curled into fists, and her eyes dropped to them before meeting my gaze in disapproval. I didn't give a shit what she thought. "We don't have years. You'll talk to her and fix this," I gritted. "The house is that way, just follow the path."

"Good thing I didn't wear my heels," she said with a hint of annoyance.

It wasn't until she was out of earshot that Alexei said, "Are you okay?"

I nodded, more worried about Louisa than my own state of mind right now. "When you came for me," I said, meeting his gaze, "I was the only one in the room. Right?"

"You were," he confirmed. "You kept pointing to a spot, asking me to save her, but there was nobody there." Fucking Sofia and her sick games. I would have never thought she'd be capable of torturing her daughter to the point of madness. "I have some news you probably won't like," Alexei added pensively.

"Oh how I love starting my day with bad news," I retorted wryly, facing him.

"Well, it seems you haven't slept much as it is, so consider it yesterday's news." Alexei hesitated before he continued in a low voice. "The girl we saved... Louisa. It turns out her name wasn't Louisa at all. She was beaten until it was the only name she responded to."

Interesting... Initially, I thought it a strange coincidence, but with everything that'd happened, with how fucked up the past few months had turned, it didn't feel crazy to believe it played a part in all of this.

"Do we have her real name?"

He shook his head. "No, she refuses to talk to anyone."

A long sigh left me. I suspected as much. She hadn't uttered a word on the drive from the warehouse, but she'd clung to Liana—

correction, *Louisa* the whole time. Alexei watched me intently. Waiting, it seemed.

"She'll talk to Louisa."

He nodded. "I thought it'd be our best bet." His gaze darted in the direction of my home. "But how will you handle everything else?"

"I'll help her remember."

Because we'd been in love almost as long as we'd been alive.

Chapter 52
Liana

"**I**'m here to talk to you about your twin."

I stared suspiciously at Dr. Freud, who stood on the terrace outside Kingston's home.

"What about her?"

"What do you remember about her?"

I narrowed my eyes. Who in the hell was this chick, thinking she could poke and prod about my sister?

"Let's sit down," she offered, and frustration flickered inside me. This wasn't her office nor her home. She didn't wait for me to take a seat, but she must have read my expression because she added, "Please. I've had a rough day, what with being forced out of my bed and dragged here."

"Oh, you should've led with that..." I lowered myself opposite of her. "Who forced you out of bed?"

"This scary dude with blue eyes, covered in tattoos," she muttered.

The corners of my lips twitched. "Alexei."

"Yes, him. I want nothing to do with him."

"Well, here's to hoping."

The note of sarcasm in my voice didn't escape her, and she brought her pen to her lips, watching me closely.

"Are there hopes that were ruined for you?" she inquired. My mind rebelled as I thought back, the mental blocks making my temples throb. The harder I tried, the worse the pain got. "Do you remember?"

I narrowed my eyes on her.

"I remember everything." She held a pad in her hands, her pen moving over the page furiously. "What are you writing down?"

"Just notes." As we sat on the terrace, the sun made its way up the clear blue sky. "I'm trying to ascertain the differences in your personalities, in your behaviors and interests."

I scoffed, but still gave her as much as I could, and then it was one question after another, making my head spin and my ears buzz.

Until she lifted her head and shifted subjects as she said, "And you and Kingston—"

"That's Mr. Ashford to you," I hissed. It was too early in the morning for this shit or for any woman to be anywhere near my... *my* Kingston. Yes, that sounded right. He was mine, and this lady better get lost. He was none of her concern. My turn for questions. "What are you doing here?" I snapped. "And how do you know about my twin?"

"Kingston—" I glowered and she cleared her throat, a small smile twitching on her lips. "Pardon, *Mr. Ashford* gave me some insight earlier."

Why was he talking to this woman? She was too pretty for him not to notice. Then realization sunk in. I was jealous. The green-eyed monster bubbled in my chest, ready to eliminate any woman who could be a potential threat. But why? I wasn't territorial.

"He had no right," I grumbled, my jaw tensing. Why would he be telling a perfect stranger anything? We'd have to set some ground rules about that. "And you'll forget everything he said."

"Or what?" Jesus, was the woman actually challenging me? She had a death wish, I was certain of it.

I eyed the space around me, surveying any possible objects to use as weapons. There was nothing aside from silverware, a plate, and a porcelain cup. I sighed. The butter knife wouldn't do; I'd tried to kill a man with it once. It didn't work for me. A fork would have to do. Messy but necessary.

Just as I leaned forward, Kingston appeared, his attention locked on my hand.

"Sunshine, put that down," Kingston ordered, and I narrowed my eyes on him. He better not be defending the beautiful doctor.

A muscle in my jaw twitched. We might've had an incredible night, but he sure was pissing me off this morning.

"Why is she here?" I growled, waving the fork in the air. "And why are you telling her my history? *Our* history." The one *I* didn't even remember. I couldn't remember him as my and Louisa's bodyguard, and it left me feeling like I was missing a limb. "I don't like it, Kingston."

"What hand did you use to grab the fork?"

My brows furrowed at the jarring change of subject. I wasn't easily frazzled, but he managed it every single time.

My gaze lowered to find my left hand clutching the fork. "What does that—"

"You used your left hand," he said. "Which twin is left-handed?" My mind blanked. I could almost see my invisible, mental walls slamming into place. "What's your favorite ice cream flavor?"

I shook my head, trying to clear my mind. I brought my free hand to my temple and cleared my throat.

The images of my mother breaking my wrist each time I used my left hand played in my mind like a distorted movie. That dull ache in my left wrist throbbed. *Don't break,* my mind chanted on repeat. *Don't break. Don't break.*

"Can I make a recommendation?" Dr. Freud inserted herself.

"No," I snapped.

"Go ahead." Kingston really wasn't earning any brownie points today.

"Hypnosis."

"You're not fucking with my mind." I'd had enough of that shit to last me a lifetime.

She ignored me. "It's just to unlock the barriers."

"What fucking barriers are you talking about?" I glared at Kingston. "Why did you bring her here?"

He closed the distance between us and kneeled down. "Do you trust me?"

"Yes. No. I don't know." I'd been self-reliant for so long, I didn't know how to trust anyone.

"What does your instinct tell you?" Dr. Freud interrupted, chiming in when she really shouldn't. Although, I had to admit it was a valid question.

"Sunshine, you have to do this." Kingston was relentless. "You know these memory gaps aren't normal. Hypnosis could help."

I shuddered, my chest suddenly heavy. "I don't want to be at her mercy."

"I won't let her or anyone else hurt you," he vowed. "I'll be here with you, every step of the way."

My gaze darted to the beautiful woman who waited patiently for us to make a decision. She was a stranger, a potential threat. But Kingston seemed to trust her, which made me trust her too.

"Don't make me regret this," I hissed. "Because I'll end you without flinching."

The corner of her lips lifted. "Duly noted."

Inhaling a deep breath, I exhaled, slowing my heart rate. Or attempting to. "Okay, now what?"

Kingston stood up from his kneeling position and came to stand next to me, like a protective cloud.

"You're going to relax and listen to my voice. Concentrate on one memory you had with your sister." Closing my eyes, I followed her instructions, last night's dream fleeting to the forefront of my mind. "Tell me what you see."

As if in a daze, my mind hazy, I narrated the dream. The bracelet of teeth that meant so much to me. Its calming effect when I was scared. "The bracelet," I murmured. There was a rustle, but I was too deep in this changed state of awareness to care.

"Who gave you the bracelet?" Dr. Freud asked.

"Kingston, my ghost." My brows knitted in confusion. He gave it to me last night. But I had it in my dream when I hid with my sister.

"Don't think," the doctor said softly. "Reasons and logic don't matter right now. Just follow that train of thought." I focused on the noises around me. Birds chirping. Waves washing against the shoreline. The rustle of the breeze in the trees. "Focus on your breathing."

With each breath, I felt myself relaxing. Time slowed.

In a sleep-like yet hyper-aware state, images started flashing through my mind like a movie on fast-forward. So many. So confusing. My heart raced in my chest, yet my breathing never sped up.

My eyes shot open. I stared at my wrist, almost expecting my mother to appear out of thin air and snatch the bracelet. The familiar crunching of bones would follow, accompanied by that immediate pain. I slapped a hand over my mouth as a flashback hit me with deadly force.

A light tapping woke me up and I jolted. I blinked several times, erasing sleep from my eyes when I saw him sitting in the corner by the window. Silver moonlight threw shadows across his face, and a heavy tension settled in the space between us.

Something was wrong. Kingston never snuck into my room at night. He always said it was too risky.

"What are you doing here?" I whispered, glancing around the empty room before returning to watch him sitting in the chair like a king. He always reminded me of a king—strong, protective, and deadly—despite being my mother's prisoner.

"I've been waiting for you to wake up." The vehemence in his tone sent a chilling alert through me. Glancing at the clock, three a.m. stared back at me in red. "You were right." Confusion flickered through me, sleep still tugging heavily on my brain. "We have to run."

I swung my legs off the side of the bed, then padded barefoot toward him, wedging myself between his knees.

"Okay." I took his clenched fingers in my hands and smoothed them out. "Then we run."

His eyes dulled, but it didn't hide the fear that permeated from them. "It won't be safe for you."

I'd seen Kingston kill. I knew he'd keep me safe. Nobody and nothing ever made me feel as protected as he did.

"Anywhere with you is better than here without you, Kingston." This place was hell for him. I swallowed, my heart trembling within my chest. "Can we bring my sister along?" Trepidation flickered to life in my chest. "I... I can't leave her behind."

"Are you sure she even wants to leave?"

A heaviness tugged at my chest. Lately my twin had become harder somehow. She was distant, shutting me out constantly. Mother liked it; I didn't. But she was my sister, a part of me, and I'd never forgive myself if I didn't at least try.

"She wants to leave," I said with a certainty I didn't feel. With my free hand, I traced my finger along his lips, down his chin until I reached the smeared red lipstick that stared back at me. I inhaled a shuddering breath, unable to bury my head in the sand. "I'll kill her for you one day, Kingston."

He shook his head.

"No, sunshine. I'll kill her." He lifted our interlocked fingers and kissed my knuckles one by one. "I want your hands clean."

Our eyes locked, and he stroked my cheek.

"Tomorrow night, we run and never look back," I whispered, and for once, my hopes and dreams felt like physical things I could hold in my hands.

"Tomorrow night, we run."

I was thrust back to the present, my limbs trembling as I slumped over before Kingston caught me. My breath lodged in my throat as I stared up at him. It wasn't possible, was it? I was Liana. Right? I gripped my head with both hands, curling my fingers into my hair. My panicked eyes sought out Kingston like he was a lifeline.

"Fuck, I'm sorry, sunshine," he swore, his voice gravelly but deep and warm. "I never wanted to hurt you like this." Emboldened by his words, I raised my chin and we locked eyes. "I've never stopped loving you. There hasn't been another woman. You're it for me, Louisa. My beginning. My middle. My end."

There was nothing but sincerity and devotion in his expression and his voice. Was everything I thought I knew a lie? A faux reality? What should I believe?

My heart. My instincts.

For the past eight years, I'd lived with things I couldn't explain. Dreams and gaps in memories. Maybe those were fragments of my old self; my subconsciousness holding on to myself. And then it occurred to me... It was always there—in my sketches, in my heart, and in my dreams.

"I remember," I whispered, tears racing down my cheeks. And then the anger hit.

My name was Louisa Volkov, and I intended to murder my mother for what she'd done to me. What she'd done to all of us.

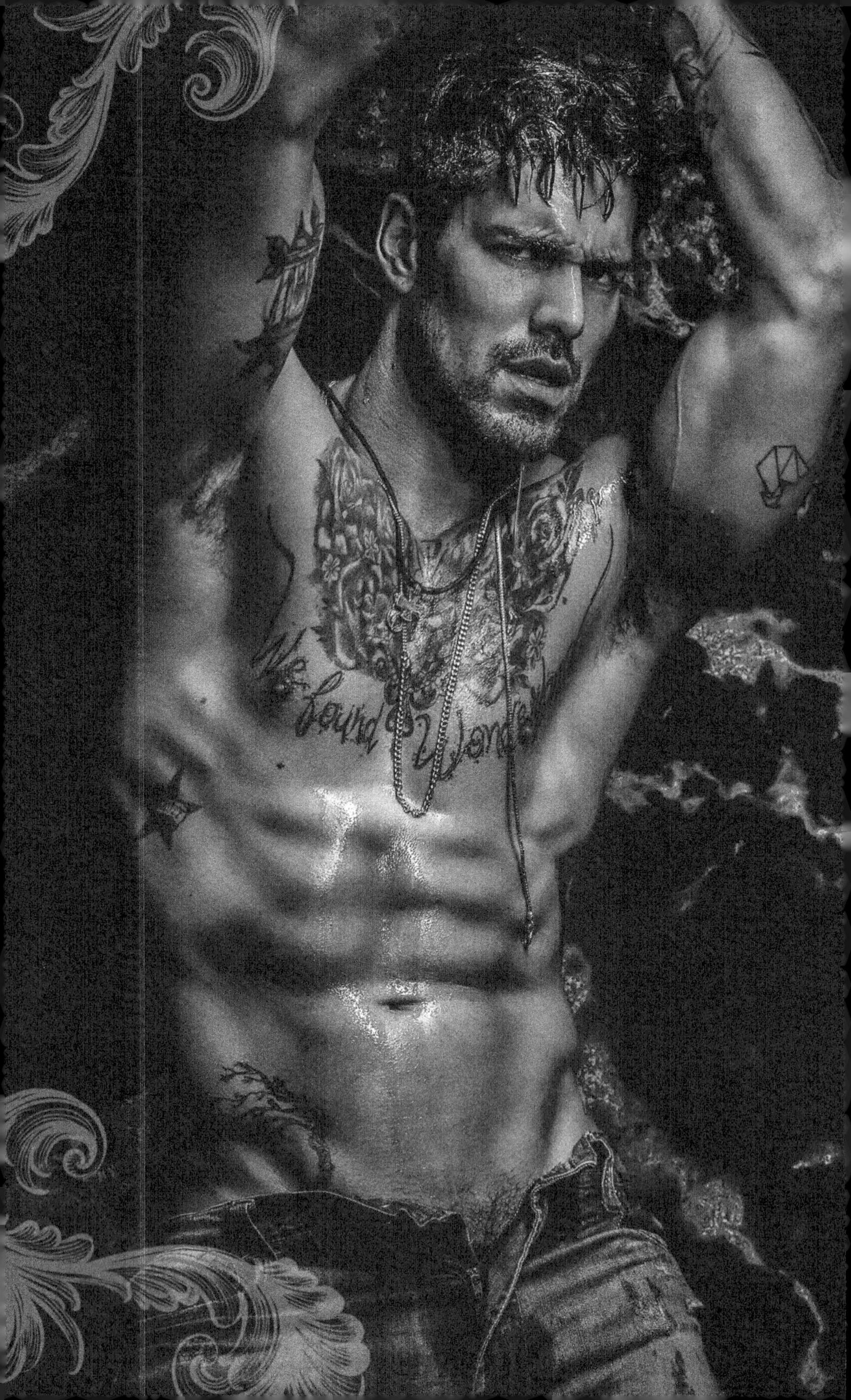

Chapter 53
Louisa, 18 Years Old

Staying here would destroy us. We had to get out of here—all three of us.

"Are you sure?" Liana said. "If Mother's men catch you two—"

I knew what she meant, but we couldn't stay. Not if the man I loved was a prisoner. We weren't much better. Yes, we were spared rape and beatings—for the most part—but we wouldn't be for long. The Tijuana cartel had been in negotiations with Ivan to arrange a marriage with one of us—the prized mafia princesses.

We knew that sooner or later, we'd be sold off just like the humans they trafficked.

Liana and I detested what our mother represented. Years of learning about every criminal alliance in the underworld had taught us that she was high up in the food chain and drove a lot of despicable deals.

Yes, she protected us, but at the cost of others. She didn't care that they were innocent; she let them suffer. She encouraged their punishments. She encouraged the gladiator games. And she encouraged human auctions.

"We have to try. Should we go over the plan again?"

She shook her head, flashing me that smile that usually got her what she wanted. "I'll meet you two in the agreed-upon spot." She leaned in and pecked my cheek. "I love you, sestra."

"Love you too, sestra," I repeated softly, staring at my twin. We were identical—both of us blonde, with freckles on our noses and golden-brown eyes. Nobody could ever tell us apart, aside from her being right-handed and me left-handed. "This will work," I whispered. "Then we'll be free of these walls and chains. Kingston will be free."

"And if she catches us?" she asked, eyes darting around.

My chest tightened with the knowledge of what would happen if she did. Torture and beating for Kingston. Possibly for us too. Each breath pierced my lungs as foreboding filled my veins.

"If she catches us," I started calmly, "I will kill her. For her part in what was done to Kingston and all the other innocents."

Liana smiled. "He makes you brave."

"I'd kill for him," I admitted. I'd die for him too, but I didn't voice that. "He's it for me, Liana. I hope you find someone who'll make you feel the same way. I know you'll understand then."

I was drawn to his heart, his every broken piece.

Her eyes flicked to my bracelet and her shoulders slumped. "He might be the right man for you, but it's the wrong time. Same with this escape plan."

I hugged her tightly. "There's no right time for anything in this life. We have to make it, grab it, and seize our own happiness, even if we have to lie, steal, and cheat."

Then, I turned around and left my twin behind without another glance, not doubting for a second that I'd see her again.

"Sunshine, I promise." Kingston was restless. Our time was running out. "We'll come back for her, but unless we leave now, we won't make it."

I didn't want to leave my twin behind, but I knew Kingston was right. They didn't call him Ghost for nothing. Nobody matched his skill when it came to disappearing, hunting, and ending a target.

"Okay," I agreed. My twin was my other half. Leaving without her was like leaving part of myself behind.

His hand gripped mine, squeezing in understanding.

Then we ran.

Our feet sunk into the thick layers of snow as the castle, that caused all of our nightmares, disappeared behind us. I stumbled, falling to my knees, but Kingston's firm grip quickly yanked me up.

The sky was gloomy, nearly invisible as snow descended from the skies above. The heavier it fell, the less likely they'd be to track our footprints. The sharp, crisp air felt like a whip against my face. The air fogged around us with every exhale as we raced hand in hand, the Siberian landscape swallowing us whole.

"Almost there," Kingston urged, sensing my fatigue. He was in excellent shape; he had to be to survive here. Unlike me.

Each breath split my chest in half.

The wind wailed, bringing with it the dreaded barking of Ivan's dogs. I sent up a prayer that maybe he'd set Puma on our trail. She wouldn't hurt Kingston or me. She was the best dog out of all his vicious animals.

"Kingston," I cried, snowflakes piling onto my eyelashes and wind biting my cheeks. "I'm... I'm... Leave me behind. I'm slowing you... d-down."

My chest heaved and I trembled as I let out silent sobs into the night.

"No, we do this together. Keep running, Lou. We're almost—"

He never finished the statement.

Bang.

A single shot was all it took for Kingston's body to drop and begin to jerk in slow motion. I stumbled face-first into the snow, my fingers gripping his hand. I lifted my head to find ruby-red snow stacked around Kingston's body.

My world came crashing down as an animalistic scream tore from my lungs and the world titled on its axis.

I woke up bruised and battered in the basement of our castle where Mother tortured all the innocents. Made them killers. We'd endured hours and hours of beating; I didn't know how much more I could take before I broke.

My eyes flicked to Kingston, who was unconscious next to me. I stared at his chest, watching for any sign of life. Was he breathing? It was hard to focus with how mangled he looked.

"You disappoint me, Louisa." Mother's voice pulled me to where she stood across the room, her hair in a perfect updo and her fur coat unsullied. But it was her face, twisted with anger, that held my attention. Her heels clicked, a countdown to my doom, as she made her way to me, an iPad in her hand. "Look at what you've done."

An image stared back at me and I blinked a few times. Then she pressed the Play button and the video started.

I thrashed and pulled at my chains, shouting until my throat turned raw and blood trickled from the corner of my mind. I finally managed to slump away from my mother and throw up all over the dirty ground. The images swam behind my eyes when I was finally able to close them, and I wished it were me—that I had been the one on the screen.

Unconsciousness pulled me under.

When I woke up, my Kingston wasn't with me.

I blinked, disoriented and dizzy as I glanced around the sterile room. It was empty and bright. The only decor was a flat-screen television in the far corner. I moved to rub at my temples when I realized

I was strapped to a chair, my feet and wrists bound by special leather belts.

I was terrified, fear clawing up my throat. My heart sped into overdrive.

The door opened and all hope shuttered at the vision of my mother walking in. Her eyes were blank, her gray strands a matted mess—she was a shell of herself.

The diamonds around her neck glittered, trying—and failing—to make up for their wearer's emptiness.

Hate slithered through my veins, cold and venomous.

"You're the cause of this all, Mother," I spat out. "You destroy everything you touch." My control was gone. My fear was through the roof. Panic set into my bones. I jerked against the restraints frantically. My life and my sanity depended on it. "Fucking everything," I bellowed, my voice turning raw.

She stepped closer, her eyes empty.

"Let's begin."

The television flickered on, and my blood chilled. I watched my sister fighting against the men, scratching and clawing. Biting them. I jerked against my restraints, dread sluicing through me at what was coming.

And then the screams began. Hers. Mine. Ours.

I tasted her fear. I felt her pain. I lived her torture.

The first electroshock jolted through me, and a wretched sob escaped me.

The second electroshock followed. Breathe. Focus. Survive.

Then the third shock came. I shut my eyes and soaked in the finality of my twin's death.

A fourth.

I lost count. All I could do was scream.

Heartbeats blurred. Words twisted. Days blurred.

"You took her from me." I didn't know why Mother was so furious. "I need her back. Understand me?" I nodded despite not comprehending what she meant. "Very well, Liana. Let's start."

Start what? I thought I moved my lips, but I didn't hear the sound of my voice. My mind was in shambles. The ringing in my skull refused to cease.

Then the shocks came again, wrenching agony from my throat. It pierced my skull, splitting it in half.

That time I heard my voice. Although I wished I hadn't.

The old me died that night.

The new me was born out of the ashes, a phoenix thirsty for revenge.

Chapter 54
Louisa, Present

Eight years.
    Memories pierced through me like a sharp blade.
    I had lost eight years of being me; eight years of loving the boy who protected me and my sister; eight years of looking for my twin.

    I desperately tried to hold my tears back but was quickly losing the battle. One tear rolled down my cheek, then another, until it was impossible to stop them.

    Finding Kingston's dark gaze on me, we both ignored Dr. Freud's eyes on us as the past danced around us. My eyes filled with tears again as I stared at him like I hadn't seen him in eight years.

    The boy was gone. A harsh man was in his place.

    I couldn't stop remembering the boy, memories breaking my heart slowly, wreaking havoc from the inside out.

    I shook my head. "I... I need—"

    I couldn't breathe.

    Rushing out of there, I heard Kingston call for me. "Louisa!"

    "A minute," I croaked.

    My mind was a jumbled mess. I couldn't think with his eyes on me. I couldn't breathe when he was near. Most importantly, I couldn't shake off the guilt of forgetting him.

"I'll be right behind you, sunshine," he called out. "Take all the time you need, but I'm following right behind you."

This was not how it was supposed to be.

My heart squeezed, so many memories bouncing off my skull and suddenly making sense. The faceless man. The brutality of our childhood. The pain of his torture—and mine.

I walked aimlessly around the island, Kingston's footsteps distant but steady behind me. My skull screamed, my muscles protested, and my left wrist ached. Fuck, no wonder it hurt. My mother broke it so many times, forcing me to use my right hand.

A headache slowly formed between my temples, the throbbing pain matching the one in my heart.

I stumbled through the shrubs, staring at my surroundings through my blurry vision. Birds chirped. The waves soothed this raging storm inside me.

I failed them.

For eight long years, I'd been failing Kingston and my twin. I let my merciless mother twist me into something I never was.

A shadow fell over me, and I lifted my head.

Kingston—my ghost and personal shadow—lurked over me.

"It's going to be the only promise I can't keep," he rasped. "Please tell me you're okay."

"I'm okay." I managed an awkward smile, unable to tear my eyes from the man he'd become. It felt like a twilight zone.

"You're not okay."

"I shot at you," I blurted, feeling like sobbing my heart out. "Twice. Then Russian—"

I was such a mess. A killer who was unable to keep her shit together. No wonder Mother didn't want me as Louisa. *No, don't think like that.*

"And I hated you." Kingston's soft admission pulled me out of my spiraling thoughts. "I thought you were Liana, and I hated that my

Lou was dead while she was alive. I wanted to kill her... you... but a promise I made *you* kept me on track."

My fingernails curled into fists, digging into the palms of my hands. My pulse roared in my ears.

"But you kept your promise," I whispered. "How could I have forgotten you?" I croaked. "My sister?"

He cocooned me against his strong chest, the familiar warmth and spiced-vanilla scent enveloping me into a protective bubble.

"You survived." A broken moan left my lips and I buried my face against his chest. "You kept your promise because you survived and came back to me."

"No, Kingston. You found me."

Another tear rolled down the side of my face, but this one held hope.

My ghost—my Kingston—had found me despite the universe conspiring against us. The warmth of his love and the lines of his face kept me going in my dreams, only for him to find me again.

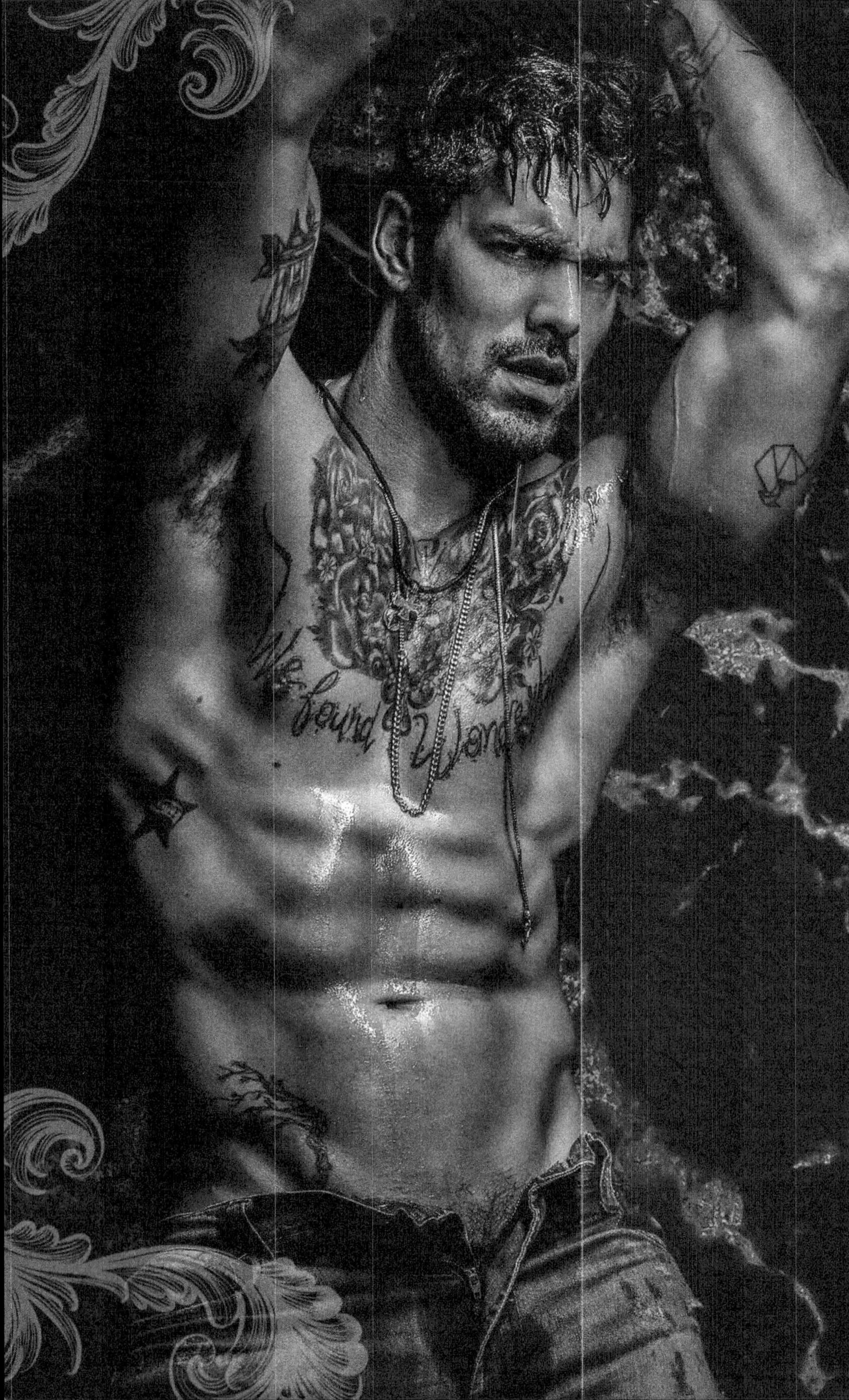

Chapter 55
Kingston

My obsession with Louisa became oxygen and water. It was born out of emotions that the world had almost erased.

I couldn't pinpoint when I fell in love with Louisa. It just happened—like a breeze becoming wind and then turning into a hurricane. It grew with each touch and kiss, each stolen moment.

My heart bled and ached during the years when I believed she was gone. I was a dead man walking, as cliché as it sounded. And then fate brought her back into my life. It was our second chance, and I wouldn't waste it. I'd hunt down every threat and eliminate it.

Starting with Sofia Volkov.

Something had bothered me about this whole situation. It lacked any logic. Why would Sofia have orchestrated this whole thing?

And now, this random girl turned up beaten and confused, claiming her name was Louisa.

It was all connected. The question of *how* remained.

When we got back to the house, I barely spared Dr. Freud a glance when I said, "Your ride home's waiting. Send me the bill."

I lifted Louisa by the hips and sat down with her on my lap as Dr.

Freud hightailed it out of there. She turned out to be very useful, although I wished she'd been able to offer me a way to spare Lou from it all. She kept staring at me as if she'd seen a ghost.

"Tell me how I can help," I murmured, brushing my nose against hers.

"I'm Louisa?" She was still shellshocked, her eyes twitching and her mouth turned down in a frown. "You're not going to break my wrist?"

I clenched my jaw so hard my molars almost shattered. That bitch must have forced all Lou's old habits out of her.

Inhaling a calming breath, I forced a smile on before I said, "No. Nobody will ever hurt you again." Her forehead came to rest against mine, her breathing shallow. "Take your time. Breathe. Everything else will come."

"How could I forget?" she whispered. "How could I forget you?" She swallowed hard. "Me? Us?"

I stayed silent for a moment, thinking of the best way to answer. Maybe I should have kept Dr. Freud on for a bit longer, but now that Lou was back, I didn't want any witnesses to our reunion.

"It was probably a combination of Sofia's torture and your mind's coping mechanisms."

"Am I crazy?" Her voice trembled.

"No, sunshine. You're not crazy." My grip around her waist tightened. "You're a survivor. You're the strongest woman I know. Hell, one of the strongest human beings *period*."

"I feel like I'm losing it," she whispered. "I don't know what's true and what isn't. It's insanity."

"Then you ask me, and we'll figure it out together."

"Together," she repeated softly, as if tasting the word on her lips.

"Yes, together."

She shifted, her golden-brown eyes on me. "How did you survive?" She blinked several times. "I remember... the torture. Yours. Mine. I thought you died, and I wanted to die too."

"Alexei saved me." I took her chin between my fingers. "I thought you died. I touched you and..." Fuck, my voice cracked. "I passed out, and when I woke up, you were gone."

"Sofia played us."

My jaw clenched.

"She did." She shuddered, goosebumps visible on her skin. I ran a hand down her arm, then wrapped her in a hug. "But she'll never get to you again," I vowed.

"You... We always wanted this, didn't we?" Her voice was muffled against my neck. "The beach and the sun... just the two of us. True?"

I rubbed my hand over her back soothingly.

"True."

"Did... did we... You were my first and I was yours?" A light blush crept up her cheek. Her fair skin always betrayed her, and those eyes... Fuck, I should have known. Lou's eyes were always the windows to her soul.

This time, when a memory came, I welcomed it. I watched it happen and let myself remember it with everything I had. It was eight years ago, when we'd been able to sneak away after trying for so many months. She stood there in the abandoned hallway, under the blanket of darkness, her golden locks lighting my world.

Leaning against the stone wall, my arms folded over my chest and my breaths fogging the air, I watched as she danced across the floor, lost in her own little world. It terrified me that one day one of Ivan's men would sneak up on her and hurt her, so I'd made it my mission to train her to be vigilant.

Lou was sometimes too focused on one thing, oblivious to her surroundings, but we'd been working on it. She was getting better each day.

The oil lamp flickered, throwing shadows over me, and she finally spotted me.

My chest stirred, the same way it did every time I saw her. The girl had me wrapped around her little finger.

"Happy birthday, sunshine." Her smile lit up the dark and cold hallway. "Shouldn't you be in bed?"

She ran the rest of the way, her dainty feet soundless against the marble floor. My pulse rocketed, achingly beating only for her. She single-handedly made my time here bearable. If it wasn't for her, I would have attempted to run—and likely gotten killed—years ago.

I opened my arms and she fell into them, burying her face into my chest as I lifted her.

"How does it feel to be eighteen?"

She looked up, her smile somewhat sad. "The same. Except that now we're legal adults, we should have the freedom to live our lives freely."

I nodded, wishing I could take us far away from here, where she'd be protected from all the ugliness she was forced to witness. I worried about the toll it was taking on her soft heart. Her sister was the tougher one of the two.

"How does Liana feel about turning eighteen?"

She shrugged.

"Pretty much the same. She's still mad Mother forbid her to go to MIT." It was always a far-fetched dream. Sofia was far too controlling to allow her daughters out of her sight. "Anyhow, I kissed Lia, wishing her a happy birthday at midnight, then headed here." Her voice was breathy and excited. She never hid her emotions around me, which was so damn refreshing. "You're home to me, and even though we're both here, it means something."

"I want to give you a real home."

"Soon," she murmured.

"Soon," I vowed.

Sliding her down my body, she hit the ground and brought her arms around my neck.

"Were you waiting for me?" she asked, her lips brushing against mine. She always tasted sweet. It'd become my favorite taste. Fuck chocolate. Fuck strawberries. Give me vanilla any time of day or night.

"Yes." There was no sense in pretending that I wasn't. If there was anything we learned living under this roof, it was that tomorrow might never come. "I have your birthday present."

I reached into my pocket and pulled out a bracelet.

"You don't need to make me gifts, Kingston. You're all I need." Her hand came down from my neck, her fingers trembling as she traced the bracelet with the pad of her thumb. "So many men you had to kill for me."

Brushing my mouth against her forehead, I murmured, "I'd kill them all again for you, sunshine."

She released a shuddering breath. "I need to protect you, Kingston."

"Shhh." I breathed hard, my fingers shaking as they stroked the side of her face. "I've got you. I'll always have you."

Something clogged in my chest, knowing how little I could offer her. Her life hung in the balance between her mother's and Ivan's threats, but I would always be here to protect her. Until we ran.

Lou was a sacrifice worth making.

"Kingston?"

"Yes?"

"I'm eighteen now, and I know you think I'm too young and immature—"

I cupped her cheeks. "You're not too immature," I corrected her. "You've seen shit most men have never seen. You survived them too."

"But I am young." I nodded. "Even though I feel like we age a decade for each year that goes by in this prison."

I chuckled softly. "So what does that make us?"

"Like... one hundred and eighty?" We laughed, but it wasn't exactly a happy laugh.

"I love you, Kingston." Her whisper echoed against the hallway. "Don't make me wait anymore. We could die tomorrow. At least don't let me die a virgin."

My chest tightened. I wanted better for her.

"I'm too tainted for you." The anguish in my voice was hard to miss.

Lifting her hands, she cupped my cheeks.

"No, Kingston. You're perfect for me." *She'd brushed her lips against mine then, stealing my breath and my heart. "You deserve the world. And if we have to lie, steal, and cheat, we'll get our happy ending. Because we fucking deserve it."*

The same unflinching determination I now recognized in the woman before me had danced across her face that night, and just the thought of it had my chest shattering from how much time we'd lost.

"Is it true we were each other's firsts?" she repeated, yanking me back to the present.

"True." Her shoulders tensed, and I suspected the reason. Lou had never been the sharing type. It was what I loved about her. "There hasn't been anyone since, sunshine. I thought you were dead, but I couldn't handle anyone else's touch. I decided I'd wait for you in hopes that we'd at least get an afterlife together." A choked sob sounded against me, and my heart cracked a fraction more. "Then I saw you again, thinking you were Liana. I hated you—her. You were so familiar yet not."

"Me too. All of it," she whispered her admission, so soft I could have missed it. "I didn't understand why I never bothered with any men until we crossed paths."

I smirked down at her, satisfaction filling me. I wouldn't have held it against her if she'd been in a relationship—it had been over *eight years* after all—but I'd be lying if I said it didn't please me.

"Maybe our hearts were smarter than our minds," she mused.

"I think you're right," I agreed.

Chapter 56
Louisa

Kingston and I took his jet to Greece, heading for the shelter where we dropped off all the women nearly a week ago. I didn't know what awaited us, but Kingston was right. We had to find out more about the young woman.

Over the last two days, since memories of my past had started to sharpen into focus, I told Kingston *everything* that I'd done over the last eight years, including my reason for trying to infiltrate Cortes's operation.

I explained how I worked with Giovanni Agosti to kill the old Santiago, and how I learned that my sister was used by Perez to be sold using a Marabella Mobster arrangement.

Kingston held me through my tears, promising we'd find her, wherever she was in this world. My gaze brushed over his forearm, tracing the tattoo of angel wings wrapped around his arm.

There was so much history left to uncover between us, but I trusted Kingston to be here with me every step of the way. Somehow we got through torture, death, and separation, only to be brought back again. That had to count for something, right?

"How did you finally realize I wasn't Liana?" I asked curiously.

His eyes darted over my face before they came to linger on my throat. "On the nape of your neck, there's a tattoo I gave you." I reached my hand back to feel for it, tracing it like he had. "It was our secret. Nobody else knew about it, not even Liana."

A memory probed at my skull. "The angel wings?"

"Yes, sunshine. It always fascinated you."

"The wings of your guardian angel," I whispered, remembering why he got the tattoo. "So they can always protect you."

He wiped at the tears clinging to my eyelashes. "You always represented my guardian angel, sunshine."

My heart clung to it, beating for him, and for the first time in years, I felt whole. If not for one missing piece: my twin.

"Mother has taken so much from us," I rasped.

His fingers brushed over my jawline, down to my collarbone, then to the back of my neck. I imagined he was probably tracing the tattoo just like I was tracing his.

"We'll get it back," he said with conviction, his voice serene. "And then we'll make her pay."

I took his hand into mine and squeezed. "On one condition."

The corners of his lips twitched. "Name it."

"I get to kill her." He stiffened, but before he could protest, I continued. "You protected me for so many years. You've killed again and again to keep me and Liana safe." I brought his palm to my mouth and kissed it. "Your hands are drenched in blood. It's my turn to keep you safe."

"No." His eyes burned into me.

"Kingston," I sighed out. "My hands aren't clean anymore." His eyes darted to my palms, and I watched him clenching and unclenching his fists. "I've killed more than once."

"You were protecting innocent, vulnerable women. I'm not innoc—"

"Don't you say it," I warned. The ache in my chest grew at the knowledge that it was my mother who'd made him believe he was less than. "Nobody in this fucking world is innocent. The only way we can make this"—I gestured between us with my fisted hand—"work is by protecting each other. I've seen the teeth, and I still don't give a shit how many men you've killed. They deserved it."

"It was *my* job to protect you, and I failed," he hissed.

I shook my head. "It was our parents' job to protect us, and *they* failed, Kingston. That's not on us. We did our best and we survived."

His body tensed, the muscles of his shoulders rigid, but then he shook his head. "You're right, sunshine." Kingston's mouth tilted up. "I have to get used to this new fierce and strong Lou."

I swallowed, my pulse thundering. "I know it's different... I'm different from that girl you fell in love with—"

He silenced me with a kiss. "We're both different." His lips molded to mine. "I'll love any version of you, in every lifetime, in every death, in every universe."

And then he kissed me like the world was coming to an end.

Wearing a casual black T-shirt, jeans, and combat boots, Kingston walked next to me, holding my hand as we made our way through the compound that was built by Lykos Costello for victims of human trafficking.

"We're gonna be one of those couples who dress the same?" I mused, squeezing his hand gently as his gaze roved over me in the same outfit. He towered over most people, including me, but tucked into his side, I'd never felt safer.

"We share a heart," he whispered into my ear as he led us through the hallways. "It seemed appropriate."

I caught a few curious glances thrown our way, nurses and women alike, probably recognizing danger. When you grew up around people like Ivan and Sofia, it was impossible not to carry some of it everywhere you went.

"Maybe when all this is over, we can go on a date," I teased. "I've never been on one."

I sensed his amusement as he glanced at me. "What a coincidence... Neither have I. You think there'll be sex on our first date, or should we wait for the second?"

My face heated. We were quite the pair, both of us missing out on so many normal events in our lives.

"Let's do it on the first date," I said, grinning. "Since we kind of live together already."

Kingston raised his brows at that. "Kind of?" He pressed his lips to the top of my earlobe. "Sunshine, that ship has sailed."

A little smile tugged at my lips. "Where should we go for our first date?"

"A restaurant?" he suggested.

"Maybe we can go wild and see a concert."

He chuckled. "A concert, huh?"

"Have you ever been to one?" He shook his head and I smiled. "Me neither. We have some catching up to do."

But before we could iron out the details, I felt his body snap to attention, and I followed his line of sight right to Lykos Costello. At least my mother's teachings proved to be handy in some aspects.

"Handgun?"

"Yes." I watched Kingston's entire posture switch to a predatory mode. "Do we not trust Costello?"

"We trust nobody in the underworld."

I nodded, and we remained silent as we closed the distance.

"Mr. Costello," I greeted him, extending my hand. "Thank you again for letting the women stay here."

His dark eyes studied me, his face half covered by stubble. "Miss..."

He waited for me to give him my full name, but that wasn't happening.

"Miss is fine." I smiled tightly. "We're here to see the girls."

The man's eyes were alight with humor at my not-so-subtle dismissal.

He gave a pointed look down the hallway. "All five of them are together in the last room on the left."

A door behind him opened and surprise flooded me when I saw a woman, her hands and wrists bound to her bed, children around her.

Kingston's hand on the small of my back urged me forward. "Let's go."

I shared a glance with him, picking up on his warning to stay quiet, and we continued forward. The moment we were out of earshot, I asked under my breath, "What was that?"

"Nothing we want to get involved in." My steps tripped over the smooth surface, but Kingston caught me by my elbow. "Let's focus on what we came for," he warned.

When we reached the last door, we found the women, and my eyes traveled over each of them. They looked like different people. Their faces were clean, they wore new clothes, and color had bloomed on their cheeks. They looked *healthy*. Until you looked at their eyes.

You could always tell by one's eyes how much they'd suffered.

My throat felt thick with unshed tears as I said to Kingston, "They'll open up easier if you're not here."

He nodded. "Keep the door ajar."

I knocked on the doorframe, and five sets of eyes turned to look at me when I entered.

"Hello," I greeted them softly. "Is it okay if I come in?"

Four of them offered soft smiles, while one set of eyes remained staring out the window.

"Hello, Liana," the girls greeted me in unison, causing me to wince at the name. How in the hell would I ever explain?

"There's one empty seat," Visha said.

I perched down at the little table where the girls were gathered around.

"Are you doing okay?" I asked, regretting that I couldn't take them with me to the island. Alexei had assured me that they'd be safe here, but it wasn't the same as having them tucked in our territory.

"Yes," Delilah answered. "We've been well taken care of here."

I nodded, feeling Kingston's presence even though he wasn't in the room.

"I have to tell you something," I said, bringing both my hands to the table and twisting my left wrist. "And then I'm going to ask you for help, but I want you to know, if it's too... hard or painful or anything like that, you don't have to tell me anything."

Uneasiness permeated the air. The girls smiled, millions of tiny goosebumps breaking over their arms, remaining quiet. They were suddenly nervous and I hated being the source of it.

I lowered my head, my heart racing in my chest.

"First, I guess let me start by saying, I..." I swallowed. "Well, it turns out, my name is Louisa."

Tension filled the room while I considered the girls. Their expressions were mostly marred with confusion, except for the youngest. Her brown eyes flickered with terror.

"Did you... forget or something?" Mae asked hesitantly, her eyes darting to the girl who had been beaten into thinking her name was Louisa according to the intel Kingston got.

I took a deep breath, twisting my fingers. It made me sick to my stomach to admit the woman who was responsible for their misery was my mother, but there was no way around it.

"I have a twin sister," I started softly. "Her name's Liana. I still have some gaps in my memory—" I watched the girl who clung to me when we saved her, hoping she'd hear my sincerity and sorrow in my speech. "My mother's Sofia Volkov." The girls gasped and reared back. "There aren't too many people who know my face, but I owe you this much. Believe me, a week ago, I fully believed I was my twin."

"But how?" Mae asked, her brows drawn.

"Eight years ago, my sister, me, and m-my—" Unsure what to call Kingston, I stuttered. "And the man I love tried to escape my mother.

My sister never made it to our meeting spot, so my boyfriend and I ran alone, but we were caught." My bottom lip trembled and I sunk my teeth into it, the copper taste of blood flooding my mouth. "M-my mother had me tortured. She showed me the video of my sister's death and—"

"She tortured you until you were convinced you were your twin," the brown-eyed girl whispered.

I nodded. "For eight years, I believed I was my twin," I rasped. "I don't even know if she's alive."

"She's alive." The conviction in her voice stole my breath. "I heard them... the men... whispering about Liana, they said her name in the same breath as Sofia's. That can't be a coincidence. They sounded scared of her." I found her almond-shaped eyes on me.

My throat tightened as I stared at her, pain coiling in my belly. God, what in the hell was happening here?

"But how do we know they weren't talking about *you* as Liana?" Visha pondered.

I tilted my head to the side, blinking at them, and something heavy settled in my gut.

"I've killed human traffickers." I shot to my feet. I started pacing around, my mind turning over faster than I knew what to do with it. "But it's no more than what others are doing. Liana though..." I breathed in and out, hand on my chest. "She was... is stronger than me."

My heart thundered, my breathing uneven as I made my way to the brown-eyed woman, lowering myself to my knees.

"I'm sorry for what Sofia did to you," I told her quietly, tears gathering in my eyes. "I want to stop her. I have to stop her."

My disdain for my mother and everything she stood for colored my voice. I didn't even bother to hide it.

"What do you need?" Her voice was raspy, like she'd been choked too many times and her vocal cords were damaged.

"What's your real name?" I asked, and suddenly the temperature in the room dipped ten degrees.

I waited with bated breath, unsure whether I pushed too fast and too hard. She'd suffered enough.

"Lara Cortes." I gave my head a shake. It couldn't be any relation to... "My father is... Perez Cortes."

I stared at her in disbelief, knowing in my heart she wasn't lying, but I was unable to wrap my head around it. A familiar hand came to my shoulder, squeezing in comfort.

"It can't be the same man," I breathed, yet somehow it made complete sense. He took me, so my mother took her.

Lara's eyes found me and she let out a heavy exhale. "The very same one who sells girls via the Marabella Mobster arrangement."

The pain inside my chest worsened. My hands started to shake, and a tear rolled down my cheek, soon followed by another. Tears streamed down my face, steady and fast.

"I'm sorry." Lara's soft voice, her cries, pierced through my own pain, and I pulled her into a hug.

"Our parents sure made a mess of things, didn't they?" I croaked, feeling my lips tremble.

Kingston's hand tightened on my shoulder. "Revenge?"

One word, but it was all I needed to strengthen my resolve. I clenched and unclenched my fists, the cruelty of the underworld echoing in the bitterness on my tongue and hollowness in my stomach.

I glanced at Lara, who must have been in agreement. Heart stuttering at this new piece of information, I tried to process it all and understand it, but there were still so many missing pieces.

But there was one thing I was certain of: Lara needed protection. The moment the underworld learned Perez Cortes had a daughter, they'd be after her.

Chapter 57
Kingston

I'd been dealing in information and collecting secrets for years, my end goal always being to be untouchable when I came out on the other side. I had become a ghost so nobody could ever get close to me—my siblings and Alexei being the only exceptions.

Soon after the truth had come out at the women's shelter, we left Greece and headed for my property in Portugal—Lara in tow. After learning her true identity, we couldn't leave her. Louisa and I agreed she'd fare better under our protection.

The girl had suffered because of who her father was. Once others learned of Lara's existence, there'd be no mercy shown. Fuck, they'd probably come after Louisa, but I'd protect them both. With Louisa by my side, we would fight anyone who dipped their toe into the filth that was human trafficking. While we were all murderers and sinners, we wouldn't allow certain lines to ever be crossed.

The atrocities of evil men and women would continue, but we'd never give up. The young boys and girls who found themselves in the clutches of human traffickers would be our responsibility to eliminate. We wanted a better world for these children; one that wasn't afforded to us.

"I still can't believe Perez had a kid," Alexei said, his legs stretched out as he sat in my study. I was at the window looking out at my woman, my sister, and Lara by the coastline. The tightness in my chest eased up, watching Lou smile at my sister and holding Lara's hand in her own.

Lara gravitated to Lou, and after what they'd both been through, I knew they'd be good for each other. She was under our protection now. We offered the same to the other girls, but they were content to stay in Greece.

"It's a fucked-up story," I muttered.

"Do we know why the other girls were taken?" Alexei pierced me with his pale blue eyes. Every child was taken for some reason or another—revenge, blackmail, as a pawn. The other four girls kept their stories close to their chests. It made sense; they were older and probably guarded more secrets. Lara was the youngest, which was probably why she cracked first.

"No, but I have a feeling we'll be finding out more information."

They'd all need rehabilitation. They'd need help—physical and mental. The same thing that Alexei provided me with when he saved me.

"Are you going to tell the Omertà about Perez's kid?" he questioned.

"No." He didn't seem surprised. "The girl's fifteen. She deserves to have a life—a safe one—and her last name will make her a target. Especially after the shit that happened with the latest auction."

He nodded. "Nobody knows she exists. Let's leave it that way."

My mind was still reeling from all we'd learned in the past twenty-four hours. The results for that mystery finger came in today, and they were unexpected.

The DNA was matched to Liana Volkov. I hadn't shared the information with Louisa yet. She'd been through enough shit, and until we had more details, I didn't want her to assume the worst.

"When will you know whether that finger came from a dead body or not?" Alexei's voice pulled me from my thoughts.

Reign of a Billionaire

"Not sure." I had asked the very same question, but Winston's contact seemed to have some work to do before he could provide us with an answer.

"You seem different," Alexei pointed out. "More... settled."

"You're different since you married my sister," was my answer as my eyes found the source of my change, her hair shining like gold under the Portuguese sun. Everything in my life started and ended with this woman. I loved her a decade ago, and today, I loved the woman she'd become.

Despite growing up amongst vipers and wolves, she maintained her light and held her strength like an armor, and she didn't even know it. She said her hands were sullied. They weren't; they were pure and beautiful, just like her soul. I was a lucky fucking bastard that she picked me to love out of all the people in this world.

"She wants to kill her mother," I said.

Even after everything she'd been through and the demons she still fought, she was capable of the deepest love. I feared that killing Sofia would leave a stain on Lou's soul.

"Someone's got to end her," Alexei, ever the voice of reason, pointed out.

"I know." A shrieking laugh had both of us turning to the window to find my nephew, Kostya, running circles around the smiling women. "Looks like his video games can only capture his interest for so long," I remarked.

"He gets through the levels too fast."

"I'm not surprised. He's smart like his uncle Winston." He'd been the only one in our family to be seriously good at it, but the day of our mother's death, he'd just given it up.

"You love Sofia's daughter," Alexei stated matter-of-factly.

I had no shame admitting how utterly infatuated I was with Louisa. It was a pure, unadulterated emotion in my veins that had driven me to survive, to fight eight years of living without her, and now that she was back, to protect her.

"I do," I finally said, getting to my feet. "And I'll bring every goddamned alliance in the underworld down if it means protecting her."

Louisa

"I'm happy my brother found you." Aurora, Kingston's sister, studied me openly. "I've never seen him like this."

I flicked her a curious look. "Like what?"

She thought for a moment before saying, "Content. He seems at peace, and I know it has everything to do with you. He can't keep his eyes off you." I didn't say anything, unsure how much she actually knew about me. Did she know my mother was the one who'd tried to ruin her brother's life? Did she know my last name was stained with blood?

Lara squeezed my hand, probably attune to my feelings. Just like me, she was haunted by her parents' decisions and because of whose daughter she was. The enemy didn't care what she had endured as long as they felt like they got some kind of revenge.

I'd never let that happen.

"You know, the men in this world aren't like normal men."

"Yeah, they're fucking crazy." Lara's first words of the day were muttered, drawing chuckles from Aurora and me. "And some are evil," she agreed. "But there are also good ones too. Their love is more intense and their protectiveness fiercer."

I lifted my head to the window of Kingston's office and found him standing and looking out with a serious look on his face. It looked a lot like love. It was always love with him—first innocent and now as strong as the burning sun.

I returned my attention to my new ward and smiled. "Let's stop worrying Lara with any men and go grab something to eat instead."

That night, after Aurora and her family left and Lara was safely in her own bedroom, I stood barefoot in our bedroom, wearing nothing but Kingston's oversized T-shirt.

I found Kingston leaning against the black marble counter in the bathroom. The giant mirror reflected both of us, him in his full darkness and me surrounded by him. His phone was pressed to his ear, talking to someone in Italian, and he was wearing nothing but gray sweatpants. I had never seen anything so fucking sexy.

"*Non ne ho idea*," he uttered, dragging a palm across his stubble.

Judging by his expression, he wasn't listening much, because a flash of something unmistakably sinful lingered in his eyes. My heartbeat tripped as his gaze raked over me.

My skin burned as I walked toward him. His cologne, so warm and intoxicating, wrapped around me and I stretched up on my toes to press a kiss on the rough stubble of his chin.

My knees shook with the need to fall down to them and pleasure him.

As I leaned forward, I hooked my fingers on the hem of his sweatpants, pressing my breasts against his chest and my lips to his neck.

Skimming my lips across his ear, bringing my lust-filled gaze up to his, I breathed out, "I want to taste you."

Heat flared in his gaze and he ended the call, then threw his phone to the side. His finger stroked the pulse point on my neck back and forth as nerves danced in my veins.

When he thrust his index finger inside my mouth, I darted my tongue around it tentatively.

"What if you don't like it?" he asked, insecurity coloring his voice. His hot breath skimmed over my skin, burning me alive. "I've never had it done."

His finger slid out of my mouth. "I've never done it, so it'll be another first we share."

"On one condition."

I chuckled huskily. "I didn't know men give conditions on blow jobs."

His lips twitched. "Tell me if you don't like it."

"I promise."

I dropped to my knees and pulled his sweatpants down his muscular legs. I wrapped my fingers around his hard and thick erection, my mouth watering at the sight. He spread his thighs farther and grabbed a fistful of my hair.

I closed my eyes and licked his shaft from base to tip. A low groan escaped him, and I took it as encouragement. Opening my eyes, I repeated the motion until his eyes grew dark and hazy. Heat bloomed in my stomach, moving lower and lower, making me squeeze my thighs to ease this throbbing ache.

His grip on my hair tightened and I ran my tongue across his crown, then slid him all the way to the back of my throat. I moaned and sucked him again, gliding up and down and taking more of him into my mouth.

"Fuck, sunshine," he hissed, his grip moving my head and controlling the rhythm. "You look so beautiful choking on my cock."

My gaze flicked to his, sparks of pleasure fluttering through me at his filthy words.

He slid in deeper with the next thrust, but I remained still, letting him fuck my mouth, curious to see the way he liked it.

His breaths came out heavy, watching me with a half-lidded gaze. He fucked me, and I watched him come undone for me. There was something euphoric and empowering about the knowledge that it was because of me.

A hoarse sound left him, his breathing harsh and fast, and he came into my mouth with a groan. I swallowed, growing dizzy from his taste and smell.

"My sunshine," he breathed, grasping my face between his rough hands and caressing my cheeks.

Then he pulled his sweatpants over his softening erection and lifted me by the backs of my thighs. He pressed his mouth to mine, his tongue sliding past my lips and toying with me, as I wrapped my legs around his waist.

I dug my fingers into his hair, and he deepened the kiss, pouring everything into it. Our tongues tangled. My hands slid down his chest, resting against his racing heart.

"I love you."

Reign of a Billionaire

His eyes flared and his fingers gripped my nape firmly. Getting rid of his sweatpants first, he ripped my panties, leaving me bare underneath his shirt. The tip of his cock at my entrance, he thrust inside me, filling me to the hilt.

He pressed his forehead to mine.

"Tell me again," he demanded fiercely, and my walls clenched around his length in response.

"I love you, Kingston Ashford," I breathed, grinding against him.

When he kissed me next, the world stopped spinning. The problems ceased to exist for a moment. The horrors faded.

"I'll love you in every lifetime, sunshine," he murmured against my lips.

It was just the two of us and this feeling that bound us together—in life and death.

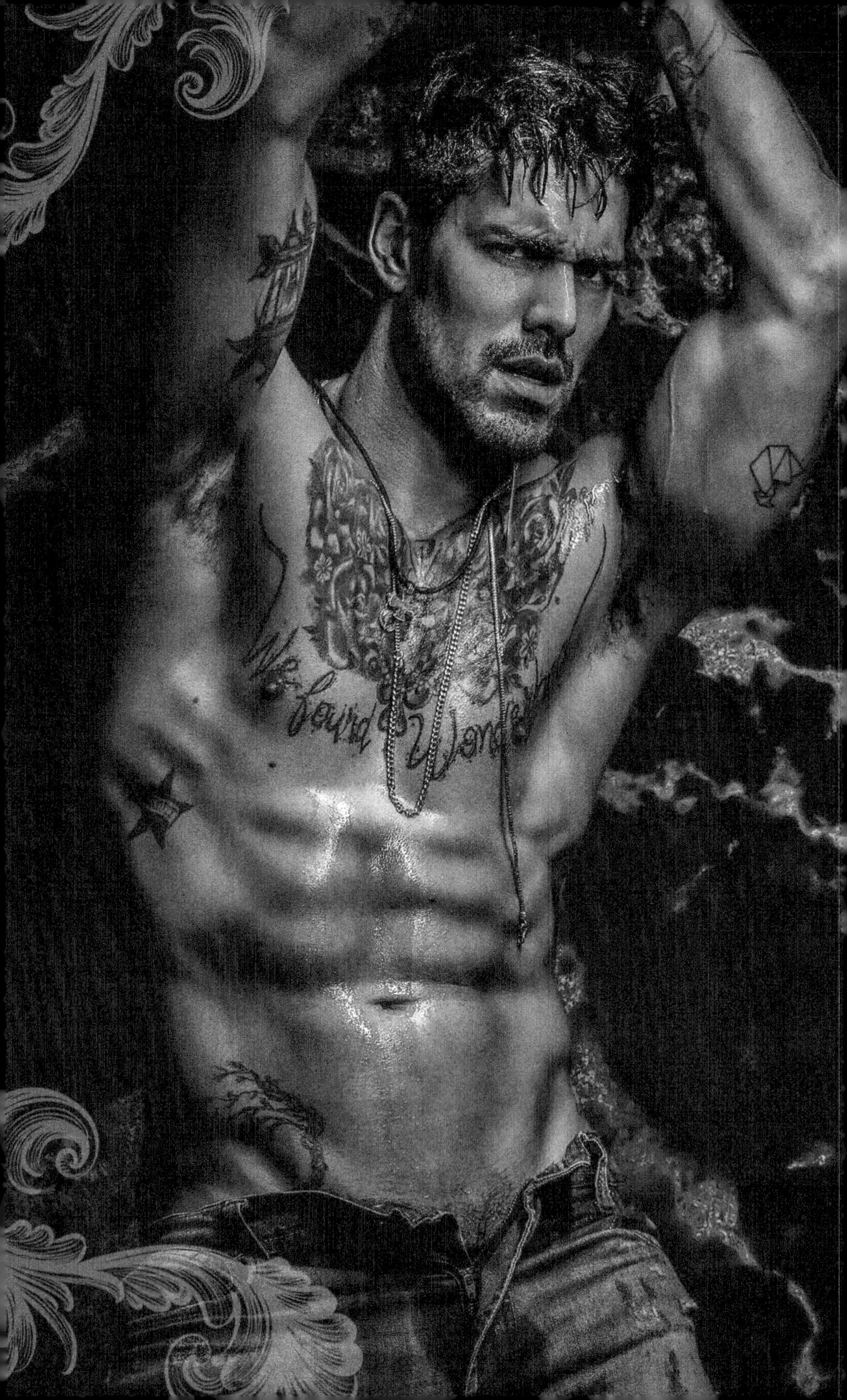

Chapter 58
Louisa

I sat in the waiting room of the medical facility that the Nikolaevs owned, waiting for Lara's counseling session to end. It had been a week since we left Greece together, and although her progress was minimal, it was there. In every flicker of a smile. In every word spoken.

Lara Cortes was a survivor and one of the strongest girls I'd ever known.

Two of Alexei's guards waited outside the building for us. Usually Kingston came with us, but he and Alexei were following a lead, and I knew it had to be important for Kingston to miss this.

There hadn't been any development on the Sofia front. I suspected she might be hiding in Russia, but I didn't know where. Her castle looked deserted on the surveillance we'd gotten.

The door opened and I lifted my head, fully expecting to be met with Lara's face, but Dr. Freud's door remained closed. I shifted around just as a man's hand slammed over my mouth and I was snatched violently from the couch.

I jammed my elbow behind me, hard enough to make him grunt but not enough to loosen his hold. I started kicking my legs, sending the crystal vase from the table flying through the air and crashing against the wall. To my horror, the door opened and Lara stood there, her eyes wide with terror.

"Get the girl too."

I sunk my teeth into the man's hand, and he howled like a dog, loosening his hold on me.

"Go back inside and lock the door," I screamed at Lara.

"But—"

"Do it!"

The man's hand wrapped around my throat just as Lara shut the door, dragging me out of there while his accomplice tried and failed to turn the door handle. He slammed his shoulder into the mahogany, but it refused to budge.

"Fuck her," one of the men grunted. "Help me with this one before she gets away."

I yanked his hand, then twisted it around as I whirled, the sound of bone snapping filled the air.

The man yelped and cradled it but not before he managed to shove a cloth into my mouth, gagging me. They began to drag me while my muffled screams filled the air. Nikolaev's guards had to be here somewhere.

I kicked backward, hoping to hit his shins, and cursed myself for not having my gun on me.

"Just knock the bitch out," one of them grunted as they struggled with me.

"She'll have our balls if we damage her," the one man wheezed, his voice full of fear.

Panic slowly started to rise within me. There was only one *she* that made men quake with fear, and that was my mother. I thrashed wildly, my lungs and body burning from the exertion. My eyes darted around for signs of help, and to my horror, death surrounded us. Dead nurses. Dead doctors. It was a goddamn massacre.

Before I had the chance to process where they were taking me, I heard the screeching of tires. The two guards who'd brought us here were lying dead on the sidewalk, their blood pooling around their bodies. I saw red and knocked one of the men out with a kick to the head. Two more jumped out of the car, and one pressed a knife to my neck.

"That's enough, bitch." My breath whooshed out of me. Drago was here. *My mother sent Drago after me.* I didn't think there was anything left that could shock me, but here I was. "Move, or I'll bleed you like a pig."

Yanking myself out of my stupor, I pulled my fist back and punched him in the face. I'd rather go back to my mother dead than alive.

But before I could attempt anything else, my vision went back.

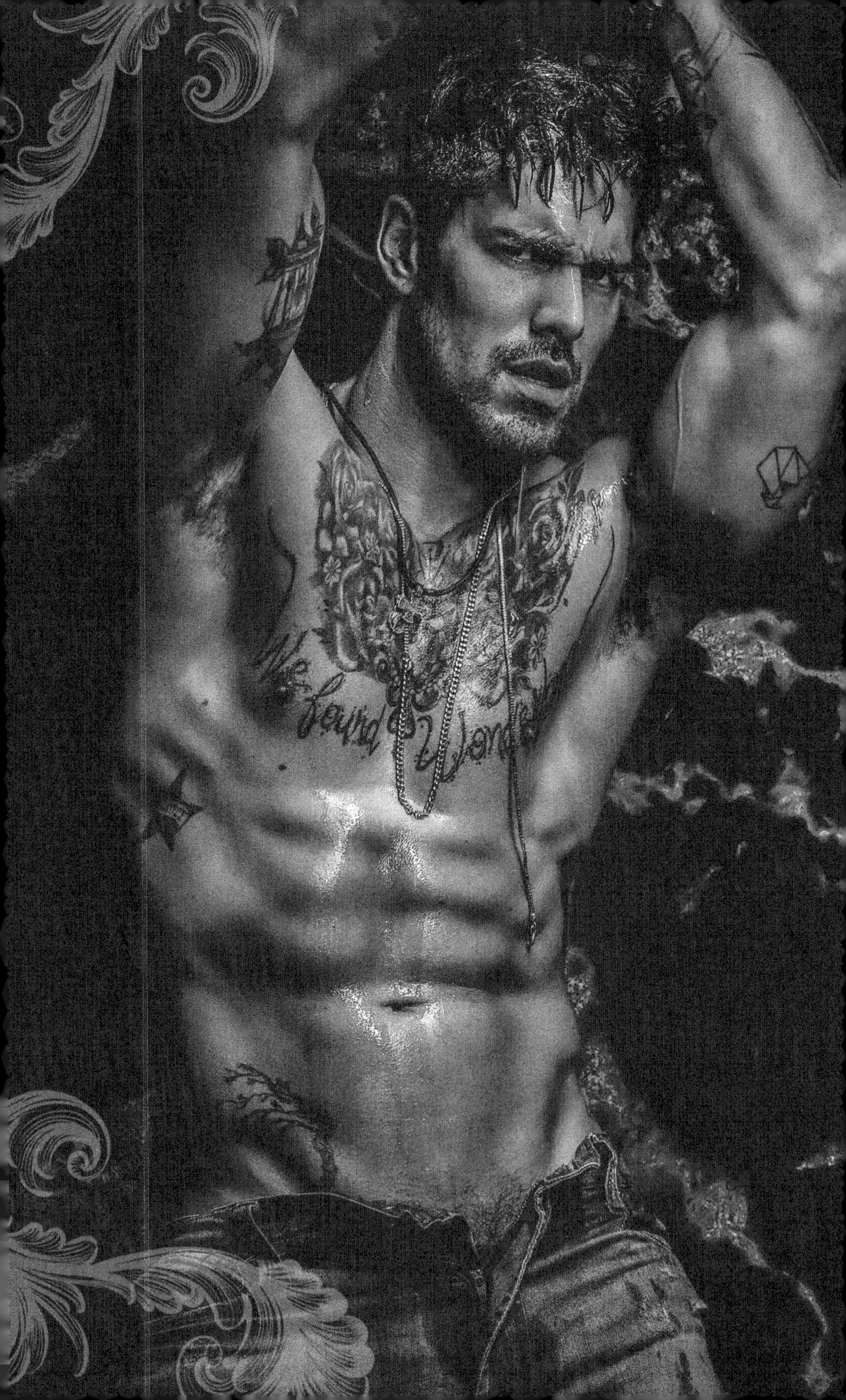

Chapter 59
Kingston

My molars ground together as I stared at the surveillance video of Louisa's kidnapping. She fought them like a tigress, but eventually they had her subdued. It was hardly a fair fight, an army of men against one woman.

The Nikolaevs and my brothers were here, prepared to offer whatever support I needed.

My sister sat in the connecting room consoling Lara, whose soft cries traveled through the space. She and her therapist were the only survivors in the whole facility. Sofia's men didn't spare anyone who happened to be visiting the facility at the moment of the attack.

My stomach churned at the images flashing on the screen, each one more grotesque than the last. Red-hot anger flared to the surface at the injustice of it all. But I knew it wouldn't help me in this instance. I had to keep my head clear to devise a strategy. That was the only way to get my girl back.

Sofia was desperate, made clear by the fact that she attacked the Nikolaevs' facility without cutting the surveillance.

But there was one thing that worried me above all else, and that was Drago.

The motherfucker was a sick and twisted pervert, rarely dragging out his torture. He'd get so unhinged the victim would die before ever offering up answers. He had no self-control, and Sofia knew that. So why did she send him to get Louisa?

The fury bubbled in my veins, quickening my pulse until my ears rang.

"We'll get her," Alexei said, his voice devoid of emotion as per usual. "Her mother won't harm her."

"Yes, she will." The room fell into resolute silence, and Alexei's and my brothers' eyes landing on me. I'd lost her once, I couldn't lose her again. "She beat her so badly in the past that Louisa needed plastic surgery."

"Jesus fucking Christ," Royce muttered under his breath. "Maybe we ought to catch her and give her a taste of her own medicine before getting rid of her."

"Where do you think they've taken her?"

A heartbeat passed. "Russia."

My gut was warning me Sofia took her back to where it all began. Her twisted, evil castle in Siberia.

"But you've always refused to go there," Sasha pointed out.

"For her, I'll go to Russia." Fuck, for her, I'd visit all nine circles of Dante's inferno.

"Are you sure Sofia would hurt her own daughter?" Byron questioned.

"Sofia had her brainwashed, making her believe she's her twin," I gritted. "She'll try it again."

I couldn't allow it to happen. I couldn't allow Sofia to erase my Lou. She was the best thing that had ever happened to me. Her strength helped me survive every fucking storm throughout my miserable life. My heart beat only for her, in the rhythm of hers, and this need for her was part of my DNA.

"I'm going after her." I slammed my fist against the table, everything on it rattling in protest.

It was so fucking hard to think rationally when I knew exactly what kind of torture Sofia was capable of. I'd endured it. It was the kind that broke your body and spirit, molding you into something unrecognizable.

The dread in my chest grew with each passing minute. I feared if I didn't go after her immediately, I'd explode.

I couldn't even hear what Alexei, Royce, and Byron were saying outside of the buzzing in my ears.

"Sofia's probably counting on it." Alexei was right, but I didn't give a shit. I'd lose my fucking mind if I didn't get to her.

I stood up and strode to the window, releasing a heavy breath as I stared at Lisbon's glittering night lights. "You never saw what she did to her eight years ago. Nobody can survive that twice."

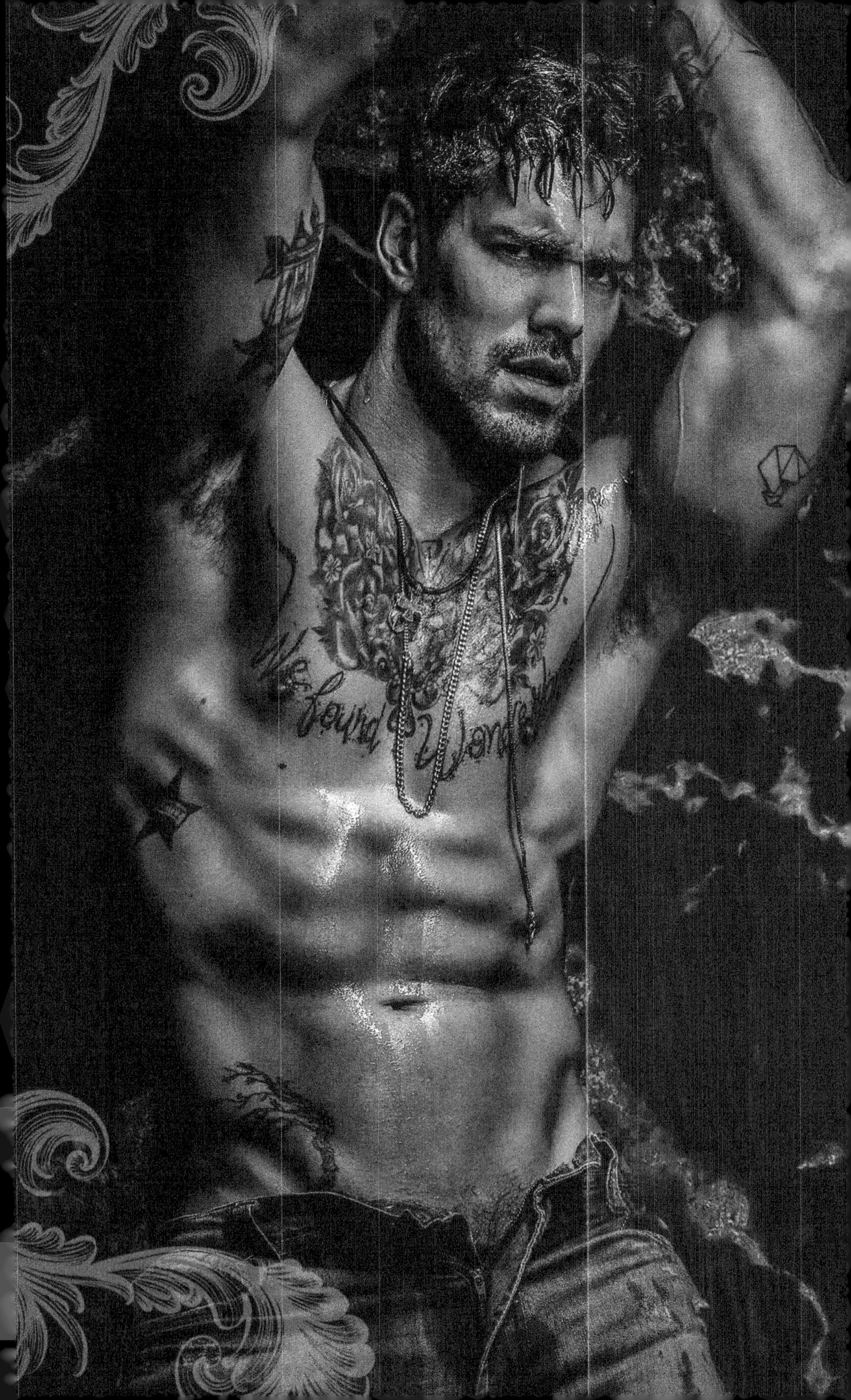
We found

Chapter 60
Louisa

I blinked against the bright light burning my eyeballs, my whole body registering pain. The stench of death and mold brought back memories, pointing to where I'd been taken, and I almost choked with fear.

My eyes roved over the room, the familiar walls coming into focus. It was the very same basement prison where I'd died eight years ago. It was still filthy, the whispers of all the innocent boys and girls who died here loud. Goosebumps broke over my skin, and I shifted to wrap my arms around me only to stop short. I was bound to a chair.

History was repeating itself.

The only saving grace was that Kingston wasn't here. Nobody could hurt him.

I looked down at my hands, scratched and bloodied, as memories came flooding in. My heart started to beat faster, my worry for Lara overwhelming, but I immediately shoved it into a corner. They couldn't have gotten to her.

On the tail end of that thought, the door opened with a loud creak and my mother walked in. Her hair was perfectly styled, and her posture belonged on the catwalk as she sauntered over to me, diamonds glittering around her neck. As if she were about to attend a royal ball, not torture her daughter.

Drago, that sick bastard, strutted behind her like a fucking dog, smiling like he was about to get a bone. A shudder rolled down my spine, realizing that I was probably that bone.

Swallowing down my panic, I straightened my shoulders and narrowed my eyes on the monster that was Sofia Volkov. There were rare moments in our childhood when my twin and I had hoped she'd take us away and give us a normal life. She protected us from Ivan's men only to use us for her own plans. Whatever they were.

She clucked her tongue. "Liana, Liana, what am I going to do with you?"

"For starters, you can call me Louisa."

Her eyes flashed with something dark as she took the seat opposite me, crossing her legs elegantly. Jesus, give her a fucking cigarette holder and send her to the opera.

"I should have ended that *stronzo*."

My mother's Italian heritage never came out except for when she was scared and panicked. The knowledge that she was both gave me enough courage to flash her a smile.

"Don't worry, Mother, that *stronzo* will finish you." She scoffed, but the worry on her face remained. There was no hiding it behind the layers of makeup or plastic surgery. "You fucked with the wrong man, now you'll taste the wrath you've been bestowing on others for so long."

"Let me teach her a lesson," Drago hissed, looking at my mother with hope as he hopped on his feet like he was in a boxing ring.

She raised her palm and he stopped. Like I said, a dog. When my mother said "Attack," that lunatic went to town.

"Where is Liana?" I demanded, locking eyes on Sofia.

"Sitting in front of me."

"Wrong, Sofia," I snapped. She wasn't a mother, she'd never been a mother, and it was time to cut ties. "Is. Liana. Alive?"

A heartbeat passed. "Yes, I believe she is."

"You... you believe?" I stuttered with disbelief, my body filling with adrenaline and so much fury I was scared I'd explode. "Since when?" She watched me as if debating how much to reveal, and I let out a bitter laugh. "You're going to kill me, so you might as well tell me what I'm dying for."

She leaned forward, putting her elbows on her knees. "You're right."

Fuck, why did it hurt to hear her say it out loud?

I straightened my spine, ignoring these useless emotions. I knew Kingston would rescue me, I just needed to buy time and keep her talking.

"Where's my twin?" I asked.

"Somewhere in South America."

"Alive?" I breathed.

"Alive."

"You haven't found her," I said, my voice shaking from my nerves and hoping that maybe—just maybe—I could get her back.

"No, Perez did a good job covering his tracks." Or maybe my twin was hiding?

My head was a jumbled mess, every lie I'd ever been told scattered around my head. It was a struggle to put all the puzzle pieces together.

"What part did the Tijuana cartel play in all of it?"

Mother took out a cigarette and put it in her mouth, Drago instantly jumping to light a match for her.

"Santiago wanted an arranged marriage between you and his son." She inhaled, then puffed out a cloud of smoke my way. I held my breath, hating the smell of smoke. "I refused, but Ivan went behind my back and arranged it." Her jaw clenched. "It's always the fucking men."

"He was *your* husband," I pointed out.

"My second and my last." A distant look entered her gaze, and I imagined she was probably remembering her first marriage and the daughter it had cost her. "Anyhow, the day you and Ghost tried to escape, Liana got caught by Santiago and his men." I held my breath, anticipating where this was going. "She lied and told them she was you."

The searing pain slashed through my chest, and I looked down, certain I was bleeding from it.

"So you see, my weak Louisa," she stated coldly. "You had to become her."

I blinked, all the alarm bells ringing in my head. Finally, it made sense. The questions she'd always ask me during my torture sessions. She'd ask me my favorite color, my favorite ice cream flavor, whether I was right-handed or left-handed. For every wrong answer, the torture got more intense.

She was conforming me into my twin.

"Did it ever occur to you that none of this would have happened if you'd just taken us away?" I breathed, my heart drumming in a hard, painful rhythm.

She huffed. "And let all those men get away with taking my first-born?" My blood chilled. "She was *everything* to me. The only thing that kept me going in this underworld."

"And us?" I asked, hating the way my voice cracked. "What were we, Mother? What were Liana and I?"

She didn't answer. She didn't need to, because I knew. Deep down, I'd always known. We were pawns in her games. Disposable.

I gave my head a subtle shake, chasing all these feelings away. It wouldn't do me any good getting all emotional. Not here. Not around her and her pet.

"What is the connection between the Tijuana cartel and Perez Cortes?" I croaked. "I'm assuming you know Perez sold my sister through a Marabella Mobster arrangement?"

"Oh, I know," she assured. "Why do you think I got my hands on his daughter?" Hate wracked through me like a hurricane. "Of course, then he went after you."

She tapped her cigarette ashes onto the bloodstained floor.

"Round and round we go," I said through clenched teeth. "You and your sick friends play, and we pay for your fuckups. Her name's Lara, not Louisa, you sick bitch."

She laughed, causing my skin to crawl. "Of course you were fucking with our shipments, costing us millions of dollars." Her cold eyes found mine. "Didn't I teach you better, Liana?"

Even now, she insisted on calling me by my twin's name. This woman was delusional, believing her own lies.

"I have no regrets, you psychotic bitch," I screamed at the top of my lungs, my breaths heaving. I should be stronger and keep my cool, but instead I was letting her get under my skin.

Mother tilted her head at Drago.

Everything in me stilled. No, I *froze* as I watched Drago smile that feral dog smile. He pulled out a knife, then made his way toward me.

"M-Mother... No..."

And so began my screams.

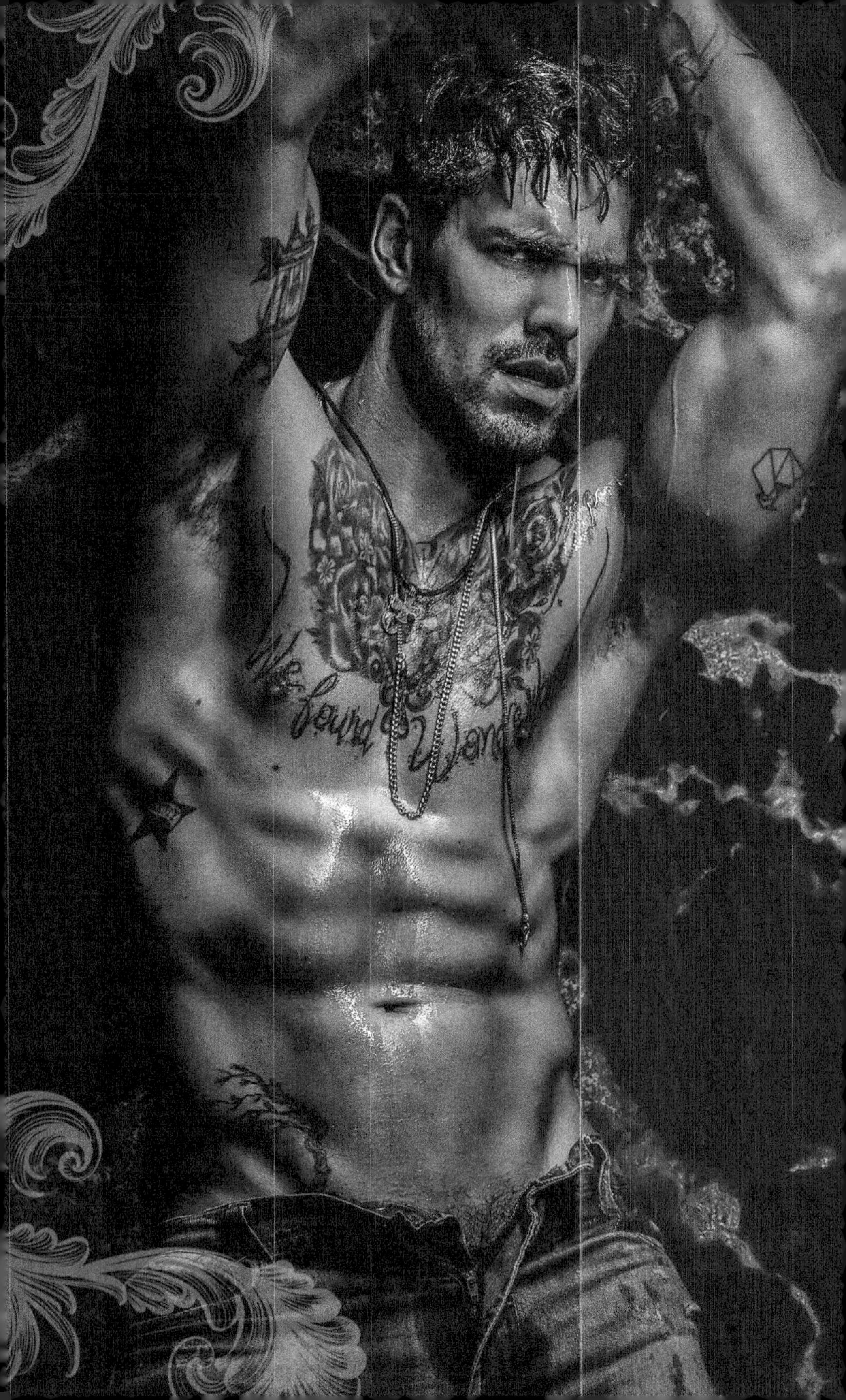
We found

Chapter 61
Kingston

My gut churned with a sick sense of dread. The memories haunted me with each step deeper into this property, even though I hadn't stepped foot in this country for eight years. I hadn't been here, to this castle built on nightmares, in eight years, yet I remembered every stone and every corner. There were many nights during that time where it felt as if I was still here. It was the reason I refused to come back to Russia. For anyone or anything.

But she wasn't just anyone or anything. She was *everything*.

"We're half an hour behind you." My brother's voice came through my earpiece. "Wait for us."

My brothers and Alexei, along with his men and probably his own brothers, Sasha and Vasili Nikolaev, didn't hesitate to join me in this rescue mission. But proper planning and scouting would have taken too much time that I feared Louisa didn't have.

"Don't be like that," Sasha grumbled. "We like to have some fun too."

"Ditto that," Royce chimed in, sounding like he was on his way to a party. "We like to dance and kick ass too."

"I'm going in," I replied, ignoring them all. "Catch up as fast as you can."

I rammed my shoulder into the reinforced door. A soft creak like the scrape of metal against metal filled the eerie silence and I held my breath, praying nobody heard it.

I lifted my gun high and entered the source of all my nightmares. The prison that stole my childhood. The prison that was trying to steal my future. Yet, knowing the ins and outs of this castle and compound gave me leverage. I knew the floor plan better than anyone.

Sofia wanted to play mind games, always loving the element of mental torment. It was what she and Ivan had in common. She knew I left this hellhole with more than physical scars.

But not even incapacitating nightmares would stop me from entering this property tonight. Nothing would stop me from saving Louisa—not even the risk of being tortured again. I failed her eight years ago; I wouldn't today.

Spurred on by adrenaline racing through my veins, I entered the castle. I moved in silence, my steps soundless on the marble floor. Painstaking hours gave my brothers and I plenty of time to devise a plan of attack. They would be following shortly, using the tracker on me. Right now, I'd get as close to Louisa as possible before Sofia and her men realized I was here.

It was our best chance.

Her mother was a coldhearted bitch who had no trouble using her own flesh and blood for her own gain. The fact that she tortured Louisa, fucked with her mind, and held her responsible for the death of her twin told me she would have no trouble putting a bullet through her heart.

Sofia blamed Lou for crippling her empire from within, so she wouldn't go for a quick death. She'd make her suffer, then probably try to brainwash her—again.

My heart thundered, adrenaline pumping through my veins and urging me forward to get my woman.

Reign of a Billionaire

I needed to get to the woman who proved to me that life was worth living despite darkness and nightmares thrown our way. She was mine, and I'd stop at nothing to bring her home.

Together, we were invincible. We were one, an unbreakable unit.

My focus returned to the task at hand when a soft voice shattered through the silence. I froze, the buzz of adrenaline easing to a dull sensation, and then I heard it again. Louisa's humming voice echoed through the silence, faint and distorted, but I was confident it was coming from the dungeons.

I headed to a set of stairs on my left. The broken stones were in desperate need of repair, so I took my time, taking one step at a time.

"There are only so many places you can hide, Mother, before your sins catch up to you." Louisa's voice was confident, but there was an odd pitch and rasp to it. Almost as if she'd smoked a pack of cigarettes.

She'd been missing for twenty hours, while scenarios of the last torture I witnessed played in my mind. Now that I heard her voice, relief rushed through me and I swayed on my feet.

I was almost halfway down the dark hallways that used to be my home, crouching in the shadows, when a barrel of a gun pressed against the back of my skull. My plan on creeping up on Sofia was ruined. I slowly straightened up to my full height and turned around to find a guard's aged face glaring at me. Behind him, four other men stood at her back, all with weapons aimed at me.

"We've been expecting you, Ghost," he greeted me in an icy tone. I couldn't help but think back to the similar scenario not so long ago when Louisa had a gun trained on me. Except, nothing about Lou reeked of this stench and evil.

"Where's Lou?" I demanded, speaking Russian for the first time in eight years.

His lips curled into a sneer. "She's dead to you." My finger on the trigger of my own gun twitched. "By the time Sofia's done with her, she won't—"

Bang.

The remainder of his sentence was silenced by a bullet between his eyes. The rest of Sofia's men swarmed around me from all directions.

"She wants him alive," someone shouted, and my lip curved into a smile. That knowledge certainly gave me leverage.

I started to shoot. With every dislodged bullet, more men appeared. It was hardly a fair fight, but Sofia never cared about fairness.

I fought through them, killing them one by one like flies as I continued my way down to the dungeon. The stench increased with each step down the hallway, the haunting memories reeking of it. Ignoring it all, I focused on the rush of getting closer to Lou.

The need to see her was scorching my veins.

I'd end Sofia Volkov once and for all, because Louisa's life would be at risk for as long as she lived. And that knowledge pushed me forward, my possessiveness burning at fever pitch.

By the time I reached the last cell, the very same one where she died—or so I'd thought—eight years ago, I was covered in sweat and blood, my heart pounding against my ribs furiously. The hallways were now empty, the guards I'd killed scattered over the ground.

My boots pounding against the centuries-old stone, I made my way to it, then jerked to a stop, spotting a shadow lurking right outside the cell.

Sofia Volkov.

Her icy eyes locked on me with that cold, cold smile.

"Where is she?" I asked, although I was fairly certain I knew. Confirming my suspicions, Sofia nudged her head toward the last door in the hallway.

"Take me to her," I gritted.

"I will," she agreed, surprising me. "But neither one of you will be leaving this place."

My teeth gritted as anger lined my face. I wanted to pounce on her and decapitate her to ensure she'd never come back to life. She wasn't a vampire, but she sure as fuck acted like one—vicious, bloodsucking cunt.

The sex trafficking ring was the reason for this woman's downfall. She should have learned her lesson when it cost her her firstborn. The rumor on the street was that Sofia lost her mind once she lost her daughter to the Irish mafia. Not that it mattered to me. None of it did. Only Louisa.

Not waiting for her to respond, I pointed my gun at her and nudged it into her back, pushing her forward. My heartbeat in sync with my footsteps, I watched her slim shoulders move. She was a full head and a half shorter than me, yet the woman managed to destroy so many lives, causing pain and destruction wherever she went.

Size really didn't matter in this world. Sofia had come to be one of the most ruthless human beings in the underworld, kidnapping and torturing children. Including her own.

That ended today, one way or another.

The moment we entered the cell, we were curtained in darkness. The scent of death lingered in the air. Sofia ran her hand down the wall, and dim lights flickered on.

The sight that greeted me sent fire through my veins, fury raging like an active volcano. Louisa was tied up, her back exposed and whipped raw, her wrists tied above her head. Her head dangled, her eyes closed and her face red.

Drago stepped into the dimmed light and I aimed the barrel of my gun between his lifeless eyes. It turned out all he was good for was to be Sofia's pet. I'd take him out right now if his gun wasn't jabbed into Louisa's chest.

Sofia's chuckle had Louisa opening her eyes.

"Kingston," she gasped, her lips swollen and bruised, the sheer panic on her face had my heart twisting painfully. "Why did you come?"

My brows drawn, I studied her.

"I'll always come," I rasped, keeping my tone comforting even though my rage was volatile. "Every lifetime, every scenario, life or death, I'll always come. My heart beats within yours, and yours within mine."

She shook her head violently, tears springing down her face. "No, no, no," she whimpered. "You should've sent someone else. Save yourself."

My desire to protect her was stronger than my nightmares. My safety was nothing compared to hers.

"It's okay," I assured her, locking eyes with her. "We'll get out of this together."

She swallowed. "Promise?"

"He can't promise you anything," Sofia snickered, and Louisa's eyes darted behind me, all her fire and rage burning inside those golden depths.

"Touch him, Mother, and I'll end you." My little warrior queen was so fierce. It'd be different this time. Nobody would hurt her ever again. "And it won't be a quick death."

And I'd ensure my woman's wishes came true.

"Last chance, Sofia," I said, my voice flat. "Let Louisa and I go or you're dead."

"You're in no position to call the shots. It's time to end this."

And here we go.

Chapter 62
Louisa

Dread filled me as a flashback tried to overtake me—the two of us bloodied and bruised on this very ground.

I ignored it, working on my bindings instead. If I got my hands free, I could snatch Drago's gun and Kingston would take care of the rest.

"Ivan warned me about you two," Mother said, her voice fainter than I was used to. Maybe all this torture she ordered on me was exhausting her.

I met my mother's malicious gaze with my own. "Ivan played you like a fiddle," I hissed. My goal was to piss her off, but it was Drago who was getting mad, shoving the gun harder into my chest. "You thought he danced to your tune, when really it was you dancing to his all along."

"How so?" she asked while I scrambled my mind for anything to keep this conversation going, because surely Kingston had a plan.

Somewhere in the broken corners of my mind, I remembered everything that happened the last time we were together in this room. Parts of us died here, yet Kingston's eyes urged me to be brave.

"He wanted you to arrange the marriage to the Tijuana cartel," I pointed out, my bindings slowly getting looser. "You fought him, but in the end, you caved. See, he got what he wanted."

"You think he wanted that?" she scoffed incredulously. "It was all me."

My brows furrowed. "But—"

"I wanted bigger and better than what Benito King had," she answered. "They used me to settle the Belles and Mobsters debt, so I kicked off the Marabella Mobsters arrangement."

My mouth dropped. "Perez—"

She threw her head back. "I used Perez as a puppet, but it was me pulling the strings all along."

"So you sold Liana?" I wanted to kick myself because a part of me had refused to believe that a mother would do that to her child.

"No, you idiot." There was something nudging at my mind, but my brain refused to process it. "I sold *you*."

A puzzle piece snapped into place as I stared dumbfounded at my mother, no shadow of a doubt that she was telling the truth.

"That's why you didn't bother saving me when I was snatched by Santiago," I whispered.

"Now she gets it." She flashed me a frigid smile as she approached me, then leaned forward so that her face was level with mine. And the whole time, Kingston's aim was on Drago. "In my defense, I initially thought they killed you, but then your name was circulating the dark web, so I knew you survived. I snatched Perez's scrawny daughter and was going to use her to get my real Liana back."

My head was spinning from all of it. But one thing was clear, if Kingston hadn't come for me, I'd be at the mercy of some sick fuckers.

"You were always so weak, Louisa. A problem that needed to be handled."

I spit on her malicious face as fury shot through me. "Narcissistic bitch. Your firstborn would have hated you. I'm glad she was snatched from you."

"Don't touch her." Kingston's voice was full of fury, but before I could do anything, my mother slapped me so hard my ears rang and I reeled in my chair. My cheek burned and my eyes stung, but in the next breath, a loud explosion shook the ground.

"That'll be your final mistake," Kingston gritted, the sound of fighting, bullets, and explosions somewhere in the castle drawing near. "You'll never touch her again."

"Just because you brought reinforcements doesn't mean you won," Mother snickered with a twisted smile. "You're not getting her. I stopped you eight years ago, I'll stop you again."

Kingston flashed her a cold sneer. "Not this time."

The fight must have almost reached our cell. Punches, grunts, and cracking of bones could be heard, and it wasn't long before Mother's men poured into the cell with more behind them. And then a familiar face.

Alexei Nikolaev.

More bullets sounded in the air.

Everything happened too fast. Blood splattered on my face. My ears rang. My chair fell over and my head hit the stone floor so hard I swore I saw stars.

Ignoring it all, I ripped the loosened bindings, then yanked the chair and swung it at Drago. He roared in pain and dropped his gun, sliding it across the floor.

From the corner of my eye, I spotted Kingston, Alexei, and his brothers fighting Sofia's men.

I stumbled for Drago's gun, reaching it at the same time as my mother. Then, gripping the gun, I straightened and pointed it at her.

"Tell them all to stop," I ordered.

"No." Her eyes roved over the room, pausing on Kingston who had four men rounding up on him. "Ghost won't last much longer," she remarked in a bored tone.

I aimed and pulled the trigger, hitting one man between his eyes. "Tell your men to stop or you'll be the next," I shouted, my eyes darting between Kingston, his brother, and my mother. If the situation wasn't so dire, I'd be impressed.

More bodies fell to the ground, the numbers slowly getting even.

"Last warning, Mother," I said, my chest heaving and rage burning my cheeks. "This problem child won't hesitate to end you once and for all."

"Louisa," Kingston called out, but his voice sounded like he was underwater. "Sunshine, don't do it." I looked up, finding him hopping over the dead bodies to get to me. My slender fingers shook around the trigger, needing to end this. For Kingston. For my twin. For Lara.

His big hand wrapped around mine, his body tight, tense, and controlled.

"Let me, sunshine," he whispered. Alexei was by his side, his brothers eliminating the rest of my mother's guards. The burning ache in my left wrist registered and my shoulders slumped. "Look away, Lou," he ordered, his expression deadly and his whole focus on my mother as he told her, "The last faces you see before you die will be ours."

My fingers wrapped around his forearm and I squeezed, causing him to pause. His gaze darted to me with a raised brow.

"Don't kill her," I whispered, looking into his dark eyes. "Quick death... It's too good for her."

His shoulders tensed, the hunger for revenge in his dark eyes hard to miss. "You sure?"

"Yes." I flicked a glance at the woman who destroyed so much. "She wants a quick death. Don't give her what she wants."

"Attagirl," Kingston's brother Royce said, snapping the last guard's neck and dumping him onto the ground. "Give that bitch a taste of her own medicine."

Alexei's eyes blazed with vengeance. So did Kingston's brothers'. We'd ended this, once and for all. Their support meant more than I'd ever be able to repay. They'd have my loyalty for the remainder of my days.

Locking eyes with my mother, I breathed, "Let's see how long you last."

My mother got her wish. She created monsters.

Chapter 63
Louisa

Sofia securely imprisoned and no longer a threat, we left Siberia. Kingston and I agreed that we'd never go back to that hellhole in Russia. Sun, sea, and warm climate would be in store for us from now on.

Two days later, we were finally back in Lisbon where we were met with Lara's bloodshot eyes and Aurora's compassionate dark gaze. She squeezed my shoulder and then her brother's hand before leaving to go meet her husband, who stayed behind with the Nikolaevs.

Karma finally caught up to Sofia Volkov. We'd watched as the Nikolaevs dragged my mother into the basement. She'd live out her days chained like a dog in a cold, windowless room. It was only a matter of time before she met a bitter end.

"Are you okay?" Lara's soft voice pulled my attention, her hand slipping into mine.

I squeezed it. "I am."

A visible relief washed over her, and she released a long breath. "I was so worried about you." Her eyes darted to Kingston. "Both of you."

Tears filled my eyes as she fell into me, and Kingston wrapped us both into his strong arms.

"It's our job to worry about you, not the other way around," Kingston said, his voice rough with emotions.

"How about we all worry about each other?" Lara suggested softly, not pulling away from us.

I smiled tiredly. "I'd like that," I murmured, clutching her hand. "I'd like that very much."

"Is something wrong?" Lara asked tentatively, her perception and empathy often in-tune with the emotions surrounding her.

"You were right," I said, my stomach churning with the recent findings. "My twin is alive. Somewhere in South America."

She clutched my hand. "You'll find her."

I met Kingston's gaze over Lara's head. We'd talked about my twin a lot since he'd rescued me. He told me about the finger he'd received, the DNA matching my sister's. There was no guarantee what shape we'd find her in, but we wouldn't give up.

Not until we found her.

"We will," I said, my voice shaking.

"Do... Do you still want me to stay?" Lara blurted.

"Look at me, Lara," Kingston ordered. She lifted her head, her pretty eyes locking with ours. "We want you to stay with us forever. You leave when you're ready to leave."

I smiled softly. "And when that happens, we'll ensure you're independent but also safe. You're part of our circle now."

"The Ashford circle."

I chuckled. "I was thinking more of Kingston and Lou's circle, but the Ashford circle sounds even better. It's bigger."

"Now let's go inside. I don't know about you two, but I could sleep the winter away."

Lara giggled as we made our way inside our home.

The threads of mystery surrounding my sister weighed heavily on our minds, but we'd solve it.

Together.

Reign of a Billionaire

The steady rush of water should have calmed me.

Yet a storm brewed inside my chest as I stood in the luxurious bathroom fit for a queen, staring at the tub slowly filling with water.

The events of the past few days finally caught up and my biceps started to tremble. My twin was alive, somewhere on this earth.

How could our mother be so evil to bring us to this point? She had destroyed so many lives, including our own, and she felt zero remorse about it.

Wearing nothing but a T-shirt that reached my knees, I watched the steam gather over the tub. I caught my blurry reflection in the mirror, and my breaths turned shallow and harsh. A ball lodged itself in my throat, suffocating me.

Mother hated us so much that she condemned us to death. Kingston saved me. Who was saving Liana? I had to find her. For the past eight years, I'd come to terms with living without my twin, even though it left a gaping hole in my chest. But now that I knew she could be alive, that hole started to fill with hopes and dreams, and that scared me more.

A set of strong, inked arms wrapped around me, and it was only then that I realized how badly I was shaking.

"Hold on to me." His strong, warm voice cocooned me as he scooped me into his arms and stepped us into the hot bathtub, my shirt clinging to my body. "We'll find her."

I buried my face in his neck as I desperately gulped for air, inhaling his scent into my lungs.

"If she..." My mouth trembled. "I can't lose her again."

His strong hand gripped my nape and he squeezed, turning my head to look at him.

Our eyes locked, my heart thundering in my chest. "We'll find her," he told me, his voice leaving no room for doubt. "Together.

We'll scout every inch of this earth if we have to, but I promise you, we'll find her. You know why?"

His eyes burned with so much love it made my heart flutter, like new wings on a butterfly. Or a bird about to take its first flight. Except, we'd been here before, and I knew for a fact he was the reason I was born.

To be his.

"Because you're mine. *My* woman. Because your heart beats in my chest, and mine in yours. We're one and the same, Lou. And now that you're back in my life, there isn't anything I wouldn't do to make you happy."

I hugged him tightly, like I'd die without him. Because I would.

"You... You, Kingston, make me happy."

Chapter 64
Louisa

Two weeks had gone by since Kingston came to Russia and rescued me.

I observed the Nikolaevs and the Ashfords seated around the table, Kingston's grave expression marring his features. He hadn't shaved since we'd been back, and I couldn't help but notice that the scruff suited him. Dressed in jeans and a white T-shirt, he looked a little intimidating and a lot hot.

We hadn't made a lot of headway on locating my sister. Nico Morrelli had offered to help us track down every Marabella Agreement ever made, and knowing his skillset, I took him up on it. My sister wasn't the only victim of Perez's and my mother's schemes. There were many innocent boys and girls who needed to be found and saved.

"Kingston said he's taking you out on a date," Lara whispered, smiling smugly. The two of us sat on the carpet, our backs against the couch as we watched the living room at the Nikolaevs' Lisbon home buzz with life. Kids found their cliques and played without paying any mind to the adults while the two of us observed it all. "And that it's something neither one of you has ever done."

My lips curved up, happy to see Lara slowly but surely coming into her own. We still had a very long road ahead of us, but together, we'd get through it.

"Can you give me a hint?" I whispered back. "Just so I know what to wear."

She smiled. "Wear something nice."

I scoffed. "That's not telling me much."

"What are you two whispering about?" Aurora asked from the other side of the room, drawing everyone's attention our way.

"Nothing," we answered at the same time, our cheeks flushing with the obvious lie.

Sasha stood from the table and reached his wife, Branka, in a few short steps, engulfing her into his bulky embrace. The guy was built from stone. I truly believed he missed his calling. He should have been an MMA fighter.

"So, are you two going to get married?" Sasha asked casually.

I glanced around, curious who he was talking to when I noted everyone's eyes were on me.

"Leave her alone, Sasha," said Aurora, coming to my aid. "You're turning into a gossiping old hag."

He grinned. "At least I'm a hot hag."

"Keep telling yourself that," Lara muttered loud enough for everyone to hear, and laughter filled the room.

"I must say, I'm curious myself," Royce chimed in.

Kingston and I shared a look. "When we find Liana."

"When we find Liana," I repeated.

I wasn't alone anymore. I had a family—a very big one—but until we found Liana, our lives wouldn't be complete.

So we'd wait. Together.

I tucked Lara in, pressing a kiss to her forehead.

She admitted she was too old to be tucked in, but some days, she needed that reassurance. We all did, and I saw no harm in it.

"You'll be careful, right?" she asked, her voice full of trepidation.

"Always," I promised. "Kingston's bringing a knife and a handgun. I'll have a gun too."

"What if you—"

"Shhh." I pressed my finger against her lips. "Nothing will happen to us. And I'll send you a message every hour." I glanced at her nightstand. "Your phone's charged up?"

She nodded, her tension slowly easing.

"You look pretty," she said as I stood up. "Kingston won't be able to keep his eyes off you."

I chuckled. "Thank you for helping me pick the perfect outfit."

Blowing her one last kiss, I made it out of the room and closed the door softly behind me. But instead of heading to the study where Kingston was, I made my way down to the basement.

It was my first visit since we'd been back, and I had spent the last few hours mentally preparing myself for this confrontation.

I made my way into the dungeon alone, my steps soundless against the hundred-year-old stone. Maybe it was my glutton-for-punishment tendencies or a fruitless hope to extract more information that would help me find my sister sooner.

"I need to see Sofia," I said, giving the two guards stationed outside my mother's cell a tight smile. The guys exchanged hesitant looks before I added, "Either open the door or step aside."

One of them nodded while the other opened the door and I slipped inside, holding the hem of my pink bohemian dress off the ground. My gun holster strapped around my thigh played peekaboo—some habits were hard to break—as I made my way deeper into the dark space.

My eyes slowly adjusted as the dark, cold, and destitute dungeon came into view. Just like the one from my nightmares. Just like the one from Kingston's. Except this time, Sofia Volkov was the one chained to the wall.

Without her fur coat and expensive clothes, she looked harmless. Like another victim suffering the wrath of evil men. Except *she* was the evil here, confined to a room where she could do no harm.

I came to a stop a few feet from her, locking my eyes with her, every memory of my torture coming to the forefront of my mind. I'd come to terms that it'd be something that would remain with me for the rest of my life.

"Hello, Liana."

"It's Louisa," I corrected her. A vein in her temple pulsed in response, but she remained silent. I was doing this for my twin. For my man. For our future children. "Hello, Sofia."

Her lip curled with a sneer, but her rejection no longer hurt. There was no love lost between this woman and me. That ship had sailed a long time ago.

"You've finally found your bravery." There was a hint of pride in her voice, and I fucking hated it. I never wanted to be anything she wanted, because that meant I'd ventured to the wrong side.

"We're scouring through your Marabella Agreements," I stated casually.

She scoffed. "You won't find anything about your sister in those."

"Why are you so sure?"

"Because I've already gone through them."

I didn't think she was lying. "Well, we need to find those other victims too. We're going to save them all."

Behind me, the door opened and her eyes darted over my shoulder. I didn't need to turn around to see who it was. I could feel Kingston's eyes on my back as he moved to come stand behind me.

His hand came to rest on my lower back, lending support and strength. He always knew what to do, and I loved him even more for it. I leaned into him, a calm strength washing over me. He was the reason for my sanity, for my life, for my healing.

I'd be all that and more for my sister once we found her.

"I want to know all the theories you've come up with relating to Liana," I stated calmly.

Reign of a Billionaire

When she remained silent, I asked, "The video? The one that you've shown me for years while"—I swallowed hard—"torturing me." There was no mistaking what she was doing to me. "Who was it?"

Yes, it was photoshopped according to Santiago Tijuana, but someone had to have endured that to be used for the video.

She shrugged. "Some girl."

I balled my fists, fighting the urge to punch my own mother. "What girl?"

"I don't remember her name." This wasn't helping her case at all. "Last name Freud-something."

My brows knitted. "Dr. Freud?" I blurted. "It has something to do with Dr. Freud?"

"I don't know any Dr. Freud." Just another puzzle piece thrown our way.

"Why did you keep showing me that video?" I asked instead. "You said it was my sister."

She smiled—that crazy, twisted smile. "You needed an incentive."

I hardened myself. All she did was hurt me, again and again. "Tell me what you know about my sister," I gritted.

"Why?" she asked, her voice raspy.

"Because she's my *sister*," I gritted. "She's my other half." This woman—who gave me birth and was supposed to be my mother—had been sick in the head for far longer than I'd been alive, the loss of her first child—Winter—destroying her fragile mind. But it didn't excuse her behavior toward me. It didn't excuse her abandonment of my twin. "Because I'm going to get her back, and you're going to help me by telling me everything you fucking know."

She smiled, her first warm smile in a long time. "Maybe all those years of electroshock therapy made something out of you."

"Fucking watch it," Kingston growled from behind me, ready to pounce, but the moment my hand took his, he stilled.

"You always preferred Lia to me," I stated, feeling nothing with those words. She no longer mattered to me, only my sister did. "You should want me to save her." Sofia wasn't the only manipulative bitch here. She'd taught me well, and I'd use any means necessary to find my sister. "Now tell me what you know and maybe you'll get to see Lia before you waste away in this dungeon."

She started to laugh, the sound slightly hysterical.

"If you're her best chance at survival, your sister's already dead." My heart clenched for my sister who was paying for this woman's sins.

"But I'm not alone," I said coldly. "I have Kingston and his entire family by my side."

She scoffed. "A lot of good that will do you. You need someone from the other side."

"Other side?"

"There was one thing you were right about." Her subject changes gave me whiplash, but I held on.

"What's that?"

"I had to play their tunes so she'd stay safe." My hands shook, trying not to imagine everything my twin was going through. "Every time I looked at you, you reminded me that you led her straight into their hands."

I might have come into my own with Kingston, but I'd be lying if I said those words didn't hurt like bullets. Every one of them dug into my skin, leaving behind more invisible marks. My mother might have fixed my scars cosmetically, but the invisible ones were worse.

Kingston came around me and pointed his gun at Sofia's forehead. "You might want to reconsider your words."

I brought my hand to his forearm and squeezed. "She's egging you on." Turning to face back to her, I asked, "What did you mean by needing someone from the other side?"

She shrugged. "A family that participates in human trafficking." An idea filtered in, and suddenly, I knew exactly who or what family would help me as my mother's next words spread fire through my chest. Giovanni Agosti. "I should have made you my regular fuckboy, Ghost."

Reign of a Billionaire

Rage crawled up my neck and over my cheeks, burning my ears. I brought my hand to Kingston, meeting his eyes in silent understanding. The kill was his, but the blood was mine. It was time that someone killed *for* him.

He let me take his gun, the cold metal stark against my burning fingers.

Those eyes feral on me, unlike anything I'd ever seen before, I didn't look away. "Goodbye, Sofia."

Then I pulled the trigger, the bullet finding its target between her eyes.

Blood splattered across my dress and a tormented scream left my throat as I fell down onto my knees. Not for her. Not for me. For him, my Kingston, who'd saved me so many times.

Big arms came around my waist, pulling me up to my feet and offering me their strength. The familiar masculine scent of musky cologne cut through the fog, the feeling of safety seeping into me.

I buried my face into his chest and started to sob.

Our story began with blood; it was only fitting that it ended with blood too.

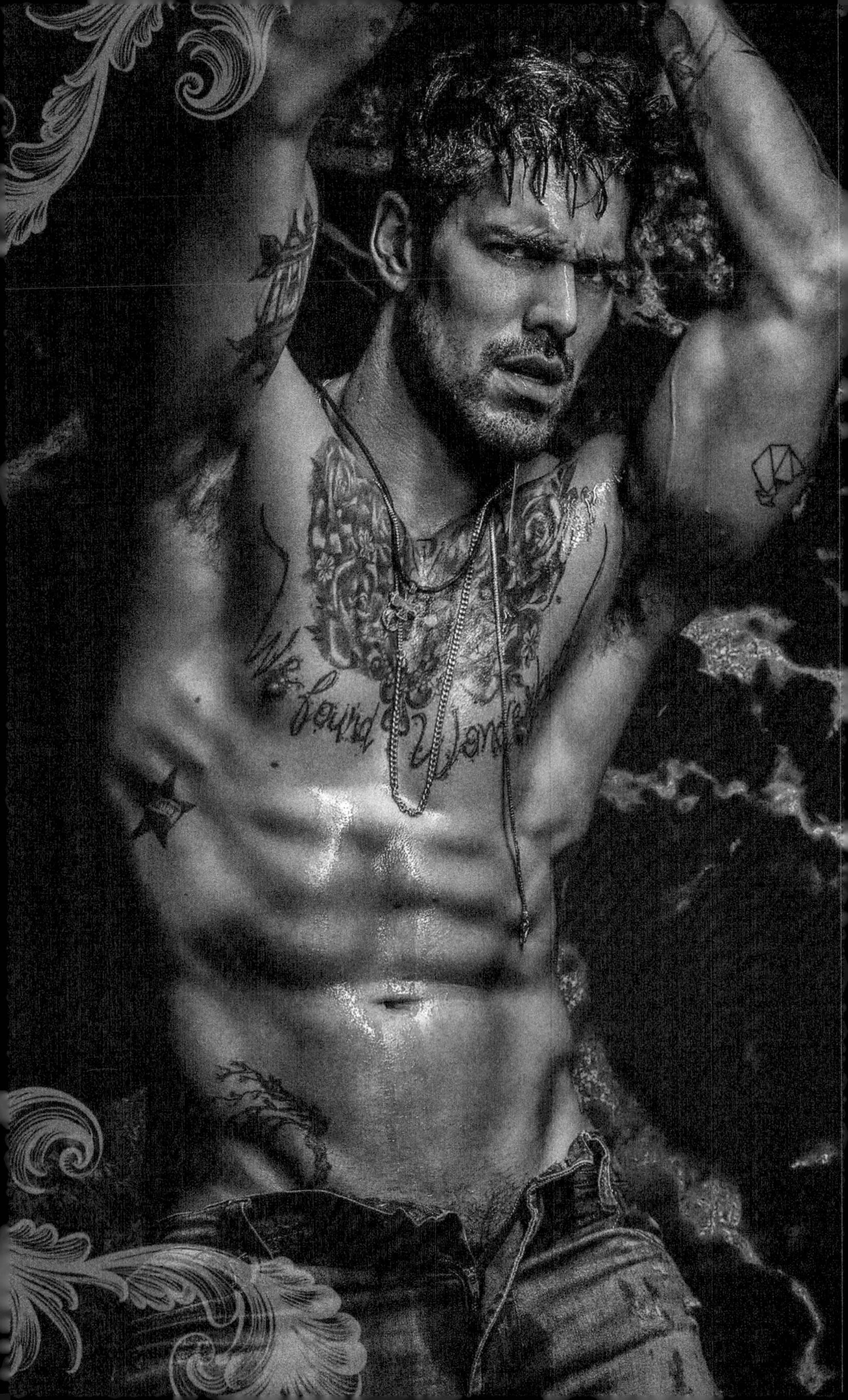
We found

Chapter 65
Kingston

S ofia's death delayed our date by a few days.
We had her buried in an unmarked grave. Lou's hand in mine and our fingers interlocked, we watched the coffin disappear into the dirt, and I couldn't help but wish that bitch made it all the way down to the last layer of Dante's hell. We didn't linger, our hearts filled with relief rather than sorrow.

Sofia was past and all I wanted to do was enjoy the here and now.

My attention on Lou, I couldn't take my eyes off the first and only girl I'd ever loved. It was our date night. Finally.

Our first date was at an outside Moroccan restaurant on *Praia da Figueirinha* beach outside Lisbon. It was fitting, considering our dream was always to escape to the beach.

We ate, and then we walked the beach hand in hand until we got to our final destination.

"What's that?" she asked, pointing ahead of us.

"Let's go check it out," I suggested. I didn't have to tell her twice. She was already tugging me along, her small steps eagerly rushing forward.

"Oh... my... Is that a concert?" Lou's eyes lit up like the stars above us, excited flush coloring her cheeks. "I've never heard of a concert on a beach."

I watched her as she ran circles around me, bubbling with excitement.

"I figured we could combine all our favorites," I mused. "Beach, date, and concert."

She looked at me with that rare happy smile and my hollow chest soaked it up. I was going to keep her this way, happy and safe, so I could see that smile on her face every day of my life.

I followed her, taking her hand back in mine. Her touch, however small, always grounded me. It assured me I wasn't dreaming, that she was really right here with me.

"How about our first concert, sunshine?" She nodded, those eyes shining with so much love it brought me to my knees. "I wasn't sure of the choice of music—"

She silenced me by raising on her toes and pressing a kiss to my lips. "It could be first graders playing a violin and I'd still love it."

She tugged me gently until we both took a seat in the sand, uncaring of our clothes. The first notes drifted through the air, mixing with the sounds of the waves in the background.

I had never felt more alive, and it had everything to do with Louisa—my own ray of sunshine. She was my kindred spirit whose darkness rivaled my own. She'd never looked at me with disdain at the deeds I'd done and had to endure to survive, because she'd been through them too.

Louisa didn't just live, she thrived. She got close with Lara and my sister. She talked more. She smiled more despite the recent events. We hadn't been able to locate her twin. But none of that mattered right now. This was our first date, and I refused to let anything ruin it.

This life was exactly what we'd envisioned. The two of us with our families, never experiencing cold weather or cruel people again. Although we knew there'd always be more of them—humans with no morals or dignity—and we made a vow to fight them together.

Reign of a Billionaire

My heart thundered harder as she leaned her head against my shoulder, her small but lethal hand in mine, memorizing this moment so it lasted us the rest of our lives.

We'd always hold on to each other.

Our pasts were drenched with blood. Our future probably would be too, but as long as we had each other, we'd conquer the world.

Tomorrow we'd resume the search for her sister, but tonight... Tonight was ours.

Lou kicked off her heels with a sigh as we entered our bedroom after checking on our sound-asleep ward.

"Thank you for the amazing first date, Kingston." She glanced at me over her shoulder, a familiar mischievous glint in her eyes stirring my cock to life. It was all it took with this woman. Just a simple look and I was ready to bend her over the bed and fuck her into oblivion. "How about we end it on an even higher note with another first?"

"Let's hear it," I said, leaning against the wall and crossing my ankles.

Lou always found ways to surprise me, and fuck, if she said let's jump into a volcano together, I'd probably do it.

There was a beat of silence before she erected her spine, her golden locks sweeping over her back. She padded over to me, closing the space between us.

Her body flush against mine, she wrapped her hands around my neck, bringing her lips so close to mine that when she spoke her next words, they brushed against mine. "Want to have another first?"

"With you, always," I answered without an ounce of hesitation as her scent invaded my nostrils. She was my personal vice.

My hand slid to her lower back, and I pressed her body against mine. A shiver rolled down her body, her breathing ragged. She tilted her head up, her lips tempting me, but I waited for her to tell me what she had in mind.

"We could try exhibitionist sex."

"You want me to let someone else see what's mine?" I growled, reeling with surprise. "I'm up for anything with you, sunshine, but after you orgasm, I'm killing anyone who saw you."

She let out a husky laugh, her lips parting for me. "Our bedroom windows are tinted. We'll see them, but they won't see us."

"In that case..."

I took her mouth in mine, her body rubbing against me and causing friction. A moan fell from her mouth and I swallowed it greedily as our tongues danced in perfect harmony. In one go, I unzipped her dress, letting it pool at her feet.

I trailed my mouth down her neck, licking her racing pulse as my fingers fumbled with her bra and panties until they too lay discarded on the ground.

My fingers found her pussy, wet and ready for me.

"Fuck, we need to make it to the window," she panted, bucking her hips against my hand.

Her fingernails dug into my nape, her lithe body shuddering and moaning. She was already close to climaxing. It was always like this with her—electric and consuming. My mouth continued its journey south, over her collarbone, down to her breast before slipping her pink, erect nipple into my mouth and sucking it. I moved to her other nipple, lapping, pulling, and biting.

Her sigh filled the space between us, her head lolling back as she murmured incoherent words in Russian and English. Or maybe I was so far gone I couldn't comprehend them.

"Every inch of you belongs to me," I claimed, teasing her with my mouth.

"I do, but for the love of God, Kingston, you have to fuck me now," she said, working my zipper fervently. I did the same with my shirt, and before long, I was as naked as her.

My fingers dipped inside her wet folds and she kissed me with the same desperation I felt, both our chests rising and falling to the rhythm of our frantic heartbeats. I took my finger out and brought it to her lips.

She sucked it clean and my control snapped.

Grabbing her hair from behind, I guided her to the French window that overlooked old Lisbon. Even though it was late in the evening, the city was still busy, passersby rushing home or to the next party.

Lou's palms splayed against the window, she was butt naked, breasts and pussy smashed against the glass and on full display.

"If someone stops and even has a glimpse of you," I murmured against her ear, "I'm going to track them down and kill them. Take their teeth for a trophy."

She whimpered, grinding her ass against me and giving me her consent. I thrust inside her wet heat in one go. She cried out as I began moving inside her, driving into her with a maddening tempo.

She turned her head, her eyes half-lidded and her lips swollen. I couldn't resist her, my mouth taking hers again, and all the while, I kept driving inside her. Again and again. She reached for her nipple with her free hand, tugging and pinching, driving me insane.

I kept one eye on the busy street. I meant what I said. If anyone got a glimpse of her, I'd fucking murder them.

"So good," she moaned, her voice muffled and breathy.

Maybe we were both fucking depraved, but I didn't give two fucks as long as we were depraved together. She was my perfect match, in heaven and hell, and now that we found each other again, there'd be nothing and nobody that would separate me from her.

"My sunshine likes to show the world what her man does to her," I growled into her ear, pumping harder. "Open your thighs wider, let them see your juices and greedy little pussy."

Her inner muscles clenched around my cock, squeezing me for dear life. But she obeyed, smearing her juices against our window as I fucked her hard and deep.

"Fuck, Kingston. I'm gonna... Blyad..."

Her head fell back against me, and I reached around, rubbing her drenched clit, wreaking havoc through her body and pounding into her mercilessly.

Her legs shook, and I snaked my arm around her waist, keeping her upright while I kept screwing her through her orgasm. She screamed my name, my free hand on her clit, milking her for another climax.

Her clenching pussy had my balls tightening, and I emptied myself inside her just as another orgasm wracked through my woman.

We shuddered against each other, our bodies sweaty and our breathing labored. Lou fell back against me, my own legs slightly wobbly.

"Nobody saw us," she breathed. She turned her face, locking eyes with me. "I think we should go out on dates more often."

"And do this often too?"

Lou turned around and buried her face in my chest, my palms covering her butt cheeks.

"Only if you liked it," she murmured, not daring to meet my eyes.

I took her chin between my fingers and her eyes flew up, her crimson-stained cheeks tempting me for another round of in-disguise exhibitionist sex with her. "With you, I like it all. If you fancy us fucking in blood, I'll kill and make it so. I'm up for anything with you, because I love you."

Her cute nose wrinkled. "Nothing so extreme, and no sharing."

I released a shuddering breath. "No sharing, sunshine. You're all mine."

She nodded, satisfied. "And you're mine." Her naked body pressed against mine, her kisses soft and caressing. "I want you to be my first everything, Kingston."

"Your first, your only." When you had so much taken away from you, you learned to be greedy. And this was me, greedy for all of her. "I love you, sunshine."

Reign of a Billionaire

 She lifted on her tiptoes, her lips finding mine. "Love you forever, my ghost."
 I might have owned all her firsts, but she would own all my lasts, because thanks to her, I was no longer a ghost roaming this earth.
 Lou brought me back to life.

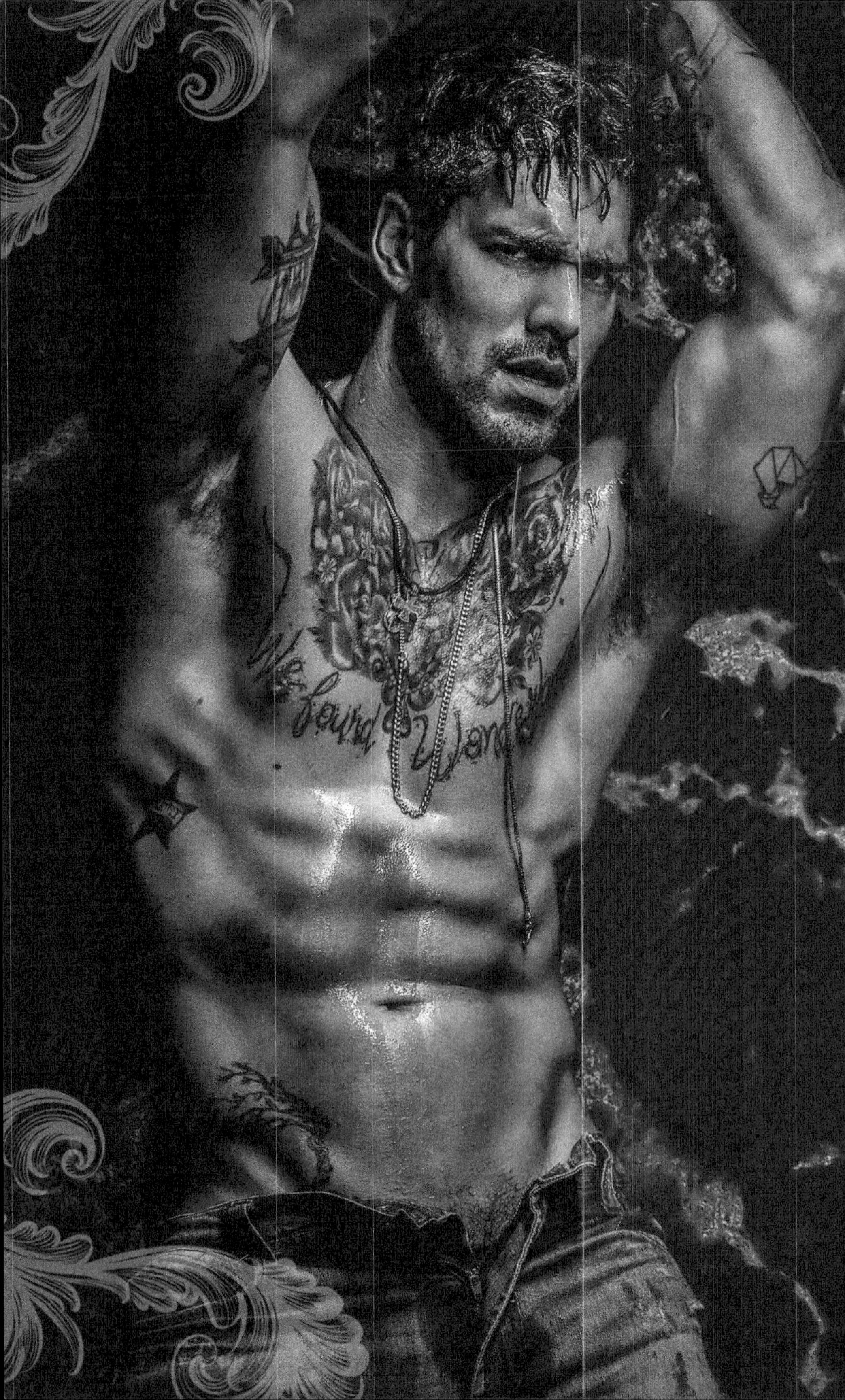

Epilogue-1
Louisa

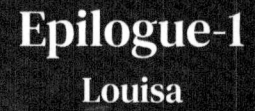

Four Years Later

Refusing to even blink, Stella stared at Alexei for the entire ride from the Nikolaev compound in New Orleans to the building where his half sister practiced medicine. Her chubby little hand gripped my fingers, cutting off my circulation.

Luna, on the other hand, refused to look away from her papa, always finding comfort when looking at him. I couldn't blame her really; I found comfort and safety in his eyes too.

My phone buzzed at the same time as Kingston's, and we shared a glance, knowing exactly who it was. He retrieved the phone and his lips curved into a smile.

"Lara sends her love. Says she's safe and can't wait for us to be back." I smiled. Life with Lara had been a priceless journey. She made our family richer and better.

"It's too bad her professor wouldn't agree to a few weeks off," I muttered. "It would be so nice if she could have come along with us."

"I should have broken his hands," Kingston grumbled. "That would have put his class on hold."

I chuckled. Although tempting in this case, we never hurt innocents, no matter what. It was our hard line, a rule that we never broke.

The bulletproof limo came to a stop, and with it, my thoughts. Alexei reached for the door handle when Stella let out a loud wail, crying bloody murder.

I jolted out of my own trance and glared at Alexei, fighting the urge to slaughter him for making my baby cry.

Sleepless nights were slowly getting to me. Our first visit to the Nikolaevs in New Orleans hadn't exactly gone as planned with the twins getting their first fever. A visit to the doctor was never on the agenda, but we wanted to make sure they got the best care.

Plus, there was comfort in doing something so mundane. So simple.

Kingston and I were just like any other normal parents in the normal world. Our childhoods were full of nightmares and torment. Our children would have better, and we were doing everything in our power to offer the normalcy we never had as children.

I held Stella in my lap, wiping her tears away, her high-pitched cries getting louder and her little face bloodred.

"You want Mommy to dropkick Uncle Alexei?" Stella's cry immediately died out and her eyes, dark and beautiful, came to mine. When she smiled, another piece of me melted. "I guess he's gonna have to die if you're going to keep smiling like that."

Alexei let out a sardonic breath, but I ignored it. I couldn't tear my gaze from my daughter's chubby cheeks.

Her grin turned bigger and my chest melted, feeling lighter. Since our twins' birth, the light shone brighter and stronger. They were the best part of our lives. But then there were nights filled with terror of what could happen if we failed to protect them from all the evil roaming this world.

"And Daddy's going to help Mommy get away with it," Kingston said, placing his hand on mine.

He caressed my cheek with his knuckles. His eyes of warm

chocolate and black diamonds made me want to cuddle up to him with our babies and forget all about the doctor.

Alexei's raspy voice slashed through the air. "Okay, killers, let's get your babies to Isabella before you start your murder spree."

The moment broken, my husband leaned over, planting a hard kiss on my lips, and Stella's cries resumed. Ironically, I could kill a man without flinching, his screams and cries leaving me feeling flat. But my daughter's cries left me feeling frazzled and helpless.

"Isabella will make them all better," Kingston assured. He trusted the Nikolaevs, and that was enough for me. They were part of my husband, and as such, part of me. Part of our family.

We'd made a pact when our twins were born that we'd slay anyone who even looked at our babies wrong. And we weren't joking. Together we'd right all the wrongs that were done to us as children. As adults.

"You and me always," he reminded me of our promise.

I nodded, soaking in his strength.

I tucked a crying Stella to my hip, wrapped in her favorite blanket, and Kingston did the same with Luna.

"At least we know her lungs are strong," I said with a shaky smile.

Kingston threaded his fingers with mine as we slid out of the limo, his towering six-foot-four frame protectively shielding our family. It didn't matter that there was no threat around. That protective streak was built into him—kicking into overdrive where our babies were concerned—and I loved him even more for it.

The brick building awaited with the elevator door already open, and I was surprised to find another couple there waiting. Sasha and Branka Nikolaev.

The young woman waved at us, smiling cheerily, holding the hand of a little boy who looked to be the spitting image of the Nikolaev family. Those Nikolaev genes had to be fucking strong because I had yet to see a Nikolaev who didn't have their traits—either that pale blond hair or those blue eyes.

"Hey, Louisa." Kingston and Sasha nodded to each other in

typical male greeting. The elevator door slid closed and began to ascend.

"Hello, Branka," I greeted, barely hearing my own voice over Stella's strong cries. "Is your little one sick too?"

She opened her mouth to answer but her son beat her to it. "I'm not little," he practically shouted. I guess the little bugger wanted to be heard over the screams. "I'm three."

Alexei ruffled his hair but said nothing while I stifled a smile.

"You sure are big," I agreed. Truthfully, he was the tallest three-year-old I'd seen, but then most of these Nikolaev men were tall and built like warriors.

His eyes came to Stella in my arms, then to Luna in Kingston's. "They're tiny."

They were. The twins were born prematurely, but they were healthy, and our pediatrician said they'd catch up in size. But this fever worried me.

I pressed Stella harder to my chest, feeling her little heart pitter-patter against me.

"You were small when you were born too," Sasha told his son. "And look how big you are now."

"Why is she screaming so much?"

The corners of Kingston's lips quirked and he kissed Stella's head before planting a kiss on my forehead. "They'll be fearless like their mama."

Suddenly Stella's cries died out and she smiled, at peace as she looked at her papa with doting eyes.

The elevator door dinged, sliding open, and we all slowly stepped outside. First Branka and me, then the men.

Isabella Nikolaev came out to meet us, wearing a white coat and a wide, warm smile.

"Welcome." She shot a wink at Branka's son, then turned to face me. "How about we see the two princesses first? Little Damien's annual checkup can wait a bit longer."

"I'm not *little*," he protested, stomping his tiny foot. "But you can see the little babies first." Damien tugged on my pants and I kneeled down. His hand brushed over Stella's warm cheek in a surprisingly gentle gesture. "Her crying hurts my ears."

A soft laughter rang in the room.

"Thank you, Damien," I said softly. "I'll be sure to tell Stella and Luna they are in your debt."

I looked around the room. Alliances. Loyalty. Trust.

And then there was my husband. The boy I loved. The man I fell in love with. We finally got our fairy tale. It might not be perfect, but it was ours, and I wouldn't change a single thing about it.

Kingston leaned forward, wrapping his free arm around me and guided us into Isabella's office. Holding on to him, I watched as Dr. Nikolaev took care of our baby, and I knew our future might be dangerous and dark, but together we'd defeat it all.

My eyes found my husband's. He was my gravity. My whole world. My fucking *everything*.

We'd found in each other something worth fighting for. Something worth living for. And something worth dying for.

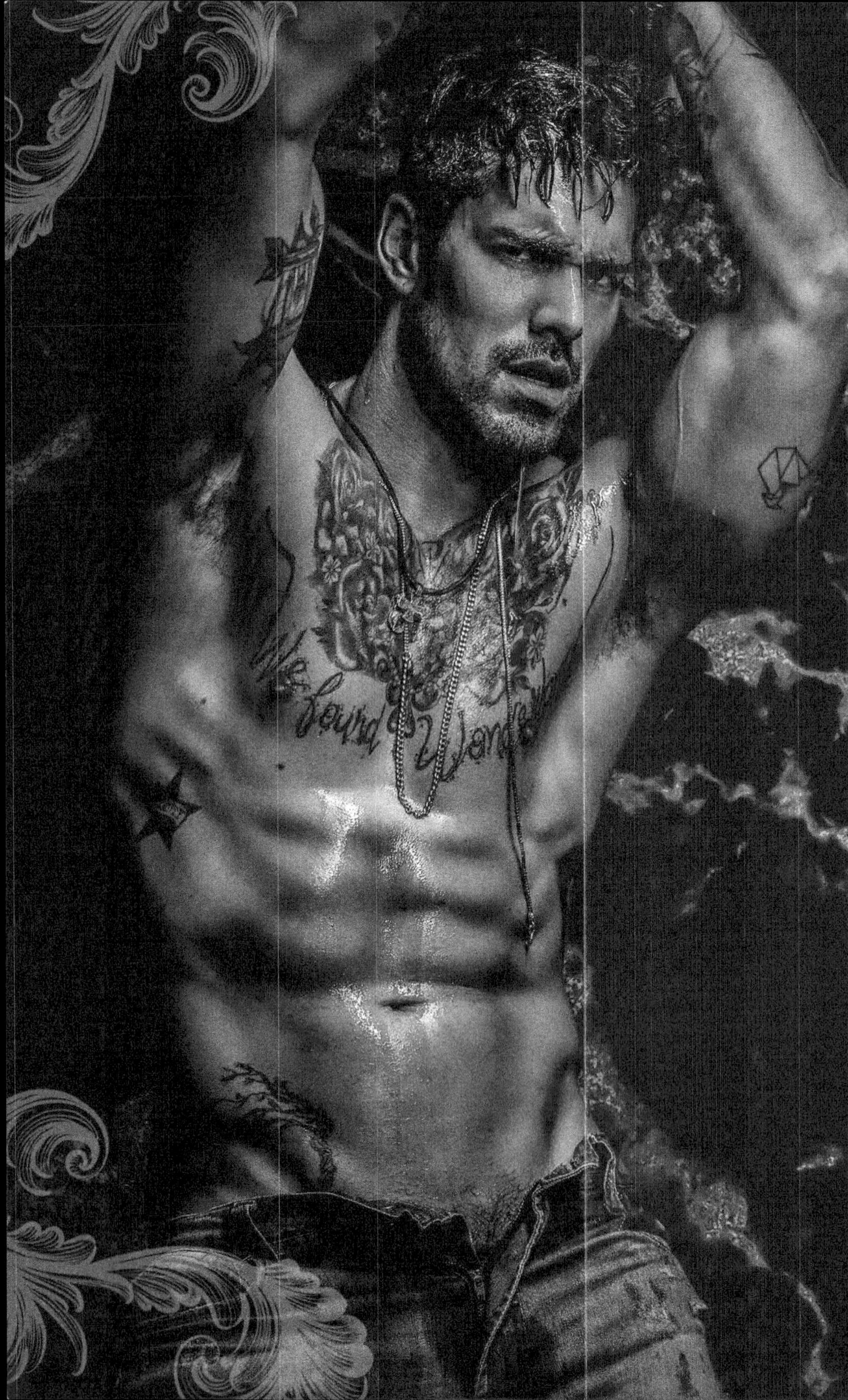

Epilogue-2
Kingston

The rain came down, pounding against the windows, banquette, and bayou of the Crescent City where the Mississippi River curved around the city of New Orleans, and the slogan *"laissez les bon temps rouler"*—let the good times roll—was a motto for life.

It had been my motto since I was granted Lou back. She and our babies were mine, and I'd never let anyone take that away from me.

My heart thumped so loud I feared the whole city would hear it as I looked down to my daughters in my arms. They slept peacefully, their heads full of curls more beautiful than anything I had ever seen. My wife's left hand was outstretched over the bed as if she was reaching for me even in her sleep, the bracelet I had given her a long time ago still there. Her soft snores filled the silence, her blonde halo hiding her profile but telling me she was at peace.

My chest shifted as it always did when I watched my family. The world felt so fucking right with them in it. I still collected the teeth of my victims—a reminder not to fuck with me and those I loved.

I was so fucking besotted with my family that I'd burn the entire world for them so we'd have a light in hell. As long as we were together.

"Kingston..." her sleepy voice croaked. I found my wife's eyes on me, shimmering with endless emotion, putting another hook into my chest. "Everything okay?"

Everything was so fucking perfect it terrified me.

As if she could read my mind, she shifted and nuzzled her nose against mine.

"None of us are going anywhere, my ghost." I looked down at the golden, bright eyes I loved so much. As long as she looked at me like that, I'd follow her to the ends of the earth. She changed my life, gave me a purpose to hold on to and a reason to live. "I promise."

And my sunshine always kept her promises.

The twins let out soft mewling sounds, their lips curving and their eyes fluttering behind their eyelids. They were safe. They were happy. And I'd ensure it remained that way, even if I had to fight their nightmares.

Everything inside me vowed to shield them from anything ugly.

Thunder rumbled across the sky. The rain came down harder, the raindrops pounding on the windows.

I leaned forward, pressing my forehead to hers. "I love you, sunshine."

She held on to me, and I felt loved. Everything I needed and wanted right here in my arms.

THE END

Acknowledgments

I want to thank my friends and family for their continued support.

To my alpha and beta readers—you are all amazing. You put up with my crazy deadlines and even crazier organization. I couldn't do this without you.

My books wouldn't be what they are without each one of you.

To the bloggers and reviewers who helped spread the word about every one of my books. I appreciate you so much and hearing you love my work, makes it that much more enjoyable!

And last but not least, **to all my readers**! This wouldn't be possible without you. Thank you for believing in me. Thank you for your amazing and supportive messages. Simply, THANK YOU.

I get to do this because all of you.

XOXO

Eva Winners

What's Next?

Thank you so much for reading **Reign of a Billionaire**! *If you liked it, please leave a review. Your support means the world to me.*

Kinks of a Billionaire *is the next book in this series, and it's Royce's kinky story. You can continue reading here https://bit.ly/3PlQUgt.*

If you're thirsty for more discussions with other readers of the series, you can join the Facebook group, Eva's Soulmates (https://bit.ly/3gHEeoe).

About the Author

Curious about Eva's other books? You can check them out here. Eva Winners's Books https://bit.ly/3SMMsrN

Eva Winners writes anything and everything romance, from enemies to lovers to books with all the feels. Her heroes are sometimes villains, because they need love too, right? Her books are sprinkled with a touch of suspense and mystery, a healthy dose of angst, a hint of violence and darkness, and lots of steamy passion.

When she's not working and writing, she spends her days either in Croatia or Maryland, daydreaming about her next story.

Find Eva below:

Visit www.evawinners.com and subscribe to my newsletter.
    FB group: https://bit.ly/3gHEeoe
    FB page: https://bit.ly/3oDzP8Q
    Insta: http://Instagram.com/evawinners
    BookBub: https://www.bookbub.com/authors/eva-winners
    Amazon: http://amazon.com/author/evawinners
    Goodreads: http://goodreads.com/evawinners
    TikTok: https://vm.tiktok.com/ZMeETK7pq/